HMS Prometheus

Alaric Bond

HMS Prometheus
Alaric Bond

Copyright © 2015 Alaric Bond

Published by Old Salt Press, LLC

www.oldsaltpress.com

ISBN 978-1-943404-06-3 paperback
978-1-943404-07-0 e.book

The cover shows a detail from *Combat de la Poursuivante contre l'Hercule, 1803* by Louis-Philippe Crépin (1772 – 1851) The original is in the *Musée national de la Marine*.

Publisher's Note: This is a work of historical fiction. Certain characters and their actions may have been inspired by historical individuals and events. The characters in the novel, however, represent the work of the author's imagination. Any resemblance to actual persons, living or dead, is entirely coincidental. Published by Old Salt Press. Old Salt Press LLC is based in Jersey City, New Jersey with an affiliate in New Zealand. For more information about our titles go to www.oldsaltpress.com.

For Pat and Norman

By the same author

The Fighting Sail Series:

His Majesty's Ship

The Jackass Frigate

True Colours

Cut and Run

The Patriot's Fate

The Torrid Zone

The Scent of Corruption

and

Turn a Blind Eye

The Guinea Boat

CONTENTS

HMS Prometheus

Prologue

It was luck of the worst possible kind, although Acting Lieutenant Hunt had already told himself so at least a dozen times and the repetition in no way eased matters.

"Starboard guns are ready, sir," the elderly master's mate reported and, at a nod from Hunt, the brig's paltry battery of six four pounders spat defiantly back at the oncoming enemy.

But the shot was light and would do little damage, Hunt was as sure of that as he was the other factors stacked against him. Nothing would help; his was a hopeless case.

"Bring her to the wind, Mr Carston," he ordered in an artificially firm voice as his prediction was proved all too correct. There were barely enough men to fight and sail his small command. Those allocated to the guns were already serving their pieces while the few left to man the braces followed the brig round as her helm was put across. And all he could do was strain to see the fall of shot against the rising sun's increasing glare, that and curse the misfortune which had placed him in such a position in the first place.

With luck they might get another broadside in – possibly two, before the xebec came alongside. Not so much as a musket shot had been received in reply from the graceful but deadly vessel, although that was not the advantage it might appear. Hunt knew he was facing Barbary Pirates, probably the most ferocious and merciless enemy expected in the entire Mediterranean, and their mode of attack was all too well known.

In this current battle they were superior in almost every quarter, and the fact that no shots had been fired did not mean the xebec was unarmed. Across the narrow stretch of water his opponent was likely to mount a veritable arsenal of nine, twelve or possibly eighteen pounders; formidable fire-power that would not disgrace a frigate. But all the pirate ship actually needed was to come alongside to do the business. She would be crewed by over three hundred fearless fighters – no match for the twenty or so British seamen at Hunt's command. His small force was bound to be overwhelmed within seconds, while the brig would make a far better prize if she were unblemished by gunfire, and contained a full crew of strong, sound and, primarily, saleable Europeans.

The lateen rigged, three masted vessel had first been spotted an hour or so back, as dawn began to break. And with an outline so extreme, so well known, the British crew's suspicions were immediately aroused. Until then, Hunt's hundred ton charge had been making reasonable progress and would soon have found safety in harbour. She was a capture, taken while trying to run the blockade off Toulon, with Hunt given temporary charge to see her to Gibraltar. But as soon as the deadly silhouette came into sight, swooping down from the east with the rising sun behind her, he sensed his first experience of independent command was about to end.

"I think we may have done some damage after all, sir," the master's mate suggested cautiously, and Hunt looked again at the hateful vessel. Yes, Rutherford was right; a good chunk of the enemy's slender prow had been knocked away by the last broadside, and Hunt acknowledged the fact with a cursory nod. But it would take more than a four pound round shot to stop such a sleek and warlike craft. There were still two hundred miles separating them from Gibraltar with no friendly territory between, and what time remained was fast running out.

Of course they might yet run. Unusually for the Med., the night breeze had not been swallowed by the sun, and still came from roughly the same direction. They were carrying all plain sail when the enemy was first sighted, and Hunt immediately ordered the helm across, so every ounce of the precious force might be taken on their quarter. He had learned much during his brief command. Despite winds which changed from light to non-existent, the brig was fast for her size, a fact that inevitably endeared her to him: Hunt had even hoped they would maintain their lead, if not extend it.

But the change of course also benefited the xebec; the wide, high, triangular sails were made for sailing the Med., as was that distinctive and gainly hull. Her frame might be light when compared with the far more durable structure of the brig and, placed together in the midst of an Atlantic storm, there was no doubting which vessel would last the longer. But these were peaceful conditions: the soft wind and gentle sun of a pleasant Mediterranean summer's morning, and the enemy continued to close on them. Hunt supposed stunsails might still be added, but that would take men from the guns, and even their meagre broadside was likely to be of more immediate benefit in the next few minutes.

"She's a pirate, sir. Sure as eggs is eggs," Rutherford, who was second in command, grumbled, and the young, fair haired officer could only agree. A pirate indeed, although that should not come as a surprise when the area was plagued by them. And Hunt was equally aware that, however much he might blame ill fortune, the whole sorry situation was really his own stupid fault.

For it had been vanity: nothing less. When entrusted with despatches and a well found brig to carry them, Hunt had been prepared to risk anything in search of a swift passage, and the pursuit of a solid wind had taken them perilously close to the African coast. At the time Hunt was sure there was little need for concern: the brig showed a fair turn of speed and was armed: in effect a minor warship: he really should fear nothing. But it was a foolish decision: one based on a young and unknown officer's desire to impress, and they were paying for it now.

Or rather, they would be very shortly; the Barbary Pirate's treatment of prisoners was as well known as their fighting tactics. If, or to be pragmatic, when they were taken, the brig and her stores would not be the full extent of their booty: Hunt, and his fellow men, could expect to spend the foreseeable future as slaves.

So they must waste no time. To fire another broadside it was necessary to yaw, and preferably now, despite the fact that several of the servers were yet to signal their pieces ready. At his shouted command, the brig fell off to starboard and began to wallow as the men he had so casually designated gun captains peered over the weapons' crude sights. To Hunt, who only a week before had been second in command of a third rate's battery of thirty-two pounders, the guns appeared ludicrously small although, once despatched with another ear-splitting clatter, he hoped they would still have some effect on the enemy.

"Holed her fore that time," Rutherford announced with satisfaction, and indeed a dark patch in the vessel's forward sail showed where she had been hit. But there was no split; the sail continued to draw to some extent, and neither had the mast, nor any of its supporting lines been struck; something that might have bought more time, and perhaps altered the odds in their favour. Hunt turned away from the sight, conscious that the aloof and confident persona expected of even a young commander was becoming hard to maintain. His brig was coming back to the wind and already picking up speed, but the enemy now lay hardly a cable and a half off, and the next broadside the British fired would be their last.

He tried not to think about what was to come; to the months, probably years to be spent as a captive. Algiers was the nearest port; should the enemy hail from there it was a dismal prospect. There would be no honour in being a prisoner; none of the mutual respect or reciprocal arrangements usual in European conflict. He supposed amongst people who held scant regard for their own lives, those of defeated unbelievers were bound to figure low. The British would be put to work, and work hard; his men probably being sent to serve in just such a vessel as the one that was shortly to capture them. There they would find the hardships of Royal Naval service nothing compared to what was demanded. Stories abounded of men being put to the oars for hours at a stretch; many died of exhaustion or malnutrition, and the Barbary nations were no respecters of rank or position: even as an officer, Hunt would be lucky not to join them.

He gritted his teeth and tried to clear his mind of further dismal thoughts, concentrating instead on what every captain should do during the last few minutes of command. In the binnacle drawer lay Admiral Bickerton's despatches which he had brought up from his cabin as soon as the sighting was reported. He collected them now, and held the tarred canvas bundle tightly against his chest. Rutherford was apparently watching the oncoming enemy, but Hunt knew the older man had noticed his action, and would agree the end was close. When capture became inevitable, the parcel must be consigned to the deep, its ballast of small shot ensuring all sank well beyond enemy reach.

Indeed, there seemed little point in delaying longer; Hunt took two steps towards the lee bulwark before tossing the bundle over. It fell with barely a splash: Hunt had no idea what the local Dey would have made of communications from Sir Richard Bickerton, but he was not going to get the chance now. And then there were the three sacks of general mail that lay ready by the taffrail. Some might conceivably contain items of small commercial value but, even if not, no one liked the thought of personal messages falling into enemy hands, and one of Hunt's last responsibilities to his colleagues was to see they did not.

By the time all were disposed of, the brig's guns were almost loaded once more. On this occasion when they yawed, Hunt knew there would be little point in turning back. The xebec was making good speed and lay less than a cable off their stern. The British would get their broadside in before the collision, but could not prepare another before the inevitable rush of boarders. He caught the eye of the quartermaster who clearly waited for his order, and was actually drawing breath to give it when a call came from the masthead.

"Deck there, I have a sighting to the east."

The young officer froze, his mouth comically open, but the report was creating far too much excitement for anyone to notice.

"It's a frigate, or at least something substantial, an' no more'n three mile off," the man continued, over the babble of excited comments. "She were hidden by the enemy but I have her now. Under all plain sail an' settin' stuns'ls."

"Any colours?" Rutherford asked, but it was a futile question. If the sighting was indeed a frigate, it was likely to belong to a friendly power, although even a Frenchman would be welcome at that particular moment.

Hunt glanced back at the oncoming pirate; there was now no point in their yawing, they must maintain the chase for as long as possible. For a second the terrible thought that the enemy might also have failed to spot the newcomer flashed through his mind, then he noticed the xebec's yards move slightly as his pursuer altered course.

"They're going to pass to starboard," the master's mate murmured softly. It would be foolish in the extreme for the pirate's commander to continue attacking the brig when any delay was likely to see his own ship captured. Instead, with the situation neatly reversed, he was now altering course to place the xebec in the optimum position for a stern chase, and a lateen rig would be more effective with the wind a littler firmer on the beam.

Soon it was clear the subtle change had indeed increased their speed. The pirate was going to pass close, but not so as to allow them to board, although Hunt might expect attention from their cannon. And a vessel of such a size would be expected to produce a broadside substantial enough to sink his little brig with a single dose.

"Looks like we're to exchange one drubbing for another," the master's mate snorted, as if in agreement with the younger man's thoughts. Hunt did not respond; what Rutherford said was correct although he, for one, preferred taking his chance against enemy fire to facing the prospect of a lifetime's bondage.

"Sightin's a Jonathan!" the lookout called in glee. "An' a big one!"

Hunt accepted the information without comment. The Americans were currently fighting an intense campaign on the nearby North African coast. It was something the Barbary States were pleased to call a holy war, or *Jihad*, and the British Navy stubbornly ignored, in the face of a bigger conflict that threatened their own shores. He was fortunate to have chanced upon one of their larger ships, and that his attacker had taken notice and was doing the sensible thing by running. But before he could welcome the change in luck, there was the small matter of a parting broadside which, Hunt guessed, the xebec would deliver and was likely to be significant. But if that were the case, the young man was determined to get his shots in first.

"Ready lads, aim at her spars and make 'em count!" Rutherford cautioned as the xebec's brightly painted hull crept into the brig's arc of fire. There was no point in delaying; should the pirates beat them to it, some British guns could be disabled, whereas a lucky hit might wound the enemy's tophamper sufficiently to allow the Americans a chance to deal with her properly.

At a call from Hunt, the guns were discharged in a series of staccato snaps that covered several seconds. One shot fell disastrously wide and two merely punctured the mainsail but Hunt was reasonably sure the xebec's mizzen was also struck. Then the pirate's full armament was being run out, and Hunt found himself looking straight into the mouths of twelve heavy cannon. They were significant pieces; eighteen pounders by their look: more than enough to annihilate his command.

And then, even as he considered the prospect, the enemy opened fire.

Chapter One

So this was Gibraltar. Kate Manning stood on the quayside basking in the hot sun as she took in the sights and smells of a busy harbour. Besides the general packet that had carried her so far, several other traders clustered together in the centre as if for security while, to the north, a line of supply hoys, uniformly painted and moored with precise regularity, lay ready for work. The Royal Navy was also in evidence, with a two decker, pristine in fresh paint and apparently polished to perfection appearing ready to sail. She was anchored a respectable distance from the private shipping with just a few of her type, but smaller and not so magnificent, allowed near. A variety of light craft under oddly shaped and gaily coloured sails passed between, and a heavily laden lighter was in the process of being unloaded at a nearby wharf. But one ship and one ship alone captured Kate's attention and she was probably the least impressive of any on display.

Soundly secured to a mole at the southern side of the harbour, and sheltering under the protection of several canvas awnings, the aged third rate looked more fit for a breaker's dock than the open sea. Kate had seen her before, but the last occasion had been many months ago and under very different circumstances. Still, she recognised the lines immediately, and knew for certain her journey was at an end.

Actually it had been a remarkably fast passage from England. So much so that it seemed the decision to join Robert was hardly made before she arrived, and with his ship in plain view. She was in no hurry, however. In a time when to have anything other than the whitest of skin was frowned upon, Kate held no petty inhibitions and took her pleasure wherever it could be found. The summer sun was agreeably hot; about her the stones positively glowed with warmth, but they merely emphasised the coolest of breezes, and she was content to stand a while longer, enjoying the pleasing contrast. Her journey that far might have been brisk, but it would be finished in a more leisurely fashion and there was no possibility of her arriving in a fluster. When she met with Robert, their reunion would be as dignified as possible.

And it was strange that she should be so concerned; Kate was nothing if not pragmatic; abstract or groundless worries rarely bothered her. Their parting had been perfectly genial, after all; Robert was even keen for her to accompany him to sea, as on earlier commissions. But there were more subtle reasons why Kate preferred to stay in England, not the least being she felt herself in danger of becoming a professional sea-wife: one of those worthy types whose life apparently centred about her husband, and the ships he served aboard. More than a few such creatures had crossed her path and, in truth, she did not despise them greatly. But Kate knew herself, and that she could never be satisfied with such an existence.

Then there had been the letter. Due to the somewhat erratic nature of *Prometheus'* commission, post had been sparse while little of great sensitivity can be trusted to a note sent over a thousand miles which was to pass through many tar-stained hands. But one had come, the last, which concerned her greatly. And it was not so much what it contained that worried her so, rather what had been left out.

Kate's concerns increased steadily as the small craft headed across Biscay and down the Portuguese coast, until they now reached the point when, even though she stood at what must surely be her journey's end, a considerable part of her wished it might never be completed.

But if they were unable to discuss more personal matters, Robert had certainly told her of the battle. His ship, *Prometheus*, was one of two third rates that took on three French liners, sinking one and capturing the others. Word of the action had arrived in England just as she received that last letter and, as her packet sailed from Falmouth, all talk was of the brave Sir Richard Banks and his remarkable achievement. Naturally the opinions of a few Fleet Street journalists did not impress her; Kate was glad the British had been victorious of course and, more so, that Robert was unharmed. But all the jubilations and flag waving hardly affected her at all. Her concerns were far deeper.

"Shall I find a hackney for us, ma'am?"

The young voice broke into her thoughts. Kate was still unused to having a maid and being called so, although ma'am was a distinct improvement on 'mum' which had been the girl's original form of address, and one she could never tolerate.

"Yes, Poppy, do," she said, breaking her mood. "And ask the driver to come for our luggage."

Whatever her reception, Robert would not be over pleased at finding his wife in company with a maid. Were they both to ship aboard *Prometheus*, it would doubtless cause problems, and he was yet to learn that she was even in Gibraltar. So be it; if Robert was that distressed they would simply pay for Poppy to return in the next home bound merchant. And if she herself were as unwelcome, then the two of them would travel together.

"*Buen día, señora.*"

She gave a neutral smile as the short, stocky man bent down and lifted her sea chest onto his shoulder, before scooping up another bag with his free hand. Kate draped the new uniform she was to surprise Robert with over her own arm, then collected her personal portmanteau. Poppy dealt with the rest of their luggage and soon the three of them were making steady progress towards the open carriage that awaited them.

And then it was just a matter of minutes before they rounded a corner and began to trundle along the quay and towards the New Mole. Kate understood this to be quite a structure; something between breakwater and harbour wall, but was unprepared for the actual size. The spit of artificial land extended deep into the bay and even carried a respectable wooden roadway. There were a collection of assorted vessels secured alongside including Robert's ship, and it was then that she finally saw the liner's tattered sides in greater detail.

Prometheus' bows were facing the open sea and Kate drew a deep, unconscious breath as she reviewed the damage. Much work was being undertaken, three separate stages lay against her hull, and fresh wood was being hammered into place even as she watched. But when last seen the magnificent warship had been in far better order, with gleaming paint, new cordage and fresh canvas. Robert had grumbled about the sick berth not being finished to his total satisfaction, but one look at her wickedly scored and punctured sides and the tangle of old and new line hanging from strangely foreshortened masts told her story adequately enough. Even at such a distance the very air, rich with the scent of hot pitch and marine glue, spoke of a fierce action. That the ship remained afloat was remarkable in itself, and considerable time would be needed before the magnificent beast could be let loose upon open water again.

And the battle must have been all of six weeks ago, Kate reminded herself with a start: probably more. The carriage stopped by a small barricade guarding the entrance to the mole and, for a rare moment, Kate was at a loss.

"Turn back," she told the driver briskly, her mind finally made up. "You can place my luggage over there, in the shade of that warehouse." Kate reached for her purse as the carriage swung round and began to clatter back towards the nearby buildings. There had been no change of heart: the low wooden structure was simply a far more suitable place to leave Poppy and her possessions. Little comfort would be found from the sun at such an hour but it was a good distance from the Royal Marine guard at the mole, and Kate knew the girl would be keen to make a close acquaintance with any likely male.

"Wait for me here," she told her after they had alighted and the driver was paid. "I shall not be long; if my husband is aboard you will be sent for immediately, otherwise we can seek him out elsewhere together."

Poppy settled herself on the sea chest readily enough, and proceeded to flash her dark eyes at a nearby group of seamen. Kate considered her for a moment before deciding she might be trusted for a while at least. Chances were high Robert would be aboard, and all then could be sorted relatively quickly. Either she was at fault, and had taken the tone of his letter in completely the wrong way, or whatever problems he felt unable to discuss had healed during the time spent travelling. In which case they could continue as before, and she may well complete the commission in his company. And if not: if, as she secretly suspected, something dreadful was to tear them apart, be it a woman, someone he met ashore – perhaps an officer's wife, or maybe some terrible ailment which he could not speak of, she would accept that as well. Then, rather than having just completed a journey, the women would find themselves at the start of another, with their destination very firmly set as England.

* * *

Clement had noticed the young girl as she sat amid the dunnage, as did Butler and Jameson, the seamen who walked with him. Actually it would have been difficult to avoid doing so, her thick, auburn hair caught the sun in such a way that it drew even the most indifferent eye, while the freckled face beneath was so young, so full of life, yet with an obvious element of mischief that it brought a smile to all three. But though she openly returned the compliment, neither man gave her more than a second glance. Clement was a boatswain's mate; a responsible position aboard any ship, and more so in one with a tophamper that was a veritable cat's cradle of confusion. And they were running low on half inch line; Knolls, the boatswain, had sent the three men ashore to collect two more sixty-fathom lengths which would be needed to finish serving the mizzen shrouds. It was a small requirement, and hardly noticeable amongst the many miles of cordage that supported and controlled the motive power of a third rate. But if Clement could see to those shrouds it was another job done, and another day closer to that on which their precious barky could return to the sea.

It was late morning, just shy of noon when their main meal was due, and they were keen to get a shake on. The food was not the incentive, however. Being a Wednesday, one of three banyan days in the week when no meat was served, little could be expected. And what they did get would be cold, for while the ship remained trussed up to the shore and with most of the regular hands in barracks, the slushy rarely bothered to light his ovens. But Up Spirits would be piped before the meal, and that gave more than enough reason to see this simple trip to the stores done with, and themselves back to the ship.

They turned off the main quay and made for a side road that ran past the nearby storehouses. Clement was ahead of the other two although this in no way indicated his seniority; the three would have been far happier walking in line abreast, as seamen ashore tended to prefer. But the narrow lane was filled with all manner of traffic heading against them, and to do so would have slowed their progress considerably.

Their journey wound through various tight turns that were the hallmark of the area, and past several side streets, but the three had followed the same route often and knew it well. As soon as the weather-boarded building came into view, their pace increased and when they arrived they did not hesitate, but walked straight into its cool and dark welcome.

The warehouse supplied most of the dockyard's smaller requirements, and its storekeeper greeted Clement respectfully enough. The requested line was soon routed out, and the requisition signed. Then, with the two seamen lugging a coil on each of their right shoulders, while the boatswain's mate remained unencumbered – a recognition of rank that was accepted by all – they set off both for their ship and that day's first allowance of grog.

And all went well on the return journey. The boatswain's mate was ahead once more and, once more, became lost in thoughts of the repair in progress. He knew the two men following better than to expect they would be doing the same, but was still not unduly bothered and it was only upon reaching the quay, when he finally turned back, that Clement realised one was missing.

"Where's Butler?" he asked, suspiciously, but Jameson simply looked back with a completely blank expression. "Well come on," Clement demanded. "You was walking next to the cove, you must 'ave seen where 'e went."

"No, Mr Clement," Jameson replied earnestly. "I didn't see nothing."

"Did you not?" the warrant officer challenged as he took a step towards his one remaining helper. This would not go down well back at the ship. *Prometheus* had a good record, with hardly any hands being lost since the ship was taken over by the dockyard mateys and he was bound to be held responsible.

"Straight up, Mr Clement," Jameson assured him. "I just looked round, and he were gone."

"An' I suppose you 'ad no idea he was gonna try anything?" Clement persisted.

"Not an inklin', I swear to God," the seaman declared, and this time his voice even carried a trace of concern that he was not being believed. "I only discovered he'd run when you did," the young man added.

"Is that right?" Clement questioned. "Then how come you's carryin' 'is line?"

* * *

"I'm to see the surgeon, my husband, Robert Manning," she told the young private who guarded *Prometheus*' gangplank. But the man made no response; it was as if she had not spoken – did not exist and Kate was about to repeat in a louder voice when a second marine approached. He was equally bedecked in red and white but also wore shoulder knots and a laced hat.

"He's not permitted to speak, miss," he told her. "Not been on picket duty for more than a week or so, an' we don't like the younger ones having too much to think about."

"I see," Kate replied, her gaze remaining on the sentry for a moment, before switching to what she assumed to be some measure of an officer. "Well can you allow me aboard?" she asked.

"Indeed," the sergeant replied. "It might not be totally level, but I am the last to keep a man from his wife. Though you should have a guide," he added thoughtfully. "A ship in refit is not the safest place, don't you know?"

"I shall be perfectly safe, thank you," Kate answered stiffly.

"Very well, though I'd be happy to provide an escort."

Kate looked briefly at the mute sentry. "If they are all as quiet as this one, I should be better on my own," she said testily before bustling onto the wide plank that led to the ship's entry port.

But once aboard Kate regretted her decision. Though she had grown up around merchant ships and actually sailed in both sixth and fifth rates, *Prometheus* was by far the largest warship she had ever encountered. And her last visit had been many months back, when Robert was present to show her around. Still, she knew the sick berth was to be found on the orlop and to the stern so, after waiting for a pair of men carrying several planks of wood to pass, she set off for the aft companionway.

Below, it was even more confusing. The ship was a mass of activity, with workers hammering noisily at almost every station. The next stairway was in sight however, and Kate made for it without hesitation. And she was actually halfway down, before her path became blocked. Instinctively she stepped to one side to allow the two heavily built fellows by, but they were more intent on standing in her path, and apparently found the act amusing.

"Why Tosh," one said, speaking to his mate. "We seems to have the wedding garland hoisted, ain't that the thing?"

The other simpered like any regular toad, and Kate had their mark immediately.

"Have you a fancy man, my lovely?" the first asked. Both were several steps below her, and it was no effort for him to reach forward and take hold of her skirt, as if examining the fabric.

"Stand away there, Rogers!" the voice came from behind and carried both authority and confidence. The seaman let go of the material in an instant before standing straight and staring into the far distance. Kate sensed a uniformed man stepping down beside her, but her own gaze remained on the seamen. "If you're in a working party I suggest you return to it," the firm tone continued. "If not I shall surely find you employment..."

Kate finally glanced to one side, but the officer was unknown to her and, as she was surprised to note, no more senior than a midshipman. The two seamen knuckled their foreheads respectfully though, before turning back down the companionway and vanishing into the crowd.

"I apologise for that, ma'am," the man spoke gruffly. He was well built, probably in his thirties, and definitely old for such a rank. "Ship is not under proper discipline at the moment, and those two reprobates are scarcely the best examples of our people." He smiled, and there was the hint of a more gentle soul within. "If you have business aboard, you would be better to have a youngster to guide you."

"Thank you," Kate replied. "I did think I knew the way but was mistaken. I am the surgeon's wife, and wished to find my husband."

"Mr Manning will be in the sick berth," the midshipman replied. "Here, we are so close I may as well show you. My name is Franklin, by the way," he said as they stepped together. "I berth in the aft cockpit, just for'ard from here."

"Well thank you, Mr Franklin," Kate said, smiling politely and offering her hand. "It was good of you to rescue me, I am most grateful."

* * *

It might have come as a surprise to Jameson and Clement, but Butler had actually gone ashore with every intention of deserting. He first arrived aboard *Prometheus* several months back as she was commissioning. His ship, a transport, had been entering home waters after a lengthy voyage to New South Wales when a pressing tender set upon her. All bar the master, a mate and two ship's boys were taken, leaving ticket men in their places. At the time Butler was struck by an almost inexpressible anger; for all his adult life he had served aboard both Navy and merchant shipping and, whatever the law may decree, felt it a fundamental right to choose between the two. And with his woman ashore, and not ten miles from their Tor Bay anchorage hardly made matters any the easier.

But he had finally accepted his fate in the philosophical manner seamen were accustomed to, and settled aboard *Prometheus*, a ship he grudgingly recognized as being a relatively happy one. But all that changed within a few short hours. A general packet had come in bringing post which was distributed during breakfast. His contained news of home and there was little so very terrible in what he learned. Mary was well, and missed him greatly. His child, a boy, named William in his honour, was doing famously. An aunt had died, his best friend's ship was worryingly late in returning from the East, all the usual tattle-tale that made a seaman's life more bearable. Certainly nothing momentous, or likely to persuade a dependable hand and potential captain of the maintop to run.

But run he did; and it was the normality of the letters which had caused him to do so. The reminder that, however exotic and bohemian his life might have become, there was another, far more mundane existence that he was also a part of. And suddenly it occurred to Butler he wanted to be more than just a part. He wanted – needed – to be home, telling his wife, the girl whose face was in danger of fading from his memory, exactly how much he loved her, and hold his son in his arms while he was still able to do so.

"You'll be regular Navy then," the master told him suspiciously as he stood on the deck of the same packet Kate Manning and her maid had so recently vacated.

"I might be," Butler hedged, although his rig and lack of possessions said much about his status.

"Well I won't pretend I can't use another hand," the man admitted. "But I been bobbed in the past. There'll be no wages paid in advance; not a penny 'till we see England."

"Fair enough," Butler agreed.

"And a topman you say?"

The seaman nodded and the master's face betrayed his pleasure. "Then you'd better find yourself a berth," he said, without further hesitation.

Butler drew a sigh of relief. It had been much easier than he thought. Less than half an hour before he was one of Clement's party, and *Prometheus* still lay in clear sight to the south of the harbour.

"If the Navy comes a lookin' we've places you can be hid," the master continued. "The mate will show you where when he returns. And I won't say a word, not about you being aboard, nor how you comes to be so, if you're found."

That was fine by Butler; in fact it could hardly be bettered.

"We're to sail at first light tomorrow," Butler's new captain was warming to the capable young man who could have come as a gift from the gods. "Once we makes it clear of harbour, I'd say you're safe. We has one call on the Med. Squadron, then can start for glorious Albion."

Butler grew tense but said nothing.

"We've a commission to carry despatches, but that shouldn't affect you none," the master assured him. "*Sprite* can raise Toulon in four an' a half days with the wind right, an' we'll be delivering to the Navy. No one comes aboard as a rule an', if they does, we can hide you once again. In less than ten days we should be passing back through the Strait, then it is just a call at the Tagus, cross Biscay and on to England. Falmouth's our home port, from there you'll have to make your own way to Tor Bay. That do you all right, will it?"

"Yes, sir," Butler replied. "That'll do me fine."

* * *

The strangely grown up midshipman had left her at the entrance to the dispensary and Kate paused before knocking on the light deal door. This was the last moment when she could have changed her mind. In theory at least, she might still turn away: still leave the ship, leave the port and, together with Poppy, be heading back for England before Robert even knew they had arrived. She would be running away from whatever had worried her of course, but some folk believed it easier to avoid problems, rather than confront them. Kate was not of that type, though: she always preferred to tackle obstacles head on. And, if there was difficulty with her husband, it was surely better to meet it so. There had been no reply so she tapped again, and more firmly this time.

A familiar gruff voice called for her to enter and she pressed the door open.

"Robert, you have a seaman aboard by the name of Rogers," she began, while taking a single step into the dark little room. "You must know him; an offensive ox of a man: kindly see he is soundly purged when next your attention is sought."

Manning placed the china bowl he had been holding back on the counter before turning to meet the wife he had thought so many miles away in England. "Kate, how absolutely wonderful to see you." he said.

It was not quite the welcome she had expected and the corner of her mouth lifted slightly, but Kate made no move to greet him, and stayed near to the doorway.

"But come in, do," he insisted. "I have much to tell, and you must be tired. Did you arrive in the packet?"

She went to reply, but he was obviously far too excited to give her the chance.

"I looked to her, and thought of you, but only for the letters that might be aboard. To be truthful I was sorry when none were delivered. And then here you are: why it is wonderful!"

Kate allowed herself to be led further into the room, feeling his well remembered touch while previous doubts and expectations tumbled about her mind as if suddenly robbed of a home. Whatever she may have been fearing, there was clearly nothing amiss with Robert, or his feelings for her.

"So, when did you decide to join us? In your last message you were helping in the village surgery at Alton."

"I should have written," she replied, while allowing her expression to soften. "It was wrong of me I know but, after receiving your letter it seemed better to come in person."

"My letter?" At her words much of the enthusiasm seemed to drain from the man's face and he looked older and more vulnerable. "But I have sent several. Do you know about Tom," he enquired hesitantly. "That he was wounded..."

"And that you expected him to die?" Kate added in a way that would have sounded callous to anyone who did not know her. "Has he?"

Manning shook his head. "No. No, he is alive. But it is not good, Kate – I fear I may have let him down dreadfully and cannot say how badly I feel."

But his look of sudden concern told her much. She had been partly right; something was obviously bothering her husband, although it seemed the problem did not concern her or their relationship, but rather someone else entirely.

"So he is to go shortly?" She demanded; really the man was making no sense at all.

"No, I expect him to live," he gave a slight smile. "Live and be healthy."

"But that is wonderful, Robert!" She looked at him as a mother might a troublesome child. "And, from what you said, also remarkable. There was infection in the wound, as I recall. Sure, it is the hardest task in the world to clear such things: you have nothing to reproach yourself for, I am certain."

They were now close, almost touching, although neither made a move to embrace. It was as if they had come together purely out of habit.

"Can I see him?"

"All in good time," he told her. "There is a deal to tell and he will be sleeping now, but more of you; are you staying? I am sure you shall be offered a berth, if so. I could certainly use the help: Dodgeson has been lured ashore to the new hospital, and there is more than enough work for Prior and me. We are dealing with a positive stream of accidents from the refit and I have no wish to sail with only one assistant surgeon."

She was looking at him quizzically now and, reaching forward, took both his hands quite firmly in hers.

"I shall stay for as long as you will have me, Robert," she declared.

"It is so good to see you again," he replied with equal solemnity. "I cannot tell how much you were missed."

* * *

Franklin entered the aft cockpit to find it empty. There was little surprise in that, even though the small space had been designed to be home to up to twenty men and boys – volunteers, midshipmen or junior master's mates – and was usually overcrowded, almost to the point of physical danger. Several of the young gentlemen originally appointed to *Prometheus* had already fallen, either in the recent action or earlier in her commission and, despite having been in harbour for over six weeks, only four new faces had so far been received as replacements. In addition, while the ship remained firmly in the grasp of the dockyard, most of her lower deck hands were accommodated ashore, with all the older midshipmen bar himself transferred there to supervise them. In fact Franklin was left with just those four young souls with whom to share the berth and found himself spending a good deal of time playing nursemaid.

He exhaled deeply, and ran his long and slightly ink stained fingers through his hair, then reached for the teapot that rested on a hanging shelf in the centre of the stuffy room. The pot was cold, but still heavy enough to contain sufficient for his needs, and he poured a goodly measure of the thick, brown liquid into one of the cups alongside, before selecting the only free chair not filled with clutter and lowering himself down.

When the ship was at sea and during normal service conditions the younger, some might say aspiring, officers were placed under the care of a senior midshipman or master's mate. It was a responsible position, and one open to a select few. They must be sound enough to take charge of the lads' care and education, while able to combine the roles of messmate, tutor and, all too often, parent. Aboard *Prometheus*, that responsibility had fallen upon Franklin who, although only a midshipman himself, was older than most of his rank and possessed more than enough experience for the task. It was not a position he particularly enjoyed but, after serving twice as acting lieutenant without completing that all important step to commissioned rank, Franklin was becoming increasingly disillusioned with his career as a sea officer. This had yet to reach the stage when it became obvious; when he, like many of his type, unintentionally marked himself out as unlikely to proceed further. The process was undoubtedly underway, though: already he knew himself established as one of the more permanent warrant officers; those known for a limited number of abilities and the last to be chosen for anything new while, in turn, he was inclined to view any fresh duty with a measure of cynicism.

For he was thirty-five; seventeen years beyond the time when first eligible for a commission. Instead, he was stuck as an oldster midshipman: a figure of fun when employed and pity when not, for no advantages such as half pay or pension followed those who had failed so conspicuously. Franklin was uncomfortably aware of officers more than ten years younger who were now considered made. They commanded post ships and sat safely on the captains' list, with the very real possibility of receiving their flag before he even got another sniff at a lieutenant's board. To them would go the glamour, fame and fortune every king's officer should aspire to, and he could not deny that part of him was envious.

But it was only a part, and getting smaller with every day. Others may consider those of captains' rank and above to be a success, and they were welcome to their opinion: Franklin's was different. In fact his views went far deeper than any expected of an older man with a youngster's rank. Deeper, darker; almost revolutionary, as well as being radical enough for them to be kept a carefully hidden secret.

"All alone, Mr Franklin?"

He looked around to see the genial face of one of the quartermasters poking through the opened doorway.

"Come in, Mr Maxwell," Franklin urged, using the formal mode of address despite being below deck. "Though the place is little better than a morgue and all I can offer is cold tea."

"Cold tea's a sight better than none at all," Maxwell told him cheerfully as he helped himself to the last of the pot then, at a subtle nod from Franklin, settled on one of the lad's sea chests opposite.

As a quartermaster, Maxwell was junior even to Franklin and with considerably less chance of further promotion. Franklin knew the man to have spent more than twenty-five years at sea, all in some Royal Navy vessel or other, and most whilst his country was at war. But he could detect no disillusionment as he regarded the wrinkled face that drank eagerly from his cup. The man had never expected anything, so was easily satisfied. Aspirations simply brought disappointment and Franklin would be the first to acknowledge that inner contentment was worth any amount of apparently fulfilled ambition.

"Word is we have sight of some early provisions," Maxwell told him on finishing his drink. "Just a few bosuns' stores; candles, and the like. But it's a start."

Maxwell was mainly responsible for supervising the steering of the ship, although he also assisted the sailing master with the stowing of supplies and shifting ballast; tasks that became redundant while they remained secured alongside the mole, and it was clear to Franklin the man was eager to return to normal duties.

"So soon?" he asked, with superficial interest. "Surely the ship has months of work before we should even think of provisioning?"

"It's Gib.," Maxwell replied philosophically. "Never much of anything, so you grab what you can while it's going. Besides, I've a mind we might get things moving afore long." He eyed the younger man for a moment. "And how is it with you, Mr Franklin?" he enquired. "Making you jump about a bit, are they?"

"Would that they were," the midshipman replied candidly. "Dockyard mateys have everything under control as far as repairs are concerned. Chips and his team are busy enough and, in a week or two, we may be able to bring back some of the regular hands as auxiliary painters, but there's a deal to do before that happens. I've been writing up a fresh schedule for when we come to take in water; last one took no account of the livestock's needs but, until more progress is made, it's really a question of keeping everything under supervision. There's nothing to do, as such; least nothing I can get my teeth into, and I must admit to finding it a mite wearisome."

"We'll be back on the briny in no time," Maxwell countered in a voice intentionally gruff to conceal any understanding his words might have conveyed. "Then you'll be complaining of too much on your plate. And with the older middies back in the mess, it'll be just as before, you see if it's not."

"Aye," Franklin agreed. "The old routine."

"One moment you're wiping noses," Maxwell grinned. "the next, they're giving us orders and we're both calling them sir."

"Something on those lines," Franklin agreed. He had noticed the quartermaster's unusually astute views on such matters in the past, while Maxwell regularly saw through his own personal façade, which was both disconcerting and reassuring at the same time. "But as you say, we'll be back to it afore long." Franklin continued with a feigned cheerfulness. "And it's better than being on the beach."

"That's the spirit," Maxwell beamed. "Ain't no use in wallowing in misery; there's enough about without makin' more. 'Sufficient unto the day is the evil therein,' - it's what my old mum used to say," he explained.

And then Franklin could not help but smile; his own mother had said something so very similar.

Chapter Two

The victualling yard was across nearby Rosia Bay, about half a mile to the south of the New Mole where *Prometheus* lay. It consisted of a series of single story buildings that actually held little of interest to entrepreneurs such as Charlie Bleeden. Even the newly built cutting room, a mild euphemism for the combined slaughterhouse and butcher's shop, did not attract him. There were storage problems connected with whole sides of fresh beef or pork, while the usual seamen's fare of salted meat, hard tack, or preserved vegetables would be scorned by his regulars. Slop clothing was a possibility, however: Bleeden's customers were always ready to pay out for a crisp new jacket or smart pair of trousers, especially if offered cheaper than those supplied by the purser, but again such things were not easy to store or transport.

Of course it was a different matter entirely with spirits and tobacco. High value items that were far easier to hide and much in demand; the only fly in the ointment being that all such luxuries were more securely held in bonded warehouses at the harbour itself. But there were still a few things in the victualling yard that might be of use to his buyers. And if they would pay, he was interested, for Charlie Bleeden had never been known to pass up a business opportunity.

The problem of logistics remained, however. Whatever he could liberate must be conveyed to the ship, the wooden huts where the seamen currently berthed being far too open and totally unsuitable for clandestine storage. And before then, his plunder would have to be carried past a fort strategically positioned on the nearby headland, then physically brought aboard. The last part should be no great undertaking; enough parts, supplies and men were constantly being taken on and off the liner to make the odd case of booty almost unnoticeable. Besides, Bleeden's little industry was well known: he had friends throughout *Prometheus* who would gladly turn a blind eye in return for a small consideration while, if he set his mind to it, he could probably secure himself a hand cart. In fact Bleeden found few things to be totally impossible: a bit of determination combined with the cheek of the devil could move mountains, and he scored highly on both counts.

But he had actually given up the idea of land transport long since. In his daily observations – Bleeden believed research to be a the heart of any successful operation – he noticed all who approached the victualling yard on foot were challenged. Even quite senior officers rarely passed through without at least a note of their name and business, so an ordinary seaman like himself would have no chance. He had tried to get round this by offering his services to Rigget, the purser's steward, but the man proved as incorruptible as the psalm singing hypocrite who employed him. Then Bleeden chanced across his current plan and, even if he did say so himself, it was a beauty.

"Very well, lay her alongside," he muttered to his two messmates, as the jolly boat drew near to an empty wharf. The yard was freshly built, indeed more warehouses were under construction further to the south, and Bleeden guessed the system must have an Achilles heel. Sure enough, in all his observations he had not seen one approach from the sea challenged; a remarkable oversight for any organisation whose main purpose was to serve the Navy. But it was on just such an omission that Bleeden's success had been built, and one of his talents to identify and exploit such things to the full.

He had other gifts as well. For much of his life Bleeden had crewed for a number of different smuggling gangs before latterly running his own operation. It was a lucrative activity that had only come to an end a few months before, following a most generous offer from the magistrates at Seaford. He could either sign on with a Royal Navy ship for a minimum of five years, or spend the next seven serving out a penal sentence in the colonies. And so it was that Bleeden found himself posted aboard a seventy-four, and putting his not inconsiderable skills as a seaman to far more noble use.

But on that particular day he was not intending anything that would benefit his country, and neither was he dressed in the duck trousers and checked shirt of a regular Jack. Instead, Bleeden sported the frock coat of a master's mate, something that had been simple enough to secure from a cockpit hammock man. As were the knee britches which, although somewhat tight on his sturdy frame, passed a cursory inspection. The hat proved harder; Bleeden's head was unusually large and both examples found for him sat on top in a manner that appeared far too comical. And it was a hot day, with barely a cloud in the sky, so the sight of a warrant officer carrying his scraper might be considered unusual. But Bleeden trusted he would be outside for the briefest of periods; and was not averse to taking the odd chance when necessary.

Under Cranston and Greg's expert guidance, the jolly boat drifted easily up to a low quay, finally coming to rest against the manilla edged rubbing strake with hardly a shudder. Bleeden jumped out clutching at his hat and, not waiting for the small craft to be secured, made straight for the collection of huts that sat amidst the larger storehouses. The place was crowded, crates were being opened, wagons loaded and there was a good deal of chatter and calling out between the workers, although Bleeden walked confidently through it all and was not challenged. He knew that inside one of the huts would be the agent victualler, a man ultimately responsible for all stores coming in or going out of the yard. If there had been a way to get on his right side, it would be the gateway to wealth beyond imagining, but Bleeden was not so foolish as to attempt such a thing. He had long since learned who might be bribed and who might not and, surprisingly, junior grade civil servants usually fell into the latter category. If he were better connected it would be a different story. Even in the short time they had been in Gibraltar, Bleeden had learned that most on the port captain's staff were as bent as the proverbial doornail. Once he could engineer a meeting between someone of influence, perhaps a writer in the naval storekeeper's office, or even the man himself, things would change. He was sure an arrangement could be made that suited both parties, and he would not be reduced to using more mundane means to earn a crust.

He stepped swiftly past the first hut; the place had curtains at the window and was likely to contain those who might challenge him, then straight through the open double doors of an adjoining warehouse that he judged to have more potential. Sure enough, at the far end an elderly man sat at a combination of desk and bench, his head bowed over a large, open ledger. Until that day Bleeden had only been able to observe the clerk from a distance but, by his faded hair and permanent stoop, had reckoned him to be easy meat and a closer look confirmed that assessment.

"Requisition from Captain Conn, HMS *Canopus*," Bleeden said in a voice that artfully combined authority, confidence and routine. "Half-hundredweight o' soap, half hundredweight o' butter and fourteen pounds o' raisins, any time you're ready."

The elderly man brought the form Bleeden planted on his ledger closer to him and stared at it through thick lensed spectacles.

"This ain't straight," his voice was tired and husky. "Mr Kendall, the superintendent of the wharf, 'as to make out a warrant – that's the next office." So saying the clerk passed the paper back up to Bleeden and returned to his work.

There had been a time when that might have sufficed. Faced with even the smallest opposition, Bleeden would have bowed out gracefully, grateful to retain his liberty. But one of the lessons learned since being condemned to a period as a professional seaman was the advantages his new status actually held.

When carried out by a civilian, any theft that involved a value greater than forty shillings was punishable by death, and what Bleeden proposed to steal was worth considerably more. But if a foremast Jack were caught committing such an offence, he was unlikely to meet the same fate. And neither would he be dismissed the service – more was the pity. With the shortage of skilled manpower being as it was, the worst he might expect was a dose of the cat. Not a pleasant prospect perhaps but, when a smuggler, Bleeden had lived in constant dread of far worse, so was content to take the risk and hold his ground.

"Mr Kendall's squared it with Mr Pownall," he insisted, smoothly inserting the name of the naval storekeeper for all Gibraltar into his speech. "I just come from his office. This lot were missed from the last lighter, and Captain Conn's got a promissory note sayin' all would be made up. Ship sails in less than twelve hour', he can't wait about."

"So where's the warrant?" the clerk asked.

"I can get's it," Bleeden informed him with just the right amount of certainty as he tossed the paper down in front of the clerk. "But Captain Conn ain't too happy – 'pparently there's been more than a few mix-ups provisioning the barky as it is. He's ashore now. I can say you ain't cooperating and bring 'im down if you wishes. But he's a man I wouldn't want to cross on a good day, and this is a long way off."

"There's no need," the clerk replied, then raised his eyes to meet that of the seaman directly. "Stay here; I shall not be long." So saying the old man rose from his stool and tottered from the room, stepping out into the bright afternoon sunshine and leaving Bleeden alone.

There were packing cases and crates to every side, but all were securely sealed and much too large to be moved. And, for once, Bleeden did not feel inclined to pilfer. A sixth sense, nurtured through many years' misconduct was starting to make itself known. He waited for a while, shifting from foot to foot while the doubts grew. A clock could be heard: each sturdy tick seemed to emphasise time as it passed, while Bleeden's bluster dissolved further with every second. His note still lay on the ledger: he was about to retrieve it and make for the boat when the sunshine that came flooding in from outside suddenly darkened and Bleeden turned to see the silhouette of the old man standing in the doorway. But he was not alone: another, taller, figure stood next to him.

"There he is, Mr Kendall," the elderly voice wheezed. "That's the man."

In an instant Bleeden was on the move. There was no other way out of the warehouse, he would have to rush the door and common sense told him it was best to do so straight away. Blasting through, the two men fell to either side as he ran between them. He felt the borrowed britches rip as his long legs stretched, but it was just a simple matter of crossing the yard – less than a hundred and fifty feet, although the ground was rough, and he stumbled more than once. There seemed to be figures everywhere, and some turned to look in his direction as he went. But no one thought to stop him and soon the boat was in sight, along with Cranston and Greg, sitting nonchalantly on the quay.

"Cast off!" he gasped, thundering nearer. Mooring lines were being slipped as he approached and the craft was actually moving when Bleeden flung himself off, landing squarely in the bottom between both thwarts. For a moment the hull tipped alarmingly and he lay still and panting while his mates did their best to stabilise the vessel.

"After you, was they?" one enquired, grinning. Bleeden raised himself, and looked back towards the victualling yard. Everyone in sight had returned to their work and there was no sign of either the clerk, or his superior; the one object out-of-place being Bleeden's black bicorne hat that was rolling, abandoned, amid the dirt.

"I were smoked," he confessed. "Best get a shake on, in case they comes after us with the guffies."

The men laid into their sculls and soon they were crossing Rosia Bay, where a subtle change of course allowed them to mingle with other small craft. But there was no pursuit. Even when they passed the grim, grey outline of the fort, the only interest paid was from a bored sentry who watched them idly as they shot by. In no time they rounded the end of the mole and *Prometheus*, with all her reassuring bulk, came into sight.

"Any joy?" Ashley, the coxswain, was waiting for them. He had authorised the use of the jolly boat and beamed expectantly as they slotted the tiny craft next to its larger peers.

"Na, we drew a dead un," Greg smirked. "An could be in bilboes b'now, if Charlie Boy here weren't such a dandy runner."

Bleeden accepted the compliment with scant acknowledgement.

"Ah well, it were a long shot," Ashley sighed. "But worth the effort."

"Oh, I ain't given up," Bleeden told him. "They only won the first round. We'll be back, and see 'em cleaned out proper." He was just starting to smart, both from the defeat and what had been a decidedly undignified exit. But he was serious in his assertion. Bleeden had run from both revenue, and dragoons in his time; one old man and his boss weren't going to get the better of him.

* * *

"Franklin is the obvious choice," the first lieutenant said. "He has served as acting lieutenant before, and been at sea as long as either of us."

Prometheus would remain in the dockyard's hands for several more weeks but Banks and Caulfield had been discussing the changes needed when she once more became operational. And they were using the great cabin; the captain's quarters having been one of the few areas that received minimal damage during the recent battle. Already much had been corrected and the magnificent apartment restored to a close approximation of its former glory.

"Franklin – that would be the oldster." Captain Banks pondered, remembering. "He has charge of the aft cockpit, does he not?"

"Senior of the berth, and keeps good order," the first lieutenant confirmed. "Gets respect from the more experienced while the squealers treat him very much as a sea daddy."

"You do not think he is already serving a useful purpose?"

"Possibly," Caulfield allowed. "Although there would doubtless be others who would perform as well. And with most young gentlemen ashore, we have only the four newest currently in the berth: they should be able to look after each other well enough for the time being."

"What age is he?"

"Thirty four or five, I should chance," Caulfield replied.

"It is old to be a midshipman," Banks said, as he considered further. "Has he sought advancement?"

"Sat his board twice, as a matter of fact." Caulfield cleared his throat. "And was rejected both times."

"There is little shame in that," Banks gave a brief smile. "A lot may depend on the examining captains..."

"Indeed," The first lieutenant agreed and went to add more before thinking better of it. He had failed his own lieutenant's examination at the first visit, yet happened to know Banks breezed through his, and when he was considerably younger than eighteen, the statutory minimum for a commission.

"Still he carries out his duties well," Caulfield mused. "And I've not heard a bad word said about him, except..."

Banks gave an enquiring look.

"Except that he may be a dissenter," the first lieutenant added.

"In truth?" the captain was surprised. "I had no idea."

"He attends divine service," the first lieutenant continued guardedly, "and is always alert when the Articles of War are read."

"And the prayers?"

"The prayers also," Caulfield confirmed awkwardly.

"So is it my sermons that concern him?" Banks asked in sudden realisation.

"I fear so," Caulfield admitted. "They may not be entirely to his taste."

"There is no reason why not," Banks protested. "All are supposedly written by a God fearing man; a Church of England Bishop, or so I recall. And I feel them delivered soundly; could it be a difficulty in hearing, do you suppose?"

Caulfield said nothing. As far as he was concerned, the captain's weekly bellowing fulfilled its purpose and most of the men seemed equally satisfied; there were even some who failed to notice whenever he reached the end of his book, and started again at the beginning. And he could not help but feel that *Prometheus* was lucky in avoiding the appointment of a chaplain. Such people were more nuisance than they were worth to his mind, and too often inclined to impose a judgemental atmosphere on the wardroom. But there was no doubting the captain's sermons lacked sensitivity and were not a patch on their previous sailing master's efforts.

"Perhaps it were better when Fraiser was aboard," Banks added after thought, and Caulfield gave a silent nod.

"So what is he?" the captain continued. "Methodist? Papist? Surely not a Quaker?"

"I have no idea," Caulfield's expression was blank. "He is known to drink wine and eat pig like a regular Christian. In fact, were it not for tattle-tale and his obvious inattention, I would not be concerned at all and consider him as devout as you or me."

"You might wish to speak to him about it?" Banks suggested.

"I might," Caulfield agreed. "Though a man's faith is usually considered a private matter; providing he has one of course," he added quickly. "And Mr Midshipman Franklin is not alone; there are several others who do not attend too closely."

"Are there, indeed?" Banks asked suspiciously. As a post captain, he was the senior king's representative aboard *Prometheus* so naturally assumed himself to represent God into the bargain. And until that moment he had been quite proud of his weekly sermons. That they were delivered also gave him an additional source of income, as he felt entirely justified in claiming the monthly groat extracted from each man for religious instruction, and so many regular fourpences was not a sum to be carelessly tossed aside. But Banks was also aware it would take just one right-minded individual to complain for him to attract severe censure. There might be times when the lower deck were given inferior rations or treated badly in other respects, with subsequent protest falling on deaf ears. But a foolishly tolerant Admiralty had decreed spiritual guidance relatively cheap to administer, and this was one instance where the regular Jacks were likely to see their will exercised over his.

"So Franklin considers himself a man of faith?" Banks scratched at his chin in thought. "There is nothing to that effect in his personal papers."

"Such a thing should surely not deter advancement," Caulfield commented delicately. "Though he may have problems taking the Test Act. I recall a particularly vehement Presbyterian who refused to swear an oath and never progressed beyond warrant rank. But if Franklin were made acting lieutenant it would only be while King were unwell; he might not remain in position long enough to sit another board."

"I would not be so certain of that," Banks rested back in his chair. "We are awaiting a replacement for Benson after all."

Ten days before, Lieutenant Benson had been lured away by the dash of a visiting frigate. The act itself was bad enough, but the young man removed himself without formal notice or arranging an exchange; a fact that still rankled with both men.

"The naval commissioner has not provided?" Caulfield asked.

"He undertook to find a suitable body though none have volunteered as yet." Banks replied. "Doubtless a man will be appointed in time, but I would prefer one who came willingly."

"You are assuming Tom King shall be able to function," the first lieutenant's voice was slightly hesitant. "When fully recovered, I am meaning. It is what we all wish obviously, but..."

"I realise he may never heal completely," the captain grunted. "But many who lose a limb do, we have to look no further than our current commander as an example. Though there is a deal of difference between the duties of an admiral, and that of a second lieutenant..."

"With Franklin's help he may have more chance." Caulfield's tone remained soft.

"Then dissenter or not, we must give him a try," Banks said, decisively. "In fact every effort should be made to see King back as an active member of the wardroom. *Prometheus* would be a very different ship without him."

* * *

Kate opened the door to the sick berth proper and silently let herself in. Robert had gone to speak with the captain in the hope she could once more ship as surgeon's mate. With luck he may also be able to arrange accommodation for Poppy. The girl should still be waiting for her on the shore and, if past experiences were anything to go by, probably getting herself into a deal of trouble, but Kate had no inclination to find out. And while most of her possessions were in the dubious care of her maid, there was precious little else to do. Consequently she had decided not to wait for her husband, but seek out Tom King by herself.

Of course she would have been prepared to delay, but knowing that what was probably her closest friend apart from Robert lay in the next room proved too much. And with the ship reverberating to the sounds of saw, hammer and chisel, it would be interesting to see how deeply asleep the cove actually was.

But she had not expected the darkness: the small, stuffy room was almost pitch black. She stopped, uncertainly on the threshold, and it was simply because Robert chose the same moment to return that she did not turn back immediately.

"Kate, I said we would visit him later," her husband told her in a harsh whisper, while collecting a pusser's dip.

"Why so dark?" she enquired, unabashed.

"I keep it so in the early afternoon," Robert explained as he lit the wick from a taper, before closing down the glass. "So my patients have a chance to rest after their midday..." A series of loud hammer blows applied directly above their heads interrupted him and the surgeon smiled ruefully. "Though with the ship being refitted, it hardly makes a deal of difference."

"Then why did you not transfer everyone ashore?"

"Because some do not care to leave the ship." The familiar voice came from the depths of the room, and Kate peered down to see the dim features of Tom King's face beaming up at her. "It is good to see you, Kate: what cheer?"

"Good to see you also, Tom," she told him, settling herself down on the deck to be at the same level as his bunk. "Though sorry to find you poorly. Why won't you go ashore?"

"I've heard too many tales of what they does to you in hospitals," he explained. "And would rather stay aboard the ship, even if it means remaining in your husband's care."

The two men exchanged expressions of mock disdain, but Kate took little notice. Her eyes were becoming used to the gloom and, with the aid of Robert's light, she was able to make out Tom more clearly. The lad, and Kate could never think of him as anything but, had lost a good deal of weight; his face was drawn, and there were dark patches under both eyes. But the main difference was something far more obvious and she could not help but take a sharp breath as she realised what must have happened. King regarded her with the cynical look of one accustomed to such a reaction, and Kate did all she could to regain some composure, although the dreadful truth remained with her. Tom had always been such a fit young man, and as active and energetic as any. Yet now would have to put up with this...

But there was no disguising the fact; his blankets were pulled down in deference to the heat and she could see the left sleeve of his night shirt clearly. And that it was quite empty.

* * *

Franklin approached the double doors of the wardroom and resisted the temptation to knock. He had been inside the senior officers' quarters on several occasions, but never dreamed the place would ever become his home. He pushed the door open, and entered. Beneath his feet he felt the stiff white canvas that was carefully painted with black squares to represent tiles. Although hardly the height of sophistication, it was a pleasant touch and, when compared with his previous berth, luxury indeed.

Of course the wardroom might not be his home for very long, Franklin reminded himself. All too soon, either due to some foolish mistake on his part, or simple logic, he could find himself back in that adolescent nursery on the deck below. And he would return to teaching the lads; those who were richer, younger and better connected, the ways of the sea, only to have them leave him behind in their wake.

A steward appeared, and seemed surprised to see what he would take to be an elderly midshipman in such illustrious surroundings.

"May I assist?" the young man asked with an odd look in his

eye. He might not have been more than a junior member of the catering staff, but knew his place, and clearly believed Franklin to be out of his.

"I am appointed acting lieutenant," Franklin told him, a little stiffly. "And will be berthing here."

"Mr Franklin, welcome!" It was an older voice and it came from a far smarter senior steward who seemed to have appeared from nowhere. Franklin had noticed the man, but only in passing; apart from his immaculate uniform, there was little to distinguish him from the other servants. Now that he regarded him more closely though he detected an unusual air; a presence, almost, and the purposeful look in the clear blue eyes could not be ignored.

"I heard you were to join us, sir," the steward continued, while surreptitiously bustling the boy out of the way. "And expect you will be taking Mr Carlton's cabin. It is cleared out and ready. My name is Kennedy, I have charge of all officers' domestic arrangements; if you would care to follow me?"

Franklin found himself being led into the wardroom proper. A large table sat lengthways down the main room, ending just before the mizzen mast, which was decorated with a sheet of highly polished copper laid about it. And light – a rare and valued commodity in any ship of war – streamed in through the massive stern windows, adding an extra gleam to the glistening plate that was already set out for the day's main meal. He paused to take it all in; the wardroom had a generous deckhead and was comfortably spacious, despite also containing two lines of cabins on either side, and it was to one of these that the steward led him. There was a small door and, reaching it, Kennedy stood politely to one side.

Franklin ducked in through the low entrance. It was undoubtedly a tiny room, no more than six feet by five, but the lack of space meant he need not share it with a cannon. There was a canvas basin, what some might generously call a locker and a hanging cot. Beneath was space for a sea chest on which he would be able to sit when at the narrow desk wedged into the opposite corner.

"I can have your dunnage brought up from the cockpit,"

Kennedy, who had followed, suggested. "And appoint a marine to attend you."

Franklin turned to the steward once more to thank him and was again struck by his presence. Kennedy emanated a rare sense of assurance: comfort almost. This might be nothing out of the ordinary; Franklin was totally unaccustomed to dealing with professional servants, but still the man seemed subtly different to most stewards.

He looked around once more when finally alone and allowed himself a private smile. In his two previous spells as acting lieutenant, Franklin had never been provided with such luxury. The first time was a shore posting, when he shared a barrack room with a fellow regulating officer, and the other aboard a frigate. On that occasion the second lieutenant, for whom he had been deputising, was taken ill, and retired to his cabin, forcing Franklin to remain berthed in the cockpit. But now, finally, he had achieved something few aboard a ship-of-war ever experienced. It wasn't his own personal servant, the elite atmosphere of a wardroom, or even knowing he was, once more, so very close to achieving the status of a commissioned officer. At any moment he may be sent back to join the boys for what he assumed would be the rest of his service life, but until that happened he had the luxury of his own private space. And for as long as he did, Franklin would be a happy man indeed.

Chapter Three

She had seen heavy action without a doubt, but even though *Prometheus* was forced to wait until the less damaged *Canopus* had been attended to, the Gibraltar dockyard was making good progress. With the aid of the sheer hulk, one lower mast and several less significant spars were already replaced and the riggers had exchanged much of her tattered cordage. In doing so they worked in close cooperation with Knolls, the boatswain. He was a standing officer; one who had been with the ship for most of his professional life and reserved the affection many gave to children or dogs for her and her alone. Knolls hoped to set the tophamper to rights within two weeks and, as far better materials were being used than those originally supplied at the last refit, he was especially enthusiastic in his work.

But other problems were not so easily solved. *Prometheus'* hull had been penetrated in several places although all, bar one, were above the waterline. The exception, made by a heavy French round shot, was a jagged hole by her main hold, just below the sail room. This was currently sealed by a fothered canvas patch until a more permanent repair could be effected. As soon as the rest of the hull was watertight, the ship would be partially careened, allowing the damage to be properly addressed.

The remaining work was more easily attended to. She was an old ship, made at a time when massive beams of English oak were not such a rarity, and her frame was uncommonly strong. By the nature of her construction any repair, though lengthy, was not exceedingly complicated, it being more a matter of tackling the defects in order, and replacing damaged timbers using as few scarphs as possible.

There were some individual items, such as parts of the galley stove and the forward capstan that needed new metalwork and this often entailed their actual manufacture. To that end a temporary blacksmith's shop had been set up on the mole, where teams of hefty men carried out their gruelling work under the broiling Mediterranean sun. Replacement sails were supplied from the ship herself, *Prometheus* having been fully provisioned and stored less than two months before the action, and the sailmaker's team were already making up those required from their spare canvas.

But, beneath the awnings, the splintered wood and what was a veritable army of shore workers, *Prometheus* remained a powerful warship in the eyes of her crew. She may have several empty ports, but the missing cannon would be replaced from Gibraltar's extensive armoury: soon they would have two full decks of thirty-two and eighteen pound long guns to play with once more. This formidable fire power would be augmented by heavy calibre carronades, nicknamed smashers by their servers, and when her Royal Marine force of considerably over one hundred officers and men were once more embarked, *Prometheus* would become a menacing opponent to any enemy, be they on land or at sea.

But one difficulty still remained, and it was a substantial one. There were some materials in short supply; a few could be substituted, manufactured or even dispensed with, but nothing would solve Lieutenant Caulfield's eternal problem of the lack of manpower.

When she first left England, *Prometheus'* complement was short by about seventy trained hands. Good fortune later made up this deficit, but she had been in action several times since and, even without the losses sustained during the last two occasions, would normally be expected to require fresh men at such a stage in her commission.

In any vessel powered by the wind and subject to all forms of weather, hands could succumb to a number of debilitating injuries, ranging from broken limbs, rupture or the often deadly consequences of falling from a yard. When illnesses, disease and the ever present pox entered the equation, and the casualties added to her battle losses, *Prometheus* was judged to be just under one hundred able men light.

And it was a dilemma without any obvious solution. Trained seamen were as rare as fresh water on Gibraltar: the small supply of both being jealously guarded and only doled out under extreme duress. But if *Prometheus* were to sail again it would be to join Nelson. She would either be added to the Toulon blockade, or sent to the purple waters of the east, both places that offered very little chance of making up numbers. Caulfield glanced around the men currently gathered at the wardroom dining table: his two fit and fully commissioned lieutenants, Corbett and Lewis; Franklin, in what was clearly a borrowed uniform as well as Brehaut, the sailing master, and Marine Captain Reynolds. It was their regular Monday conference, but on that particular occasion there was only one item on the agenda.

"Would it be too extreme to raid a homebound India convoy?" Reynolds asked. As a military man, he alone could pose such a question, although Caulfield was in no mood to be gentle.

"It would be a foolish move indeed," he told him, firmly. "In sight of Dover Castle maybe, but with still over a thousand miles to cover, our actions should not be tolerated and doubtless must evoke a reprimand from the Admiralty at the very least."

"There is no possibility from the shore?" This was from Lieutenant Corbett, a new man, but one Caulfield had taken to. And, as usual, it was a reasoned contribution.

"The captain is currently with the naval commissioner," Caulfield answered. "It is hoped he may allow us a few men, but obviously that cannot be guaranteed. There were numbers to make up from *Canopus*, after all."

"There were indeed," Corbett confirmed with a smile. He had come under exchange from *Canopus*, and appeared remarkably happy to be free of her.

"And if he does not, shall we be able to function?" Brehaut this time, and Caulfield looked at the provisional watch bill once more before replying. It was in no way complete, several men posted still being on the wounded list, but served as an indication at least.

"I should say so, yes," he conceded at last. "Though it would not be ideal, and further losses hard to bear." That was the point; fortune had smiled upon them in the past but it was far more usual for a crew to deplete than increase. Within a few months they may find themselves seriously short of hands through nothing more than the expected erosion caused by being at sea. Should a serious case of ship fever strike, it would be a different story, and even a dose of mild influenza could bring trouble. But there was one ailment that Caulfield worried over most of all, and every day *Prometheus* lay in the dockyard's hands gave more opportunity for it to drain his manpower dramatically.

Known as Gibraltar fever, it was first recognised over ten years before. Since then the epidemic had been responsible for many thousands of deaths, including that of a previous governor and, in 1800, forced the postponement of Admiral Keith's planned attack on Cádiz. Measures had been taken to prevent what quickly became an endemic disease with improved ventilation being a feature of the fine new hospital, while fresh water and an adequate diet would soon be available to both civilians and the military. Any ship arriving from Spain or the Barbary coast was placed under strict quarantine, yet every year the ailment reappeared, and the preceding summer had been one of the worst. Such a comprehensive refit meant the bulk of *Prometheus'* men needed to be transferred ashore and were now cooped up in wooden huts within the military barracks. Should any of them become affected, the disease would spread like the proverbial wildfire, and Caulfield might find himself almost entirely without a crew.

And then, as he was well aware, his problems really would begin.

* * *

"I wished to speak to you first," Manning told her, once they had quit the sick berth and returned to the dispensary.

"You wrote of his injuries being to the chest," Kate said, ignoring what might have been a rare rebuke from her husband. "Why then the loss of an arm?"

Manning sighed. "His chest cavity did indeed cause my concern," he admitted. "The entire area was extensively punctured and penetrated. It was a splinter wound: you are aware how they can present?"

She said nothing: they both knew only too well.

"We did all we could to keep the lesion clean, though it seemed hopeless, and damage is still to be seen."

"But the arm." Kate persisted.

"Yes, the arm," Manning agreed. "I fear that was somewhat overlooked."

She waited while he gathered his thoughts, although the pause continued for longer than was usual.

"What happened, Robert," she asked at last. "Was it..."

"It were an oversight," he interrupted harshly. "Indications of corruption became noticeable after about a week, and I thought them to be in the major lesion. There was a young girl assisting at the time, and we gave him every attention. The wound actually appeared healthy enough, but was drained and cauterised wherever putrefaction might lie; the usual practice: you will understand."

She did: poor Tom must have gone through agonies, yet all Kate could do was nod in silent agreement.

"And it wasn't for a good while later that I realised it to be the arm that was affected all along."

Robert was now close to tears. Leaning forward on the stool, he wrung his hands together but would not meet her eyes, and what she could see of his face was a picture of misery.

"I just didn't think to check," he repeated pathetically. "Judy changed the dressings, but would not be expected to know the signs. It seemed obvious the infection must lie in the chest. I was so sure..."

"And it was gangrene?" Kate prompted.

Robert inclined his head as if in defeat. "The smallest of cuts that could have been attended to in an instant, were I not distracted by the larger damage elsewhere – were I paying sufficient attention..."

"You had other responsibilities," she reminded him. "And he was surely not the only wounded man under your care."

"But that is no excuse," he replied, wretchedly. Then his eyes were finally raised to meet hers, but they held nothing but torment. "Tom is my friend; my best, were it to be known," he confessed. "Yet I am to blame for the loss of his arm. What will he think of me when he discovers?"

* * *

"I fear experienced seamen are not so easy to find, Sir Richard," Captain Otway, the naval commissioner for Gibraltar told Banks. "All the liners in the Med. Squadron are a hundred or so below their wartime complements; why only last week that youngster, Conn was pestering me for hands. *Canopus* might be carrying Rear Admiral Campbell to join Nelson, but even he was allowed the bare minimum."

It was a light and airy room that overlooked the harbour; their seats were comfortable and Gordon Stewart, an old friend from his midshipman days, had joined them. But so important was the subject under discussion that Banks felt no inclination to relax; instead he knew himself to be tense, fractious and extremely vulnerable. However hard his officers may work, a ship without sufficient men can never be effective, and if he were to be denied even a few able hands the interview was liable to end in argument.

"But I can perhaps provide twenty." Otway continued, grudgingly. "Some – most, I would hope – will be trained, but there shall inevitably be a few landsmen amongst them."

At the naval commissioner's words, a wave of relief flowed down Banks' shoulders, and suddenly the late afternoon sunshine became pleasurable. Even ignoring the last point, twenty sound bodies would make a considerable difference. It was actually more than he had hoped for: but Banks was yet to relax fully, as much depended on the source of such a windfall.

"Would these be from the fleet?" he asked cautiously. Every captain had those amongst their crew they would prefer to see the back of, and an influx of cast-offs, likely to be trouble makers or other discontents, might not be the blessing it appeared.

"Nothing of the sort, Sir Richard; it would be wrong of me to foist any such rubbish upon you." The elderly man huffed. "In the main they shall be John Company men, currently in barracks. The *Earl of Essex* came in a month back and needs attention from our dockyard; *Prometheus* and *Canopus* received priority, of course but, to my mind, a ship that cannot sail is in no need of a crew. Accordingly, I think we might borrow a number of her people to see you satisfied."

That was good news indeed as far as he was concerned, although Banks could not help considering the merchant's master. Twenty men would likely account for a large proportion of his crew.

"That would not be the entire draft, Sir Richard," Commander Stewart added. "We have a few regular Navy men available. Those that are to be discharged from the hospital."

Stewart, a former shipmate, now acted as second to the commissioner. Banks wondered if his friend was pulling any strings on his behalf, and found he cared little either way. Twenty men was a fine number, and *Prometheus* would be a better ship because of them.

"From the naval hospital?" Banks asked. "I assume them to be sound?"

"Oh indeed," Stewart hurried to assure him. "Most had Gib. fever, though a couple were suffering from typhus. As you know, once cured they can be considered immune from further attack, so should be doubly welcome."

Banks was suitably relieved, although he did make a mental note to have Manning check the new hands carefully.

"I would it were more, Sir Richard," Otway continued, his tone now slightly mollified. "The action you fought was much needed; should those liners have been allowed to dock in France it would have stretched what resources we have still further. Even if a Spanish port were chosen, we should have had to lose at least one third rate, probably more, to keep watch on them."

Banks was about to reply when a double tap was heard at the outer door, and all three men turned to see a smartly uniformed lieutenant enter.

"Forgive the intrusion, gentleman," he said, bowing his head slightly to Banks and Stewart. Then, to the naval commissioner: "The captain of the brig is with me now, sir. You wished to interview him; shall he wait outside?"

"No, Hoskins; ask him to join us." Otway looked back as the lieutenant bustled out. "You will not mind, I am certain," he told Banks. "The young fellow came in early this morning with a captured brig sent down from Toulon. More holes than a colander, by the looks of her. Seems they ran in with a corsair but made it away, which would appear to do the boy a deal of credit. No doubt there is a story to tell, and you may as well hear it."

Banks had noticed a small, two masted vessel in the process of being secured when he rose at first light. She was in a far worse condition than *Prometheus* had been and indeed appeared barely afloat. Several deep holes marked her sides, two sails were fothered about the hull and a constant stream of clear water flowed from her scuppers. The door opened again, admitting a young, thin, fair-haired man who seemed slightly too long for his tattered midshipman's uniform.

"Acting Lieutenant Hunt," Hoskins announced, and both were waved to chairs at the table.

"Very pleased to see your safe arrival, Mr Hunt," Otway told him when they were settled. "Your command has certainly known better days; met with an enemy xebec, or so I hears?"

"Indeed, sir," Hunt agreed. His voice was hesitant and his right eye twitched erratically as he spoke. "I was commissioned to carry despatches from Admiral Bickerton," he went on to explain. "We ran in with a pirate at dawn six days back."

"And when did you leave Sir Richard?" Otway asked.

"On the tenth, sir."

That was twelve days ago: Banks considered the lad. If, as seemed likely, the prize was one of his first commands, he would have slept little before the encounter. And, by the look of him, even less since.

"You fought her?" the naval commissioner persisted, although his habitually gruff tone had softened slightly.

"I did, though caused little damage, sir. She were finally seen off by the arrival of an American frigate."

"An American?" The change in Otway's pitch was noticeable. Having powerful neutral vessels on his station must be a cause for concern, but Banks detected something more personal in the man's reaction. Perhaps they had been enemies in the past?

"The *Philadelphia*, sir, Captain Bainbridge," Hunt explained. "They came to our rescue and damn near caught the devils into the bargain."

"Then it seems our former cousins can be of some use," Otway grunted, and Banks knew he had been correct in his assumption. "But even one of their mighty frigates could not take a xebec, eh?"

"The xebec is a swift craft, sir," Stewart suggested gently, although his superior chose not to hear.

"Anyways, you took a deal of damage," Otway continued. "What was your butcher's bill?"

"Four dead, sir." Hunt replied. "And three died later – we had no surgeon. One was the master's mate who acted as my second in command. And there were four wounded who made it to harbour."

"They have been transferred to the naval hospital, sir." Hoskins intervened smoothly.

A captured brig of such a size would have needed a reasonable crew to travel from Toulon to Gibraltar, but probably no more than twenty, Banks decided. That meant the action had accounted for more than half her people; a high ratio.

"You did well to make it so far in such a condition," Otway allowed. "Why did Sir Richard send you: where is Lord Nelson?"

"Admiral Nelson is conducting a loose blockade," Hunt told them. "I was with Admiral Bickerton's squadron, so it was he who gave me the despatches."

"Bickerton gave you despatches?" the naval commissioner's expression lifted.

"Yes, sir," Hunt replied, and was about to say more, but Otway was still speaking.

"That is good news indeed; we have been awaiting word," he

said. "Has the dockyard supervisor inspected your vessel?"

"He has, sir, but believes no repair will serve," once more Hunt had been about to continue, but it was Hoskins who interrupted this time.

"Mr Cawsgrove suggests it be condemned," the lieutenant informed them. "As soon as any fittings have been removed, of course."

"And how many sound men do you have?" Otway snapped back at Hunt.

"Seven, sir," the young man replied. "Eight if you count Allinson, who is only slightly wounded."

The commissioner turned to Banks with a look of triumph on his face. "That's a further eight for you, Sir Richard," he said. "And a likely young lieutenant – you were a man down, as I recall?"

Eight more men would certainly be welcome, Banks decided, although he was less sure about another acting lieutenant. Hunt carried himself well, and was obviously capable, but a more experienced man would have been preferable.

"And we can certainly take what we can from your capture, Hunt," Otway was now positively beaming. "Pluck the guns from her, and anything else we find of use."

"I am afraid they had to be abandoned, sir," Hunt told him doubtfully. "As well as most of our dry provisions."

Otway shot the lad an enquiring look, and he continued.

"Captain Bainbridge was most helpful, sir. He sent his surgeon to attend our wounded and a team of carpenters for the damage, but they could not seal the hull. We thrummed two sails and fothered them about but still needed to pump three hours out of every four to keep her swimming."

"So you abandoned them?" the old man sighed. "It is understandable, though a waste of victuals and ordinance nonetheless."

"No, sir, I passed them to the Americans," Hunt replied innocently.

There was a stillness and Banks was strangely aware of a chill that must have come in through the partially opened windows.

"You gave British guns to Americans?" he asked, as if the young man had committed some terrible act of debauchery.

"Indeed, sir," the lad's eye began twitching again. "It seemed a waste to destroy them, and the Americans had saved the ship, as well as us. Why, without their help we would all have been taken and made slaves."

The pause that followed suggested Otway may possibly have preferred such an outcome.

"The Americans are our allies, sir." Stewart suggested diplomatically. "Their intervention with the Ottoman Empire means we can still water in Tetuan. And if the brig was a capture, the guns would surely have been French, not British..."

"Then much good it will do them," the old man grumbled. "Though I would rather see them at the bottom of the Med. than in the hands of those turncoats. I still cannot forgive them the loss of the *Lark*; fine ship and an even finer crew. And I know what you're going to say," he added before anyone could. "That was twenty-five years ago – but let me tell you gentlemen, some things you don't forget..."

"You mentioned despatches," Banks prompted, in an effort to change the subject. The lad appeared to have suffered enough and good news might restore something of Otway's humour. But he could tell immediately the attempt had failed. The boy's expression grew even more miserable and for a moment Banks thought he might crumble.

"No, sir." he mumbled. "When it were likely we would be taken I – I..."

"So they *did* go over the side?" Otway finished for him.

The silence returned and the others looked awkwardly about the room, not daring to meet anyone else's eyes. And then finally the naval commissioner spoke once more.

"I suppose we should all be grateful you didn't give them to the Americans as well," he sighed.

* * *

Kennedy felt extremely satisfied with his afternoon's work. The new man, Acting Lieutenant Franklin, had been heaven sent and was perfect. On returning from seeing him to his quarters, the steward made for his own tiny cabin just outside the wardroom entrance. It was one he shared with the warranted cook, but Olivier would be on duty, and Kennedy knew he had the next few hours to himself.

He opened the narrow panelled door and squeezed inside, then sat on the cook's sea chest, which was the only form of seating in a space little larger than a cupboard. The post had been delivered earlier and Kennedy was especially keen to open the light package that was for him.

The wafer broke under the slightest pressure from his thumb; Kennedy made a mental note to tell his brothers to be more careful in sealing correspondence in future. Although there was really no need, he reassured himself, not when the contents would be of such little use to anyone else.

He reached inside and pulled out a banker's draft drawn on Barclay's, the Quaker bank, to the sum of ten pounds. But the paper was not complete, and Kennedy examined it more carefully. It had been neatly cut down the middle, with just one half included. The steward nodded his head in approval; it was a system they had used in the past. He would receive a similar package in the next post, although that should contain the opposite half of the draft. Once joined with diachylon tape it would become legal currency, allowing him to buy supplies. And ten pounds was a splendid start, especially when supplemented by the thirty shillings he intended to contribute from his own pay.

Forwarding funds was always a risky business, as it was not unknown for mail to be intercepted. But half a draft had no value as nothing could be transferred. In the past similar systems had been used when sending cash, with pound notes being cut in two. But that carried a disadvantage: losing one half effectively destroyed all value. His brothers preferred not to use more official channels and this was surely better than sending complete notes; money that might be pocketed in full by the enemy. Kennedy readily admitted to having sinned many times, but no one could ever accuse him of being unpatriotic.

* * *

The ship was a very different prospect to the post office packet that brought her and Mrs Manning from England, and Poppy was not sure if she approved. For a start it seemed to be falling apart. Up until that point, most of her time had been spent on the orlop deck, either in the sick berth, the dispensary, or her own tiny cabin that she suspected was once a storeroom. But on the rare occasions when she and Mrs Manning ventured further the upper decks were always filled with men either knocking things down or building them up, and making a deal of noise while doing so. And that day was just the same, except that she was finally to be allowed out on her own.

Poppy had spent much of the morning washing clothes, which was hardly her favourite task. Their quarters lacked both ventilation and a proper water supply; every drop of the latter needing to be carried in by pail and then heated on a spirit stove that stank abominably.

"It will be easier when the ship's cooking range is in operation," Mrs Manning told her when the dispensary floor was finally swabbed dry. "They allow almost constant hot water to the sick berth and there is the possibility of shifting the entire medical department to an upper deck. It is the practice aboard newer ships," the woman continued. "Mr Manning is considering speaking to the captain of the matter."

Poppy viewed the prospect cautiously. She instinctively mistrusted optimism, and was especially wary on the rare occasions when her mistress indulged in such a thing.

"Nevertheless, you have done a good job, and now can put this little lot out to dry."

"Shall I hang it in the dispensary, ma'am?"

Mrs Manning was about to agree when she appeared to have a change of heart. "No, Poppy, I think not. This place is poorly aired and on such a lovely day it would be criminal to waste the sunshine. Hang it on the poop."

Poppy's expression changed to one of bewilderment.

"It is the highest deck in the ship," Kate explained, the impatience creeping back into her voice. "Right at the stern – the back," she added. "There are no guns and you are unlikely to be in anyone's way. But if the warrant officer of the watch, or even a lieutenant should object, come straight back to me and I shall speak with them. And Poppy..."

The girl considered her warily, conscious of the dangerous change of tone in her mistress' voice.

"If there is any repetition of your previous behaviour, you shall not be able to sit for a week, do I make myself clear?"

She nodded obediently and began to assemble the damp laundry into a basket. Poppy had much to learn about the ship and, after going so very mildly astray aboard the packet, it was something of a relief to be allowed out to explore this one on her own. Mrs Manning even seemed willing to forgive the incident and actually support her, which was a bonus.

The girl squeezed her load through the narrow door, and walked out along the corridor that led to the aft staircase. The first deck she came to was filled with the usual sweating men who were far too busy pulling the ship to pieces to notice her, and it was little different on the next. But then she was up and in the glorious daylight, and paused for a moment in the fresh air, before making for the small ladder aft.

"And where would you be going, young lady?" an older man asked. Poppy had no idea of his rank, but he wore a coat and hat and, in a world where nearly everyone was dressed in filthy work clothes, looked reasonably smart.

"I'm to hang out washing for Mrs Manning," she told him importantly.

"Washing?" the officer asked, his face splitting into a grin. "My the old girl has come down a peg or two!"

Poppy regarded the man with her dark eyes, uncertain if this was some oblique reference to her mistress, although there appeared to be no malice in his statement.

"Sunk one Frenchie," he sighed, "and taken two more besides, plus others in previous actions, I have no doubt. Yet now she's to be used as a line for hanging out a woman's laundry."

Poppy smiled, as it seemed the polite thing to do, but was unsure if she were allowed to continue. Mrs Manning might be summoned, she supposed, although the officer appeared an amiable sort, and there was surely no call to get him into trouble.

"Normally the first lieutenant wouldn't allow such goings on in harbour," he explained. "But no one could call us tiddly at the moment. And if washing has to be hung, the poop's probably the best place for it. Here, Mr Brown!"

A ginger-haired lad in a high black hat appeared as if by magic. "This young lady needs assistance with her washing. Take her on the poop, and rig a line if you has to. But be as subtle as you can. And remember, the captain's skylight's near at hand; he can hear every word you say, so don't spend too long a yarning."

The boy, who was little older than Poppy, grinned while managing to touch his hat to both her, and the officer, at the same time.

"Very good," he said. "Come with me, miss, and I'll be sure to look after you."

Chapter Four

"You do not have any feelings in your left hand?" Kate asked the question at exactly the same moment as she proffered the spoon to King's mouth. He paused, while deciding which should be responded to, before opting for the soup.

"How could I?" King replied, after swallowing. "When it is no longer there?"

"Some do," Kate gathered another measure from the bowl. "Even though a limb has been removed, they believe they can make their fingers or toes move, and have itches that cannot be scratched."

"If they say that they're playing you for a chub," King told her firmly, before opening his mouth for more soup.

"I think not," Kate replied, holding back the spoon. "And if a certain someone continues to believe so, they can feed their-selves in future. You have another hand which is sound so could do readily enough, I have no doubt."

They continued in silence for several more mouthfuls. Kate had been living aboard *Prometheus* for more than six weeks by then, and was comfortably settled into a routine that became inevitable when an old friend was the only permanent patient under her charge. But their time in dockyard hands was coming to an end. All major damage caused below the waterline had been attended to, with a corresponding reduction in much of the hammering, while junior officers were starting to reclaim their berths and even a few of the lower deck hands now slept aboard.

And she was returning to normality as well. The scare with Robert that had brought her so far was now forgotten, although she still held concerns over King, and the ill feelings he may have over the loss of his arm. But many of her former attitudes and habits were back, including the mildly bullying manner she was inclined to adopt when being either a nurse or a friend. And it was due to this that King waited a good while before he risked speaking further.

"There is talk of the ship being ready for sea in a week or two." he said, finally breaking the silence. "Will you be with us when she sails?"

"I shall," she replied. "Robert has been unable to recruit any help from the hospital; we are still one surgeon's mate short, and could ideally use more loblolly boys if the truth be known."

Actually it was an open secret between the couple that Manning had not applied for an assistant, but she did not feel the need to elaborate, even to King.

"And my maid will be accompanying me," she added with a significant look in his direction. Poppy was far too young, yet Kate had noted signs of interest from King's direction and such things were known to aid recovery. "And will you?" she asked a minute or so later.

"Most certainly; if the wound be healed," King replied. "Though I wonder at times what use a one armed lieutenant will be."

"More than a one armed fiddler," Kate told him with her customary lack of tact. "And, since most lieutenant's duties involve little more than shouting, I cannot see it will make much difference."

King said nothing, although his gaze had grown distant, and she could tell he was still considering the matter.

"You need not concern yourself about the stump," she blundered on. "That is healing well: indeed it is a perfect specimen of the surgeon's craft. Why, you could show it to anyone."

Something in King's expression told her that had not been the right thing to say and, for a moment, Kate searched her mind for the correct words. But such delicacy was not in her nature and, as the soup was almost finished, she resigned herself to letting things settle of their own accord. And then King spoke again.

"I was considering the wound," he said. There was no one else in the berth, but still his voice was low. "You do not think it will give further trouble?"

"I do not," Kate replied, pleased to provide positive information.

"But it was infection that caused the problem," he persisted. "And I have heard tales of men having to suffer subsequent amputations as the malady spreads."

"Well you need not worry on that count," she said with rare delicacy. "Robert did a perfect job, and took all such foulness away. Your wound is healing commendably."

But he was not reassured, and she strained for something more that might make matters better. "Robert is both your friend and a fine surgeon," she said as if sealing the matter. "And you are having the best of care. There is no unhealthiness and further operations shall not be necessary. So why are you concerned?"

"Because there was infection last time," King told her. "And he missed it."

* * *

Butler had been lucky on a number of counts, but the most important was not having been discovered. He spent his first day aboard the packet below, well out of the sight of spying eyes and, even though they were visited by a party of marines, with the brig subjected to a reasonably thorough search, provision had been made for such an emergency. A false bulkhead by the bread room concealed a chamber just large enough to take him and the other three hands who were there on equally suspect grounds, and they were not found.

And he was also fortunate in their passengers; no berth having been sought by sea officers wishing to rejoin the Med. Squadron, and the only supercargo they were expecting on their trip back to Falmouth consisted of some returning factors from an East India liner currently awaiting repair in the harbour. According to *Sprite*'s purser, none seemed to be connected to the service, and were unlikely to tell a man-of-war's hand from any seasoned Jack.

The two hundred ton vessel carried twenty men as crew, a small number when compared to the Royal Navy's regular requirement for such a vessel, but just the right size for Butler to become integrated in a short time. And so it was that, after they made their cautious rendezvous with the British fleet off Toulon, with outward mail transferred and fresh taken in return, he allowed himself to relax. The packet had her bows set for Gibraltar once more. It would be but a brief stop there, then England with all her comforts less than a month away. There was nothing he could do to bring it closer, so he may as well settle into the well known and reassuring routine of a sea voyage and actually begin to enjoy life.

But that regularity had come to an end suddenly, and when they were still two hundred miles short of Gibraltar. The first sign they were no longer alone came in the afternoon, although not so late as to allow nightfall to grant them safety. Another vessel was heading at speed to cut them off. She was clearly faster, and likely to be more heavily armed as well as better manned.

Their master had done all he could: the packet was immediately lightened of all but her most essential stores and when, less than an hour later, her pursuer was identified as a pirate xebec, even the guns were abandoned. A broadside of privately purchased four pounders could do little against what was tantamount to a frigate, and all aboard agreed their one chance of escape lay in flight.

But lightening proved futile; their enemy seemed to carve up the blue water as if she were powered from within – something that would have been perfectly possible as her graceful hull concealed a bank of oar ports along each brightly painted side. But with the wind set in her favour, no further assistance was necessary: the xebec came down on them at almost double the packet's meagre speed, and those aboard were left with nothing to do other than await her arrival.

As it was, they assembled quite formally and in their appropriate places for the expected event, with officers to the quarterdeck and men further forward, on the main and forecastle. Some were clearly hoping to barter in exchange for their lives and carried their possessions in canvas bags or the occasional sea chest. But Butler was amongst those who knew no such trade would be on the pirates' minds. Each man could expect to lose everything, including their liberty, and he might as well forget any thoughts of a homecoming to England.

"It's rum luck, and no mistake," the master told them as the xebec drew closer. "But have hope, lads; America is waging war on the Barbarians, and our own ships are steadily taking control of the Med. We may find ourselves prisoners for a while, but it need not be forever."

There was a rumble of acknowledgement from the hands; all accepted their captain meant well although none were truly deceived. The few who had escaped from pirate slavery had told more than enough tales for them to know they faced a bleak future indeed.

The xebec was drawing level with them and on a course that would see the two vessels collide in minutes. Already those aboard the brig could make out the turbaned heads and bare, muscular shoulders of their enemies as they roared and snarled defiance against the *kuffar,* and it was a vision that did not inspire hope. Butler cursed inwardly – his escape had appeared laughably easy and fortune seemed to have been with him, but now he realised his error. He should have stuck it out with the Royal Navy: his mess were a fair bunch and *Prometheus* would have been paid off eventually.

Then the two vessels struck with a splintering crash, before grinding together as the first of the pirates leapt onto the brig's crowded deck.

"Thank God we have no women aboard," the captain murmured softly.

* * *

Butler's old mess was actually at rest. In one of the wooden barrack huts that had been a home for them and several hundred other seamen for what felt like forever, they lay sprawled in various attitudes of indolence and repose. This was not such an unusual event; for almost their entire time ashore these normally active bodies had been given precious little to do. And with the heat of summer resting heavily upon them, it was something that should have worried their officers.

"If it were down to me, there wouldn't be no war," Cranston, a gunner, proclaimed lazily from his supine position in a nearby hammock. "They'd just blow a whistle, say, 'it's all over lads; you can go 'ome: we're callin' it a tie.'"

Flint, seated at the table, said nothing. All but three of his messmates were similarly recumbent, while the rest played a listless and apparently eternal game of crown and anchor on the wooden floor. Hammocks should have been struck some hours ago, but no petty officer had visited that day and Flint felt unusually reluctant to bring order to men who were hot, bored, and probably spoiling for a fight.

In the past it might have been different; as head of the mess he would have concocted something for all to get involved in; set them to sprucing up their allotted area – there was paint a plenty left over from the hut's construction, and everyone knew seamen liked nothing better than a spot of creative brushwork. Even a jape would be preferable to this mildly belligerent lethargy.

But Flint had been feeling increasingly unwell for some while, with that day proving worse than most, and he was simply unable to summon the energy. He kept such matters to himself, of course: if he told them how he felt, most of his messmates would simply have considered him lazy, like the rest of them. And, were it the truth, Flint would have been delighted.

"End to the war – now there is a novel thought," he said, feeling mildly guilty for not being more positive.

"But if they did call a halt, who'd believe them?" Ben, the youngster, asked from another hammock.

"Aye, an' we'd be right not to," Greg, next to him, agreed. "It'd be a trick; it always is. Shut the door, you bloody farmer!"

The last remark was addressed to Bleeden, who had entered from the red-hot parade ground, and was allowing a draught into the stuffy room. More shouts followed. What was Bleeden thinking of? No true seaman wanted fresh air when a congenial fug was available. But their verbal abuse hardly dulled the expression of delight and anticipation on the newcomer's face.

"'Ere, we got a situation outside, if any of you is interested." he said, approaching the small, penned off area that divided Flint's mess from others in the hut. Those on the floor remained immersed in their game, but the rest favoured him enough to glance casually from the comfort of their hammocks. Only Flint paid proper attention.

"It's Wainwright, the bootneck," Bleeden said, once he had identified his audience. "He's sparko again!"

With most of *Prometheus'* seamen safely billeted within the Southern Bastion, a place that was, in turn, guarded by the regular army, there seemed little point in mounting marine sentries on every hut, especially when all were relatively free to come and go inside the confines of the shore base. But some confusion between their officers and NCOs meant each of the huts that housed the lower deck men boasted a round-the-clock guard.

"Havin' a caulk, is he?" Flint asked, unimpressed. "Better say nothing, he must be your top customer."

"That's probably why he's asleep," Cranston agreed from the safety of his bed. "Too much of that rot-gut Spanish *vino* you been toutin' about."

That a marine should be both drunk and dozing whilst on duty was not the major crime it might seem. Flint was well aware that most of the sentries were practised in snoozing standing up – something that became almost essential on such a boring and pointless picket. But at least they had employment, which was better than this current mind-numbing boredom which gave him far too much time to think.

If only Bleeden had brought real news; that the ship was ready to embark, or further hands were required to assist with her painting. Men from Sanders' and Bolton's hut had already landed a work detail, and most duties would be an improvement on sitting idle.

"I tell you he's out cold!" Bleeden declared.

"Ain't nowt new in that," Cranston grumbled. "Even Jollies get tired of standin' about after a while."

"Yeah? Well how's about a bit of fun while we're waitin'?" the former smuggler asked, and Flint looked up at once. Something – anything – would be welcome as a distraction. And if Bleeden had an idea, he was more than prepared to back it.

* * *

Her mistress and Mr Manning were dining with the captain; it appeared to be a last minute arrangement and one that had caused a great deal of confusion in the medical department, with shirts being hurriedly ironed and fresh water needed for bathing. But now they had gone, Poppy knew she would be alone for at least two hours; probably longer. It was a rare thing to happen during the day; on the odd occasion when Mrs Manning sent her on errands she had to return immediately while, if left, Poppy was not to venture beyond the sick berth, and the wounded officer, Mr King, was always around to see she did not. But this time he had been invited as well: Poppy found herself absolutely, totally and completely on her own, and it was an opportunity not to be wasted.

During her time aboard *Prometheus,* much of her world had centred about the orlop. She found it a deeply unpleasant place, and one made worse by the work being carried out on the decks above. There was never any air not sullied by the stink of paint, glue, or ancient bilge water, while the Mediterranean sun kept them baking in what became a large wooden oven, with not a breath of the cooling breeze felt on higher stations in the ship. And so it was strange that, when she finally found freedom, the girl decided to go no further than the same dark deck which had been her home for so long.

She opened the dispensary door and peered out. *Prometheus'* deep underworld was permanently lit by bulkhead mounted lanterns, but their power was not sufficient to fill the many hidden nooks, and for a moment Poppy felt reluctant to go further. Not that she was afraid, she quickly assured herself. Before meeting with Mrs Manning her life had been far more perilous and the fact she survived at all could be blamed on her talent for self-preservation. But still she had grown used to company; there rarely being a time when at least one person was not in the same or next room. Actually Poppy could see herself becoming dependent on others and felt disgusted that striking out on her own should make her in any way nervous. It was hardly far, she told herself testily and, once arrived, she would not be in the least bit alone.

The heavy bulk of the mizzen mast was immediately outside and marked the end of usable space aft, before the bread room. But the passage ran forward with a line of doors to either side that led to a series of small cabins and storerooms. Occasionally she had seen lights burning inside and knew seaman officers inhabited them. There was even one who was young and had the deepest brown eyes; he had smiled at her on several occasions, until Mrs Manning complained about his singing early in the mornings. But on that particular Sunday afternoon Poppy sensed she was completely on her own and, despite the heat, found herself shivering slightly as the dispensary door closed behind her with a solid click.

She felt better as soon as she was outside though and, after a few steps, could actually see daylight as it filtered down the aft companionway. But fresh air and the prospect of sunshine were not what drew her on. Directly ahead lay the aft cockpit. Poppy guessed it would be every bit as stuffy as the room just left, but also knew the berth to be inhabited by four young boys, two of whom she had spoken to several times already. These had only been hurried conversations when chance caught her out of Mrs Manning's earshot, but the lads seemed pleasant and keen to entertain her. Not that there was anything wrong with the company in the sick berth: the surgeon and his wife could be dry old sticks, but she had already formed a good friendship with Mr King. Poppy was barely seventeen, though; all her life she had mixed with older people, and it would be a change to associate with others more her own age. A bit of gentle banter, maybe a jape or two, but no funny stuff, and certainly nothing on a commercial basis – she now accepted that, as long as Mrs Manning stayed close, her former trade must be abandoned. This would be a simple social gathering, and one that Poppy was rather looking forward to.

* * *

Repairs to the ship were finally coming to a close and Banks felt mildly satisfied. Fresh wood now replaced all the unsightly holes and had been swamped in several layers of heavy oil paint that stank to high heaven and would probably remain sticky for an age. The final coats were applied only a few hours before and little else could be done that day for fear of raising dust. Consequently, he had allowed additional shore leave for those working aboard and arranged this impromptu, but pleasant, gathering for the officers.

"Mr Vice, the King," he growled softly and from the far end of the room Acting Lieutenant Franklin, who was the junior sea officer present, stood and formally raised his glass. All followed his example, with Caulfield adding a sturdy "God Bless Him," before the men returned to their seats and conversations resumed.

Men, because there was one woman amongst them. Mrs Manning, who Banks had first met when she was Miss Black, and tried, unsuccessfully, to woo. That must be over five years ago, he hurriedly assured himself as his glance fell discreetly in her direction. Since then they had both taken other partners with Sarah, his wife, producing one child and another on the way. The woman was currently talking animatedly with Tom King. Time had not treated her well, the long dark hair he remembered was fast turning grey, and what were once attractively high cheek bones now appeared sharp, giving her face a far more severe look. But she was smiling pleasantly at that moment, and reminded Banks of the girl he had once known.

And it was good to see young King enjoying himself, he thought, hastily moving on. If anything his complexion had grown more ruddy since the loss of the arm and, even though this was his first time in uniform, the surgeon had declared him close to taking up normal duties again.

The captain's eyes continued to travel round his guests. Corbett, the third lieutenant, was a fresh face, and Banks had held initial concerns over him. An Essex man, Corbett came from *Canopus*, the seventy-four that had accompanied them in their last action and was a few weeks ahead of *Prometheus* in refit. There was a history of disagreements between Corbett and their premier, an officer known for being an obstructive old cuss, and the young man approached them in search of a berth.

John Conn, who had *Canopus*, would only let him go in exchange however, and that proved more of a problem as Gibraltar seemed particularly lacking in fresh blood at that time. For the first weeks of their refit they had survived with only two active lieutenants, and then the answer came in the form of a minor miracle.

One of *Prometheus'* number, a man serving on her lower deck, once held a commission as lieutenant. The former officer had been broken at court martial, hence his fall from grace, but the court decision was successfully challenged, and his old rank restored. There could be no possibility of a commissioned officer walking the quarterdeck of the same ship he had served in as an ordinary hand, so the reinstated lieutenant needed to go. Corbett could take his place, however, and any suspicions of the animosity aboard *Canopus* being two sided were soon dismissed. Corbett had taken to *Prometheus'* wardroom well and was turning out to be a reliable and trustworthy officer.

His glance reached the end of the table where it fell on Franklin, the promoted midshipman who, he had heard, was taking his new responsibilities extremely seriously. And the youngster, Hunt was settling down equally well. Both were men with every reason to progress and flourish. Banks retained reservations about the former; having no faith himself, he felt an instinctive distrust of any who believed in a deity. But then he once harboured similar doubts about Fraiser, his former sailing master and, Christian or not, the man proved totally reliable. On balance Banks reckoned he was fortunate as far as his officers were concerned, and soon would have a wardroom to be proud of.

"Are you ready for sea, Michael?" he asked, turning to the first lieutenant who sat to his right.

"Oh indeed, sir," Caulfield replied instantly. "The dockyard treated us well once more, and we have come through our refit in record time. But then a man does not sign on to be in harbour..."

Banks nodded in sympathy and went to make a comment when there was an outburst of hilarity from further down the table. Hunt, the new acting lieutenant, must have come to the end of some anecdote that caused Franklin, King and both Mannings to double up in laughter, with Tom almost falling off his chair in the process. Banks smiled politely; it had been a splendid meal, and any earlier reservations about the new wardroom officers were almost forgotten. And he was genuinely fond of the familiar faces; Caulfield, King and Manning had served with him for many years while the fresh men were quickly settling in and he felt sure would soon become an integral part of the ship.

And shortly they would be with Admiral Nelson; a commander known for bold moves and prompt action. In the past few years he had beaten the enemy in two major battles and seemed destined to add another to his list, if only the blockaded battleships could be tempted out. Meanwhile there were rumours all over the Rock of further French forces appearing from elsewhere; should these prove true, it may be a fight that hastened the end of the war.

Nelson was not well equipped; what ships he had being undermanned and many requiring refit. But *Prometheus* was battle tested, and fresh from the dockyard, her return would be a positive boost to the British fleet, and almost guarantee her a prominent role in any forthcoming action. And at that particular moment, Banks could think of no finer prospect.

* * *

"What's going on here, then?" Lieutenant Lewis asked in surprise. There was a grunt from behind; so suddenly had he stopped that Bentley, the midshipman following, almost cannoned into his back. The two officers had been posted to shore duty at the Southern Bastion and were taking advantage of a quiet afternoon to go sightseeing around the fortress. The large stone structure's height gave a wonderful view across the bay, and both were rather guiltily making their way down again when they came upon the line of familiar seamen blocking their path.

"We was just going to the top, Mr Lewis," Bleeden, at the head, told him. Lewis considered the group, most of whom appeared to be from Flint's mess, although he could also see a veritable crowd of other hands watching, apparently enthralled, from the parade ground below.

"Why would you be doing such a thing?" the lieutenant asked. "And what exactly are you carrying?"

Bleeden glanced down at his load, then quickly adopted a look of astonishment, as if unaware he had been holding anything at all.

"It's a parcel, Mr Lewis," Flint said more solidly from further down the line. And indeed it was. A parcel: wrapped in a hammock, tightly bound and containing something that might once have been a man.

"And what is inside?" Lewis persisted.

"Well, I recon's it'll be supplies," Bleeden said, as if discussing the possibility. "What do you say, lads?" he asked, and his mates began nodding forcefully and mumbling affirmative expressions as they did.

"We've to take it to the upper lookout point," the seaman added with a mildly wicked expression. "The one what faces out to sea..."

Lewis was about to ask the manner of supplies when something inside the bundle gave a long, drawn out, moan.

"Take it back down to the casement," he said instead, wearily indicating the ledge just below them. He and the midshipman followed as the seamen turned awkwardly on the narrow stairway, then began to retrace their steps.

The light was better on the stone gallery and Lewis thought the parcel may be moving slightly, although he had no wish to jeopardise his authority by saying so.

"Better take a look," he told the midshipman.

Bentley stepped forward uncertainly. He was the youngest to have been allowed ashore as well as the smallest present. He also lacked experience in his rank, still finding it hard to trust older, stronger men, who were deemed inferior to him, and even privately fearing they may cause him physical harm.

"Open it up at once," he ordered, in his adolescent tenor.

The load was lowered none too gently onto the floor of the casement and, as it hit the stone flags, there was a distinct cry. Bleeden fumbled with the line that secured it until Flint brushed him aside and released the knots far more efficiently. The canvas fell back, revealing the upper body of a comatose man wearing a marine's uniform and boasting a huge moustache that was crudely scrawled across his face in black paint.

"Who is it?" Lewis sighed.

"That's Wainwright," Flint told him.

"We found him asleep by our hut," Bleeden added. "And thought we'd better bring him up for some fresh air."

"So when he awoke, he'd be at the top of the fort, rather than outside your quarters?" the lieutenant asked. "And would wonder how in Hades he had gotten there?" Lewis had begun his career as a lower deck man, and understood their humour perfectly.

"Something like that, sir." Flint agreed.

"Or why 'e hadn't bothered to shave," another added, to a ripple of suppressed laughter.

"He's drunk," the midshipman declared, to more sniggers. Indeed, the smell of brandy was unmistakeable, and the boy, being nearest, was receiving the full force.

"Not exactly drunk, Mr Bentley," Flint suggested apologetically. "He was, there can be no doubting it, but now he's just asleep."

"An' it's surely better for him to be asleep on duty than drunk?" Bleeden asked earnestly.

Lewis closed his eyes and drew another deep breath. There was something else that could not be doubted: the men were more than ready to go back to sea.

* * *

Her afternoon in the midshipman's berth had all the makings of a success and Poppy soon lost track of time. Despite giving them such scant warning, the four boys had tidied up their stuffy little home and did much to make her comfortable. She was plied with food; everyone ate rather a lot actually. And it was chicken: a whole one that Brown, the ginger haired lad with nice eyes, claimed to have squirrelled from the gun room. Poppy, who was experienced enough in stealing to know it should rarely be boasted about, didn't argue this last point; she was not being asked to pay for the bird, so what did it matter if her host made up stories?

But whether thief or a liar, Brown was undoubtedly the group's natural leader. Poppy judged him about a year older than herself and already wondered if he would make an agreeable companion, at least for the duration of the present voyage.

There was drink as well: some rum and a bottle of red wine. Briars, probably the youngest, provided that, though readily admitted it less romantically purchased from a seaman who traded in such things. Poppy's preferred cup was Hollands; the rum was unusually harsh and, even though she persevered with Briars' wine, it still tasted weak and sour. But no one objected when she let her third glass go untouched. No one made her do anything, in fact – it was just a pleasant time with a bunch of young lads eager to treat her like a lady.

And they looked so smart in their uniforms; any one of them being infinitely more presentable than the customers she was used to associating with before Mrs Manning had changed her life. The middle aged men who thought sagging bellies and balding heads became invisible when a few pieces of silver were passed. Even accepting the poor light from two pusser's dips and some obvious grime on the canvas covered table they were seated about, Poppy told herself she might have been dining in the captain's cabin, just like Mr and Mrs Manning. And of the two groups, she could guess which was having the more fun.

After their meal they chatted for a while and the spotty young Briars sang a song, although his voice kept cracking, and the others teased him. Cross professed to know a comic rhyme about a cat caught up a tree which he declared at length to critical laughter, even if it seemed two of his audience knew the poem better than he did. Then they played a hand or two of cards – *Vingt-et-un*, – but it soon paled as none of them had any money to gamble with. And it was at that point Brown suggested the game.

It sprang from their mutual lack of funds and sounded jolly; a little daring even, so all agreed. Each would take turns in dealing the cards and when someone received the pack's only joker they must remove an item of clothing. Poppy was as keen as any of them; a quick calculation told her she was wearing more than the midshipmen, and playing as they would be ruled out the advantage of skill. Besides, her previous life had left her immune from the horror of naked flesh: hers or anyone else's.

At first the boys had been disconcerted to realise that midshipmen's britches were better removed before their precious stockings, unless they wished to create ladders. This caused a deal of merriment and any remaining thoughts about the others cheating were dismissed. With each player taking their turn to deal it was blatantly fair, and when Brown, the oldest and original instigator, was reduced to his stockings and a pair of slightly off-white cotton drawers, she had been laughing too much to worry further.

And it was fun. Brown's run of bad luck continued until he was forced to step out of his small clothes and stand, wickedly bare, in the flickering light, to a chorus of cat-calls, jeers and girlish giggles. The boy was embarrassed of course; something that made his state of undress even more delightful to Poppy, who secretly appreciated the early opportunity of viewing him in the skin. But Brown's self-consciousness soon faded, and when Briars later joined him, their nudity became almost common place.

After fifteen minutes play, Poppy had lost gaiters, stockings and shoes, but still retained her dress as well as the floral bodice Mrs Manning had passed on when they left England. And beneath everything she wore a linen chemise, so was well ahead of the remaining two: the tubby Carley being down to his small clothes with Cross not so very far behind.

The bodice went with the next hand, then it was Poppy's turn to deal again. She remembered shuffling the greasy cards especially well, so was horrified when the joker appeared in front of her almost straight away. The dress took a while to come off, and did so to the sound of good natured whistles and smirks from the boys. Her chemise was perfectly decent in the low light though; she might not be wearing anything beneath; Mrs Manning' view being that such things were only for ladies of questionable virtue, but Poppy still felt fortune to be on her side. And when subsequent hands saw Carley red faced and as nature intended, while Cross had shed everything bar a single stocking and some rather baggy drawers, she was starting to become hopeful of seeing the afternoon out in relative modesty.

Then her luck had run out. The next round was hers to deal once more and, once more, she drew the joker. Poppy must have stared at that card for a full ten seconds while the others about her tittered and sniggered although, when she finally stood up, it was to absolute silence.

But it had been such a pleasant afternoon, and she could hardly let down her gender, not when the boys had already proved themselves sporting. Besides, Poppy could not see what harm it would do to show a bit of flesh. It might even be looked upon as paying for her meal, and she had done considerably more for a good deal less in the past.

So, despite the stillness, Poppy did not hesitate in reaching down and pulling the light garment over her head. There was the usual difficulty when drawing her auburn mane through the stiff linen, but it was soon done and she could toss the thing carelessly to one side and look again to her audience.

The four below her were staring hard, and she had smiled cautiously. But a remarkable change seemed to have come over the group and even the poor light could not hide their individual expressions. The innocent young boys of a few seconds ago were now changed into something very different: monsters apparently devouring her pale body with their hungry eyes. Then she had laughed, hoping they would laugh also, but there was no trace of humour on any of the faces. And when they rose up from the table, Poppy suddenly wondered if she had made a terrible mistake.

Chapter Five

Precisely eight days later HMS *Prometheus,* still tacky from her tender paint, was warped from the mole and brought round to anchor properly in Rosia Bay. Then the job of victualling could begin, and the ship began to be assailed by a series of lighters and hoys, an attack that was maintained throughout the daylight hours and did not cease until most of her holds and store rooms were filled to capacity. Some items were not to hand, of course; the purser had been right in grabbing candles when they were available: the few crates he had been able to secure would have to last them until their next provisioning, and there was the usual scarcity of soap. But within a week the ship had taken on everything possible, and a bloated *Prometheus* edged cautiously out to sea.

Her next stop was Tetuan; they set sail at first light and a favourable wind took them swiftly across the Strait, so that it was mid afternoon when they anchored under the watchful gaze of the white, turreted tower, and began sampling what turned out to be a reasonable supply of fresh water. At least a day and a half would be needed to take on the two hundred tons a third rate carried so, while the men were still sweating over pumps and tackle, Dawson, the purser, went ashore to try the local market.

With him he took his steward, Rigget, as well as a former East India hand who claimed to be fluent in the variation of Arabic spoken thereabouts, along with a guard of marines in case he was not. But they were successful and, by noon of the third day, *Prometheus* had taken on a good supply of citrus fruits, as well as pomegranates and almonds for the officers' stores, and could set sail once more.

They covered the seven hundred odd miles to Toulon in just under a week. *Prometheus* sailed well, despite diffident winds, and even such a brief spell of freedom proved enough to settle all on board, especially the many who had been almost pining for the air and space of sea travel. Then, just before dawn on the seventh morning, their journey ended. There was a thick haze to show that summer, which had been endured rather than enjoyed, might finally be coming to an end. As it cleared, and the first stray strands of dawn spread from the east, they revealed the spars and mastheads of the British inshore squadron. That near perfect meeting was the final blessing, and Banks felt he could be certain, both of his ship, and the men he had been given to manage her.

"Eleven guns, I think is proper," he said softly as they drew nearer, and the first lieutenant touched his hat in acknowledgement. By then dawn had broken and colours were flying, so the salute could start without delay. Already *Prometheus* had made and answered the private signal and her number soon broke out from *Victory*'s mizzen at the head of some form of message. The deep boom of the first saluting gun sounded almost immediately, indicating that Hurle, their new gunner, was also fully alert and aware of his duties.

"Flag is signalling," Franklin confirmed, as the sound of their cannon continued to roll out. All on the quarterdeck looked across to where *Victory* lay on the starboard tack, barely making steerage way behind a column of two deckers. "Captain to repair on board."

Banks had not eaten breakfast and still wore the bottle green leather waistcoat Sarah had given him for chilly mornings. His gig was already being swung out, however; a request from the commander-in-chief being important to the honour of the ship and need not wait for confirmation. Nelson was certainly keeping to his maxim for not losing a minute; it was fortunate that David had laid out Banks' britches and stockings that morning. He should have time to don his full dress tunic but, as he turned for his quarters, it was to meet his servant emerging with the jacket in hand, and he was not sorry.

* * *

"Sir Richard – such a pleasure to see you again," the admiral informed him. "Why it must be five years or more!"

Banks felt himself blushing from the compliment. If he were being pedantic, it was actually more like six, but Nelson had achieved so much in the intervening time that his simply remembering their previous meeting was remarkable in itself.

The dining cabin in *Victory* was filled with people. No less than eight stewards stood in permanent attendance at a table that held a collection of officers ranging in rank from cockpit to flag, although most wore uniforms of the finest cut. And there were a fair few civilians present: again, impeccably turned out and appearing remarkably relaxed in such auspicious company. But one amongst them, the slightest by far, appeared strangely ill at ease. He was dressed in the shabbiest of uniforms, yet naturally drew the eye, and it came as a shock when Banks remembered the scruffy little man was also the most senior in the room.

"Pray, sit down, do. Have you taken breakfast?" Nelson asked. "We have only just finished, and will wait while yours is served. There is bound to be much to tell and probably easier to do so here."

The table appeared to have been laid for what must have been a minor feast, with the smell of fresh bread and cooked meat still hanging tantalisingly in the air, so it was easy for Banks to allow one of the immaculate stewards to guide him to a chair directly in front of his commander-in-chief.

"Captain Murray, my first captain, and Captain Hardy who is acting as second – I am sure you remember Thomas from our last meeting," Nelson continued, nodding to the tall, assured man on his right. And this is Dr Scott my Chaplain, and Mr Scott my secretary." For a moment the tired face lit up in unexpected humour. "Such a clash of names does make for confusion at times," the admiral explained, "though there are greater matters of concern, to be sure. But you must eat, Sir Richard. There are rolls and some splendid tongue, help yourself, do – steward, light along a fresh brew of the tea."

Banks settled into the high backed chair and selected a roll still delightfully warm to the touch. He broke it open in his fingers and briefly enjoyed the aroma as yet another servant placed a cup of milk-less tea beside him.

"We are fortunate that a small supply of soft tack can be baked on a daily basis," Nelson said, as Banks bit into the roll, although he could not help but notice the plate still lying in front of the admiral lacked any crumbs. And as his glance naturally rose to the man himself, it became clear the time between their meetings had taken its toll.

Since then, and in the very same ship, Nelson had been through many changes. The loss of an arm, Banks had been expecting, but hair that once was full and dark now lacked colour and seemed worryingly thin. A livid scar ran along his forehead, and the skin itself was fragile, pallid and stretched so tightly across the sharp bones of the admiral's face, that it appeared in danger of being split.

"So, what news of England? Do you carry despatches?" Nelson asked. "Or, if not home, Gibraltar or Malta then? Have Ball or Otway anything to say?"

"Nothing, I fear, my Lord," Banks replied, feeling genuinely sorry as Nelson's expression fell.

"It is of no matter. We received a brig not ten days back, but news is always of the greatest importance. What of your command, captain?" Nelson asked, switching the emphasis suddenly. "She has fared well at the hands of the dockyard I assume?"

"I am delighted at the speed and efficiency of our refit," Banks replied sincerely.

The admiral lowered his head slightly, giving the absurd impression he was accepting a compliment addressed to himself. "Indeed, they are an exemplary yard, and do much with so little facilities. Why, they fixed our ships after Egypt in record time; I doubt if another could have done so well."

"So your ship is quite recovered from the taking of those liners, Sir Richard?" This was Hardy asking and, although a senior captain, Banks was surprised he should effectively interrupt his admiral's questions.

"She is in good order, sir," he replied. "And we have been lucky with replacement hands; *Prometheus* is near to her wartime complement."

Hardy closed his eyes and nodded, apparently satisfied.

"And it was a bold action, Sir Richard," Nelson continued. "I have already said as much to John Conn, though he was right and honourable to attribute credit where it were most deserved."

At this, Banks almost choked. For an admiral to heap praise publicly was rare in itself, but hearing the captain of *Canopus*, the ship that accompanied them in their last battle, had done likewise was a surprise indeed. Conn was junior to him, and it would surely have been better if he had praised his own actions, rather than those of a superior.

But Banks had spoken with others, and understood that Nelson employed a novel method of command, his captains being expected to praise and encourage each other. They received respect in return and were trusted to act with an unusual degree of initiative. It was a policy Banks used with his own officers to some extent and thought himself not alone in doing so. But a single ship must be a very different matter to a fleet and he had never encountered the approach on a grand scale before.

And instinctively he could not ignore the feeling that, when dealing with such a large and diverse command, the practice might even be dangerous. In circumstances where ship's captains were not forever under observation, the good may become lazy and the incompetent, vain. There was no doubting it had worked for Nelson in the past however. One only need look at his two famous victories – Foley leading a column to take the anchored French on the landward side at Aboukir Bay and Nelson himself ignoring the permission of a superior admiral to discontinue the action at Copenhagen. There was also no mistaking the atmosphere in *Victory*'s dining cabin; the place was unusually alive and everyone seemed extremely positive.

"T-thank you, my Lord," Banks, stumbled awkwardly before adding, in a flash of inspiration. "I was well supported by my officers," which drew a nod of appreciation from the admiral.

"Perhaps Captain Hardy may be persuaded to update you on our current situation," Nelson suggested although, as the tall, serious officer prepared to speak once more, Banks noted his gaze did not leave him, and he felt under intense observation.

"The station has obvious disadvantages," Hardy began. "There is no safe anchorage; Barcelona, as you are doubtless aware, remains closed to us by government order, even though the French are pleased to take their captures there, and Genoa is as much French as Italian. Tuscany grows more hostile by the day while, even if it currently claims neutrality, we fear Sardinia shall go the same way. The only base within striking distance is Naples, and trouble lies there which I am certain my Lord Nelson will acquaint you with, should it become necessary."

Banks' expression did not alter, although the news concerned him greatly. He knew the Mediterranean Fleet to be poorly supported, but had failed to appreciate the extent. Maintaining any force of warships on blockade required an almost constant supply of food, water and materials, to say nothing of communication with nearby bases. Nelson must be surviving on little more than goodwill, and this from countries that might change their allegiance at any moment. The majority of his ships were due for refit, and Otway, the naval commissioner, had already hinted there was a shortage of manpower, yet the nearest British port lay over six hundred miles away at Malta, with Gibraltar, the only viable link to London, a week or more off.

"Meanwhile the coast hereabouts offers little in the way of protection," Hardy was continuing, "while we remain under constant observation from the heights, which give enemy coasters and small craft opportunity to avoid our attentions."

"Their fleet occasionally carry out exercises in the outer harbour," Nelson interrupted. "And have apparently made preparations to sail on more than one occasion – though sadly, all have come to nought."

Banks noticed Hardy nodding almost imperceivably while the admiral spoke, before taking up the thread once more.

"Their force has officially been recorded as seven of-the-line, with three more in the inner harbour fitting out. In addition, further large ships of war are believed to be on the stocks in the shipyard –

one was launched very recently, while intelligence suggests two more may follow, although our sources are not seamen and we cannot be certain."

There was a general acceptance of these statements from all at the table, several made small, additional remarks, and the atmosphere was oddly autonomous. Banks would not have been surprised if a more junior officer had added to the conversation, or even one of the stewards.

"We are currently keeping watch with the ships you see here," Hardy rumbled on. "*Belleisle, Renown, Superb, Kent* and *Triumph. Canopus and Monmouth* being on independent deployment that need not concern us at present. Sir Richard Bickerton has the remainder of our force further at sea and beyond sight of the French. It was hoped such tactics would tempt the enemy out to fight, although they seem uncommonly reluctant to do so." Polite laughter rippled about the table. "But soon it will be fall, and then we intend to entice them further."

"Indeed," Nelson again, and Banks wondered whether he could ever stay quiet for very long. "If such a paltry force is to be ignored, we must continue to reduce until a size they find irresistible is discovered."

Banks looked doubtfully at the two. A loose blockade was one thing, but Nelson seemed to be advocating abandoning the station entirely.

"We intend to withdraw to Agincourt Sound within the next month," Hardy explained. "It is a safe haven in the Maddalena Islands, off Sardinia. Captain Ryves charted it during the peace. The fleet may water there and, with luck, replenish other supplies, leaving a pair of frigates with watch over the French."

Still Banks kept his expression set, even though the words disconcerted him further. As blockading tactics went, Nelson's seemed to be verging on the careless. He was yet to study the chart himself, of course, and had no real idea of the distances involved, but Sardinia was surely not a convenient place to house a battle fleet.

"First we have to leave them with something to think of,"

Nelson continued, "and Mr Fife, *Belleisle*'s premier, has come up with a splendid suggestion. Captain Hardy mentioned the brand new seventy-four recently launched. She has been named *Fraternité*, and currently sits in the outer harbour, awaiting a time when she may be coppered: it is his intention to disrupt their plans. We can give more detail in due course, but I hope that you, and your fine ship will be involved, Sir Richard."

"I shall be delighted, my Lord," Banks replied, with total honesty.

"If we are successful, it should leave them itching to come out and fight," Hardy continued, in a level tone. "And if not, our subsequent withdrawal may lull them into believing our main force has given up and gone for good." The senior captain's right eyebrow rose, giving a mildly ironic look to his usually serious face. "And either outcome may eventually be regarded as a victory."

Now that was a mode of thought Banks was totally unfamiliar with. To plan for success, while being able to bear a loss could be considered prudent, but anticipating a somewhat callous benefit from both fell well beyond anything he had previously encountered.

"You must understand, Sir Richard," Nelson's voice again, and Banks had the uncomfortable feeling the admiral had been reading his mind. "Above all else, we wish the French to sail, and would risk much to encourage them to do so. Nothing can be achieved until they are brought to battle, and any similar ideas you, or your officers, may have to that end would be very acceptable."

* * *

"You were correct in consulting me, Flint," the surgeon told him. "Indeed, I wish you had done so sooner. Six months, you say?"

"About that, sir," Flint agreed. "I noticed the first signs before we left Tor Bay and hoped a spell at sea would put matters to rights."

"Ah, fresh air and salt water," Manning rolled his eyes. "The sailor's cure for all ailments."

"Something like that, sir," Flint was rising stiffly from the examination table.

"Well, I fear they will not do on this occasion," the surgeon continued more seriously as he washed his hands in a pewter bowl. This was not the usual daily surgery that he or Prior, the official surgeon's mate, held of a morning by the forecastle. They were in the dispensary: Flint had requested to speak more privately and now Manning understood the reason.

"I believe you to have a tumour of the large intestine," he continued. "It would explain many of the symptoms, though is less usual in one of your age."

"Will I need to be cut apart?" the seaman's tone was dispassionate, although he could not hide the concern upon his face.

"I think not," Manning replied. "Surgical procedures for such cases have become more common of late, though I would caution against them as the science is very much in its infancy. I shall of course read up on the subject, but suspect it may be better to leave well alone."

"So it might leave of its own accord?" Flint asked, his expression lifting.

"Sadly not," Manning stated firmly. "And you must dismiss all such thoughts. The condition is as serious as can be imagined: I would not give you false hope."

"Will it grow worse?"

"I am afraid so."

"And how long might that take?"

Manning could see beyond the man's apparent casualness and knew Flint's true state.

"I could not say." he replied in as gentle a manner as was possible. "Allow me to undertake my research, though I can arrange for you to leave the ship at the earliest opportunity, if that is your wish."

Such an offer might have appealed to the majority of lower deck hands and possibly a few junior officers, but Flint's eyes said otherwise.

"No, sir. Not for now, if you would be so kind," his tone was strangely formal. "And I would prefer it if the others remain unaware."

"I shall have to tell your divisional lieutenant," Manning warned. "And he will certainly inform the captain."

"I understand that but, with respect, you don't rightly know yet. And I would rather it kept between ourselves until you do – until you are certain, like."

"Very well, it can be kept as our secret for now," Manning agreed, even though he already knew enough to inform the entire crew.

Flint thanked the surgeon and collected his jacket, before departing in a thoughtful silence, leaving Manning momentarily alone in the dispensary. He would, as promised, read up on the condition, but suspected there was little that could be done. Unless his books told him something surprising, Flint was almost certain to find himself in the next transport home. And when he reached England he could not expect much.

Flint had not been wounded in action, in fact it was an ailment that lacked any kudos of injury in service, so there would be no benefit. The man may have given his working life to his country, yet the best he might hope for was a lonely death in some workhouse or charity hospital. And Manning privately suspected such an end was not so very far away.

A knock at the door roused him from his melancholy and he looked up to see the beaming face of Lieutenant King as he entered. He smiled cautiously in return; if anything was to erase the memory of his previous patient it would be this particular visitor.

"How goes it, Tom?" he asked. "Settling into the wardroom, so I hear; your wound is not giving trouble?"

"None whatsoever," King replied.

"And you are finding it easy to dress yourself, and eating reasonably?"

"Keats manages me adequately, and I am now considered old

enough to feed myself, though I do miss your good lady's daily sermons. I was actually here to ask if I may take up regular duties once more."

"I see," Manning answered cautiously, indicating the stool which had so recently supported him. For King to feel well enough for active service was good indeed, although the surgeon was still concerned. Ignoring the loss of an arm, there had been serious trauma to his chest and upper body that would remain tender for some while. And he knew King of old; should any of his injuries require subsequent attention, he would be the last to seek it: neither would he return to the sick berth, unless forced to do so.

King had slipped off his tunic, and was unbuttoning his shirt with one hand. Manning's instinct was to help but he thought better of it, waiting instead until the lieutenant was finished before bringing the lanthorn closer and inspecting the heavily scarred chest.

There was nothing of concern; the flesh had melded admirably. And that was despite the dreadful mauling handed out by a splinter of wood, or his own hands in closing the wound, then ridding it of suspected infection. That he had been wrong, and the warning scent of corruption actually stemmed from King's injured arm, still haunted him, although the subject had never been directly addressed by either man.

He turned his attention to the arm next. Again, the stump was healthy, and healing well. It was simply a pity more care had not been paid to the injury before; if so, his friend might yet possess two functioning limbs.

"That is all highly satisfactory," he said at last, and King grinned again.

"So I may return to duty?" he asked.

"You may, though the wound should not be allowed to become damp, or exposed to any cold."

There was scant chance of avoiding either as they both knew. The popular conception of a sea officer's business was to fire, and be fired upon, but getting wet and experiencing extremes of weather also figured prominently on the list of requirements.

"And there is no infection in the stump?" King confirmed.

"None that I can find, and I would say that any should have made itself known by now."

"So no further operations?"

"I think not," the surgeon replied. "Such things should all be behind us."

"Then that is fine news, indeed, Bob," King grinned, as he wriggled back into the shirt with commendable ease. "I shall tell the premier, and can become accustomed to standing a watch truly single handed."

"Tom," Manning began hesitantly. "I did wish to speak with you about the wound."

His friend was looking at him with interest now but no real concern, and it would have been so easy to go no further. But something drew Manning on, be it friendship, guilt, or simply his own need for order in all matters.

"I fear I may have let you down," he said, examining his own fingers as if they were entirely novel. "The infection certainly began in the arm, yet I was sure it to be elsewhere, which is why I had to cauterise so." He sensed King was about to speak, and carried on before he could. "Had I spent less time worrying over the chest, and more monitoring the arm you may not have had cause to lose it. I cannot say how sorry I am, Tom, and will understand fully if you take against me."

King was his oldest friend and they had been through much together, so Manning expected at least a modicum of comfort now there were no secrets between them. But confession brought no relief, while his last statement had probably signalled the end of any future affection. He glanced across to the lieutenant who was easing himself back into his tunic.

"I ain't dead, Robert," he said lightly, and Manning was momentarily taken aback. "I ain't dead, and I ain't likely to be, not unless something else comes along to take me. And that might so easily have been the case," King continued. "I spoke with Judy, and that robber Prior. They both said what a mess I were in when brought down to the cockpit, and that it was nothing short of a miracle I made it through at all."

"The surgery was a miracle indeed," Manning agreed and was about to say more but King was fixing him with an intense stare.

"Well I for one do not believe in such things," he replied seriously. "You saved me with your skill, and I will always be grateful. That I came to lose my arm later is unfortunate, but at worst it were an oversight, and I cannot blame any man for making such an error." And then the smile returned. "Not when he saved me to begin with."

* * *

Poppy had claimed a headache and asked to be excused at the beginning of the first watch but, rather than folding down the bunk which took up most of the free space in her tiny cabin, she settled herself down on the brown leather portmanteau to wait. The Mannings were creatures of habit; both being abed by four bells at the latest and Poppy hoped her retiring early might encourage them to do the same.

And so it proved; hardly more than an hour passed before she heard the last of their talking through the thin wooden wall and guessed them to have gone down. The door to her cabin opened directly onto the corridor but was inclined to make a noise so she decided to give them a little while longer to fall properly asleep. And while she waited, her thoughts naturally turned to what she intended to do.

Poppy was in no way concerned; the very reverse in fact. There was nothing that would shortly take place that she had not experienced many times before. The day she bumped into Mrs Manning had been one of the luckiest in her life, although later securing the position of lady's maid ran it a close second. Since then she had travelled much and learned a good deal. And she was grateful, although Mrs Manning kept such a watch on her that no girl could feel anything other than safe – whether she wanted to or not. Poppy was yet to earn any real money however, and experience had taught her cash provided the greatest security of all.

Which was why she had tried to go back to her old trade when aboard the post office packet and why she was doing so again now. Mrs Manning would not be pleased if she found out, but had forgiven her in the past, and would doubtless do so again. Besides, she had not been there to protect her on that particular afternoon with the boys.

Four bells rang out and was followed by the customary shouts from sentries at each guard point. Poppy wriggled uncomfortably on her improvised seat. There were, in theory, another thirty minutes to wait, but she was already of a mind to leave. Actually her arrival time did not seem so very important; that night's customer was only Prior, the other surgeon's mate who berthed down the corridor a mere fifteen feet away from where she currently sat. The cove had hardly given her a moment's peace since she came on board, with a wandering hand that made fine play whenever Mrs Manning or her husband wasn't aware. Well he could have a proper feel that night, she had decided. And would pay handsomely for the privilege.

* * *

"I should say it will take the French completely by surprise," King said, still staring at Brehaut's chart. All her senior men were assembled in *Prometheus'* great cabin including the Royal Marine officers. Banks considered the group as they crowded about the large table and found himself strangely gratified. Even King was back with them once more. He would be of little physical use in any action but remained a welcome face.

"Surprise?" Caulfield snorted. "Or should that be shock?"

There was the muttering of restrained laughter expected when seasoned men consider a fresh challenge.

"How many will be involved?" Reynolds, the marine captain, asked more cautiously.

"Just under three hundred, plus supporting officers," Banks told him from the head of the table. "We will take eighty from ourselves and *Belleisle. Victory* shall contribute the remainder and

I understand Captain Summers is in overall charge of the operation. Each of the smaller units will operate independently, however, and under command of their own officers. *Belleisle* is to tackle the eastern battery, while we take that to the west. Each are only supposed to be manned by gunners and a cursory guard. *Victory*'s men, which make up the largest force, will land at the centre of the causeway, then pass across to the opposite shore. The French liner is believed anchored just over a cable to the north in a small bay; other than her, there should only be fishers and maybe a lighter or two: there is no major garrison in the immediate vicinity that we are aware of."

"And how shall they reach her?" King asked.

"Hardly our concern, Tom," Banks smiled. "But there is a quay that always contains a good deal of lobster boats. It should be easy enough to commandeer sufficient craft, and the target is effectively in ordinary; indeed, she is barely finished, so we are not even anticipating an anchor watch in such a protected harbour."

There was a silence as all present considered this. King was right, Banks decided. Actually reaching the anchored liner was decidedly the weakest part of the plan. However well his men, and those of the *Belleisle*, performed in capturing the two major military emplacements, the whole operation would end in shambles if the main force were unable to burn the French ship. Men would die, a good many; either in taking and holding the shore batteries, or their subsequent abandonment. And, despite what Hardy may have said, any action that wasted lives could only be considered a defeat.

"The attack has been scheduled for the fifteenth of the month; that is one week's time. The moon shall already have been new a while so, with luck, those ashore will not be expecting any attention."

"And if the *Fraternité* is moved into the coppering dock before then?" Caulfield asked.

"Then we will obviously have to abandon any attempt to destroy her," Banks replied. "But the admiral considers that a better option than making our move at the start of a new moon."

"If I may ask a foolish question," Reynolds, the senior Royal Marine officer, began cautiously. "I fail to understand why a ship should be launched without first being coppered."

"Coppering is a different procedure to construction." Caulfield explained. "It is standard practice, both in France and our own yards, to carry out cladding after a hull has been in the water a fair while."

Reynolds raised his eyes in mild surprise, but said no more.

Banks looked about at the assembled faces. A land operation was not his preferred choice of action; his ship would be endangered while trying the batteries, and they might lose a few men; certainly amongst the marines. As for success, that must depend almost entirely on Reynolds and his subordinates; the only sea officers involved being those from *Victory* and maybe a junior lieutenant to collect the returning landing party. But at least *Prometheus* was going into action, and the destruction of a brand new seventy-four would undoubtedly annoy the French, as well as being a welcome addition to her battle honours. "If there are no other questions, gentlemen, I think we may adjourn," he concluded. "Mr Reynolds, you will have plenty of time to speak with your officers, and select those that are to be involved; obviously it would be better if they were all volunteers,"

"Every one of my men is a volunteer, sir," the marine officer replied with a flash of teeth, and there was a rumble of light laughter from the sea officers. The joke, though often told, remained true; all of the Royal Marines aboard *Prometheus* were, in theory at least, there entirely of their own volition; something that could rarely be said about a group of Royal Navy seamen.

"Then, we may indeed withdraw," Banks concluded.

"Actually, sir, I have a suggestion," King said, rather hesitantly, from his left. "It might be of interest, if you would care to hear of it."

"Indeed?" the captain inclined his head in the young man's direction. "Then perhaps you might remain behind, Tom: Michael, you will stay also?" he added, glancing across at the first lieutenant.

To Banks' mind, that was the icing on the cake: King had not only returned to duty, but was once more coming up with ideas. Previously these had varied from the barely possible to totally outrageous, although all bore the mark of originality, and were rarely an effort to listen to. It also signalled that King was not just healing physically; the old spirit had returned, and Banks could not have been more glad.

Chapter Six

It was just over a week later that Hunt found himself in charge of the blue cutter. They were off Cape Sicié and he had a midshipman and twenty-five hands aboard, as did Franklin in the black boat, which was a mile or so to the east. They had left *Prometheus* several hours before when darkness made their departure less obvious and, despite what had been a pleasant day, all were now extremely cold. But the chilly autumn air was not the worst of it; this would make the fourth night Hunt had been so employed, and the last that allowed Tom King's particular slant on the attack to be implemented. To Hunt's mind the amendment carried a hint of genius about it, although there were other reasons he wanted the lieutenant's plan to be successful.

The first was personal. They had met so very recently and Hunt was still only an acting lieutenant, whereas King, a seasoned man, had held his commission for all of six years. Yet he had done much to welcome Hunt into the wardroom, and proved not too proud to befriend what many would regard as a jumped up midshipman.

And there were more practical grounds. Since joining the inshore squadron, all aboard *Prometheus* were becoming increasingly frustrated by the succession of coasters that regularly risked the short passage from Marseilles to Toulon; something which had clearly inspired King in his scheme. The runners made their move by night, and at all stages of the moon, relying heavily on protection from the concealed rocks, shallow waters and devilish currents that haunted the area while, nearer to the port, both field and permanent shore batteries kept the larger ships of war at bay.

There were breaks in the man-made defences, of course, although none that allowed a line-of-battleship to manoeuvre in safety. Smaller vessels might be brought in, but the rip remained strong; something that Hunt already knew all about. For any craft not under oars to approach the coast was dangerous, and little could be achieved without warning being given. But ships' boats under the cover of darkness were a different matter and so, at the admiral's consent, he and Franklin, as well as fifty or so of *Prometheus*' prime seamen, had spent the previous evenings in the cold, open cutters while they negotiated an area already remembered by the British Navy as the site of one of their more ignominious defeats.

They would in no way be avenging the rout of almost sixty years ago, however; all any of Hunt's blackened faced men hoped for was to snap up a coaster, preferably one carrying valuable spars, ordinance or other bulky supplies for the shipping at Toulon. These were items less suited to the long, overland journey, yet desperately needed by the French fleet.

But at that moment his potential prey's cargo was of little concern to Acting Lieutenant Hunt. Despite his temporary status, he was in command of the operation, Franklin being of the same rank but lacking exactly nine days' seniority. To Hunt it was far more important they should be successful.

Were he to carry off a smooth and slick capture of a small enemy vessel, perhaps a polacre or maybe a *chasse marée* it would, in turn, enable a far more ambitious plan to be launched. Such things could easily sway an undecided examination board, and see his commission confirmed: a result that would undoubtedly warrant the cold dark hours and constant danger the victory had cost.

But that was assuming there would be a victory. So far they had achieved nothing, each night having been spent running in towards the deadly rocks, then battling equally evil currents without the merest sliver of moon to assist. It had been four evenings of what he could only think of as monotonous peril; and that night, the fifth, looked like being no different. They might change the boat crews, but he and Franklin turned out on each occasion, as did their two midshipmen. And with no apparent end in sight, he knew the other three were getting just as tired of the process as he was.

"Take her back to the Two Brothers," he said without any attempt at the French name for the twin rocks. Brown, who sat beside him in the cutter's stern sheets, duly called an order out to the rowers, before pressing the tiller across. They were once more reaching the small headland that marked the westward end of their watch, and would now spend the next twenty minutes doggedly pulling back in roughly the opposite direction. If there had been a convenient bay in which to shelter, matters would have been very much easier, but the coastline was as dangerous as the current, and they could only truly consider themselves safe while their boat was in motion. The lad brought the cutter's head round to face the eastward boundary of their patrol, and Hunt resigned himself to yet one more leg. Then, five minutes later, one of the seamen broke the silence.

"I think I can make out a ship aft, sir." It was only a brief comment but spoken by Flint, who was pulling stroke, had the effect of lifting the young officer free of his apathy. Both he and Brown turned in their seats and, sure enough, there was the slightly darker mass of a vessel under sail closing on them from astern.

"Take us inshore, and row easy," Hunt hissed, and the cutter began to turn immediately, her way falling off as she encountered the contrary current. Franklin was further to the east: he must also spot the vessel, although it would be harder for his boat to arrive in time for a simultaneous attack. So be it, Hunt had more than enough to overwhelm the crew of a normal sized coaster. Especially one in the midst of considerable navigational difficulties, that was also trying to avoid the dangers of a British inshore squadron.

"Bring her round," he whispered, and the boat turned once more until her bows faced out to sea. Then he could see the vessel in greater detail; a brig, probably no more than a hundred and fifty tons, and under easy sail. His cutter sat low in the water; it should be all but invisible, especially as any spare attention from the enemy's lookout would be spent watching for an attack from seaward, and Hunt felt strangely confident as he gave a nod to Flint sitting opposite.

The boat began to accelerate across the rip. Their quarry had passed: they would be taking her from behind, which was the ideal station, especially when Franklin's cutter should be in the perfect position to lead an attack from the bows. Hunt crouched low on his seat; there was no need to say anything: all aboard knew their tasks well enough. Each was armed with a cutlass, no firearms having been issued as it was hoped the exercise might be carried out in relative silence. But the coaster would only be carrying a crew of ten, fifteen at the most; a show of force was probably all that would be needed. And it was strange that, as they shot forward through the crested seas, all feelings of cold had left him completely.

* * *

They were spotted when Hunt's cutter was within musket range of the enemy, a fact both announced and demonstrated by the discharge of a firearm from the brig's quarterdeck. The shot ran true and scored a hit, landing with a solid thud, square in the centre of the boat and in front of the two officers, after presumably neatly dividing the banks of rowers. But no one paid any attention; their little craft was speeding forward under the combined strength of eight powerful men, and soon drew alongside the brig's larboard quarter.

Sanders, who had been rowing behind Flint, took a grip on the counter while a figure only dimly seen at the bows locked on with a boat hook. Between them they secured the cutter while the rest of its crew swarmed up the brig's side. Hunt and Brown stood ready to take their turn, the former momentarily relieved that he had specified a force of able seamen, rather than any bootnecks. Then a space became clear; the two young officers jumped, and began scrambling up the vessel's tiny quarter gallery.

They were over the bulwark and standing on the quarterdeck in seconds where, despite the darkness, a fight was already in full flow. Flint had no sword but could just be seen slugging it out in true brawler's fashion: as they watched the British seaman knocked his uniformed opponent out cold with a powerful fist. But further French were coming from below and forward, all apparently clambering to get their hands on the boarders.

Hunt drew his hanger before pushing his way forward and soon had engaged with a heavily set seaman who carried what looked like a wooden belaying pin. His opponent boasted a magnificent moustache, which was almost a better defining mark than the darkened faces of the British but, though undoubtedly strong, he was also slow. After parrying two strikes, Hunt was able to fell him with an unconventional blow from his sword, smacking the man square in the face with the full power of his right arm behind the weapon's steel guard. Then came a cheer, followed by the sound of rushing feet from the forecastle; Franklin's men must be boarding, and the added force would surely quench any vestige of resistance in the French. And so it proved; in no time the brig's crew were subdued, allowing themselves to be roughly disarmed and secured in small groups on the main deck.

"Brown, take the wheel," Hunt snapped at the nearby midshipman adding, "Belay that light," to Sanders, one of the last to board, who was now fiddling with a closed lantern. Franklin emerged out of the gloom, a bright, and apparently unused, boarding cutlass in his hand.

"The ship is ours, Tony," the older officer told him, his teeth shining in triumph. "Both cutters are secure and I've posted men at the braces; we can alter course whenever you wishes."

"Thank you for that," Hunt replied. "And your prompt attention; you came in the nick of time." Franklin muttered something depreciating, although Hunt chose not to listen. He had nothing against the man, and his assistance had indeed been welcome, but there was something in his manner that told Hunt he was not a conventional fighting officer. He peered forward; the deadly pair of rocks that sat at the end of the nearby headland were growing close and he must make sure the whole episode did not end in foolish disaster.

"Port your helm," he called to the midshipman at the wheel. "Take her five points to starboard."

His order was repeated and the brig turned as sweetly as if she had been sailing under the union flag all her life. Under stars alone it was unlikely anyone ashore had noticed their capture and they should be comfortably over the horizon or at least unidentifiable by morning. But the greatest satisfaction to Hunt lay in his personal success. His cutter had led the attack and now there would be a trophy to dangle before the examination board while, with an enemy coaster in British hands, nothing remained to stop King's addition to the plan being implemented. The young officer realised he was grinning inanely in the near darkness and quickly assumed a more suitable expression; one worthy of a cool headed commander at the conclusion of a pleasing operation. But the truth was, he had seldom felt happier.

* * *

"I think we must all congratulate Mr Hunt and Mr Franklin," the captain told them in the early hours of the following morning. "Not forgetting Mr Brown, of course," he added, with a nod to the ginger haired midshipman who still boasted a fair amount of burnt cork on his face. "A well found brig loaded with general stores including, I am led to believe, powder, which will be ideal for what we have in mind. And, with luck, the officers captured will enlighten us further as to the state of play ashore – providing our questions are worded correctly, of course."

Banks was seated at the head of the long dining table, with Caulfield on his right and the remaining officers to either side. These included all but one of those who were involved in the previous night's action.

"Which reminds me, have the brig's officers been taken to the flag?" The captain asked.

"Yes, sir; they were transferred not half an hour ago," Caulfield told him. "There are also eighteen seamen uninjured; who are being held below, although one appears keen for service with the king. The three wounded are with Mr Manning; he reports them to be in no immediate danger. None of our men reported injury."

"Very good," Banks grunted. "And the prize?"

"I have appointed Mr Adams in temporary charge, sir," Caulfield replied. "He was the other midshipman involved and is experienced enough to keep her from prying eyes for the rest of the morrow."

The captain nodded, pleased that his second in command was proving as solid as ever. "We have to await confirmation that the vessel is suitable," Banks continued. "Doubtless the admiral will send a party to inspect her during the day. But I would be so bold as to predict tonight's operation will be conducted according to Mr King's amendment, and we should all offer him our vote of thanks."

King flushed deeply as the officers around him rumbled in approval, while some thumped the polished wood of the table to emphasise their support.

"Very well," Banks continued. "We all have preparations to make. Mr Reynolds, your men are in order?"

"Yes, sir." The marine answered instantly.

"Mr Caulfield, there are no concerns with the ship?"

"None, sir. We are ready."

"Good. Then, if there is nothing else?"

"You have not decided who should command the prize, sir," the first lieutenant reminded him.

Banks was caught temporarily aback; Caulfield was right, the subject had completely slipped his mind, so intent had he been on confirming the capture would indeed be suitable.

Of course King was the obvious choice. It had been his plan that called for the use of a coaster in the first place and, now they had secured one, there was little to stop it being implemented. If successful, the chance of all *Prometheus'* marines returning safely was greatly increased, although he must balance that against the ten or so hands needed to man the captured brig. They should be prime seamen and the likelihood of all coming back was far smaller.

He glanced about the table; both acting lieutenants appeared as eager for the chance to captain the brig as he would have predicted. Despite the risk, such an active part in an attack on a French line-of-battleship must look well at their forthcoming boards. Then Lewis was an option; he held a full commission as lieutenant although, to Banks' mind at least, remained a lower deck man at heart and may well lack the leadership qualities necessary on such a complex mission. Corbett also appeared keen, but had yet to prove himself in action, and Banks was loath to risk him in such an important role. And then there was King, only recently returned to duty, yet obviously as keen as any to put his plan to the test. This was not a decision to be taken lightly and, as Banks grimly realised, it may also be one he lived to regret.

* * *

Flint was the only one of his mess to have been present on the raid. Indeed, he had volunteered as boat's crew every time they laid in wait for a coaster, and was usually chosen by officers grateful to have such a skilled and willing recruit. And it had been a cracking night, one made more so by the disappointment of those preceding it. Flint had actually got to grips with the enemy: felt their flesh, breathed their breath – even spilled their blood, so he was well pleased.

Though it was also strange that he should relish action so: in the past, Flint had never been much of a firebrand. On many occasions fighting was the last thing on his mind, and there had been a time, best forgotten, when he all but turned chicken hearted. But a great many changes had come over Flint of late: one of the lesser being he now craved any form of danger. Yearned for it, in fact, and with the same sense of insatiable longing a miser felt for gold.

Flint had not worked aloft for many years but suddenly sky-larking, the practice of gambolling amidst the tophamper and usually the preserve of topmen along with other young fools, had become almost an obsession, while live firing exercises with the great guns, or small arms drill, were eagerly anticipated and carried out with bestial enthusiasm. But, again like the miser, however much of his own particular wealth he might accumulate, it was never quite enough and he seldom felt totally sated. There was always a bit more needed, a further opportunity to lose himself in the moment's exhilaration; to risk what life remained on personal skill in grabbing a shroud, balancing atop a spar, or firing off an agreeably hot cannon. And the fact that he was undeniably ill, that the surgeon intended sending him back to England to await a death that would be neither dramatic nor glorious, had nothing to do with the matter whatsoever.

"Been in a ruck, then, 'as you?" Cranston asked, when he joined the rest of his mess about the well known table, and felt the warmth of their unspoken welcome. "Least now we taken one Frenchie the cap'n might be satisfied, and there'll be no more small boat work for a week or two."

Jameson passed across a filled tankard with a chunk of cheese which would have been left over from supper. And that was another thing Flint would miss: he had been head of a mess for as long as he could remember. It was an honorary position; one appointed by his fellows and retained only for as long as it remained merited. It was also the only form of promotion he had ever sought. But soon Flint must say goodbye to that as well; he would be ashore: just another disabled shellback, one with no responsibilities, no charges, and no mates.

"From what I hears, satisfaction is the last thing we should be expectin' of the cap'n," Greg, who was a gun room steward, informed them. "Word is they're gonna use that Frenchie tub for more devilment. Young King is back in harness, and he has plans – or so the tattle-tale goes."

Flint had appreciated Jameson's gesture with the cheese, but collected a dry biscuit from the bread barge instead. Food had not seemed so attractive for some while. It was a situation that would doubtless pass but, for now, hard tack was about the only thing he could stomach. News of King sparked his interest, however. He knew the officer of old, as well as his plans, having been involved in many. They usually contained both excitement and danger, elements Flint had been prepared to enjoy in small measures as part of the lot of any lower deck hand. But now such things represented a good deal more. Another bout of exhilaration; another burst of energy: another chance to forget.

And, if he were totally honest, another chance to die an honourable death – on a deck – in battle. Belonging to a ship, rather than wither away in dismal isolation ashore.

"Ask me, that young fellow 'as too many ideas," Bleeden was grumbling. "Ain't properly set from losing 'is arm and darn near 'is life, now 'es a planning to give the Frogs another seeing to."

"Aye," Jameson agreed. "He should 'ave taken his smart money and be done with it."

"Officers don't get no smart money," Greg informed them loftily. "There's a pension instead. It's only the likes of us what has to beg for charity."

"And if you loses a leg for the king, they makes you prove it every year," Bleeden agreed. "Just in case somethin' grows back."

"So what's the plan?" Flint asked, his mouth still half filled with biscuit.

"Sounds like a land action," Greg grunted. "Though if Toulon's the target, it's one I'd rather steer clear of. The Frogs seem to be adding batteries by the day – you'd think our takin' it at the start of the last war has made 'em jumpy or somethin'."

"If that's the case, I'll give it a wide berth an' all," Bleeden agreed. "There's more than enough excitement on this particular trick, and it's only just begun."

Flint looked about the faces of his mates, and sensed similar feelings on each. Then he placed the remains of his biscuit down, uneaten.

"Well you can count me in," he told them with a grin.

* * *

Mr Midshipman Brown made his way from the illustrious surroundings of the captain's quarters, and headed for the aft companionway. It had been his first time in action and, although little had been called for from him other than to assist Hunt, he felt unusually elated. Down the steps he went, and past the entrance to the wardroom. There was a crowd collected at the bottom of the staircase and he pushed through it, briefly acknowledging the fatherly congratulations from a couple of the older hands. Word had got round about the night's success: only a coaster had been taken, but *Prometheus* was a happy ship, and all were eager to share in the minor victory.

It was less busy when he reached the orlop. Hero or not, Brown was due to stand watch in less than two hours, and hoped to get a brief caulk in before then. But his friends Carley and Cross were just leaving the berth, and caught him as he was about to enter.

"Hail, the conquering hero comes!" Cross greeted, with just the right amount of affable contempt. "Seized a blazing powder hulk single handed, or so I hears."

"And didn't manage to blow himself sky high into the bargain," Carley added. "That must be cause for celebration in itself!"

"It were a brig, and armed – eight six pounders!" Brown told him defiantly. "But we took it nonetheless. And in force!"

"So let's see the blood on your dirk, then!" Carley scoffed, although it was clear both were impressed.

"And did you fight?" Cross asked more seriously, but Brown shook his head.

"I was prepared to," he said, as Briars, the youngest of the midshipmen, emerged from the berth to join them. "But there were so many prime Jacks about, it didn't seem worth the effort."

The other three understood. However proud they might be of their rank, each were little more than lads, and hand-to-hand combat was undoubtedly a man's game.

"I steered the capture away, though," he added. "And kept the wheel 'till it were taken over by the prize crew."

"And Adams has her now," Cross reflected. "I suppose that is fitting, he is older than any of us, and likely to rate an acting commission afore long. But it might as easily have been you," he said looking to his friend once more.

Then a change seemed to come over Brown's friends; all three suddenly altered their focus, and began staring over his shoulder with mixed expressions of surprise and what might have been fear.

Brown turned, expecting to see a senior officer with evil in mind, but his eyes settled instead on the slight young girl with auburn hair who had appeared from her cabin next to the surgeon's dispensary.

It was Poppy and, by the light from a nearby lantern, they could see an entirely neutral expression on her face. She began to walk purposefully in their direction and was surely looking straight at them. The boys were momentarily hypnotised by her gaze and watched in horror as she grew closer, while the delicate mouth they had all so rudely kissed started to open. But they didn't stop to hear what she might say; without a word to the others, each made straight for the narrow door of their berth, even to the extent of fighting to find safety and anonymity inside.

And so they were unaware that Poppy harboured no intention of speaking with any them, but had a far more important destination in mind.

Chapter Seven

"I still consider it harsh that the captain did not give you command of the prize," Hunt told King with transparent honesty.

He gave a stoic shrug in reply; King actually felt it was rather worse than harsh: this particular section of the scheme was his idea and he had so wanted to lead it. "I've been given my chances in the past," he added, more philosophically. "And Sir Richard assures me there will be more to come."

The last part was true enough, although he held little faith in the captain's words. His wounds were still tender but, even when fully healed, the loss of an arm would remain of no advantage on an active mission. King had served with Banks for many years, and knew the cove well. He may as well resign himself to the fact he was to be ruled out of anything other than the more mundane duties of a lieutenant in future.

And Hunt was right, he had been the obvious choice: but from now on King was an ideas man only; never again to be sent out with a landing party, given command of a prize, or called to lead a team of boarders. He considered it fortunate indeed to be allowed this small part in the proceedings, but held little hope of any greater responsibility coming his way, and certainly not while he remained under Sir Richard Banks' command.

"I have no doubt you shall cope famously," King continued, careful to hide any trace of resentment. "And a further successful action will speak well for your board."

Now that was certainly true, and a pleasure to say. Hunt must be five years younger than King – probably more, and had only been part of the wardroom a short time. But he had taken to the fellow instantly and sensed him to have all the attributes of a first rate lieutenant. King was prepared to do much if it aided his promotion, but the fact remained he would have liked to have led the attack himself, if only to prove he really was healed of his wounds. And that a one armed officer could still be effective.

"Besides, I shall be seeing you to the brig," King added. "So will not be a total parson's mate."

Prometheus was barely in sight of land, while their coaster seized the previous evening lay considerably further out and well beyond the watchful eyes of those on Mount Faron, the momentous peak that overlooked all of Toulon. Banks had relented enough to allow King to deliver the small number of volunteers Hunt would be leading in the attack. Then he was to collect the current prize crew and return them to the ship. Later, and if all went to plan, Hunt's men would be picked up along with *Prometheus'* marines that were to be used. And King was confident the captain would include him in the debriefing, although that hardly compensated for being excluded from the actual action.

"Blue cutter's a ready, Mr King," Ashley, the coxswain, reported, and both officers began to make for the small boat that was currently filling with men. Flint was once more amongst the crew, King noted, and in his usual place, pulling stroke. The man had become a permanent fixture in the blue cutter, although that was no bad thing: King, for one, felt reassured by the powerful seaman's presence.

But, now that he thought about it, Flint always seemed to be volunteering for duty of late. And it was doubly strange, as Robert Manning had hinted something about his health giving concern.

Further thoughts were banished from King's mind, however: Hunt's men were embarked and it was time to go. Dusk was drawing in, darkness itself would follow in half an hour, and it seemed unlikely that anyone on shore would spot one small boat as it headed out towards the open sea. And there was Cross, the young midshipman, who was to go in with the brig. King considered him and the part he would play with mild jealousy. Cross was hardly more than a boy and King could not help but wonder if he were strong enough for such a mission. Perhaps a full set of limbs made a difference?

"I wish you luck, Mr Hunt." Both men turned to see Banks standing behind them, his hand outstretched. "And expect to see you shortly, Mr King," he added more firmly. Then they were clambering down *Prometheus'* steep tumblehome, and King was taking hold of the tiller as their boat was released from the reassuring bulk of the battleship. There was the hint of cloud to the south, which would doubtless be brought in by the strong, onshore wind. It looked like being perfect conditions for the attack, but the fact gave King no pleasure whatsoever. Actually he felt totally, and quite unreasonably, out of humour.

* * *

They resisted stepping the masts for a good while but, when darkness finally fell and enveloped *Prometheus,* along with the far distant shore, in its anonymous embrace, there seemed no reason not to. King relaxed in the sternsheets of the boat, allowing the strong and constant wind to carry them, close-hauled, over the leaden waters. Now they were underway his mood was improving. It was good to be off the ship and he actually felt wonderfully free. His task might only be to see Hunt and his force safely to the brig, but it was one he had been given total charge of, and the return to command, albeit minor and decidedly temporary, was welcome. King supposed such supporting roles would become acceptable in time, and valiantly ignored the foolish notion he would always crave the thrill that leading men into battle brought.

They sighted the brig after an hour; Adams had been told to await their arrival, and was showing the smallest of lanterns at her main, although the midshipman would have no idea if the plan was accepted, or what his part in it would be. King gratefully steered for the light, all too conscious that missing the rendezvous would have meant the whole episode ending in ludicrous failure: something that may even have cured him of any future desire for responsibility.

The cutter drew alongside and her crew clambered up and into the coaster.

"What news is there?" Adams asked earnestly as Hunt and then, more awkwardly, King, followed.

"Belay that," King said gruffly. Flint, had been about to help him over the top rail and really should have known better. "I can manage well enough," he continued, shaking the man's grip from his shoulder. "And were you not to stay in the cutter?" he added, glaring at the seaman.

"I thought I'd come along as well, sir," Flint told him cheerfully. "Volunteers were called for, after all, an' there are plenty from the prize crew who can see the cutter home."

"Volunteers were also selected," King replied crisply. "You cannot just appoint yourself to a mission such as this."

"Will someone tell me what is planned?" Adams asked plaintively, and Hunt took pity on him.

"We're cleared for Toulon," he said. "And it is as we thought, the brig is to go in and lay alongside the Frenchman."

"I had hoped to see her to Gib.," the midshipman replied, brightly. "But a shore attack sounds the more entertaining."

"You will not be required," King snapped. Now that everything was about to start, his previous ill temper was returning and he found himself growing increasingly fractious. In five minutes Hunt and the rest would be heading into action, whereas a trip back to *Prometheus* was the best he could look forward to. And all the time there was an idea forming in his mind. It had been instilled by something so recently said and too incredible to deserve further consideration, although the frustration it evoked was more than enough to make him grumpy.

"Mr King's plan calls for volunteers," Hunt informed Adams. "You had taken command of the brig and were gone before anyone could enquire. And as you know, no man is ever assumed to have offered their services, especially for duty in a fire-ship."

The rules of war stated that those captured while serving aboard such vessels would not be granted rights of a normal prisoner. In effect they could be treated as spies – and hanged or otherwise executed at their captor's discretion. And with the callousness the French regime had displayed of late, such an outcome was strong.

"But to burn so fine a brig as this..." the youngster responded in disgust and it was clear the idea of his first command being destroyed appalled him.

"Never fear, there will be others," King said with a complete absence of sympathy. "Now assemble your men; they may take passage back to *Prometheus*. We shall continue from here."

The lad, though clearly disappointed, allowed himself to be shepherded into the cutter behind its former crew, then King turned back to Hunt.

"Very well, Tony; the wind is in our favour," he said, smiling suddenly. "For now at least; what say we square away?"

Hunt looked his confusion. "But you must take the cutter back to the ship," he protested. "I am to continue alone."

"Young Adams is competent enough for such a task," King's temper was improving with every second and he felt it would not take much to make him laugh out loud. "And as Flint said, the mission called for volunteers..."

* * *

"Where is Mr King?" Caulfield demanded of a flustered Adams as soon as the young man appeared through *Prometheus'* entry port.

"H-he has command of the prize," the midshipman stammered in reply.

"What in God's name..." The first lieutenant seemed to physically rear up at the news, and the boy added a hasty, "sir."

"Is there a problem, Michael?" It was a quiet voice, and one that belonged to the only person permanently allowed address the first lieutenant so. Caulfield turned to see Captain Banks directly behind him, and went to explain. But they were on deck; Adams and his men having just disembarked from the cutter, and hardly private.

"Mr King has remained with the prize, sir." Caulfield told the captain hotly, although Banks gave no visible reaction to the news.

"I see," he replied. "Then we shall be short of an officer commanding the lower guns."

"Indeed we will, sir," Caulfield agreed his anger mounting. Whatever his part in planning the attack, King had no business in absenting himself from his ship, especially when they were about to go into action. Such an act must surely be the subject of a court martial. But as he turned to express his disgust to the captain he could tell there would be no support from that quarter. Banks was anything but cross and might even have been smiling slightly. He certainly bore the air of one who had expected nothing less.

* * *

King and Hunt stood together on the brig's tiny quarterdeck. There was no moon, and none of any merit was expected, while the masthead lantern had been doused over an hour before. But the stars were sufficiently bright to reveal all that was needed to be seen within the craft and, when clear vision really mattered, there would be the lights of the port they were intending to attack.

On leaving the cutter, the brig had sailed to the north west, until it reached the coast in roughly the same position it was captured, not quite twenty-four hours before. And now they were steering on a similar course: Cape Sicié stood out boldly to larboard while, almost directly ahead, the peaks of the *Deux frères* were in plain sight, with phosphorescent water surging between the two massive rocks, making the hazard more obvious. At the same time, further out to sea and considerably off their starboard bow, the loom of a familiar British third rate could be seen as she came sweeping down towards them. The ship was on the larboard tack and about as close inshore as one of her bulk might manage. No captain would risk his vessel so without a target in mind and, if there were eyes on shore, the little brig would appear to be exactly that.

"Tide is near perfect – such as it is in the Med., and the wind will serve for the present," Hunt murmured. They were the first words that had passed between the two officers for some time. Even when *Prometheus* was first sighted, an event signalled by Cross, the midshipman, releasing something between a shout and a shriek, neither had spoken.

"Aye," King agreed, after considering for a moment longer.

"Though it will hardly serve as well when we are inside the bay."

Indeed, the breeze was fair and just on their beam, but would be dead against them when it came to encountering shipping to the southern side of the harbour. The wind commonly backed with the chill of night, but both were experienced seamen and needed no glass to tell them when a change was due. And they were equally aware that, should the temperature remain high, or some other quirk of nature keep matters as they were, it might spell the difference between success and failure. Or, to be brutally accurate, whether they lived or died.

"*Prometheus* is wearing," Cross squeaked again and, sure enough, they could make out the mighty liner as she began to bear round. Unseen hands gathered in her forecourse, and the ship herself seemed to have taken on an abstract entity that had nothing to do with the home and workplace they all knew so well.

"Then we may expect attention at any moment," King grunted.

"For what we are about to receive," Hunt added in heavy irony. Then, even as the words were spoken, it happened.

A series of lights that were painfully bright ran down the side of the liner, causing all aboard the smaller vessel to wince in horror. A second or so's pause, then the sea ahead of them was torn up as if struck by a dozen separate whirlwinds, while the whole devastating display was accompanied by the deep-throated roar as the sound of a battleship in anger reached them.

"Steady, lads," Flint's voice came from the forecastle, and the nervous chatter of the brig's crew gradually diminished. The experience of being aboard an unknown vessel, especially one so recently taken from the French, had already caused a deal of excitement. King was glad to see that Flint, dependable as ever, was keeping control. But now *Prometheus* was apparently firing upon them, it would be strange if at least one of their number did not start to regret his decision to volunteer. All were well primed and expected nothing less but when the broadside rolled out, even King was aware of his heartbeat increasing.

They were making good speed though, and would soon be in the lee of the two rocks ahead. Banks was playing his hand well:

Prometheus had continued to turn and was now heaving to, with her broadside facing considerably forward of the little craft. Clearly he was intending to stand off and await their arrival. Had they really been a blockade runner, it would have been the ideal position for a powerful enemy to take up. For them to reach harbour and apparent safety, the coaster must pass directly through the arc of a deadly barrage and, however friendly the ship might actually be, it was not a pleasant prospect.

The possibility of the battleship firing blank charges had been mooted, although such a ruse would be easily spotted from the shore, and King wanted the engagement to appear as authentic as possible. That had been during a casual discussion amongst fellow officers who were also his friends, with the decision taken amid the reassuring solidity of *Prometheus'* great cabin. Now, as he stood on the frail coaster's deck and was about to receive a battleship's broadside for the second time, he wondered if he should not have been quite so insistent. It would only take one gun captain, either out of spite or through mishap, to lay their weapon slightly askew and the brig would be seriously damaged. They might even have to call off the entire attack although, with several tons of powder aboard, the outcome could be considerably worse.

"Starboard your helm," Hunt grunted, and the oncoming rocks moved steadily across their bow, while the brig eased in gently towards the shore and found the shallow water only she was able to traverse.

King remained silent; his last minute decision to join the expedition had rather thrown out the order of command. He was the senior officer present and, as the instigator of the plan, had every right to take control of further proceedings, although an inward sense of justice could not be ignored. Hunt had originally volunteered to lead, and it was a position confirmed by both the captain and, ultimately, Admiral Nelson himself. Whatever the outcome of tonight's escapade, King would have some explaining to do, but before then it should be decided between themselves exactly who was in charge.

He cursed inwardly; forcing himself along had been an

impulsive, yet idiotic act; he could see that now. In taking it, he had potentially wrecked the mission and whatever remained of his career. Hunt and he were friends, they worked well together, at least until that point. But eventually one must defer to the other, and any argument or conflict would only cause confusion. He turned to the younger man, and went to speak, but before he could, Hunt settled everything.

"Do you wish us to call for soundings, Tom?" he asked, and King felt the relief flow about him like warm water added to a cold bath.

"With the current taking us so, we have plenty of depth," he replied. "And such an action might betray our caution to those watching from the shore."

"You do not mind my asking?" Hunt enquired gently. "This is my first such mission, and I welcome your command."

"I do not mind at all," King told him before adding a quieter, "thank you."

* * *

He wasn't exactly looking to go in a blaze of glory. In fact, despite his somewhat rash behaviour of late, Flint still retained a very healthy fear of death. He would actually have preferred to see that night out, and then spend the next with his mates in the mess. But the growing pain and hunger – food remained difficult to handle – had started to wear him down. And he was also uncomfortably aware that, however much he might argue against it, Mr Manning would soon be placing him in a transport home.

But it would not be home – England had long ceased to represent any such image to him and Flint was set upon a totally different tack. Whatever vessel carried him from active service was bound to call at Gibraltar or Malta. The former was by far the more likely, but both were garrison towns and, even though he would be many miles from his native Sussex, he could be more certain of finding a hospital berth in either than the place of his birth.

"Queer trick, being fired upon by the barky," Jameson sniffed, and Flint smiled vaguely in reply. The lad had been one of the more conventional volunteers; he stepped forward when asked, and was chosen as an experienced topman; someone who possessed the skills likely to be in demand during that night's activities. Flint, who also tried to join at that stage, had not worked aloft for some while, and was ignored.

Yet Jameson's presence was partly the reason he forced himself aboard. The two had shipped together for almost ten years, weathering many kinds of excitement, from fleet actions, to single ship engagements; storms, groundings and even a mutiny. Flint's support and their shared experiences had boosted Jameson from a blinking-eyed volunteer third class to his present position as one of the most respected of seamen, whereas Flint remained in his apparently permanent able status. But the personal progression from Jameson's sea daddy to tie mate was more important to him than any official rank and, as the two were about to become separated for what must be forever, he had been determined to accompany him on this final adventure. One more time when they shared the excitement of action, and let a draught of danger quench any fears he may have of his own impending death.

It was not something he could share with Jameson. Even now, Flint doubted if someone so young and full of life would have an inkling of what his friend would shortly face. But face it he must and, if the chance were given, would rather do so alongside those he cared for. And, however much a future night with his messmates appealed, Flint was also philosophical enough accept it might as well be that evening as any.

* * *

Now the two jagged outposts of rock were growing rapidly nearer – a true measure of the little vessel's pace although, to starboard, *Prometheus* remained in a position to fire upon them when they drew level. Before her refit, the battleship's gunners had boasted about releasing two broadsides in as many minutes. They were out of practice now though, and speed was anything but important.

Still, the British ship must fire within a reasonable time, if only to avert suspicion.

Then the brig was pulled to one side by an eddying current as the *Deux frères* passed to starboard, momentarily shielding the small craft from the third rate's anger. Her earlier turn had taken the battleship a little further off, but not so far as to rob the British gunners of any degree of accuracy. And it was just as the coaster was emerging from the granite shelter that *Prometheus* spoke again.

King found himself gasping as the shots fell to either side, with spray coming aboard, to the obvious consternation of the hands on the forecastle. But although neatly straddled, the prize remained untouched, and King was able to order her round and into the shallows that must see off even the most determined pursuer.

"Biggest jack-in-the-box I've ever encountered," Hunt stated glumly, and King grinned. The show was over, as far as *Prometheus* was concerned. The battleship would continue to pursue them, but must stand off as they were reaching the point where the first shore batteries were positioned. Shot thrown from the land could be counted on to fly that much further and with greater accuracy than anything a third rate could return, and stone built embrasures were stronger than the defences of a wooden warship.

But King knew Banks would not be put off by such statistics, and neither was he withdrawing by any means. In company with *Belleisle*, who was due to make an appearance at any moment, *Prometheus* was actually intending to draw the shore batteries' fire. It was hoped the attentions of two Royal Navy vessels would befuddle the issue; that their presence alone might distract any attention the French gave to one small brig. In fact, as King had blithely predicted, the coaster could expect to be allowed through in the confusion. There may be challenging signals, and their lack of response was bound to cause doubt, but one that had faced the anger of British liners must be given a deal of leeway. If he could only ease the prize past what Brehaut's captured charts labelled the

*Pointe du Rasca*s, a major problem would have been solved.

There was one significant flaw in his plan, however; he was assuming the French had not guessed what they were about. For all he knew, the coaster's capture had been spotted. At that very moment, as his vulnerable little brig steered through the shallows, aiming for the apparent safety of shore based enemy defences, their gunners might be lining up heavy weapons and simply waiting for the order to open fire.

There was more than two miles to cover before then, and they would be under threat while they did. From a good way off *Prometheus* chanced another broadside, but her shot fell comfortably short and, so intently was he watching for a sign of action from the shore, King barely heard the deep rumble of the battleship's fire.

"So far, so good," Hunt mumbled, and it was clear he was also concentrating solely on the batteries. Then a flash of light from the nearest emplacement made them all jump, and was instantly followed by more until the entire battery apparently erupted in a sea of flame.

* * *

But they were not the target. The shots must have passed perilously close, and would be heavy; each probably thirty-six pounds and, allowing for the French method of weighing ordinance, possibly more. However the brig sailed on in relative safety, although *Prometheus*, about half a mile further out, was neatly straddled.

It was a good start, King decided. If those on shore believed the British had control of the coaster, that fire would have been directed at them. All plans for attacking the port must then be abandoned while the vessel on which he currently stood would be lucky not to find herself in a thousand separate pieces. At least the French were in doubt and, as the all important headland was now less than a mile off, there was not a great deal of time for them to consider the matter further.

"There's a light, sir!" It was Cross; the midshipman was

standing on the forecastle and pointing eagerly over the larboard bow. Sure enough, King could make out the eerie glow of a blue lamp that came from the *Pointe du Rascas*, and appeared to be sited just above a battery. The signal was shielded once, before disappearing completely as another barrage followed. King had been focusing intensely on the light, so the savage brightness of cannon fire blinded him temporarily. Once more *Prometheus* was the target, although this time her position had been poorly estimated, and the shots fell short.

King turned to Hunt. "There is no point in replying to their signal," he said firmly, aware that the temptation was unbelievably strong. Both men knew to predict the combination of lights, colour and station that made up that evening's response was all but impossible, and a wrong answer must immediately confirm any doubts the enemy may be harbouring. Even if the brig was following another vessel, and copied her reply, provisions were probably in place for such an eventuality.

No, it was surely better to say nothing. But now a recognition signal had been ignored, they were more likely to receive fire from the shore and, with the *Pointe du Rascas* growing ever closer, King's excitement was at the stage when he was finding it hard to stay still.

Hunt was holding his watch close to the dim light of the binnacle. "The French took six minutes to reload," he announced. King was surprised – if asked he would have estimated approximately half that time.

The signal was repeated and, now that they were drawing into point blank range, it became harder than ever to ignore. Such a bright blue light was impossible to miss, and to fail to acknowledge or reply could be fatal. King remembered the hurried plans he had drawn up and explained to his captain. A brief outline had been forwarded to the admiral, and all agreed the scheme held merit if only, as Banks rather dourly pointed out, to remind the French the British were still there. But he had not thought out the problems of recognition signals properly, and simply believing the coaster being under chase would be enough now appeared to have been dangerously naïve.

Then the waters in front of them erupted once more and, for one dreadful second, King feared they had been smoked.

"It's *Belleisle*!" Hunt bellowed and King followed the direction of his pointed finger. Sure enough, the British two decker could be seen off their starboard bow, and worryingly close to the battery. To anyone on shore it would appear the coaster was her prey, whereas in reality she was fighting to reach the spot where her marines could be despatched. The ship was heeling significantly, but progress was being made, and she had loosened off a broadside, potentially at the brig, at just the right time. Hunt was peering at his watch again.

"The French are due to fire at any time," he muttered, "And we can only wait and wonder what target they will choose."

Belleisle was under a mile out to sea and now passing them; should the battery fire on her, the shots must pass overhead, and may even damage the brig's tophamper. A third rate was substantial enough to take at least one close range barrage from shore based guns, and obviously Hargood, her captain, was prepared to do so, or he would not have risked his ship in such a manner. But were the prize chosen instead, there would be little warning. The coast was less than three hundred yards off their larboard beam; such a distance could be covered by cannon fire in less than a second and, with her cargo containing gunpowder, it would not take much longer to account for the brig and everyone aboard.

Yet Hunt was right; all they could do was wait and wonder.

Chapter Eight

"Hargood is playing a close hand," Banks grumbled from the quarterdeck of *Prometheus*. They had put out to sea, tacked, and now were heading back for their designated station, well to the west of the causeway where the main landing party was to be despatched. The ship seemed unnaturally crowded, although most of the officers who thronged the bulwarks, their eyes straining out into the night to catch what action they could, had every right to be there. And even below in the waist, the marines, splendid in red and white with their pipe-clayed leather almost glowing in the dark, were waiting to board the boats. A mile to the east, *Belleisle* was easy to see by the light of cannon fire directed against her. She was far closer in than Banks had risked and Caulfield, who stood next to his captain, nodded in the darkness.

"He were ever the impulsive type," he murmured. "Though that last barrage must be dampening his ire somewhat."

"What of the coaster?" Banks bellowed, although it was the masthead that he addressed.

"She's just weathering the cape, sir."

They had done well to come so far in the time; King and Hunt must be getting quite a bit of speed out of the capture, something that would not surprise the enemy, considering she had apparently been under fire from two British liners. But with *Belleisle* now beyond range and his own ship considerably out of the running, she was no longer being chased and was likely to receive rather more attention from the shore.

"*Belleisle*'s turning a point or two to larboard," Caulfield said, looking forward again at the far off third rate. Indeed, the heavy fire seemed to have finally worn her captain down, and the ship was standing off.

"But where is *Victory*?" Banks asked. Both men instinctively looked out where the flagship was due to appear. Once the three decker came into sight, *Prometheus* and *Belleisle* would be at liberty to close and properly engage the gun emplacements; first with their own cannon and then later, when the boats reached the shore, in hand to hand combat. But until then they could only wait, and even *Belleisle* was taking the sensible path, and claiming sea room.

"Masthead, any sight of the flag?" Caulfield bellowed.

"Nothing to be seen to the south," the lookout replied. "Though it is precious dark, and there is mist coming in with the wind."

That was logical enough. They had expected the breeze to back, indeed, it had been as essential to the plan as any state of the weather could be. But still it came stubbornly from astern, and the addition of cloud, surely an indication that a Mediterranean storm was brewing, would give cover just where it were not needed.

"We could embark the marines," Caulfield suggested. "They might run in under sail easy enough, leaving us more able to take on the batteries..."

That was certainly an option, and Banks felt obliged to consider it. Releasing their shore party early would also mean *Prometheus* could manoeuvre when attacking the batteries; that or withdraw if need be. But the possibility was soon discounted; it went directly against plans so carefully drawn up and, without support from the ship, their marines would find storming the gun emplacements that much harder. No, he would have to wait. Wait for *Victory* to appear, and the chance to take his ship into action. And waiting, as always, was the hardest part.

* * *

The brig had escaped fire from the shore batteries and rounded the promontory without hindrance of any kind so King was feeling a little more easy. In his plan he had emphasised the fact that a mildly unorthodox approach by an apparently friendly, and harassed, coaster might be ignored, especially if there were sufficient distraction elsewhere. That was exactly what the British liners were providing, so why was he concerned? But again it was one thing to make cosy assumptions when safe in the security of a man-of-war, quite another to stand on the heeling deck of a captured brig as it edged closer to an enemy harbour.

There was less than two miles to cover before they reached their eventual target; at their current speed this would barely take fifteen minutes. If the brig had been a conventional fire-ship, it would not be long before they would have to light the fuses, so she was properly ablaze when coming alongside. However, such an action would be obvious, and bound to confirm doubt in the minds of the enemy. For the moment they were being left in peace and he hoped might remain so; besides, the coaster could in no way be considered a conventional fire-ship.

Their change of course had brought the wind more onto the quarter; the brig was fairly skimming through the water, and so close to the land that a group of figures carrying lanterns were seen quite clearly as they sped past.

"Chart shows another battery hereabouts," Hunt murmured, as they peered into the dark. "Though no one has reported anything in the past, and I'm blowed if I can see it now."

King said nothing. As was so often the case, worries were returning to haunt him. Try as he might he could not ignore the feeling that, if there was a further fortress nearby, they would discover it soon enough, and the revelation would not be pleasant. There may be some on shore who still thought the brig to be a friendly vessel; one that had been due the night before and was now making a late arrival. But three direct signals had been ignored, and the French gunners would surely be within their rights to open fire at any time.

"Starboard the helm," he ordered to the unseen helmsman. "Bring her as close as she will go." The brig turned, as if obedient to his instructions, while those at the sheets trimmed her sails. King looked across to Hunt.

"I figured we should maintain our speed," he said, almost apologetically.

"Indeed so," Hunt agreed readily. "The quicker and nearer we pass, the easier it will be for the Frogs to miss us."

But there was another matter to consider as well; travelling so fast meant that, were they to touch bottom, the brig would be firmly aground, and possibly dismasted into the bargain. Their captured charts showed a reasonable depth; despite being near to the shore: there should be a good fifteen feet of water beneath the keel. But charts were known to be wrong and, even if not, there remained the chance of a rock that had been missed, or some debris subsequently abandoned.

"Stand by to alter course!" King bellowed. No further emplacements had been spotted and they were now coming to the northern most point of the Sepet peninsula. Soon the brig must enter the massive bay that was the entrance to Toulon's equally huge harbour. He had every intention of staying close to land, so they must shortly turn to larboard. Then the wind, that had proved so disobligingly obstinate, would start to be taken more on their beam, slowing the brig, and placing them in far greater danger. There were no batteries marked for half a mile, but the two which stood on the headland that his chart had as the *Pointe de la Piastre* would have plenty of notice of their arrival, and that was when their current run of fortune was likely to end.

"Starboard your helm, take us three points to larboard!"

They turned almost as soon as the nearby shore fell away and, although there was an appreciable decrease in speed, the brig still seemed to be travelling excessively fast. And this was land that lay unobserved from the sea; a large and well lit building stood out further up, and there was a collection of fishing boats anchored in the lee of a small mole. But nothing that would apparently endanger them, and both officers breathed out once more.

"And a further point," King added as they neatly rounded the next headland and the wind, now partially blocked, fell away to less than half its previous force. There was a darkened bay to larboard that would have made an ideal shelter for gunboats, but none came into view. The only danger visible was the outpost of rock that must mark where the next gun emplacements were to be found. Once passed, they should finally meet with their objective and, if the liners had done their duty, a welcoming force of marines. But first they must clear those batteries, then alter course once more, and bring the brig into the bay.

They would have to claw their way in – it was even possible their target, the *Fraternité,* would lie in the wind's eye, in which case there would be nothing to do but abandon the coaster, and make for the landing party. And before that, they might touch bottom, or take a shot or two from the land – little more would be needed to disable a vessel as frail as theirs.

"Wind's dropping," Hunt said softly, although all aboard knew well the predicament they were in.

Again King made no reply. Yes, it might all be in vain, but he was not going to be deterred; there was still a chance of making it round the oncoming headland, and while any possibility of success existed, he was determined to see matters through to the very end.

* * *

Meanwhile, to the south of the causeway, things were also progressing. *Victory* had not disappointed: the flagship came up at exactly the prescribed time and now, with *Belleisle* on her starboard beam and *Prometheus* to larboard, the three were approaching the coast in line abreast. Behind them, and hopefully invisible to the shore, the nine small boats that carried a powerful British landing party were keeping pace, and would be ready to burst out between them, before staking their claim on the nearby beaches. But first the batteries had to be engaged, and that would take both gall and cunning. The enemy must be fooled into making the liners their target, and so give the launches and cutters a chance. That would mean exposing wooden ships to a heavy bombardment from land based artillery and, as Banks was all too aware, the opening shots could be expected at any moment.

"There's the first signal!" Midshipman Bentley, one of the signals party, shouted as a red light was momentarily allowed to illuminate *Victory*'s poop.

"We are to turn upon the second, sir," Brehaut reminded Banks.

"Ready starboard battery!" Caulfield cautioned more loudly,

and received a wave from Corbett on the upper gun deck in reply.

"It is the pity King is not present," the first lieutenant grumbled. "With two senior officers absent, we are stretched; why Lewis has command of the lower battery, and is unsupported."

"There are three midshipmen and a gunner's mate," Banks replied soothingly. "And is it not a station that has been commanded by an able seaman in the past?" he added with a smile.

They were less than a mile offshore, and had been expecting to give, and take, fire some while back. The silence was almost as disconcerting as gunfire, then four jets of flame erupted from the stone walls of the westward battery, lighting up the shoreline, and revealing the beach that was their marines' ultimate objective. Further shots were seen from the eastward emplacement, but the three ships sailed steadily on, and no further signal came from the flagship.

"The admiral is biding his time," Caulfield's words were punctuated by an iron clang as their larboard bower was struck, and two servers dropped to the deck when a studding sail boom, knocked free from the forecourse yard, fell amongst them. But there was no important damage to the ship, and she continued like a boxer simply disregarding minor punches.

"It has always been his nature," Banks replied stoically. "Though I would wish us to turn, and present our full broadside."

"Blue lights aloft from flag, sir!" Bentley's voice again and both officers were in time to see *Victory*'s spars bathed in an ethereal glow.

"Then the boats will be going in," Caulfield commented to no one in particular.

"Be ready, Mr Brehaut," Banks warned, but the sailing master was watching the flagship with as much attention as any of the signals department. There was a wait of maybe two minutes, then a red light showed for a moment and, as the first drops of rain began to fall, the three ships finally turned.

There was silence from the shore; all their guns had been discharged and the French were obviously not practised in rapid serving. Until they fired again, the British gunners would remain uncertain of their mark while, with the bad weather coming up from the south, they themselves would soon be covered and unable to create the distraction needed. But the cloud would not shield the boats; there was still starlight enough to the north to reveal the tiny flotilla that was purposefully making for the enemy's coast.

All aboard *Prometheus* wondered if the landing party had been spotted. The French were undoubtedly slow in response, and such a delay may easily be caused by gunners altering their pieces to train on the fragile craft. But there was nothing to be gained in speculation: they would simply have to wait for the enemy to fire, then see which target had been chosen.

The night was eventually split by the second offering from the batteries, and it came almost as a relief to note the three British warships remained their objective. Those commanding the land based artillery had allowed too much for the decreasing range, and the waters beside erupted in a series of dramatic, but impotent, splashes. The battleships' gun captains had been given their mark though and, barely seconds later, and with the combined power of three full decks, *Victory* opened up on the westward battery. It was still moderately long range, but over fifty guns must make some impact and, when *Prometheus'* broadside added to the number, followed by *Belleisle* with the first shots to the eastern emplacements, Banks guessed where further retaliation, if it were indeed possible, would be directed.

And so it proved; the range gradually decreased further and soon ship and shore were exchanging deadly salvoes that lit up the dark night. The French guns, firmly based and set amid stone embrasures, were fewer but better protected, while their target was undoubtedly the easier to sight. But the British made up for any deficiencies by sheer number of cannon and, in the glare of almost constant gunfire, it was hoped the boats were approaching the beach unnoticed and unharmed.

"Well that should give Reynolds and his men a fair start," Banks shouted to Caulfield after the din of yet another broadside. "With luck the same can be said for the brig."

* * *

Actually it was far bleaker on the northern side of the causeway. All could hear the fire from the British battleships who were waging what appeared to be a separate war to the south, but none paid it any attention; they had other, more immediate, problems to consider. The wind had dropped still further, and rain was starting to fall.

"I should have liked to take her farther off shore," King shouted to Hunt "Though the chart is singularly vague about depth in this area and I cannot anticipate the currents. With the wind as it is, it will be hard enough to beat south, and I would prefer not to make matters easier for the land based guns."

Hunt nodded in complete understanding. They only had a rough idea where the *Fraternité* was moored; she might be relatively deep into the bay, which would make their own escape more simple. The wind was still to shift, though, and may yet save her. Nevertheless, there was good news as well: the batteries they had been dreading did not seem to be quite so threatening. Cloud was rapidly thickening, although those aboard the brig had already seen enough to give reassurance. Both emplacements were set high; perfect for sweeping across the strait that divided outer and inner harbours, but a small craft like theirs should be able to creep beneath without encountering heavy gunfire at all.

They were still depending upon the fickle wind though; even if it did not back, it must certainly continue, and that was by no means certain. In fact there was little they could rely on and, as if to emphasise the point, the rain then changed from the occasional spots, to an absolute deluge.

* * *

"Damned weather," Caulfield cursed softly. "Can't make out the hand in front of my face!"

Banks sympathised, although he was not sorry. When last seen, the landing party had almost been at the shore. It was a sandy beach, with no apparent installations, and such a force would be able to overpower all but major resistance. And once they were safely ashore, the rain was there to shield them, as it had the British ships. All three liners continued to exchange fire with the land batteries, but in the main their shots went unsighted, and simply served to distract the enemy gunners. The French were no more accurate and, if the marines were in anything like the order expected of them, would soon cease completely.

At that moment a rocket was seen to the east. It was not spectacular, and could hardly have climbed a hundred feet into the heavy night sky, but its message remained clear. The first of their troops were going in and *Belleisle*, who was engaging the eastern battery, immediately held her fire. A similar, but stronger flare then shot up from the west: Caulfield blew on his silver whistle and all *Prometheus'* guns fell silent.

The peace felt strange and vaguely disconcerting after such a din. Three more cannon erupted from the west, and the eastern battery, that had never resorted to individual fire, let off one last barrage, before thundering rain, interspersed by the distant snap of small arms, became the only sound heard.

"Well, we have done all we can," Caulfield sighed. "Now it depends on the Royals."

* * *

The coaster made it past the second battery as easily as King predicted and, as they turned to larboard, the inner bay finally opened up to them. To the south, on the all important causeway, an unseen battle was being fought and, by the flickering glow of musket shot, cannon fire, and a strange blue light that must come from strategically tossed flares, much of the bay could be made out. But even if it were not for that, and despite the rain which now fell in a continuous sheet, their objective would still have been plain. To the west, and surrounded by small craft apparently so placed to emphasise her bulk, the outline of a warship's hull was obvious, and the brig made for it without delay.

"That's our prize," Flint told his friend. His eyes were unusually alive and he appeared far happier than Jameson had known him for some while.

"And no opposition, or so it seems," the younger man agreed.

The wind was now almost non existent; but still they moved. They must be travelling on some form of current; not strong enough to be a tide, yet seemingly predictable, although that was not the only factor in their favour.

As the two men peered forward into the night, it soon became obvious the rain was dying almost as quickly as it had been born; going from a torrent, to something that actually allowed them to breathe, in hardly more than a minute. Then it dwindled further to individual drops, and it was at that point the wind took charge once more.

No words were necessary; Flint grinned at Jameson as a faint burble came from the brig's stem. They were properly underway again and, with less than half a cable to cover, would soon be alongside the Frenchman. There came a chorus of shouting from astern, with both King and Hunt apparently vying to give the most orders in the shortest time, but the seamen were not particularly bothered. Jameson had the cheerful air of most of his type, and could foresee nothing but success. They would board the Frenchman, set their charges, then meet up with the land forces; within half an hour every man should be safe in the boats and being rowed back to the barky. And Flint's thoughts were every bit as optimistic: not so detailed, perhaps, but he too could see a glorious end to the night's activities.

* * *

"Port your helm," King roared, "Lay her over!"

"Braces, there – the wind's rising!" Hunt added.

"Mr Cross!" In the half light, King saw the midshipman spin round at the call of his name. "Prepare the fuses, if you please!" The lad touched his hat, and made aft, while there was a creaking from the yards and the flap of canvas.

"Boat-keepers, ready the gig!" Hunt again; they were underway once more, but must leave the brig within minutes, and time was becoming increasingly important.

A pair of seamen pushed past to attend to the small boat that swung from davits to the stern, while King studied the bleak sides of the hull they meant to destroy. There were no lights showing as was to be expected; the ship being freshly launched and probably little more than a shell. But neither were there any signs of sentries, not even cursory precautions having been taken to guard what would one day be a powerful liner.

"Appears we have the ship to ourselves," Hunt commented dryly.

"Indeed so," King agreed. "Within a defended dockyard, I would chance they may have grown complacent."

Certainly the British had been allowed to approach unchallenged, but then the intense battle that was still in full flow to the southern side of the causeway could have some influence on the matter.

Cross was examining the twin lengths of fuses that lay amidships. Previously Hurle, the gunner, had sewn a short length of slow match to each. They only need light the ends to allow fifteen minutes before the joint was reached. Then a deadly flame would flash down into the depths of the hold where it was safely secured within an opened cask of powder. Having two fuses halved the chance of a fault in the quick match, although King was hardly relying on such a crude means of ignition. The brig was tinder dry, and could be expected to take fire as fast as any vessel of her age. Simply being beside the Frenchman's freshly payed and painted timbers should do the business; the flames would spread, and probably find the powder of their own accord long before either fuse did their work.

"Braces there!" Hunt again. "And prepare to clap on!" They were now in the lee of the moored hull and, with momentum enough to carry the brig to her final resting place, it was important they were secured tightly to one another.

There was a groaning and splintering of wood as the two

ground together, then a flurry of activity fore and aft. Each of the British seamen knew their task well enough; lines were secured to any convenient point, while the banging of hammers told where fresh purchases were being made, and soon both vessels had effectively become one.

"Very well, we must go," King cried. The journey until then had not been without incident, yet this final action which had actually caused him the most concern, seemed to have been achieved with worrying ease.

"Go to the boat, Thomas," Hunt said. "You will take longer: I can light the fuses with Cross."

King went to object, although the sense in what had been said was indisputable. He turned away, just as three dark lanterns were opened and the oily rags that lay bundled by the bulwarks, released. Sanders, who was one of the boat keepers, stood by the brig's tiny entry port. King made for him, and would actually have been the first into the gig but, as he twisted awkwardly to clamber down the short freeboard, he saw something that made him freeze.

"Guard boat approaching," he called, turning back to those on deck. "Coming up to starboard and preparing to board!"

Chapter Nine

Those aboard the brig immediately abandoned the task in hand, and turned to meet the first of the enemy. So engrossed had they been in setting fire to the prize, only a few were armed: it took valuable seconds for the rest to grab at their cutlasses, and the French were allowed to establish themselves just aft of the forecastle. But the British were not slow in countering and soon there was the oddly agricultural sound of blade upon blade, punctuated by an occasional curse or scream, while all was lit by the bright and ever growing light of the coaster's blazing larboard bulwark.

King regained the deck and tore his hanger from its scabbard, striking mightily at the nearest Frenchman. But his aim was poor, and the effort, coupled with the lack of his left arm, made him overbalance. He stumbled clumsily and fell sideways, aware that his opponent's sword could be expected to hack down upon him at any moment. He was actually bracing himself for the cut when, instead, the clatter of a parry was heard from above. King rolled over and looked up to see Hunt silhouetted against the growing flames as he took on the Frenchman, and was clambering to his feet by the time the intruder had been knocked back over the bulwark.

Jameson and Flint were also in action: the former had been wearing his cutlass, and was one of the few able to lay into the boarders as they came over the starboard side. His first opponent went down relatively easily, but the second, who appeared to be an officer, was more practised in sword play. The young seaman found himself fending off a succession of wicked blows as he backed steadily towards the wall of flame that was growing up on the brig's larboard side. Fortunately Flint noticed his predicament, and cut in, almost literally, with his own blade. Then the two of them set upon the Frenchman in a decidedly unjust manner until he was eventually forced to the deck.

Jameson flashed a smile at his friend, but there was no time for more; the enemy still had possession of a sizeable part of the brig's deck, while the flames were spreading and now raced up the battleship's hull.

After accounting for his first victim, Hunt had moved on and found himself between Harding and Beeney, two seamen who seemed particularly adept at rough-house fighting. Together they carved a deep inroad into the tight knot of Frenchmen, two of whom were actually in the act of returning to their boat when they were taken down from behind. And soon it was all but over; the boarders had either fallen, or run, leaving the decreasing area of deck not aflame in the hands of the British.

"Cold shot!" Hunt yelled, as he and his two accomplices grabbed at the ready use iron balls that lay in garlands next to the brig's guns, and began flinging them through the bottom of the guard boat. "Now back to the gig," he said, glancing briefly down at the turmoil of struggling bodies beneath. "And claim it before the Frogs do!"

Further aft, King was shouting for the midshipman. That brief exposure to hand-to-hand combat had convinced him his fighting days were done. He had withdrawn, and was now clutching at the two lengths of slow match that snaked down to the powder below. Both were unlit, and there was no sign of the boy who was supposed to have charge of them. Hunt was hurrying the rest of the British to the starboard entry port. Two were wounded, and needed to be helped to the waiting boat below, while there were at least three bodies they would be forced to leave behind. King paused for a moment as he realised one belonged to the midshipman, Cross, then dismissed further thought. This was hardly the time for sentiment; he must leave also, but first there remained one important task to attend.

"The lantern, Flint, hurry!" he called to the last of the retreating British. The seaman turned, and seemed surprised to see King crouched on the deck over lengths of slow match. "Give me that light!" King dropped the fuses and pointed at the closed dark lantern that Cross had been carrying. Flint picked it up and was in the process of bringing it over when King snatched it from his grip. He tried to hold it, while forcing the warm metal door open with one hand but the catch needed two.

"Go to the boat," he shouted, fumbling with the thing. "And watch for more French."

The fire was now painfully hot: its light would be noticed from the shore, no matter how great a distraction the marines might be making.

"Come on, Flint!" King looked up to see Jameson, the young topman, had returned and was attempting to drag the seaman away.

But Flint did not appear to hear, and shrugged the grip from his arm quite roughly.

"The flames have her," Jameson pleaded, while King struggled gracelessly to his feet and assessed the situation once more.

"He's right, we may as well leave her," King agreed as he and Jameson made for the entry port. "Come, or the boat will go without us; the fire shall light the powder!"

"It will blow at any moment, man – leave it!" Jameson yelled, but still Flint did not go.

Instead he calmly collected the lantern from where King had left it and flipped open the metal door. King and Jameson watched for no more than a second, before clambering through the small gap. Flames had reached the centre of the brig's deck, most of her forecastle was ablaze and the heat, along with an apparent lack of air, was making it hard to breathe. It was extremely doubtful if the fuses would even be needed; should the seven tons of gunpowder in her hold fail to explode, fire from the brig must now destroy the enemy hull. But whatever happened, the intense heat was making it impossible for King and Jameson to remain, and they reluctantly lowered themselves over the side.

However, closer to the blaze, and directly above the hold, Flint was not to be rushed. He hardly acknowledged the final pleas to go, but rather concentrated solely on the job in hand, as was his custom. Each length of slow match was carefully bent in half, before being fed into the lantern's own comparatively meek little fire, and only when he was certain both were burning brightly, did he stand up and begin to amble across to the entry port. He looked back at the flames for a moment, then down into the dark waters below, and it was with no surprise that he noted the boat was no longer there.

* * *

Prometheus had sent her launch and two cutters to deliver the marines, and Acting Lieutenant Franklin was in command. It wasn't a duty he would have chosen, but so far all had gone smoothly. He had led in the launch, the larger boat creeping up and onto a beach so blessed with white sand that, even when damp and in the dark of night, it seemed to glow. Then the landing party had departed in a blur of red coats, leather and polished metal, leaving him, two midshipmen and twenty-eight seamen to manage what now appeared unusually empty and cumbersome craft. And he did not delay, but ordered them straight to the east. There they were beached for the second time, roughly midway between the two batteries, and the wait for their landing party to return began.

To one side a rather prim lieutenant had charge of *Victory*'s boats, and beyond them were those belonging to *Belleisle*. But there was no fraternisation between the three groups. Apart from Franklin's acknowledgement of his neighbour, which was returned with a derisory wave, each kept to themselves. To that point everything had been meticulously planned and timed to the second, but now they could do no more than allow matters to run their course. That, and be ready to take the troops off as soon as they appeared.

A small lantern hung before each boat, the light being shielded by the rise of the beach, and considered essential if they were to collect men in a hurry. The blue and black cutters were under the charge of midshipmen Brown and Briars respectively, while Franklin perched himself nonchalantly against the bow of the launch and the seamen sat upon the sand, delighting in the audacity of relaxing so while on enemy soil. Some had wanted to accompany the marines and Franklin had been forced to use all his authority to keep them back. But now they waited patiently enough, and he was confident his party would be ready, capable and most importantly, complete when the time came to evacuate.

The land rose steadily and no one was able to see further up the shore. But they could certainly hear, and were aware a considerable battle was in process. If the British emerged as victors and took control of the nearby shore batteries, the marines would remain in position for the briefest of times; possibly no longer than to allow the spiking of cannon. That simple act alone would guarantee a more peaceable departure, although Franklin was familiar with the enthusiasm of fighting men, and suspected they would attempt to destroy the magazines as well.

But he hoped not. He hoped – actually he prayed – they would all leave shortly. As it was, men would die, and were doing so quite close by, even as he apparently lounged against the boat. Any delay would inevitably mean more must follow, and the blowing up of a few tons of gunpowder was surely not worth anything as precious as a human life.

And if the marines were not victorious: if the French drove them off, the survivors could be expected back at any time. That would be a far harder problem to solve, as they must have wounded with them and were bound to be closely pursued. Then, with the shore batteries still in use, it would be a difficult departure indeed. Whatever threat the British battleships might make, his small force was likely to become the focus of the enemy's fire.

But the sound was steadily decreasing and soon there was relative silence. Far off shouting could still be heard, and some was in French, but as to who had been successful, no one was certain.

"Want that I take a look, sir?" Brown called hesitantly from his cutter. He was older than Briars, the other midshipman, and Franklin had noticed his apparent eagerness in the past. In fact he wondered if it were done to enforce his superiority over the younger boys, but on this occasion there was no question of independent action.

"Stay as you are, son," the older man told him gently, with the sobriquet being used quite unconsciously. He peered across to where the other boats were drawn up. "I believe *Victory* sent a youngster up a while back," he added. "And he has not returned."

Briars grinned at his friend in the next boat and was clearly about to pass comment when a bright light suddenly appeared above them. All looked up to see the low cloud illuminated in an orange glow and, even as they watched, a rumble emanated from the very ground beneath them.

"Would that be one of the batteries?" Briars asked in innocence, and Brown immediately took the chance to scoff.

"How so, when one is to the east and the other, the west?"

The hands also began discuss in urgent tones and Franklin knew he must take control.

"No, I'd say that were our brig," he said more steadily over the excited chatter. "And with luck, she will have taken the Frenchman with her."

"Aye," Brown agreed, importantly. "Along with anyone else who happened to be nearby."

* * *

King, Hunt, and the others were not exactly nearby, but still the explosion had been close enough to shock all aboard the tiny boat, and caused momentary confusion amongst the rowers. The sheet of flame was spectacular, forcing most to rub at their eyes and, even when gone, leaving the remains of *Fraternité* to blaze merrily in the bay, they felt horribly exposed. But King could also see the shore more clearly now, and knew them less than fifty yards off.

And, more importantly, he could make out the red and white of Royal Marine uniforms. There were many, and seemed to dominate the low quay their boat was heading for.

"Stand to, there," he ordered. There would be areas close by that were not in British hands and might shelter snipers. To lose further men when rescue and success were almost within their grasp would be dreadful. The rowers recovered their oars and set them in the rowlocks once more, then looked to him and Sanders, who was pulling stroke, expectantly. King drew breath to give the order and instantly felt a stab of pain that ran from one shoulder to the other. His tumble into the boat had been quite ungainly and since then there was an uncomfortable sensation in his wound. He may have torn at the lesion; doubtless Manning would put things right, but for now he must concentrate on other matters. The thought of his friend made him feel guilty, however: it was yet one more person he would have upset that evening.

"Ready, sir," Sanders prompted, but before King could speak there was another sound, and one none of them were expecting.

"Hold hard, there, hold hard!" It came from the water and was a familiar voice, although hearing it gave several inside the boat an uneasy feeling.

"We've a swimmer, sir," someone shouted from starboard and, sure enough, a man was heading for them in an artless paddle that barely kept him afloat.

"And it sounds like Flint," another added. "Though it can't be, not when he were..."

"Extend an oar, Jackson," Jameson, who was seated opposite Sanders, ordered, and soon the panting body was dragged nearer to the boat, before being heaved, spluttering and breathless, over the stern.

"I'd thought you a goner," Jameson told his friend.

"No lad," Flint replied, smiling through the gasps. "Belike you're stuck with me a while longer."

* * *

The rest of their journey to the quay was over mercifully quickly. After what seemed like no time at all, the small boat was rubbing up against the stone of the wharf. But reinforcements for the French were coming in from the west; King could make out an officer mounted on a splendid horse. The rider looked particularly dramatic, picked out in flames from the burning hull as he drew his sword to exhort the ill defined unit behind him. The pain in King's chest was increasing though, and there was a feeling of damp on his shirt while, as he clambered out of the gig, he needed to pause to draw breath. Hunt was unaccountably missing, but others, ordinary seamen, had gathered beside him and it was their presence and need for command that stirred him into action once more.

"Come on, we must join up with the landing party."

They moved off and were clear of the quay and halfway across a small road when the musket balls began to whip between them. King was now gasping for air, but could see a unit of Royal Marines that were fighting a rearguard action. His sword and hat were missing, but he held his arm high as he stumbled over the rough ground and scrub of the causeway. Then, as the small group were closing on the friendly force, Hunt joined him, along with another seaman who appeared to be wounded in the shoulder. An unknown marine lieutenant pointed the group out to his men, and immediately a line was formed that stretched out and gave covering fire to see them safely into the main body.

"We'd given you up," the officer told them bluntly as the now panting seamen were brought into the safety of the section. "Saw the ship blow, of course," he added. "Splendid sight, but rather assumed you'd all gone up with it."

The light from the fire seemed just as bright, even though the burning wreck must now be all of five hundred yards off, and was reflected in the dark eyes of the young officer. He was unusually relaxed in what King could only regard as a desperate situation, but then had not just blown up a French man-of-war, and neither did he have an excruciating pain in his chest.

"Captains Reynolds and Douglas will be abandoning the batteries," the marine lieutenant continued, just as calmly. "But we won't wait for them; Sergeant Taylor here will see you to your boats; better to leave the final evacuation to the Royals: it's what we do best."

King had no mind to argue, and allowed himself with what remained of the brig's crew to be hustled over the rest of the scrub. The loud and officious NCO bellowed to his own men, while treating King's as if they were half-wits, but there was no doubting they made good time and, after crossing yet another road, were soon tumbling down a beach filled with damp sand so soft it threatened to swallow them. Then there was Franklin, an unspeakably welcome sight, along with the familiar midshipmen and hands from *Prometheus* who crowded about, throwing anxious greetings and the occasional private insult.

"How many are you, sir?" Franklin asked, and King looked round desperately. The seamen were merging with their fellows, but he was reasonably sure of those who had fallen.

"Seven," he replied, adding, "plus myself and Hunt."

"What about Cross?" one of the midshipmen enquired.

"He fell," King snapped in reply.

"Take the blue cutter and Brown," Franklin directed. "Briars and I shall wait; the launch may need to give covering fire with her carronade."

King's chest was now throbbing badly, the pain made being looked after more acceptable, and again he felt no inclination to disagree. Instead he and Hunt stumbled after the departing figure of Brown as he made for his boat. Together they all but fell into the cutter that had just been launched and steadied themselves as the oars bit into the turgid waters. The burning hull was hidden now although the sky behind King was still strangely bright.

"Quite a fire you started, sir," Brown told him seriously as he hugged the tiller.

King was too exhausted to reply; even without the complication of his wound, there had been more than enough activity for one night. But the marines had carried out their part perfectly: there was no fire from the batteries and all might expect to be safely back aboard *Prometheus* in no time. Then there would be a good deal of talking, as well as hundreds of questions that needed to be answered straight away. Probably some form of explanation should be prepared now, King decided. He would have to justify his position aboard a captured prize, when his proper station was in charge of a third rate's lower battery. And the story had better be good if he wanted to avoid having to tell it once more at a court martial.

For the offence he had committed was certainly of such a level; forcing himself aboard the brig, with all the ramifications of creating a disputed command, was unlikely to simply be brushed aside. And to that might be added desertion of his own post in *Prometheus*, especially as the ship had seen action during his absence. But King found he really could not care about the consequences. This was his first true test since the injury. Even if he were subsequently dismissed the service and never again saw the fire of battle, at least there would be the consolation that losing an arm had not robbed him of the ability to fight. And it was, as Brown had said, quite a fire.

Chapter Ten

"I have been considering again the prospect of changing position of the sick berth," Manning said. It was two weeks after the attack which had seen the hull of the *Fraternité*, as well as a sizeable shore battery, destroyed. The wounded that had cluttered up the place since were now returned to their own messes and, in many cases, duties, so the surgeon was able to assess his department after its first proper trial following their refit.

"A good few third rates are now siting theirs on the upper deck; usually near to the stove, for warmth, and allowing more convenient access to the heads."

He looked up. As he had suspected, Kate's mind was elsewhere. She seemed to be gazing into the distance and had not heard a word; something she was prone to do of late, although such instances were not always as annoying as they appeared.

In the past the surgeon had even found them useful; much might be said which may be referred to later and, when challenged, he could honestly claim to have already informed her. This was hardly such an occasion, however, and sincerely wished for her opinion. It had been a long journey from loblolly boy to surgeon and, now established, Manning felt himself to be a made man. But approaching the captain with any major suggestion was still something that daunted him, and he was loath to do it without his wife's support.

"This place is poorly ventilated," he continued hopefully. "It is now a proven scientific fact that the humours are disrupted by foul smells, and there would be enough of those in such a sealed up hell-hole as this, even without its proximity to the bilges."

He waited, but Kate was still apparently distracted and had yet to even begin her breakfast, whereas his was almost finished. By now she would usually be annoyingly busy and for the first time he wondered if something was seriously wrong.

"Kate, have you been listening?" he asked finally.

"Why yes, Robert; of course I have." She glanced up and fixed him with a stare. They were in the dispensary; a place used as their day cabin when it was free and, even in such poor light, he could not have avoided that expression.

"You were saying the captain wishes you to move the sick berth," she said, in triumph. "And I think it to be a capital idea."

Manning shook his head in sudden anger and was about to risk remonstrating with his wife when he noticed the far away look in her eyes had returned.

"Whatever is the matter?" he asked instead and, rather than preparing for an argument, his tone was gentle.

"The matter?" she snorted. "Why nothing. What makes you ask such a question?"

"Because I have known you this long," he replied, and the truth of his words, and sincerity of intention, struck home.

"It is nothing," she repeated, although the façade was starting to crumble, and Manning was suddenly aware that tears were not so very far away.

"Tell me," he insisted, but for several seconds the woman remained mute. He waited; then she spoke.

"It is Poppy, my maid," she said slowly. "The girl is pregnant."

"Pregnant?" he cried, astonished. "How ever did that happen?"

Kate's gaze rose up from the table where it had been fixed, and something of her usual manner returned. "Really, Robert – a seventeen year old girl in a ship full of men – is that truly a sensible question? And you a medical man!"

Manning was getting a little tired of having his qualifications thrown back at him, and felt his anger return. "You know exactly what I mean," he snapped. "Have you not taken proper care of her?"

"I don't see why I should be blamed for this," she retorted. "She is my maid, not the other way about. I cannot be held responsible for everything the foolish mot does."

They both paused, conscious that the argument was in danger

of going deeper than either of them wished.

"Actually, I am not sure quite how it did occur," Kate continued, in a more mellow timbre. "She will not say, though I sense it caused her a deal of worry."

"And the father?" Manning's voice was also softer.

"She will not tell that either," Kate replied.

"Well," he sighed. "And after all you have done to change her ways – I had thought better of her..."

"I would not rush to condemn," Kate implored. "We both know her history and that she has been unreliable in the past, but I still believe her greatly improved. Besides, whoever is to blame would appear to be taking their responsibilities seriously."

"Indeed?" Manning asked, although he was only vaguely interested.

"She had placed a jacket on one side that I was to show her how to darn." Kate explained. "Two guineas and some silver fell from the pocket; it was how she came to tell of her condition."

The surgeon said nothing. The news was bad enough, how his wife discovered it was simply an irrelevance, and he was annoyed on several levels. What had been intended as a convenience for them both had been neatly turned on end: an asset changed to a liability. And that a girl they rescued from plying her trade on the streets should pay them back in such a way... But these were just superficial annoyances; their personal tragedy lay far deeper.

So far all attempts at starting a family had proved unsuccessful, with their last failure being demonstrated in the most awful and public way imaginable. And now, while it seemed further efforts were to be equally frustrated, the two of them would have to watch Poppy go through a process they both wished for so vehemently.

Kate was not the woman he had married, and he must also have changed: such things were to be expected with the passing of time. But he could not dismiss the thought that her transition from loving wife to fractious scold had more to do with their lack of children than simple ageing. It was a theory he kept to himself, of course, but one that seemed more reasonable with every passing year. Soon she would reach the age when they would be forced to abandon all hope: when that time came he had serious concerns for his wife's mental well being. And it made matters worse that the trollop had found so little difficulty in conceiving.

* * *

"We are invited to dine with the admiral," Banks told him briskly. "Tomorrow at three."

"We, sir?" King questioned cautiously.

The captain's harsh expression relaxed for less than a second. "You will be accompanying me," he said.

Since returning from the attack, King had spent no time on the quarterdeck. As soon as he regained the ship, Caulfield, who had been about to read the riot act, noticed his loss of colour, and sent him down to wait his turn with the surgeon. The subsequent days were now something of a blur; he had been unconscious for most, with Manning seeing off visitors of every rank, and only that morning was he permitted a return to light duties.

But before King could stand his first watch, he found himself summoned to the captain's quarters. The order came as no surprise; there was obviously a deal to speak of and, if Sir Richard were intending to send him for examination by court martial, King was fully prepared for most things, including being returned to his cabin under arrest. But this particular outcome had not been anticipated.

"Do not think for a moment the invitation is in any way a reward," Banks warned. "It was a successful attack: all performed well, though most did not do so at the expense of their duty."

King knew enough to keep quiet, especially when things seemed to be going his way. Certainly two weeks should be adequate time for a full report to have been made and, if he was in serious trouble, this would be when it was announced.

"And as I have already said, the example you set the men was disgraceful. No account being taken of the damage your presence caused to the order of command, neither did you show regard for

Mr Hunt, who is new to independent assignments. I trust you have sought forgiveness from him, as well as those officers who were forced to stand in your place aboard this ship?"

King mumbled something incomprehensible in reply. In fact, apart from a cold silence from Caulfield, there had been no animosity from anyone in the wardroom. His injury, caused by a strain to the old wound, was judged serious and may have altered their reaction, of course. That and the fact the French were down by one new line-of-battleship, with a shore battery also being placed out of action, while another required a total rebuild. Besides the British Navy had been victorious once more – once more demonstrated that no enemy or obstacle was safe from its might or ingenuity. And *Prometheus* had added to her battle honours: that could also have been a major factor in his reprieve.

"If there is nothing else, I shall expect you to be ready by five bells in tomorrow's afternoon watch."

Banks showed no surprise when King opened his mouth to speak.

"If I may ask, sir..."

"You want to know why I'm taking you to the flagship?" the captain enquired, mellowing slightly.

"Yes, sir."

Banks looked down at the table in front of him, and began to fiddle with a sheet of paper.

"To be candid, Tom, I have no idea," he replied. "The admiral is aware of your amendment to the plan, which I suppose might bring a commendation. But then he also knows you chose to remain with the brig, which should provoke a decidedly different reaction." He sighed. "But your attendance was specifically requested, so I suggest you simply thank good fortune, and make yourself as presentable as possible."

* * *

Mason was the marine who usually attended to him, so it was a surprise when Kennedy, the wardroom steward who had greeted him on his first day, entered Franklin's cabin.

"Apparently your regular man has an extra duty, sir," he explained, while beginning to make up the cot. "An' I had no other commitment, so volunteered in his stead."

"Good of you," Franklin said, shifting along the sea chest to give more room, and slipping the small, leather bound book he had been reading safely out of sight.

"It is no trouble, sir," Kennedy replied, as he smoothed out the blanket.

Franklin remembered the man from their previous meeting and eyed him cautiously. He was a professional servant, one used to dealing with senior officers as high as flag rank, so would have every reason to despise someone of his age, who had yet to attain so much as a commission. Even Hunt, the other acting lieutenant, was Franklin's senior, as well as more than ten years younger.

"I am happy to wait upon any man, sir," Kennedy continued, as if sensing his thoughts. "And have long since considered a servant's role to be my calling."

Now that was more curious still, and Franklin found it hard not to stare. Ostensibly the reply could have been expected from any of the stewards, but there was something in Kennedy's words that touched a nerve deep within.

"Ranks do have their importance," the man was almost ruminating now. "But, if you will forgive me, sir, they are purely man made. We are all of the same flesh, and come and go in a similar manner..."

"And end as dust," Franklin chanced, to be immediately rewarded by a look of both understanding and pleasure from the steward.

"Indeed, sir," Kennedy agreed, before taking as much of a step back as was possible in such a small space. "Mr Franklin, I wonder if you have a duty during tomorrow's afternoon watch?"

Now the conversation was taking a decidedly strange turn. By necessity, anyone who served wardroom officers would know the watch bill, and a competent steward such as Kennedy should surely not need to ask the question. Franklin was working the forenoon, but after that had no official commitments until the second dog.

"What have you in mind?" he asked, guardedly.

"It is a meeting some of us holds regularly, sir," Kennedy explained, and Franklin noted his voice was now softer. "Twice a week – to take account of the changes of watch, though often we gathers during the make and mends as well."

"Indeed? Where does this take place?"

"Usually in the stewards' room, sir."

"And a meeting, you say?" Franklin asked. Foolish thoughts of mutinous assemblies were flashing through his mind although, even if the steward had been considering something on those lines, he would hardly have invited an officer.

"Yes, sir. Those of a similar disposition." Kennedy had stopped attending to the bedding now, but made no attempt to begin another task, and neither did he show any inclination to leave. "There is nothing to be concerned about, we do not keep it a secret, and have full permission from Mr Caulfield. Attendance is by invitation, although we are always looking for new men to join us and, if I may be forgiven, sir, you come across as one who would benefit from our association."

"The stewards' room?" Franklin confirmed.

"Yes, sir. Five bells, afternoon watch."

"Very well," he conceded, "I shall see if that suits my plans."

Kennedy's expression changed once more, although this time it broke into a smile that was almost radiant. "That is good news indeed, sir," he said. "And we may all have hope for the morrow."

* * *

Any remaining ill feelings seemed to have been forgotten as King presented himself on the half deck the following day. The captain greeted him genially; he was resplendent in full dress uniform, with polished bullion epaulettes and the finest silk stockings which caused King, in brass buckled shoes and a threadbare broadcloth tunic, to feel decidedly shabby. But at least they could share the splendour of Banks' decorated barge, as well as its dedicated crew. The latter were all prime seamen made even more presentable in the matching cream and dark blue uniforms Sir Richard provided for them. The day was bright and hardly a cloud spoiled a deep blue sky, although summer was little more than a memory now. Indeed an easterly wind brought quite a chill, along with white caps to the waves as they headed over to *Victory,* lying hove to and drifting gently with the current.

The appointment was a general one, with all commanders attending, and most carried at least one junior officer with them. Banks was reasonably well up on the captains' list, but they still had to wait their turn alongside the flagship's starboard entry port, and then King was forced to submit to the indignity of being the only one making use of a boatswain's chair. But they were on the quarterdeck soon enough and a little later found themselves being presented to a slightly built, pigeon-breasted man who seemed almost swamped in rather gaudy decorations.

"Ah, Mr King; the fellow who caused so much trouble the other night," the admiral informed him blithely while extending his left hand. It was a moment of acute awkwardness for King; both Nelson's words and manner had made him cautious and, as he could only offer his right in return, for several seconds he had the strange sensation of apparently holding hands with his commander-in-chief. But there were others awaiting the great man's attention, and he was quickly edged away by an officious lieutenant before being able to reply.

A rather tinny gong then sounded and officers who were better versed in the arrangements began to gather by the large doors that led to the admiral's quarters. King and Banks followed the throng through to the coach, and on to a vast room that seemed far too palatial to be found aboard a man-of-war. The deckhead was considerably higher than most, and a set of truly substantial stern windows brought the light in wonderfully. A large table spanned the beam and, despite strong afternoon sunshine, it held at least three dozen lighted candles, all set in ornate silver candelabras. Other silverware was in evidence, as was a good selection of glasses; there being four in front of each place setting, as well as a positive mass of precisely placed cutlery. In obedience to naval protocol, King joined the junior men in making for the far end. But the table was wide, as well as long and, on taking his place, he found all officers on the opposite side, as well as the admiral who sat at the head, to be in clear view. Wardroom servants started to walk slowly down the line, reaching over each shoulder in turn to fill one style of glass and King, after ensuring others had done so before him, cautiously sipped at his. It was strong and surprisingly cold; probably some form of sherry, he decided, placing the elegant glass down. That one taste had been enough: his head was already beginning to swim. Even before his wound he had not drunk alcohol for several months, and nothing would persuade him to take more that afternoon.

A brief but serious grace was followed by the arrival of three large tureens that were placed on the already crowded table. That they contained soup became obvious when a warmed and deep china bowl was set in front of every diner, before some very superior stewards began to dip ladles into the now open dishes, and served every man at the table in a remarkably short time. When he looked back on it, King decided the food was of a higher standard than that expected from a ship on blockade duty although, when compared to what had been available in Gibraltar, not so very remarkable. The service aboard *Victory* excelled in other ways, however, as he was soon to find out.

After the thin but pleasant broth, the senior officers were given chicken, although only beef was on offer at King's end of the table.

"You may usually expect fowl," one of his neighbours grumbled to no one in particular, "and occasionally mutton at an admiral's table. But this looks to have come from the most miserable ration bullock ever."

"We grew used to game with Cornwallis," the man on King's left remarked with an ill concealed sigh, as he added roasted potatoes to a plate already heaped in steaming meat.

Then King's turn came; an equally large serving of sliced beef was placed before him and he paused for a moment, as if intimidated, before turning his attention to the vegetables. These were presented in silver tureens with weighted, captured lids that swung back to keep the contents warm, and he was unable to hold the things open while helping himself. Those to either side took no interest in his predicament although a steward noticed and stepped forward to assist in as unobtrusive a manner as possible.

Prometheus' armourer had made King a special tool that was shaped like a fork, with a cutting edge to one side, and with its help he began to wrestle manfully with his meal. But the meat, though undoubtedly fresh, proved as tough as it was stringy, and even after several minutes' hard work, King had made very little impression. He glanced to his neighbours; neither were known to him, and both seemed totally focussed on their own food. One, he noticed, was a commander only a year or so older than himself, the other an elderly lieutenant who still sported unfashionably powdered hair and, by the look of his gold buttons and silk stock, was well connected. From across the table all he could see were the lowered heads of fellow eaters, and King was temporarily at a loss. Then, remembering the vegetables, he was about to ask a steward for assistance when his plate was magically whisked away from in front of him.

He looked round in surprise, only to find it instantly replaced by another, filled with a generous portion of roasted chicken and a selection of vegetables, neatly topped with gravy. King stared at the meal, quickly noticing that all the meat, as well as the more substantial potatoes, had been subtly attended to. Their shape was in no way altered, but a series of almost surgical slices in each would allow him to take convenient portions using a fork alone.

The sullen silence that fell to either side told him this had not been missed, and King flushed as he bent down to the meal. But his senses were still primed and he found himself looking up, then along the table, to where the more senior officers were seated.

And there, at the head, sat the admiral. His clear blue eyes, both apparently perfect from such a distance, set upon his own, and with a slight smile he inclined his head in King's direction, before raising his own adapted fork in silent acknowledgement.

* * *

"I am sorry to be late," Franklin informed them as he entered the small room. "Sir Richard has only just departed for the flag," he continued, looking about him curiously. "And, even though I am off watch, there was a deal to attend to."

Quite why he gave such an explanation was beyond him. Of the ten men present, not one was above junior warrant rank, and there were several able and ordinary seamen.

"It is good of you to come, sir," Kennedy informed him formally and Franklin was quick to notice that, although he was no longer dressed as a senior steward, the man still carried a natural authority about him. "Here, make a space for our new brother," he continued, and Franklin was seated between a long standing member of the afterguard and his old friend, Maxwell.

Franklin glanced cautiously at the quartermaster, and received an ironic wink in return. It seemed a friendly enough assembly, but still he wondered quite what he had let himself in for.

* * *

"Gentlemen, we are to leave for Agincourt Sound forthwith."

They had dined well and were now relaxing over coffee so the announcement took Banks, seated nearer the head of the table, by surprise. Nelson had touched upon the possibility of withdrawal when *Prometheus* first arrived, and Agincourt Sound, the recently charted shelter off Sardinia was also mentioned. But at the time the concept of apparently abandoning a blockade appeared too extreme, even for a commander known for unconventional tactics. Nothing further was said in the subsequent weeks and, with their recent attack on the port which had been followed by a particularly bad Mediterranean storm, Banks assumed he had either misheard, or the intention was forgotten. Perhaps one or two ships may be sent in rotation; a chance to wood and water, maybe take on some green stuff, and attend a few minor repairs, but certainly no more.

As soon as the words were spoken, though, he sensed a

general withdrawal was in mind. Nelson had never hidden his desire for the French to sail and such a move was bound to encourage it. If so, they may also be lost, and allowing even a chance for such a powerful fleet to go undetected was surely madness. Banks glanced around the table anxiously, although everyone seemed to be taking the news in their stride, and he quickly suppressed his own astonishment. Which was fortunate, as the admiral had further shocks in store and one was more personal.

"*Prometheus*, with two frigates will remain. She has water more than all of us and is freshly set up. You needn't worry, Sir Richard," Nelson bowed his head towards Banks briefly. "I do not propose to be away long, and you shall be sent for replenishment directly upon our return."

But Banks was in no way reassured. He was to be left guarding a major French port, and one currently holding a sizeable fleet which could be expected to set sail at any moment. Agincourt Sound was considerably more than a day's sailing away, and with only a couple of fifth rates as support, the French could snap up his single liner in a matter of hours.

"I will be no more than two hundred miles off," Nelson continued, clearly intending the statement to be reassuring. "And, with the prevailing north westerlies, news of any departure shall reach me swiftly enough."

Banks' mind was now in a whirl. Two hundred miles to the east. All very well if the French meant to flee in that direction; the British would be able to virtually ambush them. But should the wind blow foul, and the enemy make for the Atlantic, it could prove difficult. And were such a likely series of events to occur, would it be up to *Prometheus* and two frigates, to stop them?

"I shall provide written orders that you are not expected to engage should they make a move," the admiral concluded. "Despatch one frigate to bring me word, and retain the other to assist yourself; between the two, you should be able to keep a wary eye on the enemy until I can bring them to battle."

Nelson was quite correct, Banks supposed; he should manage that. There had been several occasions in the past when he had carried out similar duties. But that was while in command of a lithe and handy little frigate; something with the heels of the fleet he shadowed. He was inordinately fond of *Prometheus*, already she had proved herself both reliable and tough. But still the prospect of scouting in a thirty year old battle-wagon scarcely appealed.

"Have you any observations, Sir Richard?" Nelson was asking, and Banks knew the eyes of every officer were upon him, and him alone. Ostensibly this was his chance to object; to say he felt daunted by the task and that it was surely one most, if not all, those present must equally wish to avoid. He might cite numbers; point out the French were vastly superior in ships, men and guns. That their fleet consisted of up to nine liners, any one of which would be a worthy opponent for *Prometheus*, as well as at least thirteen frigates, that may include the new forty-gun, eighteen pounder monsters. A brace or so of those could outsail his old barge in most winds, and take their time in knocking her to pieces. And even accepting the main force was alerted, how would they know where to head? The Med. was a fickle sea in more ways than one; Nelson himself had taken months to catch Brueys before Aboukir Bay: Banks may have to spend just as long clinging to their apron strings.

But a single glance at his commander-in-chief told him that no objection was possible. There was no look of doubt or uncertainty; Nelson was offering an opportunity that he would have gratefully accepted in Banks' position, and it would be useless to reason with one so set.

"You must understand, Sir Richard: I wish them to sail more than anything," the admiral stated softly and Banks wondered, yet again, if Nelson was privy to his thoughts. "It will be a risk, none can doubt that, but one I think you more than capable of," he added.

Lesser men may have gone on to explain that *Prometheus*, having seen a dockyard most recently, was likely to be the swiftest sailer of all their liners, although Banks was growing accustomed to his commander's manner of thinking. He already gathered that Nelson preferred to judge men rather than materials, and

Prometheus was his choice solely because he considered him, her captain, capable.

It was both an honour, and a responsibility; should the French sail, the fate of the war – of the world, for that matter – would rest upon his shoulders. Yet to reject the task; to publicly decline selection, would be the act of a fool, as well as professional suicide. Besides, Nelson had already cast his spell upon him. The frail little man with the pigeon chest was a leader no officer could fail to follow and, though he might not share the admiral's confidence, Banks had no intention of questioning his judgement.

* * *

The afternoon in the stewards' room was passing quickly, and Franklin felt more relaxed and encouraged than at any time since joining the ship. At first it had been gratifying to find himself the senior officer present although despite, or maybe because of, the disparate range of ranks, scant attention was paid to status. Apart from Kennedy's initial greeting, no one addressed him as sir, and there had been a heated discussion between an ordinary seaman and Clement, a boatswain's mate: someone who was usually given a measure of respect. But though they may hold differing ideas, there was no doubting every man present was of a similar ethos, and Franklin was amazed that such a group should exist within a fighting ship.

"Did you hear the captain this Sunday?" Wells, one of the loblolly boys, was asking. "If he reads one of Maclaine's sermons many more times we'll all be able to join in, word for word."

A murmur of agreement could be heard from most present, although none carried any threat, and this was by no means a mutinous gathering.

"Sir Richard does his best, but it is a poor one," Maxwell agreed sadly.

"Though I've listened to enough truly bad parsons in my time," Kennedy added with a smile. "And we do usually have worship."

"Had it once a day and three times Sunday when I sailed with Dismal Jimmie," an ordinary seaman, who Franklin thought might be called Gardner, muttered. "But would rather Sir Richard to most blue light captains; at least we is allowed to think what we likes, and no man must attend unless he wishes."

"That's as maybe, and one day perhaps we shall be given a proper parson." Kennedy said as he removed his watch. "But for now we must to make do with ourselves, and there is reading to be done. You have a Bible, Mr Franklin?"

"I always carry a New Testament," he replied doubtfully, producing a small, leather-bound book from his pocket.

"That is fine," Kennedy told him. "We're reading Paul at present; Romans, Chapter Seventeen; perhaps you would care to start?"

Chapter Eleven

As soon as *Prometheus* had returned to sea, the midshipmen's berth became home to those officers who had been quartered ashore, and quickly reverted to the cramped and crowded place they all knew so well. At most hours of the day there was a constant buzz of conversation, the kettle seemed perpetually about to boil, journals were written, books read and advice sought, while everyone was aware that either shared laughter or a full blown argument could break out at any moment.

Meals were not confined to set times, with those coming on or off duty frequently consuming food served out during the previous watch, while other liberties were also taken. These ranged from tending to their pets – the berth now boasted three cats, a tortoise and a rabbit – to smoking illicit pipes that added an extra cast to air already thick with the stink of burning tallow, boot blacking and unwashed bodies. And never was there the chance to speak in confidence.

Even when the slung hammocks outnumbered those left awake, no one could be sure which contained sleepers or those merely taking a light doze; the place was constantly in a state of flux and, despite being the closest any got to personal space, offered little in the way of comfort or peace.

And so it was that the more junior members of the mess were denied any chance of serious conversation. They may pass comment, or the time of day; ask favours, advice or riddles, and call each other names or for duty. But, apart from immediately after the event, none had been able say what was really in their hearts, or speak in any detail of that terrible afternoon they had spent with young Poppy.

They all had their private thoughts, though; the inner arguments, justifications and regrets that no amount of distraction could erase. But if not remove, the berth's inharmonious atmosphere certainly distorted such thinking until each was haunted by a shared demon that teased and taunted their very souls.

And then, as if in retribution, the four had become three, with Cross being taken from them without warning or even a formal funeral, leaving those that remained even more paranoid and guilt ridden than before.

Carley and Briars were the youngest; this was their first experience of life away from home and living as a supposed adult. Both came from close families, where the father protected with a stiff rule and instant justice. In the past, when guilty of a minor crime, an appeal to him would bring sudden and severe punishment, which was always followed by an effectual end to the situation. Something more major might involve resorting to the law; although in such instances the same stern, strong hand would be turned to their defence. But in either case they would not have been so totally alone.

And Brown, though the oldest, was no more used to being responsible for his own actions. Despite attempting to portray a worldly persona, his life before the Navy had been unusually sheltered and he remained every bit as unsure of the correct course of action as the other two.

They might still report the matter to a superior, although none of the lads were certain who. Should they go directly to the captain or first lieutenant, or would a divisional officer be sufficient? Of them all, King appeared the most approachable and was the allocated senior lieutenant. But once that happened, once the terrible news of what they had done became fully known, they would be on a path far more unknown and dangerous than the wrath of any father or magistrate.

The Articles of War were recited after divine service most Sundays. None implicitly referred to situations such as theirs, but a good few came close, and many cited death as the appropriate punishment. Each of the boys were also aware that, although designated as quarterdeck officers, they were about as junior, and inexperienced as was possible. Guidance would certainly be available, but if anyone mentioned a word to King it could start a process that would not end until they were all swinging from a fore topyard.

But there was one apparently good aspect; Poppy had said nothing. Each boy was certain such a dreadful breach of discipline and law, both actual and moral, would not be overlooked or suppressed, so assumed she was either biding her time, or the incident meant little to her. None were so naïve as to hope for the latter however, and individually wanted to apologise; to assure her a terrible mistake had been made, and explain how the others were to blame for creating the entire wicked scenario. It was just a shame that no such opportunity ever presented.

And so they continued in their crowded lives, welcoming the occasions when their newly acquired responsibilities gave temporary respite from guilt and worry, and only sometimes wondering when, and how, the whole darned affair would finally come to an end.

* * *

Nelson, and the bulk of the blockading force, had departed nine days before, and Banks was slowly becoming accustomed to his role as captain of the only British liner on station, as well as unofficial commodore to two fifth rate frigates. October had begun with one of the worst storms any of them could remember, although the weather stayed mercifully clement for his first week of independent command, with little cloud and clear, moonlit nights to bolster his confidence. But on that particular evening, heavy cover was closing in from the north west; the previous night's watch had been more hazardous, and with the moon now very much on the wane, he was not looking forward to the next eight hours.

A movement to his left alerted him. Caulfield had just appeared and was ambling over to the binnacle with a cup of something hot and steaming in his hand. The first lieutenant was not officially on duty, but clearly intended seeing the dark hours out on the quarterdeck and Banks was silently grateful.

They were on the eastern edge of the outer harbour. To the

west, the sun was starting to dip below the headland of San Mandrier. The last of its beams were currently shining through the low, grey cloud that covered most of Toulon in a way that some probably found attractive. But Banks could see only potential fog and a good chance of rain. He was in sole command of the entire British force, with a substantial fleet of enemy warships anchored not seven miles off his larboard bow, and felt every need to be wary.

The ship's bell sounded; the first dogwatch had barely half an hour to run and, no matter how close the enemy lay, Banks knew the ship would soon start to settle for the night. Some, who were fortunate enough to be classed with the idlers, might even be hoping for uninterrupted sleep, while those standing a watch should get at least four hours in their hammocks. It was only the senior officers, he told himself bitterly. It was only him, Caulfield, and maybe a couple of the others who would see the dangerous night out, and still be expected to function normally the following day. And as he thought, the darkness closed further about him, while the first drops of what was bound to turn into a torrent began to fall.

A few minutes later King appeared, suitably dressed in oilskins and sou'wester, to take the next watch. Hands were summoned for the change and came up from the convivial fug of the 'tween decks to whine about the state of the weather, and there was the usual muttered comments and jokes as the new men took charge. Banks started to pace the quarterdeck, rubbing his hands together for warmth as he did, while wondering vaguely if he need send for David to bring his watchcoat. *Prometheus* was under reefed topsails alone and, on a broad reach against a mild wind, made little way. Ahead, the slightly darker mass of one of the frigates could be seen as she nosed ever nearer to the harbour entrance, and at any moment there would be a ranging shot from the battery on *Pointe du Rasca*s. His servant appeared, unsummoned, and silently helped him on with a heavy cloak. Then, just as he was buttoning up the horn toggles, a light was seen from forward.

But rather than the flash of gunfire that all had been expecting, this was no more than a dull blue glow. It emanated from the frigate ahead and was masked almost as soon as it appeared. Banks continued to watch though, and felt hypnotised as the flare was revealed twice more, before dying completely.

"Signal from *Seahorse*," Brown, the ginger haired midshipman, reported promptly, before sorting through the bundle of papers he had been clutching. It was one of the disadvantages of night communications: messages were liable to be more easily intercepted by the enemy. In theory, nothing could be learned without access to that day's cypher but, on such a duty as this and with the same content being repeated several times during an evening, it would not take a genius to work out what was said. And it was equally clear that Brown, the detailed signals officer for the next two hours, had yet to learn that night's schedule, so all on the quarterdeck were forced to remain in ignorance while he fumbled with his codes.

"Enemy is making ready for sea," he finally announced in a hesitant voice.

"You are quite certain, Mr Brown?" King questioned.

"Y-yes, sir," the boy replied, adding, "it is definitely for today," before peering uncertainly at the papers once more.

"Take her three points to starboard," Banks ordered, and the ship slowed slightly as the wind began to be taken before her beam. Making ready for sea could mean anything from crossing yards to actually setting sail, but it was their duty to ascertain which, and that would probably entail taking more than a few risks.

"Ask Mr Franklin if he would be so good as to join us," Caulfield this time, and a messenger shot from under the shelter of the poop, and made straight for the aft companionway.

"Deck there, *Seahorse* is turning back for us," the masthead reported, although there was still just about light enough to see as much from the deck.

The acting lieutenant then appeared, along with Brehaut.

"Three blue lights shown in succession, Mr Franklin,"

Caulfield snapped, in lieu of a greeting. "What do you make of that?"

The officer paused for no more than a second. "By today's code, the enemy would appear to be making ready for sea," he said, with reassuring certainty. "Though not setting sail; that would be four lights. Did it come from one of the frigates, sir?"

"It did," Banks replied. "And I think we might prepare ourselves for a busy evening."

* * *

Poppy also intended to be active. As soon as her secret was out, at least as far as her employers were concerned, she had known her time aboard *Prometheus* would be limited, and the excellent money she was making must end. And since announcing her condition, Mrs Manning was actually giving her more freedom. She might pretend to be hard, but Poppy was now allowed to come and go pretty much as she pleased. It was as if Mrs Manning no longer cared, which mildly worried her although she consoled herself with the thought that the old girl had known exactly what she was taking on when offering her the position.

Working exclusively as a servant had not been not so bad, but Poppy liked earning money more. She had also strayed in the past, quite early into her employment in fact, and was taken back then. Besides, Mrs Manning claimed to be an experienced midwife, so properly appreciated the need for expectant mothers to be given special consideration. In fact Poppy was encouraged to lie down whenever possible.

But she wasn't planning any rest that night, only a further chance to add to her funds, for Poppy was smart enough not to allow any opportunity pass her by. In a ship filled with comfort starved men, there was trade wherever she looked. Such activity would hardly go unnoticed though, and Poppy restricted her patrons to a select few that she had deemed trustworthy. But of late it had occurred to her a couple more might not go amiss. On some nights she was even without custom, and she wanted to make as much hay as possible while the sun still shone. Hence, there was a new fancy man booked for that evening, although this one came without recommendation and from an unexpected quarter.

To date her trade had been plied almost exclusively amidst the foremast Jacks and marines of the lower deck, with only a single petty officer for variation. The venues varied, however; she had been smuggled into empty cabins and storerooms, dark areas of the orlop and once, with a gunner's mate, even the light room of the grand magazine. But until that night she had never been approached by any member of the wardroom staff, or invited to meet in the stewards' room. And this man was particularly insistent she should turn up, even to the extent of passing on one half of a pound note to see that she did.

* * *

"You don't seem so chipper, old cock," Cranston told him with his customary bluntness. "Maybe another trip to the sawbones is in order?"

Flint looked away, his eyes naturally falling on the small chunk of biscuit he had been aimlessly chewing on. As a matter of fact, this was as good as he had felt all day, and soon they would be clambering into their hammocks, which was probably the best time of all.

He would not sleep of course – the nights when four hours could be spent in an agreeable coma had long since passed. But the lack of movement a prime tight hammock encouraged was preferable, even if he would later have to spend an age straightening up and easing his limbs back for work.

"He's right," Bleeden confirmed, and in a voice that was unusually serious. "You been looking crook a while now, and they're not putting you on no more boat duties, 'appen a spell in sickers is in order?"

"Nothing more than a chill," Flint replied before biting into his hard tack with all the appearance of enthusiasm. He ground the hard biscuit between his teeth, doing his best to appear nonchalant and at ease. But the eyes of his mess mates were alert. Each man at the table knew him better than any in the ship – any in his life when it came to it, and Flint sensed that none were being fooled.

* * *

"A Bible?" Poppy shrieked in disgust. "You want to read to me from a bleedin' Bible?"

"I want to introduce you to the word of the Lord," Kennedy corrected her in a far softer tone.

"Well I've heard of some rum fancies in the past," Poppy reflected. "An' I'm not sayin' I ain't prepared to put in a bit of effort to please my gentlemen..."

"It's not for my pleasure, but your salvation," The senior steward told her firmly. "You and I both know why you came here tonight, and that it can only condemn your soul to eternal damnation."

"Can't say I hold with such things, miself," she snorted. "But if I did, I'd say there were already enough misery aboard this ship to need be afeared of any more."

The man looked at her with pity in his eyes. "I am truly sorry to hear you say so," he said, "and sincerely believe I may help. Perhaps if we started by reading a little from Mark? His gospel is an excellent introduction to those coming to faith. Then we might move on to Matthew, who is more for the new believer?"

"I ain't stayin' round to listen to no God botherer," she declared. "You promised a quid for an hour of my time, and you'd better pay up..."

The steward sighed, then reached in his jacket.

"It's just not what I expected," Poppy explained, as she accepted the other half of the note. "Not what I'm accustomed to; that's all."

"You could become accustomed to the Lord's teaching," Kennedy tried again. "It would help; bring you away from your sin while granting eternal life. And I have paid for your time."

"No," she told him. "Not me, I'm beyond help. But you're

right, I suppose you haven't had your sixty minutes," she conceded, and the stewards' expression lifted slightly. "Do you want to see a bit o' leg afore I go?"

* * *

Banks' prediction had proved totally correct. Three hours later, when the first watch was properly underway, the position had changed considerably, and it was becoming clear that few aboard *Prometheus* would be getting any sleep at all that night.

"Enemy to larboard," the forecastle lookout reported solidly, but he was only confirming that the leading ship, first spotted by his masthead colleagues some while back, was now visible from the deck.

The first French vessel had set sail two hours before. Almost immediately the rest followed, and began edging out of the inner road during the second dogwatch, although scant progress was being made since. And they may not be intending to go further; the little jaunt might be nothing more than a chance for their admiral to give his men some heavy weather practice in the north of the outer harbour. But it was enough for Banks to have the ship cleared for action, and draw closer himself, but from the south. And the last few minutes were bringing developments that were increasing the heartbeats of all on the quarterdeck.

The rain was still falling but in varying intensity, with short periods when it was almost clear, and proper sightings became possible. And it was through a succession of these, when reports from the fore and main mastheads gave tantalising fragments of information, that he pieced together a picture of the enemy's movements.

It seemed the French ships were manoeuvring, although not in the usual manner of an exercise: some were actually remaining relatively stationary. Banks was still not convinced but as time went on, and further intelligence came through, it became increasingly obvious that the wider waters of the outer road were being used to collect and arrange the fleet into a specified sailing order. And, try as he might, Banks could only think of one reason for such tactics: they were intending to leave Toulon.

At first he almost dismissed the thought as being wishful thinking. Were the French really proposing to flee, the act of forming up so near to land seemed unnecessary. But he was equally aware that the Royal Navy was rarely subjected to the indignity of a blockade, and had become accustomed to being the dominant power at sea. Consequently, British ships would normally take up fleet order much later, often beyond sight of land. But with the French spending far more time in harbour, and when a hostile force may lurk behind any horizon, assembling what was effectively a line of battle within safe waters was a sensible precaution. He must be sure though; they might be planning little more than dampening their canvas, but Banks was under Nelson's instructions to keep a close watch and that was exactly what he proposed to do.

"I think we should take a closer look," he said. "Bring her in, if you please, Mr Brehaut."

The sailing master responded instantly and, as the ship crept further into enemy territory, Banks became conscious of the increase in tension amongst the officers around him.

Not that he was unaware of the risks, he told himself. *Prometheus* was sweeping in every bit as sweetly as if she were doing no more than approaching a friendly anchorage, but entering an enemy harbour, even one as wide and accommodating as Toulon, would always be a hazardous business. The wind may shift, and they could find themselves trapped. Or it might die completely leaving the ship, and all aboard her, to the less than tender mercies of gunboats and shore batteries. However, Banks was commanded by an admiral accustomed to taking chances, and one who expected as much from his fellow officers. In addition to a warning that the French had sailed, Nelson would want to know what, if anything, had been left behind while, should a significant number remain, a frigate must be detailed to keep watch.

It was, he decided, an instance where intelligence was worth more than the vessel gaining it; if *Prometheus* were lost by his actions, it would be a personal disaster for him, but on a wider scale, such a risk was more than outweighed by what could be learned by exposing her to danger. And additional, if doubtful, reassurance lay elsewhere: were the French battleships undecided as to their course, a juicy British man-of-war lying temptingly within their reach might just be enough to entice them out further.

* * *

An hour later, *Prometheus* lay to the east and almost half a mile within the outer road: well inside enemy territory. The weather had grown far worse, however; rain now fell in sheets and heavy cloud obscured much of the nearby shore, although it also gave a measure of security. The French shore batteries were apparently surprised, and incensed, to find a British ship with the gall to enter their waters. There had been no response for several tantalising minutes, then both fortresses opened up with a series of barrages from either side of the wide bay. In clear conditions *Prometheus* might have been severely damaged but Banks kept to the middle channel, making the range long for both emplacements. The drifting fog also added another complication, as did the British ship's refusal to fire in return, and thus make herself a more defined target. But eventually the third rate slipped through without major damage, and was finally able to find safety, even if it were qualified. *Prometheus* was now clear of the two major batteries' arc of fire, but remained trapped inside an enemy's lair. Banks guessed they had one, perhaps two hours before a suitable reaction was organised – maybe gun boats sent in to harry them, or a temporary field battery set up that could bear upon his command. When that happened, *Prometheus* must leave, and then pass the heavy guns at the harbour mouth once more. And he could be certain that, this time, they would be ready for them.

Seahorse had been recalled before *Prometheus* ventured in: the fifth rate being far too frail to face shore battery fire and there was little sense in risking two ships on the same mission. When last seen, the frigate was considerably over to the west and heading away. Night signals were basic at best, but Banks was confident Boyle, who had her command, would now be sheltering out of sight somewhere to the south west of Cape Sepet.

The fact that he could effectively forget about the frigates was welcomed. Banks had enjoyed the brief period of commanding a small squadron, but it was far easier to concentrate on his own ship exclusively. Now he felt able to focus his mind on a single problem and, despite the obvious danger, was actually enjoying himself.

The ideal scenario would be for all the French to leave harbour, and head south for the open sea. *Prometheus,* then *Seahorse*, would allow them past, before trailing behind and remaining in contact while *Narcissus,* the second frigate, was sent to take word to Nelson. Of course the enemy may decide otherwise; his own ship was currently lying less than three miles off their potential path; even at night, and in such dreadful weather, it would take no more than an hour's work for the French to account for her, as well as the other two British vessels waiting outside the harbour. Such a powerful fleet would only suffer slight damage by such an encounter, and then be free to go wherever they wished without fear of report, so far less risk of running in with the bulk of the British force.

But Banks thought not, and neither did he consider it likely the enemy were leaving their inner harbour merely for heavy weather drill. Their navy's lack of equipment was legendary: he doubted any admiral would willingly take his ships to sea on such a filthy night simply for that purpose. And he was equally certain his opposite number would decline even a minor action, were he intending to leave harbour for good. That same dank, dark rain that was making their lives so very horrible would be affecting the French every bit as much, and he was sure they had chosen the conditions in the hope of making their move as secret as possible.

Besides, for the enemy to sail was the one scenario Nelson wanted above anything else, as well as being a fundamental requirement if both forces were to be brought together in battle.

And the more Banks considered it, the more likely it seemed he was about to witness the entire French fleet actually leaving harbour. But the final, and deciding factor was far more subtle, and one that Banks hesitated to admit, even to himself. It might mean exposing his ship to further danger, but he could not help but think how splendid it would be if he were able to confirm the news to Nelson personally.

* * *

A little later they were almost a mile into the outer road of Toulon and Caulfield, for one, was feeling distinctly uncomfortable. The batteries on both headlands had set up a murderous fire when they entered but, due mainly to their passing through while visibility was bad, *Prometheus* took little damage. It would be foolish to expect the same luck when they made to leave, however, and this was not a prospect the first lieutenant relished. As for the French shipping, as far as anyone could tell, the main body was less than three miles off their larboard bow. The wind was well set for them, as it would be for *Prometheus* when the captain finally came to his senses and retreated. But allowing such a powerful enemy to chase them away was not Caulfield's idea of a peaceful night.

Then again he was the first lieutenant, so his main concern was for the ship. All her needs, be they material or otherwise, rested upon his shoulders, and he had scant knowledge or understanding of the orders his captain had received from Admiral Nelson. But still he was relatively sure they did not require him to risk *Prometheus* unnecessarily, and that was exactly what Sir Richard appeared to be doing.

The French were on the move; which was good news indeed, and Caulfield was astute enough to understand that an enemy in open waters was far easier to defeat than one that cowered in harbour. But why *Prometheus* must keep so close a watch over them remained a mystery. They might surely retire, then send word to the main force, while doing their utmost to remain in contact. This storm would not last forever; it was late October, and more could be expected but, with the remaining frigate's support, it should still be possible to keep track of such a body until the British fleet was brought up. And even if they were lost, the Med. was not so very large a place and had but a single exit. With the starting point set, *Prometheus* and one of the frigates would be able to begin the search while the others were sent for. And it would be strange if the enemy were not found and brought to battle, before being allowed to join up with more ships from the west coast of France.

But all this was evidently beyond his captain, who seemed set on counting every last enemy vessel as they made their bid for freedom. Presumably he wished to be sure all had sailed, but such knowledge was of no value if not passed on. And that was what they risked. If Banks was determined to remain where they were, the chances of the French taking them were high. And then *Prometheus* would become the best informed British warship at the bottom of Toulon harbour.

* * *

Brehaut's thoughts were not so reasoned, but generally ran on similar lines. Sir Richard Banks was mad: there was absolutely no other conclusion to be drawn. As sailing master, he was entrusted with the safety of the ship; for the calculations that saw her to every destination without harm and, on most occasions, actual control if manoeuvring amid navigational hazards or when under fire. The captain retained overall command, of course, and it was not unknown for the ship to be ordered into situations where Brehaut, seaman first and a fighter a long way second, would never have taken her. But usually there was a modicum of sense in the action. To take an enemy or avoid defeat: something worthwhile to balance the risk they were running. Venturing this deeply into a French port at night, during a storm, and while a positive fleet of warships were heading out to sea, was blatant folly, and the sailing master was very nearly in despair.

* * *

But, on the lower deck, feelings were very different. Of all aboard *Prometheus*, the men who served the thirty-two pounders were probably the least well informed, although what could be gleaned by an occasional glimpse through a gun port was actually enough to hearten the majority.

There were the French, their hated enemy, and a vast number of them: all ostensibly waiting to be taken. One or two of the brighter hands may have worried over the odds, but the bulk held ultimate confidence in their ship and her officers. They may understand little about the current situation, but were accustomed to victory. And, if their captain had placed them so, he must be confident either of support, or some other way of foiling the devils, which was all they needed to know.

Actually the buzz was quite specific; Nelson was bound to be in the vicinity; perhaps *Prometheus* had been ordered in with the express intention of flushing the enemy out, in the same manner a single ferret might be sent to purge a colony of rabbits. And there was about to be a battle: that also cheered them greatly, for most were inwardly certain it would be won.

Only a few had doubts; only a few thought further than a group of Frenchmen, apparently ripe for the picking, and those that did were working on scant information. They knew nothing of Agincourt Sound, or that most of the British ships were likely to be more than two hundred miles away, and taking on wood and water. But they were aware that neither sight nor sound of any other friendly vessel had been made for a good while. And some even suspected *Prometheus* to be the only ship of substance currently in the area.

Flint was one of the latter. He had lived long enough and through sufficient scrapes to recognise a tricky situation when he saw one. The wind was fair for them to leave, but to do so would mean tacking in front of the enemy, and it would be strange if such an action did not bring the wrath of what he could tell was a significant force about their necks. But strangely this did not dampen his spirits, in fact he had not felt so good for many months. There was a whole French fleet out there while his ship – and he guessed his ship alone – was veritably bearding them in their own harbour.

Since the attack in the coaster, his condition had worsened, and was starting to become well known – it being difficult to hide the more visible signs of illness from those living in such proximity. Little had been said, and only slight considerations made when doling out food or extra duties, but still he feared it generally accepted he would soon be leaving. He had retained his position as head of the mess, and enjoyed being with the men although, even without the surgeon's glum forecast, Flint was aware the time he had left aboard a warship was limited. That evening might have started like any other, but had since developed to the point where he could see what appeared to be one hell of a scrap in the offing. He remained very much of the opinion it would be better to go down fighting. And, for whatever reason the captain might have, there seemed every likelihood they were all about to do exactly that.

* * *

"Any sign of *Seahorse*?" Caulfield called to the masthead, and Banks was forced to suppress a start. In truth, he was mildly shocked that the question had even been asked, and such an obvious indication of his first lieutenant's concern was the first thing that made him reassess the situation. He looked across to where the other officers had gathered next to the binnacle. Was it significant that none were choosing to stand by him?

"Nuffin' beyond the cape, sir." the lookout reported dolefully. "An' that's all but covered in cloud at present," he continued.

But as *Prometheus* edged ever nearer, the dark mass of the French battle fleet was becoming clearer to those on the quarterdeck, and Banks found his breathing growing shallow as he realised their strength. They were also coming devilishly close and, for the first time that night, he wondered if some ghastly mistake had been made.

One of his intentions had been to tempt them out of harbour; to use his ship as a lure: something that might sway a hesitant commander into taking his fleet to sea. That purpose had been served some while ago and, if he were honest, it would only have been necessary to patrol about the very edges of the outer harbour to do so. Then Banks remembered blithely telling himself that *Prometheus* would be ignored: brushed aside by the French admiral who would have more interest in seeing his charges safely to sea. But now as he looked that possibility seemed highly unlikely; the leading ship could even be a three decker, and he seriously wondered if the enemy really would allow a prime English liner to be left by the wayside, as it were.

However, the French should still be ignorant of Nelson's current position. For them to delay long enough to wipe out even a single ship would be foolish if doing so brought the might of the British fleet down upon them. No, he must maintain his composure and, difficult though it may appear, stand firm while a truly massive body of enemy warships effectively passed in front of his nose.

The wind was mainly north by north-west, ideal for those intending to leave harbour, as it would be for him, should he decide to run. But *Prometheus* was currently close hauled on the larboard tack, and creeping inexorably forward under reefed topsails alone. The eastern headland was too near for them to wear, and still avoid the batteries at Cape Carqueivanne, while inching even the minimal amount they were to the west, would only bring them closer to the line of ships that were now making their way cautiously south. It could be done, Banks decided, and his instinct that the French were as much under orders not to engage as he was, remained strong, although the sight of a British warship so temptingly close, especially one with her bows exposed in the act of tacking, may well prove a temptation too hard to ignore.

"Never been so near to a Frenchie afore," one of the nearby carronade crew commented curtly. "Not without it endin' in tears."

"Silence, there!" Caulfield bellowed, although many aboard

the British liner would have sympathised with the sentiment. The leading French ship was closing steadily. Their column still lay a good distance to larboard, but soon Banks would have no choice whether to stay or not: his exit would be effectively blocked until the French were clear of the harbour.

But then it was necessary to remain where he was for a while longer, certainly if he wished to check exactly what had sailed. And there was now the possibility that, were he to turn and run or not, *Prometheus* might still be caught.

He leant back and raised his hands to his mouth as an improvised speaking trumpet. "Masthead, what do you make of the harbour?"

There was a pause, and all aboard seemed primed for the response. Then came the squeaky voice of a midshipman.

"Still covered by cloud, sir," the lad piped. "We'll have to go a deal further to be sure."

Banks gave no reply, and indeed had never felt the loneliness of command more acutely. He was proud of his ship, and thought her able to outrun any of a similar size in normal circumstances. But when facing such a force in their own waters, and as heavy frigates were likely to be involved, he was not so sure. In fact, at that point there was little he was certain of, and it slowly began to dawn on him that he may well have come to the wrong decision.

He had done so in the past, of course: many times during what was now a long career, although this ran far deeper than a poor choice of anchorage or calling for the wrong sail. And it was then that he fully understood the next half hour would likely take the ship, and possibly his life.

The rain had held off for some time; a few stars were even starting to appear and, in the improving light, he could make out the force he faced more clearly. A cold shiver of doubt ran down his spine; he had been convinced the enemy would either be leaving harbour, or remaining in the inner road, but what if there had been another option? What if it had never been their aim to set sail *en masse*, but really were intending an exercise in the spacious waters of the outer road? And if such a thing was on the French

Admiral's mind, would it not be logical to feint a departure, especially if such a move might fool the annoying British ship-of-the-line that seemed determined to dog their every movement?

If the main bulk of the British battle fleet had been there to support him, Banks supposed there would have been little wrong in his actions. Perhaps he had been part of a powerful force for too long, and not fully appreciated how precarious his position really was. He had wished to be certain none were left in harbour, and wanted even more to impress Nelson. But, whatever his reasons, it had been a fool's action to venture so far into enemy territory.

The bleak reality seemed plain enough now and, when viewed by others in retrospect, would always appear to have been so. In a moment of chilling foresight he could imagine his fellow officers reading of his defeat in the *Naval Chronicle*, and shaking their heads in sorrow at such folly. But they would never know the certainty that had led him to such a disastrous situation; no one would ever fully understand.

He felt the need to pace the deck but stopped himself from doing so, if only to retain some credibility in front of those about him. Inwardly he was becoming more certain of his mistake; it might have been made through arrogance, pride or plain stupidity but there was no excusing the end result. If the French chose to turn now, his ship would be neatly taken, with none of the enemy even needing to step beyond the safety of their own shore batteries. And the only person he could blame was himself.

Chapter Twelve

"Leading ship is turning to larboard," the lookout at the main reported, although all on deck saw her change of rig, and the glow of the signal from her poop was unmistakable.

"Prepare to tack," Banks responded. There was room to wear ship, but that would take him perilously close to land, and the batteries installed there. He was likely to be trapped between the shore emplacements and the oncoming French, so was far better to seize the initiative and make a move towards them. Then he remembered *Prometheus* was still under reefed topsails, and had to stop himself from stamping his foot on the deck in rage. What a fool he had been – why had he let his mind become so set on one objective? Did he not know the dangers of an enemy harbour? The manoeuvre would be that much slower – that much more hazardous; canvas could only be added when it was fully completed and, for probably the first time since a midshipman, Banks had to refrain from thrusting his hands into his pockets.

"Take her round to larboard, if you please, Mr Brehaut." He cleared his throat. "You have the conn."

Despite his anger, the last order had actually been spoken in a moderate tone, and was in no way unusual. For the sailing master to have charge of the ship, whether she be in action or not, was customary; no one would think any less of him for handing over control. But Banks knew the true reason behind the request, and his personal shame increased further.

"Deck there, I have the harbour!" the midshipman at the masthead squeaked suddenly, as Brehaut began to call out the orders that would shortly see *Prometheus* in irons. "No ships of any merit appear to be present," the lad continued. "There are the three in ordinary we have spotted before, and two that need repair; otherwise only those on the slips and the big Indiaman what we thinks to be crank."

There was some consolation in that, Banks supposed. At least he had obtained the all important information, although such intelligence only became of value when it was passed on. Besides, he was already sure the French were not intending to sail for good. Whoever was in command had simply taken them into the outer road for exercise, with perhaps the chance of dealing with one of those annoying British blockaders into the bargain. And he had played right into their hands.

The rain was stopping. Banks watched as Brehaut calmly turned the ship in the night air that was becoming clearer by the second. The first Frenchman slowly crept towards *Prometheus'* larboard bow as the British liner was heaved through the wind and, now that he had passed over command, Banks instantly became critical. Thinking over the problem again, he decided that more sail might have been added, allowing *Prometheus* to gather speed before attempting the manoeuvre. But then Brehaut probably knew better, he told himself broodingly. After all, it was his own orders that placed them so far in; shaking out reefs and adding sail would only have made their eventual escape completely impossible.

"There she goes!" an unknown voice piped up from forward, and Banks was in time to see the last of the flames from the first Frenchman's bow chasers. One shot hit them with a sound smack to their prow, but *Prometheus* was starting to turn now, she would soon be on the starboard tack, and able to bear away.

"Ready starboard battery!" Caulfield's voice rang out, and immediately the gun crews stood to. The ship's routine was running like clockwork, Banks noted, despite the efforts he had apparently made to wreck it. *Prometheus* was turning faster than he had a right to expect; the leading enemy liner was coming up, and they may as well launch a broadside as they went.

"Fire!"

The flash of gunfire cut into the night and its thunder echoed about them as the ponderous ship continued to turn. The weather had cleared, although it remained too dark to see any detail of their shots. But the enemy appeared to have been bracketed, and they could not ask for more.

"Shake out them reefs and be ready to set t'gallants," Brehaut again and he spoke with a solid authority that Banks secretly envied. The procedure was sufficiently advanced for men to be sent aloft, and he was certain all on the quarterdeck breathed a sigh of relief, as the ship settled on to her new course and began to pick up speed. Any damage caused to the leading Frenchman had not slowed her; she was less than a mile off their starboard quarter and coming up fast. *Prometheus*' bows dipped slightly as her canvas caught the growing wind, and there was a muttering from her stem that had been all too absent for some while. But still the French ship was forereaching on them, and at any moment they would come within her arc of fire.

"She has the measure of us, I fear," Caulfield murmured apologetically and as Banks went to reply there was a blaze of light, and the Frenchman's broadside was released. For several seconds the ship lay in silence while all awaited what was to come, and then the barrage descended.

It came like rain caught on a gust of wind; a sudden hammering that died away completely when the breeze apparently dropped. Heavy shocks running through her timbers told how *Prometheus*' hull was hit in several places, and a solid whack to the lower mizzen brought forth a cloud of splinters and dust that covered the quarterdeck like sugar sprinkled over a cake. Three men were knocked down beside an upper deck eighteen pounder with two shouting out in pain and shock, while the third lay suspiciously quiet, and the neat row of marines that had lined the starboard bulwark was left momentarily broken, until a few stiff words from an adjacent NCO made everything tidy once more.

"Starboard battery ready!" Corbett reported.

"Fire!" Caulfield roared above the confusion, and the order was reinforced by the shrill note of whistles, a sound that was almost instantly wiped away by a deep-throated bellow from the battleship's main armament.

The ship heeled with the recoil, but their luck was in and the wind felt to be increasing; soon they were moving with true purpose.

"Caught her soundly," Caulfield reported with satisfaction,

although Banks found he could not have cared less. Two broadsides against a body of such a force would not see them out of trouble. There were still the emplacements at Cape Carqueivanne to negotiate, and the second liner was steering to add her fire to that of the first, with the three behind clearly equally eager to contribute.

A carpenter's mate was inspecting the lower mizzen mast; the shot had actually sliced its side, taking a sizeable chunk out of the of spar but, as he stepped away and grudgingly nodded his head, it seemed most of the integral strength was retained. And it was at that point that Banks noticed the change that had come over himself.

"Set the t'gallants," he snapped, breaking the self imposed silence that had already lasted for far too long. Brehaut and Caulfield were looking at him oddly; with the end of the rain, the wind was still rising. It may well grow further, and *Prometheus* was making good progress. There was almost a chance she might save herself from the grasp of the following ships, whereas the loss of even one important piece of tophamper, as the captain would be risking, must surely make them a gift to the French. But Banks had been in action more times than any of them and, on most occasions, in command. He may have made an unpardonable mistake that evening, but the poise necessary to captain any vessel was quickly restoring itself, certainly to the extent that he once more wanted control. And the ingrained confidence, a self assurance that some might call arrogance and others misplaced, told him he remained the best man for the job.

The shouting of orders, screams from the wounded and the whistle of boatswain's calls competed with a rumble of carriage trucks, as the guns were heaved up to face the enemy once more. Servers on the upper deck were depleted by those needed to attend the sails, but still the work was done in good time, and *Prometheus* could send a third broadside hurtling towards the enemy, before any further shots were received.

And then the ship's added speed began to tell. Even before the extra canvas was given chance to fill, her bows were digging deeper, and *Prometheus* started to heel slightly as the ever growing wind powered her on.

"Take her two points to starboard," Banks ordered, and the ship responded almost immediately. With the increase in speed, the enemy were becoming less distinct, and the new heading would bring the wind more firmly onto the quarter.

There came further light from astern; the first ship had yawed and was firing again, and Banks noted her position now lay considerably behind their own. In the seconds while the spheres of hot iron were flying towards them, *Prometheus'* gun teams strained to haul their pieces back into action, while the afterguard and waisters set her yards to meet the change of course. And when the broadside arrived it fell mainly aft and barely reached their poop. Banks glanced across to Caulfield, whose eyes seemed unusually alight in the gloom of night.

"The extra sail caught them napping," the first lieutenant told him with the familiarity of many years' service. "And what a stroke of luck, finding a wind so."

"We have the batteries to clear yet," the captain reminded him grimly, although he too was feeling oddly elated by the swift turnabout of fortune. "And they will be in range at any moment."

"Ready larboard battery," Caulfield shouted. The nearest Frenchman was now considerably to the stern of their arc of fire; Banks might even order the ship further across, but then there were likely to be more guns mounted on Cape Sepet to the west, than the eastern headland.

As the breeze rose further, *Prometheus* cut deep into the heavy waters and her taut lines began to scream. The eastern battery was now hard on their larboard bow, although they would pass at long range and, with luck, may avoid damage altogether. The gun crews had moved to the opposite side of the deck and stood ready beside their unused pieces. Banks glanced back; the French were decidedly in their wake and it was no surprise that a British ship should outsail them so. *Prometheus* had been on active service for several months; any group of men took time to shake down and become accustomed to sailing as a crew: he was only glad not to be in the enemy's position of having to train while avoiding what might be immediate action.

And then there came the first ranging shots from the eastward emplacements. The slender moon was just starting to rise and in its light, faint splashes were seen off their larboard bow. Banks measured the distance to land; there was range in hand for most of the ship's guns to reach with a good chance of accuracy, so they could definitely expect attention from the monsters the enemy would be mounting. And serious damage may yet leave them in danger; *Prometheus* might lose a mast, or be severely holed; either would disable her sufficiently to provide easy pickings for the oncoming French.

"We might make for the west?" Caulfield muttered, conscious he was putting a suggestion to his captain. Banks rarely objected to his second in command offering advice although, when he followed his gaze, both saw the bright cannon fire that told them the gunners on that side were equally awake. And, as a shot skipped saucily across their bows shortly afterwards, it was clear they were to benefit from both battery's attention.

"No, we shall stay as we are," Banks told Caulfield gently. "It is hard to know which is the greater danger, but you may reply to either when you so wish."

The first lieutenant snapped out an order that was relayed to Corbett, and the lieutenants on the lower deck. The weather had cleared further leaving *Prometheus* in plain view, so little would be lost in returning the fire. They could not hope to hit well emplaced artillery at such a distance with any degree of accuracy, but a broadside from a line-of-battleship, even one a mile or so off, would be disconcerting at the very least.

And when the first full enemy barrage came, it did so from the direction of Cape Carqueivanne. The shots bracketed them, causing damage to tophamper, deck and upper hull, but *Prometheus* continued with no noticeable decrease in speed, and Banks was even hopeful they may be passing out of danger by the time the same battery was able to fire again.

There remained the guns to the west, however. Whether by

accident or design, the commander of that battery waited until the last shot landed from his eastern equivalent and, though marginally further off, that fire proved even more deadly. *Prometheus* received two low body blows that made members of the carpenter's team wince in almost physical pain, and another smashed into the launch, shredding it into kindling, and drenching those unlucky enough to be standing beneath, in the water the boat had been carrying.   But nothing landed that would slow the ship significantly and, with her sheets tight and canvas stiff, *Prometheus* tore on through the night, safety now firmly in her sights.

Another long range broadside came from the east but did less damage and may even have been despatched in defiance. And then it slowly began to dawn on them all that they truly were to escape from what had appeared certain doom.

Some of the gunners even felt cheated: to have been so close to a powerful enemy, and then expected to settle for no more than a few long range barrages might almost be classed as disappointing. But the majority accepted the evening had been made lively enough, and more than compensated for the last few weeks' relative monotony. And most officers were unashamedly relieved. Even King and Lewis, isolated on the lower gun deck, had been uncomfortable while sailing, alone and completely unsupported in enemy territory, while Caulfield secretly wondered if Sir Richard had not taken the ship over that fine line that divided spirit from foolhardiness.

The doubts were soon put to one side, however. Their captain had come through yet again and, yet again, *Prometheus* was safe, after dealing damage to the enemy. They may have to remain on blockade a further few weeks, but that small taste of excitement would sate even the wildest spirits amongst her crew, whereas the French, who were declining to follow, would probably remain for a spell in the outer road. Then, when the main fleet did finally return, it would be *Prometheus'* chance to re-victual, with the additional benefit that their current wounds would force them for yet another spell of refitting in Gibraltar.

But of them all, there was none that felt quite the mixture of emotions as Sir Richard Banks. His ship had escaped and, even if the enemy still to put to sea, remained able and in a position to follow them. And, possibly more importantly, he could now relay news of exactly what had been left behind, so a more accurate assessment of the opposition's strength and sailing ability was available. But of all aboard *Prometheus*, he was the most aware of how far the bounds of daring had been stretched and, as he grudgingly accepted, it was well beyond their normal limit. Those terrible minutes when he realised the fact would remain with him for some time, and it was a lesson he was determined never to forget.

Chapter Thirteen

Independent command, that soul sustaining breath of fresh air so often denied anything larger than a frigate, had blessed them yet again and no one aboard *Prometheus* was sorry. The ship was even heading back to Gibraltar, a place that was fast becoming their second home, where they would be safe and sheltered for at least the start of the winter months. And a stay in harbour usually meant shore leave, something that never came amiss at any time of the year, although every man was equally aware that, if a holiday really was in the offing, it had been thoroughly earned during a month of relentless tension.

The morning after the French fleet moved out of harbour, *Prometheus* returned to find them still in Toulon's outer road. That was the first day of an extended game of cat and mouse which was to last almost three weeks, and robbed Banks, as well as most of his officers, of a good deal of sleep.

In the captain's case the watch was particularly tiring. Thoughts of how easily he could have lost his ship hung about him like an unwelcome smell, and he became remote and fractious. What free time he allowed himself was spent alone and in his quarters while even the most favoured officers were not invited to dine. This was noted and occasionally commented upon, although the change mattered little to those who knew him well. Caulfield and King had served with Sir Richard for many years, and even Manning and Lewis, who were less affected, accepted their captain was inclined to be moody. And few in *Prometheus'* wardroom were especially bored, not with active French shipping to keep track of. The enemy may have been merely intending to exercise their harbour-bound fleet, but every signal, change of canvas, or alteration in sailing order, had to be reported and logged, while the three British ships sent to watch over them maintained a relentless vigil and an equally respectful distance. The latter was on account of the troublesome shore batteries as well as, perversely, to allow the French every opportunity to escape should they so wish.

For the battleship's senior officers especially, the latter would have been a dubious blessing. Nelson might hope for nothing less than the entire French fleet to be at sea, but that was from the security of a force very nearly as strong. If the enemy were to venture out with only *Prometheus* and a couple of lightweights on hand, it was an entirely different prospect. One, or eventually both, frigates could be sent to raise the rest of the Mediterranean Squadron, and at least Banks, Caulfield and King were no strangers to shadowing a superior enemy. But on previous occasions they had been in fifth or sixth rates; ships specifically designed for such work. *Prometheus* might be far more powerful, but she lacked speed and agility. If the French set a fast pace, as would seem likely, they would struggle to keep up, though might just as easily find themselves running aboard the hostile ships if weather, visibility, or the ingenuity of the opposing admiral took them by surprise. And then, though they would undoubtedly put up a fight, it would be against such odds that the outcome could only be bloody and final.

But despite sleepless nights and doubt-ridden days, the French ventured no further south than Cape Sepet and, when *Victory* and the reassuring bulk of the British force were once more spotted, were still sailing apparently aimlessly about their own private enclave of Toulon's outer road.

Banks had been called aboard the flagship of course, but there was no formal dinner or meeting with officers from other vessels. After many weeks of carrying out minor repairs, as well as taking on water and wood, those of the main force were far too keen to return to the serious business of bearding the French. And with their recalcitrant enemy having left the inner harbour while they were away, all were even more determined to draw them out further, and to battle.

Nelson had listened with quiet approval while Banks gave a brief verbal summary of his written report, and hardly showed any emotion when the delicate subject of *Prometheus* almost being caught inside the enemy's den was touched upon. And there had been no censure. More cautious commanders may have taken the opportunity to berate a junior man; explain at length the value of every vessel, and warn against running further risks, but Nelson needed no such strategies to bolster his image or stature. Instead he trusted the men beneath him to make their own decisions without guidance. The fact that *Prometheus* had been able to escape with only mild damage, while bringing intelligence and dealing a blow to a vastly superior enemy in return, had been justification in itself. And that Banks was willing to take such risks actually raised Sir Richard higher in the great man's estimation; cementing him more solidly amongst the other trusted captains, that helped make an apparently inferior force worthy to stand up to the best the French could offer.

But although much of her damage was light, there was still the matter of that weakened mizzen mast, which could not be addressed while blockading Toulon, and neither were the more sheltered waters off Sardinia any more accommodating. *Prometheus* would simply have to retire to the dockyard at Gibraltar, and was despatched with instructions to refit, water, and take on any other essential supplies as quickly as possible. With luck all would be accomplished within a month, then she might return for the remainder of the dark winter months; a time that Nelson seemed convinced his enemy would choose to finally fly the coop.

So it was that they found themselves once more steering southerly with the ship, though undoubtedly battered, still able to meet any single enemy likely to be encountered on the inland sea. And there was always the chance of something less taxing. *Prometheus* was a powerful beast, if inclined to be slow when compared to other vessels. But dawn gave them a daily advantage; the rising sun so often revealed a tasty morsel, one that might be snapped up before it was fully light. And although all aboard were already due to benefit from head and prize money, there was little guaranteed to raise the general morale of a crew better, than the possibility of more.

But that morning, the fourth since leaving the waters off

Toulon, turned out as disappointing as those preceding it and, with Gibraltar now becoming less of a vague destination, Caulfield was starting to think they might not be so lucky on that particular leg of the voyage. He stretched stiffly in the lee of the larboard bulwark and breathed in the moist early morning air. It carried just the hint of storm, but whether that was from the tempest they had endured during the night, or some fresh excitement to be borne on the current north easterly, he could not tell.

The bell rang seven times and King, who would be relieving Hunt at the change of watch, appeared shortly afterwards. There was a few minutes' conversation between the young men, then Caulfield was pleased to see the second lieutenant stroll across to join him.

They had served together in two previous vessels, and considered themselves shipmates; a status that transcends many friendships formed on land. But both were also professional sea officers, and King's recent disobeying of orders aboard the captured coaster had strained their close relationship. In Caulfield's eyes, King had not only endangered himself, but the entire operation. And though they might be friends, he remained the first lieutenant; responsible for the discipline and conduct of all, be they officers or men. He might wish it differently, but could not allow personal feelings to alter such a stance.

However, the intervening time had given him the chance to consider matters more carefully, and he now grudgingly accepted there may have been mitigating circumstances. Caulfield had never suffered a serious wound, and could not imagine how he might react to being crippled, or effectively banned from independent command. And King had been closely involved in planning part of the attack, while there was little doubt his experience in guiding the coaster past the hazards of the outer harbour had proved valuable, even pivotal, to the mission's eventual success. So it was that, after a period of apparent distance, Caulfield was now pleased to note the young man held no bad feelings, and appeared as happy to join in conversation as he was to receive him.

"We should make Gib. in three days," King said, the open

smile as ever on his face. "Though I might wish it otherwise."

"Not lured by the delight of shore, Tom?" Caulfield asked lightly. The younger man turned so that they were both standing looking forward to where the recently holystoned decks were waiting to be dried by an early sun.

"Oh, I never mind the odd night in town," King admitted. "Though, with the French so primed to move, would prefer to be asea."

The first lieutenant nodded. The Mediterranean in winter was a very different place; more of its brand of particularly vicious storms could be expected and, although there were certainly worse stations, he might also think of better. But King was right, *Prometheus* was being forced away just when matters at Toulon were becoming interesting. They would doubtless bully and plead, but must expect to spend at least four weeks in repair; add another for their return, and it could be to a very different situation. All were convinced the French were on the verge of quitting harbour and, with Nelson's penchant for a loose blockade, were likely to do so undetected. Then there would be a chase to rival the last little jaunt that had ended at Aboukir Bay, with *Prometheus* doubtless arriving late, after the added complication of needing to find their own fleet, as well as that of the French.

And if the enemy's departure was detected the outcome would be equally frustrating. It could only mean an immediate major action; maybe not so sizeable as what some were beginning to call the Battle of the Nile, but surely every bit as significant. Hardly a single British officer or seaman could consider any result other than another victory for Nelson, but that would be far harder to achieve with one of his best liners languishing in harbour.

"They may not choose to leave in winter," Caulfield said, partly in an effort to reassure himself. "Indeed, I should not be surprised if they were already back safe in their lair and battening down for Christmas."

King gave a wry grin. "Aye, 'tis possible," he allowed. "Though we will be lucky to know of it before we rejoin the main force. Until then there is little for us to do but wait and worry."

* * *

"Or you can volunteer for a merchant ship." Cranston stated with unusual authority.

"Can't see how that'll do much good," Bleeden replied disparagingly. "From what I hears, deserters can end up scragged if they're not so very careful."

They had been discussing the various ways of raising money and Bleeden, usually an expert in such matters, was finding himself outflanked by his messmates

"That's all you know," Cranston told him. "Maybe in a home port but, once you get on a foreign station, they got to keep hold of every Englishman going. Besides, who said anything about running?"

The former smuggler was now very much at a loss, and remained silent as the more worldly seaman continued.

"You tells the master you're a free man, an' ask for a month's wages in advance, so as to provide for your kit. If the old man's short of a crew, he'll more'n likely agree. Then, as soon as he hands it over, you heads back to the ship, quick as anything."

"And then?" Bleeden asked cautiously.

"Well, once you're safe on board you keeps your head down – and the money, of course."

"What if they follows?"

"Oh they probably will," Cranston confirmed. "And there's bound to be a right old blow up when the cove comes a lookin'. But the RN takes care of their own; no king's officer worth his salt is going to let a merchant man aboard, or lose a hand. And the master can't take legal action, as the debt would be under twenty pounds. You're home and dry!"

* * *

Robert Manning had asked to speak with him on a personal matter, which Banks considered bad news on several levels. Foremost, he never found the surgeon particularly easy company. As far as his medical competence was concerned, there were no complaints; Manning conducted himself well and, although coming from a relatively humble position, commanded respect from both officers and men. And Banks, who was after all a peer of the realm, did all he could to make the lesser feel comfortable, but somehow they failed to see eye to eye.

There had been no major animosity to cause this; a few years back Banks might have enjoyed a brief affair with the woman who was to become Manning's wife, but that was long before the two of them were married, and surely all forgotten. But still the surgeon persisted in being awkward and ill at ease when in his presence and, despite serving several commissions together, there had never been any sign of a friendship developing.

And something of a personal nature was always likely to be difficult. Naval routine was one thing; even ignoring the Articles of War, Banks owned guidelines a plenty, both official and otherwise, that advised a captain of his formal duties. These ranged from *Regulations and Instructions Relating to His Majesty's Service at Sea* to a pamphlet, purportedly written by a serving sea officer, that gave a candid guide to phrasing reports and despatches. All contained solid advice and covered everything from quelling an impending mutiny to obtaining extra income through a variety of nefarious channels. Personal matters were given the proverbial wide berth, however, yet these were usually far harder to define and, certainly to Banks' mind, solve.

In considering the matter that morning he had come to the conclusion that a formal interview, with him seated at his desk and the surgeon standing opposite, would probably not be the height of diplomacy. Instead he had asked David to place his favourite easy chair aft of the main cabin, with it facing the upholstered lockers that sat squarely under *Prometheus'* magnificent stern windows. The two could then relax in comfort while Manning, an awkward soul at the best of times, struggled through what he had to say.

Banks hoped it was nothing more than switching the sick berth from the orlop to the upper deck. Mention had been made of the prospect in the past, and it might be accomplished easily enough during their forthcoming stay in harbour. But when the appointed time came, and Kate Manning appeared alongside her husband, he knew the subject was liable to be different, and that this would not be an easy interview.

The couple appeared preoccupied, with Manning appearing even more uncomfortable than usual. And it was then, in what was for him a rare flash of insight, that Banks wondered if his previous relationship with Kate had anything to do with the surgeon's attitude.

* * *

"I believe we have a new gentleman joining us shortly," Kennedy informed him in a whisper, before that evening's Bible study was due to start. Franklin nodded in acknowledgement and sat back in his chair. The regular meetings were growing in popularity, although Franklin felt this was hardly to be surprised at. Living so close to the elements and death itself, the average seaman was inclined to indulge in either superstition or religion. Under some blue light captains, guidance in the latter was compulsory, and could even be divided into differing branches of the Christian faith, however Franklin and Kennedy led far more general groups which were decidedly ecumenical, as they represented the only form of true religious instruction available aboard *Prometheus*.

Still it was good to see the stewards' room filling up nicely, and a further member joining augured well for the future. As it was, the room held only those men who were off watch, and would be used again at eight bells for the remainder.

But when the last man had apparently arrived, and the meeting was about to come to order, there were no new faces. Then a tentative tap was heard at the door; the room fell to a hush, and Franklin looked with interest as one of his own charges, the chubby midshipman, Carley, entered.

"Mr Carley had attended his parish church since Christening," the senior steward explained, as he led the shy young man to the front of the group. "He has a strong faith but, as with the rest of us, misses conventional divine worship, and the fellowship of fellow believers."

Franklin had been leading meetings for several weeks now, but still the acceptance shown by lower deck men impressed him. Although considered a midshipman by most, and called so out of courtesy, Carley was actually a mere volunteer, someone who drew the same pay and listing on the ship's books as an ordinary hand. And, as a first voyager, he had only a sketchy knowledge of his duties, and knew hardly any lore of the sea. Yet one day he was likely to walk the quarterdeck as a lieutenant and possibly a captain or admiral. Even now, in his uneducated state, he had the right to command Willis there, a seasoned foretop man, or Cousins; a regular Jack and old enough to be his father.

But there was no sign of resentment or disapproval from any man present. This was just one more hungry soul; the lad had been sent to hear the word as well as strengthen their numbers and, however they might behave towards him whilst on duty, he was as welcome within their fellowship as any repentant sinner.

* * *

"Pregnant?" Banks cried, astonished. "How did that happen?"

Kate Manning had to hold back a response that would have been unwise considering the circumstances. There could hardly be a greater contrast between Sir Richard Banks and her own Robert, yet both had reacted identically to Poppy's news, and she wondered briefly why it was that men so often behaved in a like manner.

"We have a healthy, red-blooded crew, sir," her husband suggested hesitantly.

"We have indeed," the captain agreed, a little more softly. He had not been looking forward to this conversation, but never expected it to take such a dramatic and embarrassing course. Now that it had though, he was determined to end matters as soon as possible. As captain of the ship, he had every right to do so, and was accustomed to having his own way. "Well, she will have to be put ashore immediately," he said, with what was intended to be the air of finality.

But at least one of his guests was not to be deterred. "Indeed?" Kate questioned. "Would that be the usual punishment for such a crime?"

"Of course not," Banks snapped, his face now burning slightly. "But you must see she cannot stay aboard. *Prometheus* is on active service: we are at war."

For a moment the two glared at each other with all differences in rank and gender, as well as any past affection, forgotten. Then the reasoned voice of Robert Manning was heard from far away and effectively broke the spell.

"I think we may be jumping ahead of the problem rather," he said, apologetically. "This would not seem to be a simple case of chance intimacy," he caught his wife's eye and swiftly corrected himself. "Not that such things are always so casual, of course."

"What is your meaning?" Banks asked.

"It would appear the young girl was forced." Kate stated firmly. "And by a member of your crew: possibly more than one."

"And has she named the person or persons responsible?"

"Not as yet," Kate conceded. "I demand you hold an enquiry forthwith."

"You will demand nothing of me," Banks shot back. "Do I need to remind you of your position?" Embarrassment was quickly giving way to anger, although strangely the atmosphere in the great cabin now seemed a good deal easier as a consequence. "I alone am captain of this ship and will decide if there shall be an enquiry."

The natural authority in Banks' voice stunned Kate into silence, and he was able to continue uninterrupted.

"Anyone suspected of committing such a crime will be arrested forthwith," he said. "And must surely face court martial or some other trial. But, as the girl has not said who is responsible, I am unable to pursue the matter further."

"You must," Kate countered. "It is your duty."

"Madam, you shall not tell me my duty." Banks retorted. The very mention of the word caught him on a raw spot and raised the stakes still further. Had he been doing his duty in taking *Prometheus* too deeply into the enemy's harbour?

"Any investigation shall, by its very nature, involve the majority of my lower deck," he continued, "and will be disruptive in the extreme. If your servant does not wish to speak, that is her concern, but I do not intend to jeopardise the well-being of my people because of it."

"And what about justice?" the woman responded.

"Justice?" he gave a brief laugh. "Do you believe you will get justice because my master at arms and his corporals start asking questions? Are you expecting whoever was responsible to simply own up, and take the charge? Or will there be gossip, supposition, and possibly far worse?" Banks sighed; this was well beyond his usual domain. In truth there was no better reason he could think of why an enquiry should not be held, although every instinct in his body rebelled against the idea. And he was equally determined no mere medic's wife was going to give him orders. Then, fortunately, her husband intervened once more.

"Tell me, Kate," the surgeon asked gently. "If Poppy has proved reluctant to talk to you, exactly how many on board are aware of her predicament?"

She shook her head but said nothing.

"I had guessed as much," Manning replied. "That being the case, is it not simply better that she is put ashore? Provision can be made at the naval hospital if need be, and she will not be abandoned."

"I am not certain..." Kate began, but her voice faltered.

"If she changes her mind and wishes to name the father, it may be reported at a later date." Robert continued; he knew his wife and, more to the point, knew how close she was to breaking. "And if any element of force was involved, that can also be taken up, with the accused brought to trial."

There was a pause, and Banks found himself grateful to the surgeon for diffusing the situation. It had been a far harder meeting than he was expecting, and part of the difficulty stemmed from Mrs Manning's behaviour. She had changed dramatically from the woman he had taken a shine to all those years ago; her face was thinner, and the note of aggression that now regularly tainted her speech was not so apparent then. But as he looked at her in the harsh light of the stern windows, there remained a vestige of the girl he had once known who had stolen his heart. And he could also see she was upset; quite why the misadventures of some foolish wench had affected her so he had no idea, but suddenly felt reluctant to press the matter further.

"You must see," he said gently. "Whatever wrong has been committed, nothing will be served by stirring matters; the very reverse in fact. And how can I allow a pregnant woman to remain aboard a ship of war; especially one that may shortly see action?"

"Then I shall go ashore with her," Kate said stubbornly.

"We still need a surgeon's mate," Manning reminded her.

"Then you can enquire for one at the naval hospital," she replied. "Or promote a loblolly boy," adding, "it has been done before, I believe," with a significant look at her husband.

"Perhaps you will allow me to decide that?" Banks asked.

"I consider you already have." Kate's voice was firm again, and now also held a measure of authority. "Did you not say that you could not carry a pregnant woman into battle? If that be so, then I must certainly leave this ship as well."

* * *

"Why ever did you not say before?" the surgeon hissed at his wife as they were shown out of the captain's quarters and on to the half deck.

"That I am with child?" she replied in far more strident tones. "I did have a mind to do so, but was waiting to be certain."

Manning felt the blush rise to his cheeks, but continued, despite the looks of interest from two passing quartermaster's mates.

"But this is surely something that should be shared," he insisted. "And shared at the first instance."

"If so, I have clearly failed you," she snapped back, with an obvious lack of regret.

He went to say more, then decided to wait for the relative privacy of their own quarters. But even when they had reached the dispensary, and met the worried look of Poppy as she rose to meet them, Manning sensed there was hardly anything to add.

The girl was reassured by Kate, who sent her off to collect water for laundry and they were left to speak as confidentially as was possible aboard a crowded wooden ship. But once the opportunity arrived, both became as tongue-tied as a couple of teenagers.

"How long have you suspected?" Manning asked finally, and it was in the tones of a surgeon, not an expectant father.

"About three weeks," Kate replied. "And I would have spoken earlier, Robert – it is just with the failures we have experienced in the past, I didn't wish to tempt fate."

He nodded, knowing so well what she meant. In fact he understood her far better than she realised. He knew the brash, forthright façade hid a very different woman; the one he had married and still loved beyond reason. And she was going to be a mother; perhaps this time matters might go more smoothly, and they would be granted a family after all. But one thing was certain; she must also leave the ship at Gibraltar. And, all things considered, he found he was actually quite glad.

* * *

The following morning proved more fruitful for Caulfield. *Prometheus* had less than two hundred miles to cover before raising Gibraltar, and the time when they might chance upon a juicy merchantman was almost over. But as the first lieutenant gained the quarterdeck and nodded to Hunt, who once more had the morning watch, he felt a very real impression that more could be expected of dawn than just the usual heavy chill.

And so it proved: as the weak, wintry light began to gain on the nearby sea, both masthead lookouts called in unison, and did so in voices rich with triumph and anticipation.

"Looks to be a xebec," Jameson, at the main, added. "And almost in range, I'd say."

The last part was hardly any responsibility of a common seaman, but Caulfield was too busy to comment.

"Forward there! Clear away the chasers. Mr Clement; pipe all hands." It might simply be a merchant craft, and possibly even a neutral, but the first lieutenant felt his instincts were on top form that morning, and was inwardly certain a pirate lay within their grasp. "My compliments to the captain," he said, turning to Carley, the duty midshipman. "Advise him that there is a potential enemy in sight, and I should like to clear for action."

"She's a pirate all right," Hunt confirmed. The young man still officially had the watch and was staring through the deck glass.

"Why so sure?" Caulfield asked.

"I've met her before, sir," Hunt said, without taking his eye off the sighting. "She was the one that all but sank my prize." Then he finally lowered the glass and turned to the first lieutenant. "She's a patched main, and I'd know those lines anywhere – I've seen 'em enough times in my sleep."

"Very well, gentlemen," Banks' voice came from behind, and both officers realised the captain must have been standing outside his quarters for some time.

"Xebec frigate, sir," Caulfield said, pointing to the vessel that was off their larboard bow and in plain sight of the deck. "Mr Hunt believes her to be a pirate."

"And I think he may be right," the captain agreed. "Colours, if you please, Mr Caulfield and clear for action by all means."

Chapter Fourteen

But however positive Hunt's identification may have been, it soon became clear the xebec would not be an easy capture. Once the sun was properly up, the wind died for the British, leaving *Prometheus* becalmed and in tranquil waters while the chase, which appeared strangely blessed, continued to draw away. It was only after several heart wrenching minutes that her sails began to flap also, then sag, and finally the enemy's hull turned slightly as she lost way altogether.

That was not the end of matters, however. As the British ship lay wallowing in the mild swell, with every hand that was able staring out towards their apparently equally stricken enemy, the xebec sprang back to life.

A line of wooden oars were seen to extend from either side; soon they were ordered and a regular pattern of strokes began to cut into the placid sea, and the slender craft was driven slowly, but inexorably, away from them.

Banks cursed quietly to himself as he watched. The pirate was more than a mile off – long range for any of his cannon. A lucky shot might reach her, but would be all but spent when it did, and with only two serviceable sea boats, they would be unable to tow the bulk of a British third rate at anything like the pace necessary.

"Launch cutters, sir?" Caulfield asked hopefully.

"Very well," he agreed. They might at least bring *Prometheus'* head round and allow a single broadside. It would sound a note of defiance, even if no practical good were done.

The hands were of a different mind, however. Most had been indulging in a spot of surreptitious whistling to summon up a suitable wind, but this was a far more constructive alternative. To them, launching the boats was a necessary part of the procedure that would bring their much loved barky's broadside to bear, and never had the routine been carried out with more speed or efficiency. Within minutes, both cutters were in the water and secured by lines to the bowsprit cap, while their crews were already straining at the oars. And both decks of long guns had been run out, their wooden quoins discarded to allow each deadly iron barrel to find its maximum range, and the captains standing by to fire on the escaping heathen craft the instant it came into their arc.

As soon as it did, a nod from Banks started the process that ended with a shot firing from each of the cannon in turn. It was a measured ripple that ran along both decks, leaving all aboard the liner temporarily deafened, while few barrages were awaited with more expectation. In the seconds that followed there was a ringing silence in which no one dared breathe, while the iron balls sped out on their deadly mission above the open waters. But when they were finally rewarded, it was with a series of splashes falling short of the target, and there came a long, collective, sigh as well as mutterings that even the curses of petty officers and ship's corporals were unable to contain.

Their disappointment was short lived, however; it was soon obvious that damage had been done, even if exactly what could not be told from such a distance. The pirate ship started to turn slightly and, though still underway, her larboard side began to present towards the British. It was possible she was simply yawing, and intended to send an answering broadside, but such craft were built for speed and to deliver punishment, not take it. Only a fool would attempt to match the firepower of a two decker from the lightweight platform of a xebec frigate.

"Arm the cutters' crew," the captain snapped, while most were still wondering what had happened.

"I suppose it possible we struck her larboard oars," Caulfield remarked, almost conversationally, although he was rewarded with a less genial response.

"Arm the cutters, I say!" Banks repeated even more forcibly. "Pistols and cutlasses, and embark a replacement crew in each along with all the seamen they will take."

Caulfield turned and gave the appropriate order, his cheeks flushed slightly from the implied rebuke. There had been no intention to criticise, however. The faintest patch of cats paws could be seen from the north and the fore topsail was barely flapping, but it was enough to tell Banks that a wind might be expected at any moment and would favour them first. But before that could be exploited, they must take advantage of the current situation, and time was vitally important.

In a rowing competition, his stately two-decker would never compete with a xebec. The enemy vessel was far lighter and made for such use, with dedicated positions being built into her design. Even when towed by all her heavy boats, the British liner would be lucky to make half her speed, and considerably less than that with only two cutters. But something had slowed the enemy; it might have been luck, one of the heavy balls could have skimmed over the waves like a pebble thrown from the beach, and struck her in some vulnerable place. Or perhaps a commonplace shipboard accident had occurred; such things were not unknown. But even without any permanent damage, the cutters would have the edge and must catch her. They might not carry manpower enough for a successful boarding, but should certainly stay in touch. And if *Prometheus* were only able to close...

"Have carronades mounted in both bows," the captain added as his thoughts developed. The light, short range guns were intended to clear an enemy's beach or perhaps sink other small craft, and would take several minutes to stow and rig. But even a six pound ball must make an impact on the frail timbers of a xebec, and Banks sensed the effort would be well spent.

By the time both boats were finally despatched, each holding over thirty men – a combined total of less than a third of the enemy's expected complement, the breeze had risen further, and *Prometheus* was able to regain steerage way. The xebec had also recovered to some extent. The wind was yet to reach her but she was moving steadily and steering a straighter course. However it seemed the damage, be it caused to either her sweeps or their mountings, had not been addressed as she was far slower and under roughly half her previous number of oars.

"We'll have the stuns'ls on her, if you please," Banks murmured. The wind had backed only marginally, and still came pretty full on their stern. *Prometheus* was showing all her square sails, bar the maincourse and stunsails, additional canvas that could be run out on spars to either side of the major yards, may not add more than half a knot. But all available speed was needed, and if the sun grew any hotter, he would turn the hands to soaking the sails, so desperate was he to bring the ship into action. After almost losing his command in Toulon harbour, Banks had resolved to attend to his duty more closely, and was determined this particular enemy should not escape.

"I think we may be keeping apace," Caulfield chanced, and Banks was glad to note his earlier brusqueness had not been taken badly.

"While Franklin and Hunt will reach her in no time," he agreed, glancing forward to where the two small boats were emerging from the cover of *Prometheus'* bows. Each was powered by oars in addition to twin lateen sails and were already setting a solid pace as they sliced through the water.

"Indeed, sir," Caulfield agreed more cautiously. "And they may well slow the enemy further." Then he considered for a moment, before adding, "though I would not care to be them if either receive a broadside in return."

* * *

Franklin was of the same opinion. He had been detailed to the blue cutter and given a crack crew; first of dedicated boat men, then reinforcements who could not only row but were openly spoiling for a fight. In fact, of all the bodies currently crammed into the tiny hull, only his did not belong to a volunteer.

Not that he would have chosen to be anywhere else, he told himself firmly. He may be a committed Christian, but that did not mean fighting was totally repugnant to him; had that been the case there were opportunities a plenty for men of his experience in the merchant service or maybe Trinity House. And for all he had learned about turning the other cheek, Franklin's concept of a just fight remained strictly Old Testament, while his understanding of right and wrong was probably enhanced. Still, having to bear down on an enemy in clear daylight, especially one as dangerous as the xebec which now faced him, was not exactly an attractive prospect, and he would have preferred any number of other tasks.

Admittedly there was the bulk and power of *Prometheus* reassuringly close behind. The battleship was of no use while her guns lay out of range though and, should the wind change; either grow, die or shift significantly, it could only benefit the pirate's sleek and nimble hull. So Franklin was resigned to the fact that it was down to him, and Hunt in the second cutter, to alter the situation.

They would catch the pirate in no time; even now it would take no more than a yaw from the xebec to see them facing a broadside of heavy guns, although Franklin was not anticipating such a move. The enemy had already received one lucky hit, and was subsequently disabled to some extent; surely they would not wish to linger and encourage another? Besides, the threat he and Hunt posed was not obvious; what possible harm could two small boats do to such a magnificent and warlike creature? But when the cutters grew nearer it would be to demonstrate that even a small boat's cannon can be effective. And once that happened, they might certainly expect some response.

Not even a full broadside would be needed from the lines of cannon, weapons that were growing more distinct with every minute: a single shot should sink either boat quite efficiently.

"Quiet in the bows there!" he ordered absent mindedly. The men were chattering like a pack of monkeys, but Franklin knew there was little he could do or say to stop them for long. To be aboard a cutter in the middle of the Med. would have been stimulating enough; giving chase to a superior enemy was just too much of a change from their usual routine to be taken with any serenity.

The boat's freeboard was unusually low; with the extra weight of a bow mounted carronade, and so many additional hands, they were almost level with the slight swell. And the wind had both backed and was actually rising further; soon they might not even need to row as the tight canvas was already giving them a credible speed. Franklin glanced back to *Prometheus,* her sails were drooping in comparison, and the ship was now falling behind faster than they were gaining on the enemy.

"I think I can reach her now, Mr Franklin."

The comment had come from Flint, at the cannon, but Franklin ignored it. Although an experienced gunner and seaman, Flint was gaining the reputation as a firebrand and might be expected to want to open fire prematurely. The last thing Franklin intended was to emphasise the fact they were closing and could indeed be dangerous, especially as their bow mounted pop-gun would be inaccurate at anything other than point blank range. But still the time for action was growing close: the xebec was less than a cable off; they would soon make that distance; then Flint could fire his cannon as often as he wished. And it would only take one shot in the right place to do the business; nothing more than light damage, preferably to her rudder or a significant stay, and the pirate would be slowed to the extent that *Prometheus* would have no difficulty in snapping her up.

The men at the oars were starting to tire, but there was still some advantage in their rowing. To be sure of delivering an effective shot would mean getting incredibly close, and the last hundred yards or so would be the hardest. It would be difficult enough if their foe were a Frenchman, but so many stories abounded about the Barbary Pirates for Franklin to know he was not dealing with a conventional enemy. They had a dedication to warfare that was quite fanatical, and what he and Hunt proposed to do was bound to stir up a reaction.

Even wounded, and with a far superior force closing on them, the heathens would fight to the very last; of that he was gloomily certain. Once the cutters achieved their purpose, both might run like salted chickens, but at least one was likely to face the wrath of the injured ship's broadside. And boarding was out of the question. In his view the captain had been foolish in weighing them down with more men; they still carried far less than a xebec's complement and, with no chance of surprise, any attempt to physically get to grips with her could never be successful.

No, Franklin decided soberly, he was a king's officer and, if given the choice, would have agreed to command the blue cutter anyway. But his heart was not in this current venture and, for probably the first time in his life, he wondered if his future truly lay with the Royal Navy.

* * *

But Hunt, in the black cutter, had no mind for doubt and cared little about statistics. He was as keen to lay in to the pirates as any man aboard his craft. More in fact: for this was somehow personal.

The vessel before him had dealt his own, precious, first command such a deadly blow that he had been forced to watch her stripped of all fittings, then taken apart for what could be salvaged of her timbers. And that was ignoring the death of Rutherford, the master's mate and his personal sea daddy of several years standing, as well as seven of the brig's crew: men he had come to know well and even regard as his own.

So with the self same xebec lying almost within his grasp, and a chance to repay what had been taken from him so tantalisingly close, he felt able to ignore odds or the likelihood of defeat. Instead, Hunt was looking forward to a total and therapeutic victory. And if a small amount of effort were required; maybe a risk or two, that was not out of the question. The men about him were certainly ready for action; the majority would be positively disappointed if they were not let loose on the enemy and, as far as Hunt was concerned, he could think of nothing better.

* * *

Flint was no less enthusiastic. He had been taken off boat duties some time back when the outward signs of illness became hard to disguise. But his determination remained as well known as his condition, and an indulgent warrant officer had allowed him in the blue cutter amongst the auxiliary crew. Once aboard, Flint quickly established himself as captain of the boat's six pound carronade. The gun was laughably small when compared to the monsters he was used to handling, but had the advantage of being a close range piece so any damage he caused would be obvious to all. And of late Flint had been keen to cause as much damage as possible.

* * *

Half an hour later the situation had changed considerably although to Banks, standing on his quarterdeck, it remained every bit as frustrating. The wind was gaining still and now came more from the east. Not so much as to lie conveniently on their quarter, but *Prometheus* was maintaining the chase well enough. However this was only through a series of uneven legs that favoured the starboard, and drew maximum benefit from such conditions. Banks realised how the frequent changes of course were wearing out both waisters and afterguard, but cared little; steering so did at least allow the ship to keep pace, even if the pirates remained beyond the reach of the luckiest of shots from his guns.

Meanwhile, Hunt and Franklin were definitely within range, and could open fire at any time. They were fortunate in one matter; the xebec appeared to lack any form of stern chasers although Banks knew that, were they to deal an effective blow, it would still mean closing to a distance that would draw musket shot.

"The boat parties must not waste a moment," Caulfield muttered softly. "Give the barbarians the chance to see what they are about, and it will be the worse for all."

"I do not expect either to delay," Banks replied in a level tone.

"They might respond to a signal," Caulfield chanced. Franklin was the ship's signals officer: he could not be expected to carry a code book, though would know the more usual hoists. But Banks shook his head. Caulfield was right, with both sides in plain sight, there was no point in putting off their inevitable attack: Nelson would certainly have closed at the earliest opportunity. Nelson would also have trusted his officers, though, and he must do the same. Hunt and Franklin were in a far better position to judge the situation than anyone aboard *Prometheus,* and risked confusing matters by offering advice that would doubtless be interpreted as an order.

"I should rather not," he replied, indicating the two boats that were now drawing close to each other. "But they appeared to be speaking," The first lieutenant nodded, although neither officer could think of anything they might attempt which would not be obvious to the enemy.

Then, as they watched, the cutters turned away on opposite tacks, with Franklin's boat shooting forward as the more favourable angle to the wind gave him extra power. Within seconds both were edging dangerously near the pirate's arc of broadside fire, but positioning so would ultimately allow them to bear down on the xebec's stern from opposing directions.

"They would appear to be attempting a simultaneous attack," Caulfield said. "A bold move, and one that may well bring results."

Banks made no immediate response. It was almost exactly what he would have done, although there were few other options. But to close so was surely inviting trouble; the boats could be seriously damaged even by small calibre fire and, if either were successful, the xebec would undoubtedly turn upon her tormentors.

"A bold move indeed," he said at last and almost to himself. "God help them."

Chapter Fifteen

Franklin, who had the helm, thrust the tiller away to take them onto the larboard tack, while bellowing for the canvas to be drawn tight. They had passed the stage when rowing was of any benefit and were gaining visibly on the angular vessel before them under sail alone. Spray flew up to either side, and he could hear whispers and curses from the men as they fingered their weapons and prepared themselves for the coming fight. A line of heads were peering over the pirate's taffrail and, at a word from Carley in the bows, several loud snaps rang out as the boat's crew began to take pot shots with their pistols. Soon they were passing little more than forty yards off the enemy ship's stern, and this was the point when Franklin's mind should have been fixed on the current task. But somehow he could not set his thoughts – he was not afraid as such, just unable to concentrate, and the hand that held the tiller was undeniably shaking.

He drew a deep breath and tried to will his racing heart down to a more orderly rate. At any moment the xebec might turn, and they would be facing a line of heavy cannon. But Franklin knew as well as any man that, should the enemy do so, they would ultimately be taken. *Prometheus* was still stoically following; any delay would see the xebec come into the range of her guns, and he refused to believe any fighting captain could be so fanatical as to risk his command in such a way.

So the plan that Hunt had bellowed across the water made perfect sense. Both boats would close at the same time, but on opposing tacks; tactics that should at least divide the small arms fire from the xebec, while causing enough confusion for them both to draw swiftly away, whether or not their task was complete. And his boat would turn after Hunt's – that had been vital to establish, when a collision immediately under the enemy's stern would be disastrous for both.

But as Franklin gripped the all important tiller he knew

himself unworthy of such responsibility. Hunt had sounded so confident; carefree almost, as he rattled out the idea with an enthusiasm Franklin would never equal. There could be no doubt in anyone's mind that the younger man would carry out his duties to perfection but, of himself, he was not so certain.

"Ready to turn, sir?" It was Carley's voice from forward, and Franklin jumped slightly, before regret and shame hit him like a punch to the stomach. It was indeed time to turn – almost too late, in fact. Franklin had been so engrossed in his own feelings that the matter had completely slipped his mind until they were perilously close to the point when they might be hit by fire from the xebec's broadside guns. Savagely, he pulled the tiller back, trusting in the men about him to adjust the sails as the nimble craft jibed. The xebec's rudder could now be properly targeted: within a minute, maybe less, it would be in point blank range. Franklin had been sailing cutters since a youngster; he knew what he must do – keep his head and the boat on course: it really was that simple. But his hand continued to shake, and he could not ignore the worrying thought that at any moment he might begin to scream, and not be able to stop.

* * *

On the upper deck Corbett, the third lieutenant, was feeling far braver, and would have changed places with Franklin in an instant. Sir Richard Banks was blessed with a reputation for courage and guile; something that had encouraged him to join the ship in the first place, and his brief time aboard *Prometheus* could never have been called boring. But, even though he enjoyed a relatively senior position, Corbett had yet to be personally involved in any action. Admittedly he commanded the upper gun deck, with twenty-eight of the ship's secondary armament directly under his charge. They had already rained merry hell on both shore emplacements and enemy shipping, even if his part had amounted to nothing more than shouting out orders. Meanwhile all independent responsibility seemed to be falling on Hunt and Franklin, who were only acting lieutenants – glorified midshipmen really, with both having earned less sea time aboard *Prometheus* than himself.

Not that he begrudged them the chance, and neither did he consider he was being purposely left out. Corbett knew he had proved himself reliable, his guns having performed well on every occasion, and there were no major problems within the division he headed. But it would have been good to become properly involved in an action; to feel the responsibility and be able to think for himself, rather than simply obey orders.

This was not a specific fault of the ship, or her captain, but a regular one in the Royal Navy. Corbett had seen far too many middling lieutenants drift away to obscurity, merely because opportunities were given to the junior, and presumably more expendable, officers. It was unfortunate that his time at the lower posts was first spent aboard a receiving ship and then in the regulating service, whereas the recent peace had been endured with him kicking his heels on land and half pay. Corbett's current seniority meant he was almost guaranteed a position of third officer or above aboard any suitably sized ship, yet he lacked sufficient experience to be a premier, and everyone knew it was only the first lieutenants who were promoted at the conclusion of a successful action.

And Corbett thought he could be brave; indeed he was certain of it. There was nothing he would have liked more than to be a hero, to stand tall amid his fellow officers with a string of successes to his name, while the wealth, women and other benefits of fame that followed would be handled, he was sure, with commensurate ease. It was why he had joined the Navy after all, and rotten bad luck that, after over fifteen year's service, the chance was yet to come.

And that was all he was lacking – an opportunity to prove himself: show the world his true mettle: let them see what a dashing fellow Simon Corbett might be. Just one independent command, he did not ask for more: the rest would be up to him.

* * *

But at the bow-mounted carronade, Flint held no illusions of bravery. He had been through enough scrapes in the past to know himself, and his limitations, only too well. For other and more personal reasons, he was still looking forward to this particular brush with the enemy though and, of all who were sailing aboard the blue cutter that day, was probably the best prepared.

At first it had been hard to grant the tiny weapon under his charge any credibility; the whole thing could not have weighed more than the carriage for a thirty-two pounder and, when it was passed to him, the six pound hollow shot seemed far too light to carry any distance. But he had seen devastating results from such weapons in the past; when loaded with grape or cannister, they could cut a swathe through groups of men that totally belied the size of the stunted barrel. And for close range work, he reckoned he could cause a fair amount of mischief; certainly to the frail timbers of the craft that was starting to tower above him.

Beside him Rogers, an oaf of a man that Flint cared little for, had several more round shot ready and was currently making childish piles from the cartridges of powder. There was limited space in the cutter's bows, and Flint had already made it clear he would need no help in reloading the gun; far better to do such a thing himself, than trust an idiot who was very likely to blow his own hand off.

He glared back at Rogers, and noticed the chubby body of Mr Carley sitting next to him. The lad was hardly more than a child and, although he doubtlessly meant well, could be of little use in what was about to occur. It would have been far better if Flint had one of his own mess or gun crew to assist; men he could trust: men who might take over if he failed in any way and, for not the first time that morning, considered it a shame that Cranston was not there.

Cranston, a messmate and second captain of the two guns Flint had charge of aboard *Prometheus*, also volunteered for the cutters, but was allocated to the other boat. He had a good eye and was steady under fire, although there were other reasons why Flint missed his company. However much he may try to deny it, the times when he did not feel so strong were becoming more common, and Flint would rather have someone reliable at hand to back him up.

He had wheedled himself aboard the cutter because the prospect of action remained irresistible, but that morning's efforts were already starting to tell. He was finding the same with other, more mundane tasks, from stoning decks to scrubbing hammocks. Somehow his old energy was lacking and he just did not have any stamina. Even the regular mustering for divisions, when his kit had to be laundered and laid out for inspection, were becoming a trial. But a further opportunity to vent his anger on the enemy, albeit with a gun that children might use to frighten rabbits, had been far too tempting to ignore.

"You straight, Flint?" the midshipman asked from behind. As he had a right to, Flint supposed; Mr Franklin had actually sent the boy to supervise his work. He knew nothing about guns of any size however and, by unspoken agreement, the organisation of the carronade was being left to his more experienced hands.

"Well enough thank you, Mr Carley," Flint replied briskly, while privately wondering what had caused the child to ask such a question. But he *would* be all right, he told himself. The boat was growing ever closer to the pirate; soon they must start to take fire from the bunch of priggers lining her taffrail, and shortly he would be able to reply. Flint knew from experience just how good that feeling would be. And it was then that the realisation came to him that fighting was about the only pleasure he had left.

* * *

And all the while Franklin, at the stern of the cutter, was doing his best to control slightly different emotions. He had searched through the hundred or so Bible passages that usually lay ready in his mind and been surprised to find none could be remembered in their entirety. But that did not mean he felt deserted, for it seemed that even seeking help from the Almighty had brought a feeling of peace. Then he prayed, but not the usual "now I lay me down to sleep" rote which had been drummed into him when a lad; this was a deep, wordless prayer; one that had more to do with intense thought than actually speaking. And, when he was finished, Franklin sensed the entire situation, and possibly even his life, was totally altered.

The late autumnal sun was certainly nothing to speak of, yet it appeared incredibly bright, and the world itself far clearer. And mundane colours – the cutter's rubbing strake or the tanned face of the man seated at stroke, glowed with added brilliance. Flint had his back to him at the bows, his arm raised to signal the gun ready; even that image held an extra store of beauty that Franklin had previously been unaware of.

But he remained a sea officer and must not become lost in ethereal musings. They were still bearing down on a dangerous enemy, and would need to close further to be certain of a hit in the right place. To his right, Hunt's cutter was on the opposing tack, and steadily drew nearer to both the xebec and his own boat. And he could see flashes of small arms from the pirate's stern. They were under fire; he might die at any moment, yet somehow the prospect did not alarm him.

The tiller beneath his arm felt locked solid, and he wondered if it could be moved, should he have a mind to do so. But there was no need; the course was fine and an inner feeling told him he would be safe: the impression remained of complete peace, and Franklin knew himself totally protected.

He had also lost all track of time; there was a regular plopping sound that came and went, which he could hardly be bothered to identify. Then a series of shouts, and a puff of smoke blew forward from the bows, to be immediately followed by the sharp report of the cutter's gun.

Another noise, this one to starboard – Hunt's boat had also fired and Franklin was surprised to notice it close by, and on a sharply converging course. He continued to watch; Hunt should have begun to turn by now, but was making no move to do so, while the heavily laden craft appeared to be aiming straight for his own boat.

Still he watched with detached interest. It was a curious problem: he could take the initiative: turn first, then be heading away from danger, and it was odd how every sense in his body urged him to do so. But Franklin did not listen; it was as if he had suddenly acquired an older, wiser head and there was no longer any doubt in his mind. If Hunt turned also, as he had every right to, both cutters must collide for certain.

There was a pain in his right hand: he realised it came from gripping the tiller too tightly and eased his hold. Then he glanced almost nonchalantly towards the xebec which seemed no nearer, and noticed, again with mild curiosity, that a neat round hole had appeared low on her stern, just level with the waterline. It was a foot or so from the rudder which, now that he examined it more closely, seemed to be wrecked, as was the stern post that supported it. That must explain the cheering, he decided: the noise had erupted quite abruptly and the other men in his boat were probably responsible.

His gaze switched to the black cutter. Time must be playing tricks; Hunt seemed hardly any nearer, but was now in the process of tacking; his helm lay across and the sails were all ahoo. Franklin was alert enough to recognise that as a good sign, although sensed no relief: no emotion at all, in fact – it was as if all facility for feeling had been removed from his body. He took a gasp of fresh, clean air and felt it cold in his lungs. The sensation brought him closer to normal life but the peace remained within him. Gradually he accepted his boat was still gaining on the xebec, but had cleared Hunt's cutter, and might turn also at any time.

He heaved the rudder back – it moved easily, and the craft responded, turning swiftly in her own length and apparently guided back onto the opposite tack as if it knew the way well. The sheets were pulled tight without any order from him, and then they were close hauled and heading towards blessed safety.

And it was only then that Franklin noticed the small fountains that were erupting in the water about him. The enemy must still be firing, and probably had been for some while. Looking forward, at least one of his men had been hit, and was currently being attended to by young Carley. He continued to take regular deep breaths: each one brought him nearer to reality until the memories of the last few seconds could have been a world away. Then the fountains stopped; the cutter must be out of musket range and that was another interesting fact, although somehow irrelevant.

Glancing back, he confirmed it to be the case, and that the absence of a rudder was already starting to affect the xebec. Without its pressure from aft, the hull was turning slightly; the enemy might attempt to take the wind more fully on their stern, but would inevitably be slowed; indeed they seemed to be drawing power almost entirely from their remaining oars. It would be hard to rig a replacement rudder whilst underway and, with *Prometheus* still squarely astern, the two boats were free to pull clear and leave the rest to the barky.

Franklin supposed this was the time to start feeling relieved; they were out of danger after all and, apart from a wounded seaman, had not suffered serious damage. But somehow the expected euphoria that so often followed an action was missing. He still felt incredibly at peace, and knew he had experienced something which would stay with him for ever, but equally sensed all was not yet over. It was as if there was more to be done, and he would be needed to do it

* * *

Hunt was in total agreement, although for different reasons. The mad dash for the stern of the xebec had been stimulating enough; coming in with Franklin's boat to larboard effectively divided the fire from the enemy's stern, and he secretly hoped their cannon was responsible for the decisive damage to the pirate's rudder. If that shot had not told, he would probably have remained in position and under fire while the weapon was reloaded, and checking the work caused him to be late in pulling away. But Franklin had provided the perfect support. If he were honest, Hunt originally nurtured doubts about the older officer – any man who spent so long a midshipman was bound to attract uncertainty, but his concerns had been misplaced: Franklin was turning out as sound a colleague under fire as he could have wished for.

Which was partly why he decided to turn back and enter the fray yet again. The xebec was damaged for sure, and it was probably only a question of time before *Prometheus* came in to settle matters finally. But the memory of that devastating broadside raining down upon his first command still haunted him. The action had robbed Hunt of a good friend as well as taking several other valuable lives, before signalling the start of a nightmare journey back to Gibraltar that remained with him still. To have fired so was quite unnecessary; with an American frigate on the horizon, the pirates should have been putting all their energy into escape. Pausing, even for a moment, for such wanton destruction was a sign of a spiteful, evil mind, and Hunt was determined whoever had been responsible was taught a lesson.

"Take her about, we're going back," he said firmly, and Briars, the midshipman at the helm, looked up in doubt. "I'll not be happy until the old girl is properly in range," Hunt explained, glancing back at the battleship. "We will close again and see if a few more shots might not settle their hash before she is."

His announcement was greeted in differing ways by the cutter's crew; a few seemed reluctant to return, but these were soon shouted down by the consensus, who wanted nothing more than another crack at the heathens. Hunt set his jaw and ignored them all as the cutter tacked round to starboard. With luck, Franklin would follow; if he turned also, the pair might make their second attack from either side of the enemy as before. Both would keep well away from the xebec's broadside guns, of course, but should cause further damage to the vulnerable stern.

Their breeze was if anything strengthening, and it seemed like no time before Hunt was able to order the cutter on to the opposite tack, and they were heading in once more. Franklin, well over to starboard, had indeed followed and was also going in for the kill. His boat was slightly behind, but the two should still divide the enemy's fire when it mattered most.

"I think I can reach her now, sir," Cranston shouted from the bows. He was manning the carronade, and had already proved himself more than capable. Hunt could see no reason to delay; there would be time enough to reload, before they came into close range, so he gave a nod, and the small boat immediately shook to the recoil of her cannon.

A small fountain slightly to starboard of the enemy showed how the shot had gone wild, but Cranston, and the youngster who assisted him, threw themselves into reloading the piece without a pause. Franklin's boat fired just as Cranston's hand was raised once more. This time there was no sign of the shot, and Hunt was about to put it down as a miss, when a voice came from forward.

"Another hit!" It was Briars; the youngster was standing and peering forward with one hand on the foremast. Hunt ordered him down, but was pleased enough at the news. And all the time the pirate's stern, an especially vulnerable area where even a six pound ball would do damage, was drawing closer.

"If we keep to this distance we can continue to fire on her." Briars again, and Hunt felt instantly guilty that the thought had not occurred to him. With the rudder taken and the ship already holed, they might certainly hold back; taking the occasional pot shot whilst staying out of range of the enemy's muskets and broadside guns. With *Prometheus* creeping steadily nearer: there was really no need to draw in close. Even if he and Franklin caused the xebec no further damage, the pirate would be under the battleship's guns within the hour – possibly less.

Cranston's hand was up once more, but only for a second; the gun discharged almost immediately and its shot, though out of Hunt's line of sight, must have been on target as a rumble of approval rose up from the others in the boat.

He decided that was good, and they had probably done enough. It might not have been the devastation he so wanted to bring down upon the pirates, but the cutter's actions had undoubtedly brought her to book. There was no time to think further, however; the men about him were shouting again, although this time their tone was far less positive. He glanced up, and saw with a feeling of cold dread that matters were not quite as settled as he had thought.

The xebec was manoeuvring on her oars: soon her mighty broadside would be aiming directly at one of the annoying little boats that had caused her downfall. Both could run, indeed they would have to, but in doing so either he, or Franklin, must expect to suffer a broadside from the pirate's heavy guns. But as he watched he also realised the enemy was actually turning to starboard, so at least his cutter was not to be the target.

* * *

"Enemy's turning," Caulfield reported, dispassionately.

Prometheus, still bearing down on the chase, was making considerable progress since the cutters had holed and disabled her. Indeed, she was probably in range: Banks had wanted to open fire some minutes ago, and was quietly cursing both small boats and the enthusiasm of their commanders for effectively blocking his broadside. But they had undoubtedly caused additional damage: the xebec was slowing further and her capture now seemed academic. Even an impious heathen must accept that further resistance would be of no benefit.

But Banks had not counted on what he could only define as vengeful tactics. One single, solid broadside from the xebec could not fail to sink a twenty-five foot cutter, as well as accounting for a good number of her crew. They may even have time to take both, which would be a wanton waste of life, as well as making a sizeable dent in *Prometheus'* complement.

"With luck we may reach her," Banks replied. "If only those damned cutters would stand off. Ready larboard battery!"

His ship was on the starboard tack, and the enemy was indeed almost certain to be in range. Between the two, Franklin's boat was sailing for all she was worth, both to clear the area, and gain refuge from the battleship's presence. In three, maybe four minutes, they would be beyond even the wildest shot from the British ship although, while *Prometheus* was at the ultimate reach of her long guns, their safety could not be guaranteed.

He looked down to Lieutenant Corbett, who had command of the upper deck, and noted he and his midshipmen were checking to see every gun was at maximum elevation. But they might take all the precautions they wished, that morning had already demonstrated the inconsistencies of naval cannon.

"The pirate may fire on Franklin's boat at any moment," the first lieutenant hinted softly. And Caulfield was right, Banks decided; a stray shot from *Prometheus* may well hit the British craft, but the xebec would be actively targeting her entire broadside on her, and was far nearer to Franklin and his men.

"Very well: open fire," the captain ordered.

There was a number of shouts, followed by the shrill scream of a whistle, then the liner began to judder to the first of a series of individual explosions that cut through the soft morning air. Thick smoke rolled forward on the wind, obscuring both pirate and cutter to all on the quarterdeck. Caulfield ran to the leeward rail and looked out, his hand waving in front of his face in a ludicrous attempt to clear the ever rising cloud, but for several seconds all aboard the British ship remained in ignorance. Then there came a cheer from the main masthead where the lookout was free of fog.

"Straddled the bastard!" he said with gloating satisfaction. "Taken down 'er main, an' caught the mizzen a proper nasty."

Those at the upper gun deck cannon began to shriek and slap each other in celebration, while the carronade crews on the quarterdeck remained cold-eyed and aloof; the shorter barrels on their pieces could not match long guns for range, and had not been used in the barrage. Caulfield looked back at Banks and grinned, but there was more to add.

"Wait, the enemy's still firing," the lookout reported to a ship that had suddenly grown silent. "Yep, a whole bloody broadside, an' aimed at our cutter – you got to hand it to the buggers: they're a game bunch..."

* * *

But there was no room for praise on Flint's mind. They had already endured being beneath one of *Prometheus'* broadsides, feeling the wind of the barrage as it passed overhead, and even mildly dampened by a stray round that fell dangerously close to their starboard beam. It was the second time Flint had been under fire from his own ship, and he would be content for it to be the last. The fact that most of her fire had gone on to strike the pirate's xebec was consolation, he supposed, but that morning's exertions were definitely catching up on him. He was incredibly tired, and the constant blubbing of Peterson, the Swede who had been wounded earlier, was beginning to annoy in a way he would never have predicted.

The cutter was on a wind and sailing fast however and, if they kept their speed, all should be back aboard *Prometheus* for midday grog. The barky was cleared for action, and it would take a while to restore the bulkheads and put all to rights, but his condition was coming to be accepted, and he could probably avoid much of the heavy work. With luck he might even swing a rest in a quiet spot, and the captain had been known to order extra spirits to celebrate success.

His mind was pondering on such inconsequential thoughts when the shout came from young Mr Carley. All hands in the cutter instinctively turned towards the enemy, and most saw the last of a ragged broadside that had apparently been pitched in their direction.

"Now we's for it."

Rogers' comment was the only sound heard during the time it took for the shots to reach them, and seemed to sum up their position perfectly. With a mighty splash, the first landed about fifteen feet from the cutter's prow and in no time several more had fallen in the general area. For upwards of five seconds the boat appeared blessed, with fountains erupting to every side as it dipped and bobbed in apparent safety. Then one hit them: squarely and amidships, and all thoughts of noontime grog were forgotten as the next nightmare began.

Chapter Sixteen

The shot struck Carley a glancing blow, wounding him severely, before going on to settle Peterson's moaning for good, and finally crashing through the larboard side of the hull. The small but heavily laden craft instantly began to crumble; water rushed in and the entire boat was soon swamped. Then, almost as quickly, the cutter had disappeared, heading bow first for the bottom of the Mediterranean.

And there was barely any wreckage; little to hold on to at all apart from oars, a half filled water cask and far too many struggling bodies. Some grabbed at each other for support, only to find that two non swimmers were no more buoyant than one. Others made for the oars, the lengths of pine might have kept one man afloat adequately enough, but with up to four claiming each, and all fighting for their place while trying to knock the rest away, they proved less than adequate. Men began to shout, then scream; a few who were able to swim instinctively headed away from their companions while the rest battled against the foaming water. Some were kept afloat through a mixture of energy and desperation: others gave up the fight and slipped beneath the waves in a brief flurry of froth and fear.

Franklin was one of the swimmers. He had learned during the long, hot summers of his childhood when the local mill pond was a focal point for all the village children. That time had ended more than twenty years ago, but still he was able to keep his head above the thrashing waves while doing his best to rally those he commanded.

He called for order, berated the greedy who were unwilling to share their supports and encouraged those who could keep afloat to assist. But he had little joy with the non swimmers; what had been practical and level headed beings seconds before, now seemed far too intent on flailing about like lunatics. Those more comfortable in the water found reasoned speech and sensible instructions were ignored in their companions' apparently pathological desire to drown, and anyone foolish enough to offer physical assistance did so at the risk of sharing their fate. Franklin seized one man, Rogers, the ox who had been with Flint at the carronade, only to be rewarded by the swipe of a ham-like arm across his face, and he could hear the curses and cries from others who were returning to save their fellows, and being dealt with in a similar manner.

But in time order became established; those determined to drown having met their fate while the less excitable had either found a swimmer to cling to or discovered that, if filled with air and treated sensibly, a human body will float and life could continue. Franklin had shed his tunic and was beginning to make his way round the small number of living bodies that represented the remains of his cutter's crew, when he came across Carley, whose head was being held clear by Flint.

"*Prometheus* will reach us shortly," he told the lad confidently, although they were low in the water and nothing could be seen of any vessel. "That or Mr Hunt's cutter." But Carley's eyes were vacant while the sea around him appeared worryingly dark and Franklin did not know if his words even registered.

"The boy's wounded," Flint told him briefly. "The shot that took us caught 'is arm."

Franklin considered the two. Carley's skin was certainly a deathly pale, although Flint was not looking exactly healthy either. But the lad seemed safe enough in the seaman's grip and he felt he might move on.

The sun was warm, despite the time of year, while the sea itself felt to be roughly the temperature of fresh milk. But Franklin knew both might be an illusion; one of many that came with shock. He was also aware that, if they were to keep the remaining non swimmers afloat, it would be better to bring the survivors together.

"Close on me!" he shouted, then repeated the order in a slightly louder voice. At first no one moved, then he noticed Flint, still clutching at his young charge, begin to paddle backwards in his direction. Soon there were five, all desperately holding on to each other and the three oars Franklin had assembled. Flint began shouting for more to follow until all the survivors were grouped about six of the cutter's oars.

"I sees the barky!" someone shouted, although Franklin was not sure who, or where the supposed help might be. But their low vantage point meant *Prometheus* could creep up on them and shortly the battleship did come into general view, her masts towering high above and a line of cheering bodies gathered about her forecastle. And it was only a few minutes later that those wonderfully familiar faces were close by. Men who were strong, dry and gloriously real; who greeted them coarsely, but extended boat hooks and hands from the liner's fore chains, and brought a welcome feeling of solidity to a world that had become all too ephemeral.

* * *

"Steady Mr Franklin," the quartermaster warned as he scrambled over *Prometheus'* top rail. "We got plenty more to fish out yet, and them heathens ain't going nowhere."

Franklin supposed Maxwell was right. His trousers and shirt were sodden and a shoe was missing but, now that he stood on the forecastle, he felt a different man from the one who had been foundering in the water barely seconds before. The xebec was in sight off the larboard bow, although her rig was dramatically altered, and apparently useless. She had oars set, but was doing little to manoeuvre, while Hunt, in the black cutter, was keeping his distance off her stern. From the amount of smoke that was being carried away by the wind, the boat must have just despatched a shot in her direction, and there were small pin-pricks of light that showed where the pirates were replying with spasmodic musket fire.

"Did you lose many men?" Caulfield's voice brought him back to reality; Franklin turned to see the first lieutenant standing beside him.

"A good few, sir," he replied. "I could not be certain."

"No, of course not," came the unexpected reply, and Franklin thought he could detect a trace of sympathy in a man he had always considered incapable of such emotion.

"Young Carley's wounded," he added.

"He has already been sent down to the surgeon," Caulfield confirmed. "As you should also, along with every man from the cutter."

Franklin found himself agreeing, although felt no wish to go below until all were brought up from the water. Flint was also standing by, and giving the occasional hand or word of encouragement to those still being dragged aboard. And then all that had survived were safe, the backed mizzen top could be reset, and *Prometheus* took to the wind once more.

"The sick berth, if you please, Mr Franklin," Caulfield reminded him in a voice more attuned to that of an executive officer. "You are clearly cold and may require medical attention."

Franklin followed Caulfield's gaze and was surprised to notice both his hands were indeed shaking. He flexed his fingers which moved only stiffly and were quite without feeling or colour, before obediently making for the companionway.

* * *

By the time *Prometheus* closed, Hunt had despatched a number of six-pound shots into the xebec, and much of the fight should surely have been knocked from her. But even though the liner now loomed above, her guns run out and promising an instant paradise to any believer who opposed, there were still those aboard who wanted to continue the action. Several musket balls were sent whipping through the British ship's rigging, while a group of robed men could be seen attempting to train one of their broadside cannon on the infidel's beast. At a curt instruction from Marine Captain Reynolds, Sergeant Jarvis ordered six of his men to account for them with more considered shooting from the quarterdeck. Then *Prometheus* was lying off the corsair's stern, and even the most fanatical mind must accept that further resistance would be foolish.

"It is curious," Corbett commented briefly, watching from his position on the upper deck. "The pirates still have oars, yet make no move to escape, neither do they try to avoid being raked."

"If the captain fires now, she'll be sunk for sure," Adams, who was second in command of the gun deck, agreed.

"And for an enemy who tried so hard not to be caught..." the lieutenant began, although felt no inclination to finish his sentence.

"Mr Hunt is going in," the midshipman pointed down to the black cutter. The boat was indeed closing and all aboard the British ship watched as she rubbed briefly against the enemy's hull, then emptied her crew into the pirate vessel.

The boarding party swarmed up and over the side, landing on the enemy's deck patently eager for combat. But they met little resistance – two shots rang out, and a bearded figure, clad in gown and turban, swung a silver blade menacingly at them, and there were cries of delight from the battleship when he was taken down by Kennet, a regular Jack, armed with a far more mundane cutlass. Then there was Hunt himself at the enemy's ornate, but battered, taffrail. Corbett swallowed dryly as his appearance was greeted with further applause from the liner, and the sound grew further when the young officer gave a casual wave of his hand, signalling the vessel's capture.

"Well that appears to be that," Corbett muttered softly as he watched the junior man acknowledge the cheers and approval. His guns had undoubtedly been used in anger, but this had not been the close action Corbett craved. Franklin and Hunt might have benefitted from it, but few others, while lives had been lost from amongst the crew, which would make everyone's work that little bit harder. He supposed some good had been done by ridding the Mediterranean of a pirate, but to his mind it had not been a satisfactory morning's work, and he hoped for better in the future.

* * *

"Drink this," Mrs Manning ordered, passing him a pewter mug, and Franklin was so taken aback by the woman's curt command that he obeyed without question. The fluid was hot, and doubly welcome, as it contained some unknown spirit that seemed to awaken his inner being, just as much as it warmed the body. The improvised sick bay on the orlop deck was almost empty, a reassuring sight to any used to seeing it heaving with wounded in the midst of an action. The rest of the cutter's crew were being cared for further aft, where Prior and a couple of loblolly boys were handing out measures of grog and dressing minor wounds. Only Franklin was allowed forward, the area where Manning rigged his operating tables, one of which now held the body of young Carley.

Franklin sipped again at his drink as he considered the lad. His chest was bare, and bore the bright red welt of a graze, but it was the arm that lay limp and apparently unattached that drew his attention. A tourniquet strapped close to the shoulder was evidently carrying out its task as there was a remarkable absence of blood. But the boy's skin appeared pale to the point of being almost transparent, and the surgeon did not attend him with the haste usually expected on such occasions.

"There is little I can do," Manning told his wife and Franklin sadly. "He must have lost a deal of blood while in the water and is in shock. I might remove the arm easily enough, but sense the act will be sufficient to claim him completely."

Franklin nodded. It was desperately sad; Carley had come to several Bible studies and obviously held a strong faith. He had also introduced two other midshipmen, Briars and Brown; boys that Franklin would never have considered having an interest in the Lord, yet both were taking to the teaching readily. He did not doubt the surgeon's words, but felt instinctively that something should be done. And, more surprisingly, that he was the one to do it.

The woman passed a small silver mirror in front of Carley's face, and examined it sadly. "There is no breath," she said.

"And I do not feel a heart," the surgeon agreed, removing his hand from the patient.

"We have no parson aboard," Franklin said, feeling foolish.

"Someone should pray, or read a passage."

"You may if you wish," the surgeon's mate replied sternly, while her husband drew the edges of a canvas sheet over the raw wound. "Such things are not the sole province of churchmen, and you would not be the first to do so in these circumstances."

Franklin inclined his head more slowly this time, before placing his mug on the deck and drawing closer. The lad had undoubtedly ceased to breathe and he noticed his pallid skin was growing ever whiter. But still he sensed an element of life remained.

There was no text to hand, his New Testament having been lost with his tunic, but that would be no obstacle. He began with the grace, spoken softly and almost to himself, as he reached forward and placed a hand upon the lad's forehead. The surgeon withdrew, and no one else spoke while Franklin, with an unusual lack of embarrassment, continued. The verses that had been denied him before now came rushing back; he recited a psalm, then from John's Gospel, and finally some words written by a tent maker to a Thessalonian church nearly eighteen hundred years before. And all the time the two medics watched in respectful silence. The lad's head was cool – cold even, and there was no movement, but the impression that an element of life persisted remained. Then Franklin felt it leave; the group that had contained four people now only held three, and he knew his job was over.

The surgeon and his wife appeared to know it too; they both stepped forward at the same moment and Kate, who was closest to him, placed her palm on Franklin's shoulder.

"That was well done," she said, her voice unusually soft. "He could not have wished for better."

* * *

Banks was seated in the empty space that usually represented his day cabin. The back of his arm chair, the one that Sarah had so thoughtfully provided at the start of the commission, was turned firmly away from the carpenter's team who were busily tapping bulkheads back into place. He found he could ignore them surprisingly easily, and would be content to let the rest of his cabin be reconstructed about him, if only he were allowed to remain undisturbed with his thoughts.

The act of capturing the xebec had initially restored some of his confidence, although Banks was aware how much of the success was down to luck. It would look impressive to enter Gibraltar with a prize in tow, and not be made to feel his only contribution to the current war was to use up valuable supplies. But, on what he thought of as mature reflection, if he took any credit for the victory he was even more the fool he currently thought himself.

For the fact remained, *Prometheus* would not have been making for home in the first place, had he kept his head when the French fleet sailed. The ship would still have needed to take on wood and water, but might instead have gone to Agincourt Sound, or even to relieve the *Kent*, currently sheltering at Malta. As it was, *Prometheus* had been detached from the Mediterranean Fleet; returned to Gibraltar for yet more repairs, and the only reason such a thing had been necessary was his own incompetence.

He was a seasoned officer, and used to feelings of disappointment following a successful action. He knew that, even if *Prometheus* had taken a more active part in the xebec's capture, and the main reason his men currently celebrated a victory was down to their captain's exceptional skill, his spirits would have been just as low. But this current mood was so much worse than any of the brown studies experienced in the past. Banks was able to disregard his lack of attention easily enough at the time, but memories of that dark night in Toulon harbour had been returning with increasing regularity ever since. *Prometheus* had come so perilously close to being handed over to the French that he felt nothing he did in the future would ever truly compensate for it.

Outside he could hear the excited cries of his men as they secured the pirate ship; all sounded happy, as they had a right to be, and would doubtless be looking forward both to prize money and the chance to spend it in one of Gibraltar's many doubtful haunts. But there was no joy in the great cabin and, for all the good fortune that day had brought, Banks' mind remained firmly set, not on their victory, but what had so nearly been a defeat.

He told himself that, rather than seated in his comfortable chair, he could now be in a stone cell, and a prisoner of the French. Or his dead body might be rotting in the sludge of Toulon's outer harbour, along with those of others who had been foolish enough to trust his expertise. It was luck and nothing else that had enabled him to escape such a fate, luck that brought about the pirate's capture and, as he dismally allowed himself to review previous successes, luck that was behind the majority of them.

Countless men relied on little more to see them through their careers but, until then, Banks had never considered himself to be one of them. Besides logic dictated that, if he continued to make mistakes, his measure of fortune would eventually run out. And at that moment it felt as if the time might finally have arrived.

* * *

The drink they had given him on the orlop was specifically ordered by the surgeon and not the grog he expected. It encouraged the deepest of sleeps Flint could remember for a long while and, when he awoke, it was to find the ship once more heading south, with much of the chaos caused by clearing for action magically restored. Noting the fact, he felt suitably shamed. A fair proportion of the drug still remained, however, and his guilt was easily balanced and even countered by an inward feeling of tranquillity, as well as the equally rare and welcome absence of pain.

As soon as he was discharged from the sick bay, Flint made for his proper berth on the deck above, cheerfully acknowledging the greetings of others met upon the way. And as he approached the well remembered benches that sat to either side of his own mess table, was probably in the most congenial mood since the day Mr Manning first identified his complaint.

Seeing some of his mates heightened the feeling further; there was Cranston, Greg and Bleeden along with Ben, who had been the mess boy but now rated ordinary, and Jameson, the lad he befriended all those years back in *Vigilant*. Jameson had made it to topman and was as regular a Jack as any, but Flint would always think of him as the wide eyed volunteer from nearly ten years ago. They turned to him as he drew nearer, and all seemed as pleased by his presence as he felt in returning. But there was something else; an excitement in the air that even Flint's dulled mind could not miss. And then, as he slumped down in his usual place at the bench, another face swam into view, and Flint gasped as he recognised it.

"Butler!"

There could be no doubt; of all the friends a man may make during his life, shipmates were the closest, with those who shared the same mess, more intimate still. No one could live in the cheek-by-jowl atmosphere of a gun deck berth without another messmate's features, habits, even their very scent becoming as familiar as those of any family member. But however well remembered Butler might be, the face that stared back at Flint was almost a parody of the healthy young topman who first joined them in Tor Bay.

"So where did you spring from?" Flint found himself asking, almost rudely.

"The xebec," Butler replied in little more than a whisper.

"He was caught some months back," Jameson explained to save his weakened friend the trouble.

"An' been forced to serve as a galley slave since." Bleeden continued, eager to be the bearer of such news.

"That's bloody," Flint grunted, his eyes now switching to the man himself. He was wearing a tattered shirt with both arms bared from the shoulders. The limbs appeared healthy and his muscles were undoubtedly well developed but, in contrast, Butler's face was almost void of flesh and seemed no more than skin over bone. It occurred to Flint as he stared at the skull-like image before him, that he was actually looking at a body in poorer condition than his own, and the realisation was oddly disconcerting.

"Whatever have the bastards done?" he asked softly.

"Treated 'im rotten," Bleeden replied. "Just as bad as the tales you hear."

"A good deal worse," Greg added. "Though 'e got 'is own back."

Flint looked enquiringly at his mates, but it was Butler who provided the explanation.

"We took a hit from the barky," he said, his voice barely audible amongst the commotion of a ship still settling from action stations. "Landed on our larboard quarter, and weakened a frame that made several rowing positions useless."

"It might 'ave wrecked the mountin's, but left all the rowers pretty much untouched." Cranston boasted proudly. "That's good shootin', I'd say!" Cranston had laid one of the guns so could, conceivably, have been responsible.

Butler nodded, then continued. "They had a go at rowing against the rudder, but that proved no better, so were forced to cut back on the starboard to balance. But by then we'd smoked there was a British ship in range and, however hard they tried, us Jacks weren't putting in much effort at the sweeps. An' then when we started being raked by the cutter, we didn't want to know. No matter what that bastard overseer did, we weren't having none of it."

"Beat some poor bugger half to death, so they did," Bleeden again. "An' he were an officer, ain't that right?"

Again Butler nodded.

"You did well," Flint told him. The drink was still having an effect and, despite its anaesthetic qualities, he felt able to speak and think more clearly than for ages. "Without your help we would never have taken them pirates," he continued. "As it is, the barky's got another prize, and we'll be due an handsome payout, 'less I'm mistaken."

They waited for Butler to say more, but either the effort so far had been too much, or there was nothing further to tell. His arms still bore the livid marks of regular beatings, and his face the memory of other mistreatments, yet his friends were able to offer little other than compassion and understanding.

"I've a sup of wine from the gun room's dinner," Greg said, in an example of generosity that was rare in him. "But the surgeon said to give 'im nothing."

"An' it's a shame 'cause there's some cheese left over since Monday what we were going to use to catch millers," Cranston added. But Butler shook his head. He was beyond any material needs and simply craved rest and security. So it was no surprise to any of them when, shortly after, he placed his arms down on the table, lowered his head, and surrendered to a sleep that was solid and deep.

Chapter Seventeen

Gibraltar was now very much a second home to them, having been their saviour or restorer on previous occasions, and all were looking forward to sighting the rock once more. It was clear that *Prometheus'* current requirements should not take long however; the sheer hulk would be needed to draw her mizzen mast from its partners, and there would be a degree of work to do on the hull, although none that meant extensive disruption, and certainly not the disembarkation of her lower deck as before.

Kate and Poppy left with little ceremony, the surgeon having found them clean lodgings ashore, as well as yet another maid who would look after both when the time came, as their projected dates were inconveniently close. He was also able to secure a replacement surgeon's mate from the naval hospital. This was a Londoner named Blake who was slightly younger than Prior, the other assistant, but seemed of a sensible disposition, and the three settled down together quickly enough. Manning's intention on reaching harbour had been to start work on moving the sick berth and dispensary to a forward part of the upper deck. But the sudden influx of patients; men liberated from the pirate xebec who now needed care, rest and monitored feeding, took both longer than expected as well as much of their current space.

Marine Captain Reynolds had reappeared to a chorus of ironic cheering and good natured banter from his fellow wardroom officers. He, along with all *Prometheus'* Royal Marine contingent, had spent the last few days guarding the xebec's prisoners aboard their former vessel, while a party of seamen from the liner made temporary repairs and saw her home. Having access to ready made secure accommodation had eased his task no end but, now that his charges were safely handed over to the shore based military, all he wanted was several glasses of an agreeably dry sherry, and a rest.

But there were no such luxuries for Hunt and Franklin. In addition to normal duties, they had been called to stand their examination board. This would either confirm their acting rank and grant a precious commission, or see them returned to the cockpit as midshipmen. *Prometheus* carried above her allocation of lieutenants, and both accepted that one of them might be failed for no other reason. Consequently, their every free hour was spent re-reading personal copies of the basic instructional books, and borrowing what others they could from their colleagues in the wardroom.

Of the two, Franklin was undoubtedly the least enthusiastic. He had sat enough boards to grow cynical of their appointments and knew that, even if he were to pass, an older lieutenant would never be as welcome as one who could bring youth and vigour to a post. And that was not all Franklin lacked; he was rapidly coming to the conclusion that much of his interest in the Navy in general was now missing.

He was not sure where the blame for this lay; whether it could be put down to the regular meetings with his fellow Christians in the stewards' room, or those brief but significant moments spent in improvised prayer as his cutter moved in to attack the xebec. The last had undoubtedly been meaningful – actually more so than he realised at the time, and the memory remained with him ever since. It was as if a hidden and ethereal door had been opened and he was invited through, assuring his faith and changing him from hopeful seeker to assured believer as he went. But whatever the cause, Franklin now felt more at peace, both with himself and his maker, than at any time in his life.

So it was that, as he ploughed through his old copy of *The Elements of Navigation* as well as a more modern guide to rigging, seamanship and naval tactics that a sporting Hunt had lent him, Franklin felt the added pressure of studying a subject that was becoming increasingly less important to him. He had no wish to return to the midshipmen's berth; to resume his previous unofficial duties as surrogate father to a bunch of ignorant and often spoiled young boys, but equally acknowledged his talents were probably better used in that direction. And there was one thing that worried him above all; since experiencing his last taste of action, Franklin was far less certain if he would ever be truly suited to the life of a sea officer.

Being at Gibraltar once more also affected the lower deck, although in diverse ways. One of the major differences between this and their previous visits was that all regular hands were required to work. And work hard: a strangely energised Captain Banks had decreed that *Prometheus'* stay should be as short as possible, so every able man was set to assisting the dockyard force and took an active part in the repairs. But even if most were fully occupied, there was little asked of Flint. He was now universally acknowledged as ill and expected to be transferred to the naval hospital at any time. Somehow he simply did not go, however; Manning spoke with him on several occasions, and once went so far as to threaten his removal by force. But they were in harbour, and it would have been an act of extreme cruelty to rob an experienced and well liked seaman of his last days aboard a warship.

And so he stayed, keeping his position as head of the mess by unspoken agreement, even if most of his day was spent yarning with his mates or taking increasingly longer breaks. Time when he would rest, but not sleep, in the lee of the gangways or huddled up next to a knee with his hat pulled firmly down upon his head.

Butler was a different matter. He was a deserter and, by rights, should have been placed on the punishment deck, or transferred ashore for court martial. But like most of the xebec's prisoners, his body was far too undernourished for anything other than the tenderest of treatment. The surgeon had taken charge of all former slaves but, in Butler's case, allowed the lower deck to look after what was indisputably one of their own. And it had actually taken only a few days of his familiar diet to start putting flesh on bones and colour back into his skin. Butler remained incredibly weak, of course, but still made himself useful picking oakum or splicing line, and all secretly hoped it might be conveniently forgotten that he had ever strayed. There was no doubting he, and the other captured British seamen, had been instrumental in the final taking of the xebec so an element of natural justice would appear to have come into play.

And the xebec was a valuable ship. Despite damage wreaked by the cutters' six pounders, she remained a fine craft and of a type particularly popular in that part of the Mediterranean. The Admiralty might have no use for her, but there would be more than enough private buyers keen to bid, as soon as she was presented at the prize court. Along with money due to them, the not inconsiderable sum their government were obliged to pay for men captured and vessels taken or destroyed, most of those aboard *Prometheus* knew they could expect a decent pay out, and were suitably buoyant.

In fact both Banks and Caulfield considered themselves lucky to have a particularly happy and healthy crew. Twelve men were lost in Franklin's cutter, and fifteen more since their last call at Gibraltar, both in action and to the usual wear and tear of shipboard life. But these had been more than made up for by those rescued from the xebec, which included many prime seamen and even a few former man-of-war hands. All were recovering as well as Butler and, as with him, it was hoped they would show their gratitude by marked enthusiasm, and a level of loyalty rarely seen in newbies.

The ship would be in harbour a month, or less, if the local dockyard mateys got a shake on. The weather might be terrible, but it would have been a lot worse off Toulon and, now they were safely put up in a British port, none could seriously believe the French would leave until the spring. And Christmas along with the New Year was coming – it would be 1804 and already seemed incredible to note the fresh century passing so quickly, although that only made the likelihood of an imminent and decisive battle the more real.

It was generally agreed the French must sail within the next twelve months. And, when they did, the British, along with a freshly serviced *Prometheus*, would be there to meet them. Even if both sides failed to attract further forces, it could only be a conclusive action. Were the Royal Navy successful it would signal an end to any plans Napoleon might have of dominating the seas.

And if not, he would gain access to the Channel and invade England. But despite the odds, there were few aboard *Prometheus* who did not wish for battle, and none that considered any outcome other than victory. It was a habit established during the last war. Howe, Duncan, and now Nelson had seen them successful; the latter on more than one occasion. And with that same energetic Admiral as their current commander in chief, how could they fail?

* * *

"I was wondering what might be done about Butler," King said softly to Caulfield. It was the end of the weekly meeting the first lieutenant held with all senior officers, and King had timed his comment so that most were either rising from the wardroom table, or had at least stopped paying attention.

"Butler?" Caulfield repeated, absent mindedly.

"The hand we took from the pirate xebec," King reminded him.

"Ah yes. He were marked as a runner; whilst we were refitting previously, as I recall." Caulfield's face cleared with the memory. "And originally pressed, or am I wrong?"

"When we commissioned," King agreed. "In Tor Bay."

"It is rare for a hand to desert after being aboard for a spell," the first lieutenant reflected. "Were you aware of any discontent?"

The younger officer raised an eyebrow. As Butler's divisional officer, King was responsible for several hundred men, many of whom were there against their wishes. He happened to know the man quite well, however, and Caulfield was right; after the first six months of joining a ship, most had become sufficiently immersed in the culture and routine to stay until they were payed off – something that was especially so when in a foreign port, where the likelihood of returning to the home they craved was smaller.

"There was little troubling him out of the ordinary," King replied at last. "He was reliable and being considered for promotion. From what I gather it were nothing more than a severe case of homesickness."

Caulfield pursed his lips. "Good hands are hard to find," he said as he pondered. "We were lucky in claiming what we did from that xebec, but are unlikely to be so again."

"I would gauge him popular with the men," King added hopefully. "And he did much to enable the pirate's capture..."

"And I suppose you feel punishing him for desertion would not go down well?" Caulfield gave a wry smile.

"I do not think it would serve any purpose," King answered with obvious sincerity. "Nor would the sound flogging that must follow, were he sent for court martial."

With the general shortage of manpower, the practice of hanging deserters was declining. But a group of dispassionate captains were quite likely to award a savage beating in cases like Butler's, and King was soft hearted enough to hope he would avoid such a fate.

"Of course, Butler would have missed quite a bit of prize money in his absence," he pointed out as tactfully as possible.

"Prize money?" Caulfield questioned.

"There is that due for the coaster, and the liner we burned," King continued. "We did not carry them back, but the Admiralty are obliged to pay an allowance even so. There would doubtless be a measure of head money to add as well."

"And the xebec herself must raise a fair amount," Caulfield agreed, warming to the idea. "Butler shall be owed no share of that, despite any assistance he or the other British may have given."

"Perhaps that might appear to be punishment enough?" King suggested.

But Caulfield shook his head. "No, it will not do, Tom. I gather your meaning, but there has to be official acknowledgement," he sighed. "No man can run from a ship without recognition of the fact. Even if lenient, we must be openly so. I shall bring it up with the captain at the next opportunity."

King nodded but said no more; he was actually quite satisfied. Butler remained weak, but his seaman's lifestyle made him inherently healthy. He should recover before long and eventually resume normal duties. On reminding the first lieutenant of the offence, Caulfield may well have ordered Butler to be placed in bilboes and await court martial. An appearance at captain's defaulters could lead to the same conclusion of course, but King thought not. He hoped – in fact he was reasonably certain – Sir Richard would see sense and deal with the matter diplomatically. Possibly a spell without grog, maybe a token dozen at the gangway; Butler would soon be able to take that, and it would be seen by all as a reasonable outcome. In such circumstances, and with a popular member of the lower deck, anything more would be resented. And King had no wish to face the storms of a Mediterranean winter with a discontented crew.

* * *

"Very well, we shall start the final part of your examination." The senior captain must have been sixty if he were a day yet, despite the wrinkled and weather beaten face, his vivid blue eyes held both life and energy and seemed to penetrate deep into Hunt's own. "Your ship is under stuns'ls with a quartering wind when the call goes out that a man is overboard; what are your actions?"

The younger officer's mouth opened for a full second before he spoke. But Hunt was prepared for just such a scenario, and his mind had been racing from the moment the board's president began to speak.

"I would see that an aid is thrown to him," he said.

"An aid?" the elderly captain asked, curtly.

"Probably a hammock, sir," Hunt replied. "Unless something more suitable were available." It was common knowledge that a properly tied hammock would float for some while, and plenty were always to hand, packed into the side nettings. Hunt actually remembered an occasion when a hen coop, complete with occupants, was thrown, but this did not seem the correct time to mention it. "Then I should call hands to stations and put the helm down."

There was no reaction from the granite face opposite; two

other captains sat, one at either side, but it was the central, and clearly bloody minded officer that Hunt involuntarily focused on.

"The aft yards would be braced up and studding sail tacks and sheets let go."

Still the same lack of response.

"Then, if a quarter boat were fitted, I would call for her crew; otherwise launch whatever craft is available the quickest."

"And that would be a fine mess, were you in company," the stern face informed him. "Amongst a fleet sailing in close order you would endanger both your ship, and any vessel following."

Hunt was now every bit aback as his imaginary ship. "I was not told we were sailing as part of a fleet," he replied, too surprised to feel embarrassed.

"He has the right of it, Sir Robert," one of the captains informed the president hesitantly. "That was omitted."

"And as it was, the answer served perfectly," the other added, evidently pleased to have caught his colleague out.

The older man's eyes closed for a moment, and then he drew breath.

"If junior officers cannot summon the wit to ask a question, the Navy is doomed for certain," he stated testily. Then the eyes opened again, and this time they held a more kindly air. "But so be it; grant him his commission, and may the Dear have mercy upon us."

* * *

All aboard *Prometheus* had been pleased to reach Gibraltar, with her promise of shore leave and rest, and were surprised when their captain, usually the most affable of commanders, announced the regime that would have them back on station before the end of the year. The dockyard superintendent had predicted four weeks for the work to be complete, but privately allowed for five; however Banks was determined all would be done within three, and set every man involved working double tides to see it was.

Some jobs were finished relatively quickly; it took less than a morning with the sheer hulk to draw their fractured mizzen mast. The spar came out like an enormous bad tooth, to a murmur of approval from the watching band of boatswain's mates and topmen. The dockyard riggers were as efficient with its replacement: a fresh length of pale, jointed pine being lowered into position just as light was starting to fade. By noon on the following day the original top had been set up, and most shrouds were in place. It was then a reasonably routine task of setting up the top and topgallant masts, and rigging yards. By the time the more subtle work needed to her hull and superstructure was halfway through, *Prometheus* already boasted a healthy tophamper and was ready to face the worst a Mediterranean winter could throw at her.

And the rest of the repairs, though not as dramatic, were also attended to with relative speed. Fresh wood was let in to replace the shattered bulwarks and scantlings, and the lower wales were given an extra coat of marine paint for good measure. Most of the internal work needed paying or painting as well, although the humid winter air meant each took an age to dry. For upwards of a week *Prometheus* was filled with the pungent smell of linseed, while her delicate surfaces attracted dust to the consternation of every officer from the first lieutenant downwards. But despite this, all major work was completed within twenty-three days of their first sighting the Rock; an incredible feat when compared to that expected of the average English dockyard and, however reluctant some members of her crew might be, the ship was subsequently pronounced fit to return to duty.

Then came the familiar loading with wood, powder, and other provisions. In their usual perverse way, the victualling yard had received fresh supplies of candles and beeswax, but were now almost entirely lacking in canvas, causing the sailmaker and his team to re-cut their second spare main course into a serviceable fore topsail, which also provided material for the several replacement hammocks that were required. Then *Prometheus* was truly ready and, despite muttered complaints from all stations, scheduled to set sail little more than a week before Christmas.

It had been a busy period and, as countless other minor jobs were still outstanding, was doomed to remain so until the last minute. So less important tasks, such as the collection of officers' laundry, and the final drawing up of the watch bill, were left until the day before they were due to leave. And it was during those final hours that Flint's absence became apparent.

"Adams is his divisional mid," King told the captain when he and Caulfield were offering the new duty schedule for approval. "He was present at the last muster, and marked so this morning, though the lad did not see him personally."

"Did he not?" Banks queried testily. There were a veritable pile of returns and other requests to authorize; he could not spend a great deal of time on a single missing seaman, especially one known to be ill, who would undoubtedly be sent ashore when discovered. But of late Banks found any disruption in official routine annoying, certainly far more than when he had commanded smaller ships. This was possibly a side effect of added responsibility, or maybe his temperament was changing. Or perhaps he was simply getting old. "Then why was Flint marked as present?" he asked crisply.

King had no answer and Caulfield remained equally mute; Adams was undoubtedly at fault, although both officers could understand why he had not looked into the man's disappearance more closely.

"Instigate a full ship search," Banks told them wearily. "And have the master-at-arms report to me personally. I want Flint found and escorted to the shore hospital by the end of tomorrow's morning watch, or a reliable report that he has already gone and will not be returning."

King agreed readily enough and both men left the captain to more pressing tasks but, as the following dawn broke on a ship amid the final confusion of putting to sea, there was still no sign or news of Flint.

"We may mark him as run," Caulfield said doubtfully, when King brought the matter to his attention in the more informal setting of an empty poop deck. "But, as he was to be discharged, it would seem a bad end to any career."

"And he would lose what wages he were entitled to," King agreed. "Not to mention prize and head money."

Flint's disappearance was actually growing from being mildly irritating to a true annoyance, yet King remained concerned that someone he had sailed with for much of his working life should apparently leave the ship without so much as a backward glance. If Caulfield authorised an 'R' to be placed against his name, Flint would become a wanted man and, ill or not, must then be pursued and face punishment.

"I think we should let the matter rest," Caulfield said suddenly. The two had been steadily pacing the deck, and King stopped and looked round in astonishment. "He may have gone ashore or, as I suspect, could be concealed within the ship," the first lieutenant continued, "but it will serve little purpose if we disrupt routine further by seeking him out."

There was no doubting the logic, but it still came as a surprise to King.

"The man is ill and expected to die," Caulfield sighed, as they began to walk again. "None of us can predict how we might behave in such circumstances. Whatever has become of him is likely to be the result of his own choice, and we should allow him to make it without further interruption."

King remained quiet, although it was not the matter of a missing seaman that filled his thoughts. There were times when Caulfield was the strict disciplinarian, a true stickler for duty and procedure such as anyone might expect of an executive officer. And times, such as now, when a far softer side was revealed. King had noticed the occasions to have been less frequent of late; certainly since he had taken on his responsibilities in a line-of-battleship. But he still found it oddly reassuring to note his friend retained an element of compassion.

"Should I delay in taking any action at all, then?" King finally asked.

"I believe so," Caulfield told him, as they reached the taffrail and turned. "But a word to the wise; it would be better if the captain is not reminded of the incident."

A second surprise, and King waited for the first lieutenant to continue with interest.

"Sir Richard has become a trifle conscientious of late," Caulfield had not started to walk, and his voice was lowered to the point where it could barely be heard, even by King. "Perhaps you may have noticed, but he appears to be playing by the rules, and the people are growing discontented. I have tried to speak with him, but he will have none of it."

That was undoubtedly the truth. All had been looking forward to a spell in harbour, although the stop at Gibraltar had proved anything but a rest. No shore leave was granted and now they would be setting off, into the very worst of the winter weather, King and every officer aboard was worried about a lowering of morale.

"I am also concerned about how he will react to Butler."

"You are thinking he may deal harshly with the man?" King asked. They had begun to pace once more and were just nearing the open skylight above Banks' quarters.

"It is a possibility," Caulfield confirmed, although this time his words were spoken far louder and with almost studied clarity. "And Sir Richard would be within his rights, of course. Desertion is surely an offence, whatever the circumstances. But in Butler's case a severe punishment would not be taken well."

"Would it not?" King asked with equal volume. He had initially been confused by the first lieutenant's behaviour but, now that he understood the reason, was more than prepared to support it.

"No, the very reverse," Caulfield replied in the same strident tone, while adding an elaborate wink to King for good measure. "If Butler is given more than twelve strikes it will lower morale considerably, and the ship shall undoubtedly end up the loser. But then I have known the captain a good many years, and respect his judgement greatly. He always has the overall good of the men in mind, and I cannot believe he would order an extreme punishment."

Chapter Eighteen

It was the first fellowship meeting since the ship set sail, and the first since Franklin had been returned to the aft cockpit after failing his examination board so ignominiously. Furthermore, the theme for that day was forgiveness and, even ignoring his recent change of circumstances, it was a subject Franklin found particularly challenging.

Not that he had ever been one to bear a grudge, and neither did he consciously remember the smaller matters that counted against him. But a few had caused him significant harm in the past, ranging from the older brother who took on, then ruined, their father's grocery business, to the only woman he had ever loved, who turned out as loyal as any Drury Lane fen; these, along with a few fellows, he had been struggling to forgive for some while. To grant them the same concession his personal redeemer wished to impart on all was well beyond a mortal such as Franklin, and he entered the crowded stewards' room in low spirits.

But inside he found much to encourage him: the place was indeed packed – there must have been at least twenty already squeezed against the spirketting or huddled uncomfortably upon the deck, and he knew for a fact there were as many attending the next meeting that Kennedy would be leading immediately afterwards.

For all his apparent humility, the steward had done wonders in waking up the spiritual heart of the ship, although Kennedy always cited Franklin as being the main instigator. But whoever was responsible, there could be no doubt that a good deal of progress was being made.

And it was not confined to those appearing at Bible study; the general attitude on the lower deck was also altering, with less squabbling and petty fights while, on the Sundays when the captain held divine worship, it was noticeable that the entire congregation was becoming more vocal. Hymns were now sung with gusto, and the assembled seamen were finally achieving that deep rumble of combined prayer that Franklin felt had been missing aboard *Prometheus* for far too long.

Still, the next hour or so would hardly be easy, and after it he would not be returning to the wardroom, but his previous berth in the crowded and stuffy aft cockpit. He consoled himself with the thought that there were plenty worse off than him, and the position of senior midshipman and head of the mess was not without its benefits.

He had found it easier to speak to other members of the crew; those who came to him to ask about the regular meetings and, on several glorious occasions, go on to confess a stumbling acceptance of the Lord. There were actually two at the current meeting for which that had recently happened, and Franklin wondered if his presence in the berth had been the final factor in bringing them to faith. Briars and Brown, two of the youngest midshipmen – Briars was in truth still only a volunteer – were sitting opposite him now as he opened with a short prayer, and Franklin was particularly happy the lads had joined.

There had originally been four youngsters posted to the ship at roughly the same time he was promoted to acting lieutenant. Two were later killed though, and such a thing is likely to have an effect upon the most seasoned of men, let alone impressionable boys. But Briars and Brown had come to accept the word with all its connotations, eagerly reading their Bibles during off duty moments, and apparently destined to become solid Christians. Such a victory was wondrous indeed and, should his presence have had anything to do with it, probably worth the reduction in rank on its own.

But that was not going to make the next hour any the easier. As far as coming closer to the Spirit was concerned, Franklin knew himself to be making progress in most directions, although forgiveness remained his least favoured subject, and one on which he felt unqualified to preach. But the general prayers were over; from across the crowded room Maxwell caught his eye, and Franklin knew it time to begin. He stood up, head bent more from the low deckhead than out of devotion, and read from Luke. Of all the gospel writers, he was probably Franklin's favourite. Doctor, scholar and gentile, Luke 's account was the one Franklin felt most at home with, and something of this must have been apparent to the assembly. For the men listened in respectful silence, and very soon Franklin became lost in a place where ranks, privileges and all other worldly matters counted for very little.

* * *

Flint made his reappearance shortly after they watered at Tetuan, although by then he was barely a shadow of the man whose spirit had filled both his mess, and most of the lower deck. None of the officers commented on his return; it being generally agreed he must have found a convenient hidey-hole. And neither did they ask why he had chosen to stay hidden; all could understand how a seasoned Jack would prefer to end his days afloat, than undergo the terrors of a land based hospital. And Flint was allowed to retain his berth, rather than shifting to the medical department as Manning briefly suggested. He was a seaman of many years' standing, one who had served with a good few of *Prometheus'* people through other commissions in different ships although, even if he had more recently joined as a raw recruit, the reaction would have been little different.

It was a recognised fact that men serving aboard the same vessel, be she brig or battleship, soon became of one mind. Even if they remained in home waters and not hearing so much as a musket fired in anger, they would inevitably meld together and become shipmates; a term frequently misused or not fully understood by land animals. As it was, this particular crew had seen action on several occasions, while their ship sailed in seas where nearly every coastline was either inhabited by the enemy, or under their influence. Consequently, *Prometheus* was now a floating island – a small slice of English territory in herself. And if one of their number was sick, he would be attended to in the manner of any caring community.

His hammock was still struck before breakfast of course: anything else would have been contrary to routine, and might start similar breaches of discipline which could end with *Prometheus'* afterguard messing in the wardroom. But he was now excused even light duties and spent the time when his watch was on deck wrapped in a blanket, his kerseymere hat pulled low, and the previous issue of grog lying untouched to one side.

And soon he would die; that was recognised and accepted by all. When the time came he would be given a seaman's burial, sewn into his hammock, with the last stitch, the snitch, being passed through the bridge of his nose by the sailmaker. At his feet would be round shot and, after a short ceremony which the captain himself presided over, then be slipped gently off a grating, over the side, and into his natural element.

All this was known, yet unspoken; acknowledged as the way of things by men who accepted their own fates were likely to be broadly similar. But while he remained amongst them, Flint would be treated with respect; allowed to continue in his honorary position as head of the mess, and entitled to any benefits due to the working hands.

When he did go they would be sorry, that was also generally agreed. Such an integral part of their lives could only leave a gap, and it would be weeks before memories took the place of the man who left them. The commission would continue, however; their ship might see further action, or be paid off, with her people dispersed to different vessels or returned to where little of the sea and its lore was known. And then even the memories would begin to fade, that or be overshadowed by other events, other sadnesses. Flint would probably remain in the minds of his close friends, his tie mate, and perhaps members of his gun crew. But even they would forget him some day, that or take a similar journey. And only then would he truly be gone.

* * *

At first the meeting had progressed in exactly the fashion Franklin expected. He read two further Bible passages, before adding his own comment; vague reflections on forgiveness that had been somewhat guiltily cribbed from notes made during a previous talk by Kennedy. And then, as had become the custom in such gatherings, the subject was thrown open for all to discuss.

One of the quarter gunners mentioned a long running dispute with a quartermaster's mate, a man known to all as something of a martinet, and there were loyal hisses of sympathy from gun crew as well as general hands. Another spoke of a purser in a former ship known to be mean with rations, to the extent that they had cause to petition the captain. Then there were other examples where the speaker was indisputably innocent, and found forgiveness hard to grant.

By the time they were half way through, and there was less than an hour left before the end of the first dogwatch, Franklin was barely listening. Experience told him they would get no further, as was invariably the case when the topic was mentioned. None came forward to admit to being the guilty party and ask for mercy themselves. That was not to say the meeting was in any way wasted; to Franklin's mind such a thing could never be, when men met together in the Lord's name. Still, he was resigned to the fact that, if any progress was to be made, it would come in the privacy of individual reflection, rather than a public announcement.

And then someone did speak up; one of the lads who had only been attending for a few weeks. When Briars raised his hand all, including Franklin, were expecting some revelation about an unfair incident with a senior officer, or perhaps something from the boy's recent childhood. No one expected the dreadful confession that was subsequently delivered.

Often such a tale, when told amid the revelry of a run ashore, or an afternoon's make and mend, would have attracted lewd comments, and raucous laughter, but the men gathered in the stewards' room were there for an entirely different purpose, and not the type, or in the mood, to give way to such base instincts. Instead they simply regarded the culprits with pity, for Brown, seated next to Briars, gave credence to the story by his red face and guilty countenance.

Franklin swallowed dryly as the last terrible details of that afternoon in the midshipmen's berth were revealed. On one level this would have been perfect fare for the session he had in mind; were the boys admitting to petty pilfery, or perhaps a minor dereliction in duty, a blind eye might have been turned to the actual crime, while the two were counselled, and no doubt became the subject of ongoing prayer. But Franklin knew at once there was no question of containing such a revelation to Bible study; whatever the spiritual ramifications, this was undoubtedly a case where he must submit to more worldly laws. A serious crime had been committed, and it was his duty as a king's officer to see Caesar was paid with a suitably earthly punishment.

The boy's divisional officer should be informed without delay, and there would be a court martial, so both lads would be placed under arrest. It was unfortunate the girl had been delivered ashore, but not inconceivable that a trial could take place when *Prometheus* rejoined the Fleet off Toulon. For there was no questioning such a full and detailed admission: they could only be found guilty; indeed it would hardly take longer to hear the evidence than announce sentence.

Although sentencing itself would be another problem. The Articles of War covered many crimes, but none the boys had specifically committed. They might be subject to criminal law, in which case a civil court should try them, and that must wait until they made harbour: really this was a nightmare on so many levels.

Franklin stood up and raised his hands for attention; there was little he could say, no words of wisdom, no passages which came to mind, just a numb feeling of disbelief that two apparently good natured young men had been so reduced. Fortunately Musgrave, a ship's corporal, was present and, reverting to his authority as a warrant officer, Franklin crisply ordered the lads to be taken into custody. Then three bells were struck; the first dogwatch would be over in half an hour at which point he was required on deck. But first he had a deal of explaining to do, and that was something Franklin did not relish.

* * *

"How long have these gatherings been taking place?" Banks asked when the two lads had been taken from the great cabin. Their crime left him only mildly surprised; such things were not unknown aboard ships of every description, and he had long since accepted that most beings carried the ability to be both good and bad in equal measure. The thought that the incident had come to light in such a way bothered the captain far more. What had been blithely referred to as a fellowship meeting held ramifications beyond mere religious instruction. A mutinous assembly might be equally so called and, as captain of the ship, it was his duty to investigate the matter fully.

Caulfield shifted uncomfortably on his chair. He was also aware that a gathering of men not subject to strict naval discipline was a potential threat, and could be seen as a black mark against his premiership. "Since about a month after we first commissioned," he replied. "There was a measure of resentment from some of the hands at our not shipping a chaplain."

"Why so?" Banks asked, genuinely surprised. "Surely the average man cares little if there is one aboard or not; some even credit them as bringing bad luck."

"That is often the case," Caulfield admitted. "Though we appear to have many with a strong faith amongst our people."

Banks snorted. "Have we indeed? And is not the weekly divine service sufficient for them?"

"Apparently not, sir," Caulfield answered with unusual formality. "In Mr Fraiser's time there were similar meetings, but that was in smaller ships with lesser crews. *Prometheus* is a third rate..."

"And I suppose should, in truth be carrying a chaplain," Banks conceded irritably. "But I fail to see why it be necessary, nor what a man of the cloth would actually do when not conducting worship."

"It is customary to combine the duties of a chaplain with those of schoolmaster," Caulfield suggested cautiously.

"So I understand," Banks snapped. "Although I consider each head of department fulfils the task adequately; there should surely not be need for more."

"Perhaps a general education?" Caulfield persisted. "Some are little older than children."

"Are they indeed?" Banks questioned. To his mind the first lieutenant was being unusually stubborn. It was bad enough that he had been forced to confine two junior warrant officers under close arrest when, with the girl gone from the ship, there must surely have been a more diplomatic way of handling things. For a major crime to have been committed aboard *Prometheus* reflected badly on all, and privately he conceded a breakdown in pastoral care was the cause. And he supposed Caulfield was right, with the offence being admitted in front of so many, it would have been hard to hide such a public admission of the ship's failings.

"But surely things had not grown so bad?" he asked finally. "Franklin did a fair job of supervising the midshipmen in the past."

"I believe he did," the first lieutenant confirmed. "And after failing his board, he returned to the aft cockpit without protest. Since then there has been a better standard of dress and deportment amongst the young gentlemen." Caulfield paused and considered the matter further before adding, "so perhaps I may have been wrong with what I said previously."

Banks raised his eyes in enquiry but made no comment.

"I felt Franklin was doing little good as senior of the mess," Caulfield continued. "It seemed a position that served no actual purpose – rather as that of a chaplain," he admitted, with an ironic look at his captain. "But it might be his presence accounted for more than we believed. And, had he not left, this whole terrible incident might never have taken place."

* * *

Butler was not with them that evening. Though still decidedly weakened from his time with the xebec, two ship's corporals had escorted him from the mess during the afternoon watch, just before the second issue of spirits, and no one was certain quite what had become of him since. News of the midshipmen's arrest then began to be known and generous descriptions of their exploits were soon causing sniggers, comment and a predictable buzz of speculation about the lower deck. But however titillating the lads' crime, the talk eventually returned to that of Butler and Butler alone. There might have been no scandal or mystery; everyone knew the circumstances as well as what he was accused of, and all were united in their disapproval.

"Don't care if he were a runner," Bleeden declared over a post supper tankard of stingo. "If he and t'others 'adn't stopped their rowing, that pirate would still be out an' causing mischief."

There was no reply from the rest; every man present shared his sentiments but were too tired to voice them yet again. Then Jameson, returning from a trip to the heads, brought news.

"Butler's on the punishment deck," he said, slipping into his customary place at the table. "Set in bilboes with a couple of bootnecks watchin' over him."

"So he's getting a flogging," Cranston's tone was level but not without feeling.

"Aye," Jameson agreed. "Two 'undred, accordin' to our old mate Wainwright. And the bugger seemed to think it funny."

"Bastard," Bleeden commented philosophically before laying into his beer.

"He's probably still cut up about that prank we pulled on 'im in Gib.," Greg mused.

"Two hundred stripes is more than the captain's properly allowed," Cranston maintained, returning to the subject. "Twelve: that's the limit."

"But he needn't take notice of that," Flint pointed out. "Captains do what they pleases, they ain't accountable to no laws."

"Aye, it'll take more'n a rule book to stop Sir Dick," Greg agreed. "Nothin' will as I sees it."

"Then he's a bastard an' all," Bleeden added, and no one disagreed.

* * *

On the following day, when Hunt was standing the morning watch, he could not have been happier. His commission was now a full three weeks old, with the last five days being spent at sea and aboard what was becoming the best ship he had ever served in. *Prometheus* might appear nothing more than an uninspiring and slightly aged third rate but, since joining her, there seemed to be no lack of action. And, most importantly, he had received the vital step to commissioned rank.

Furthermore, he was working with a set of officers he truly felt at home with. Hunt had taken the watch from Tom King, someone he now considered his best friend, although several others in the wardroom ran a close second. And there had been no objection to his moving into Franklin's old cabin which, though marginally smaller, lacked the presence of a thirty-two pounder.

Remembering Franklin brought up mild feelings of guilt. Though there may have been reservations at first, Hunt now genuinely liked the man, and knowing he may have stolen his last chance of a commission rather took some of the joy from his new wash-boards. But there appeared to be no bitterness; Franklin had cleared out of the wardroom remarkably quickly, and resumed his former duties as senior of the aft cockpit without a single word of comment or regret.

Six bells rang, the watch was three-quarters over already; in little more than an hour Hunt would be enjoying his breakfast, safe in the knowledge that, apart from unforeseen circumstances, he would most definitely be dining in the wardroom for the rest of his time aboard *Prometheus*.

But before that could happen, there was one brief but important procedure to go through. Towards the east, the sky had been lightening for some while and, just as the opening rays of a wintry sun broke through the gloom, the first lieutenant appeared on deck, his personal glass in hand.

Hunt acknowledged his senior formally, and Caulfield responded with a touch to his own hat, although neither spoke.

Daylight would be upon them in minutes, and could reveal anything from an enemy battle squadron to a fleet of French merchants ripe for the picking. But on that particular morning only one other vessel could be seen, and she was a brig that might, in theory, belong to a number of nations. The tattered ensign that was already flying said otherwise, however, and only confirmed what her rig, and the colour of her sails, had already told the two officers.

"She's making the most of what wind there is," Hunt commented as the small hull bobbed manfully a mile or so off their windward quarter. Caulfield nodded, but made no reply, although he continued to watch. The breeze was light; it came on both their starboard beams and appeared likely to increase. But the sighting, which could not have been more than a hundred and fifty tons, was under all possible sail, and healed markedly as she strove to overhaul them.

"Our friend seems intent on a race," the first lieutenant muttered. He had brought out his personal glass and was still studying the small craft. "I think we may hoist our own colours, Mr Hunt."

The sun was undoubtedly rising so there was nothing extraordinary in the request, but still Hunt felt he must have missed a significant point about the brig.

Then Caulfield took a step back and snapped his glass closed. "She's carrying despatches," he said.

Hunt stared hard; the light was improving all the time and, even without using a telescope, he could now make out the distinguishing bunting that was blowing almost directly towards them. This must be one of the regular vessels that brought communications to and from Nelson off Toulon, he decided. The brig would have left Gibraltar three or four days before, and should reach the blockading fleet at least twenty-four hours ahead of *Prometheus*. In addition to official papers, she would be carrying personal mail, perhaps a few essential supplies, together with any officers or men who were to return to Admiral Nelson's force. Nothing unusual, nothing in any way of interest really, except that the first lieutenant had taken to staring at her through his glass once more.

"She's signalling," Caulfield said without surprise, and Hunt snapped to attention. Bentley, the duty signal midshipman was on hand, but Hunt's new position as official fifth and junior lieutenant carried additional responsibilities, one of which placed him in charge of all ship's communications.

"Seven six nine; that would appear to be the private signal for today." The wind's angle made identification difficult, and Bentley spoke hesitantly from the poop, while Caulfield looked at Hunt for confirmation.

"Yes, that's today's code," it was a different voice, and both lieutenants turned to see Franklin, who had joined them on the quarterdeck.

"Very good, Mr Franklin," Caulfield replied gently, noting the exchange of glances between the two officers. "Kindly see we make the appropriate response."

"One four seven over our number, Mr Bentley," Franklin ordered, and the midshipman disappeared to do his bidding.

"If they are charged with despatches no detours are permitted unless they be of a significant nature," Caulfield mused. The brig was steadily drawing on them and now lay almost directly in front of the growing sun. "But kindly summon the captain, I believe she is intending to close on us after all."

* * *

Once more Caulfield's instincts had proved correct. By the time Banks, clad in trousers, shirt and leather waistcoat under a quilted silk dressing gown, appeared on deck, the brig was already less than a cable off, and clearly intending to come alongside.

"She's listed as *Aries*," Caulfield told him. "A government charter, I know not who has command."

Banks gave an ill-tempered grunt. Whoever it was would be a lieutenant, or possibly a commander. They may be carrying news, or require something of *Prometheus*, but it could hardly be important. And his breakfast had been interrupted.

"I think they wish to speak," Caulfield continued, aware he might have upset his captain in some way.

"*Prometheus* ahoy!" Despite being heavily distorted by a brass speaking trumpet, it was a young voice. And the slight figure that held it, apparently the brig's captain, looked less than eighteen.

"What brig is that?" Banks responded in a solid bellow that needed no assistance. He knew the answer but it was first light and his mood made him pedantic.

"His Majesty's Hired Vessel *Aries*; my name is Jefferson: we are three days out of Gibraltar."

Three days; they had made a good passage, and were obviously keen to continue as the brig was steadily headreaching on the third rate.

"I'm carrying despatches for Lord Nelson, but have a message for you also from the naval commissioner."

Banks snorted; it would be one of the manifests he had somehow forgotten to return; that or an error in a way-bill; certainly nothing to warrant delaying a despatch vessel, and he was surprised at Otway for doing so. "Go ahead," he replied, while reaching out to David for his first cup of coffee of the morning, and preparing himself for what was bound to be a rather public reprimand.

"A French squadron passed through the Strait two days after you left."

Banks narrowly avoided dropping the china cup. An enemy squadron. Nelson had been obsessed with allowing the French to sail; that they would, and must surely then head for Gibraltar before the open Atlantic, had lain at the forefront of all their minds for a good while. But this was something different. This was additional shipping, presumably sent to take on the blockading British and, were they to succeed, it might mean the end of the Mediterranean Fleet.

"What force are they?" Banks found himself asking, although his voice was nothing like as strong as before.

"Three third rates, two frigates and a sloop," Jefferson replied.

"We passed them yesterday even'. The sloop gave chase, but we managed to keep out of their way, though the whole squadron cannot be far behind."

Banks managed to stop himself from instinctively looking south, but the news was enough to evoke a dozen equally foolish reactions. They were probably still a good two days from Toulon with the current wind; even if *Prometheus* packed on all sail and this little brig made exceptional time, the only help they could expect from the inshore squadron would be a chance ship returning to Gibraltar.

"Were there any serviceable British ships at Gib.?" Banks asked. When he had left the answer had been no, but it may conceivably have changed in the meantime.

"Nothing that would give you support, sir," the voice answered and, even through the distortion, Banks thought he could detect a note of sympathy from the young man. "Captain Otway has authorised *Prometheus* to shadow the enemy, but you are not expected to engage," Jefferson continued.

"Very good," Banks replied, his tone now level. "Then you must continue to find Admiral Nelson, and I wish you God speed."

The brig was now considerably ahead and her captain answered with nothing more than a wave of the speaking trumpet as the two vessels drew further apart. Banks turned to the first lieutenant.   "We would appear to be expecting company from the south, Mr Caulfield," he said. "Perhaps you would be so kind as to set the stuns'ls?"

Chapter Nineteen

Banks had spoken at length with Caulfield and Brehaut. *Prometheus* was currently off the Spanish coast, with approximately a hundred and seventy miles to run before they raised Toulon. That would take at least two days at their current rate, or less if only the breeze would increase.

As well it might; the glass was dropping and there was definitely the scent of change in the air. But should what was coming turn out to be a heavy winter squall, it could as easily work against them. At least what airs there were lay in the south east; a rare occurrence for those waters, and they were making the best speed possible while it did. The same wind would be powering the French, however and, as they included a number of small craft, some might be expected to come into sight at any time.

But whether or not they were about to be overrun by a squadron of enemy warships, life aboard *Prometheus* must continue, and Banks could see no reason to clear for action. He had learned from experience that the very act was enough to begin sapping energy from his crew and, as this chase might last for some time, the longer they retained creature comforts such as hot food and draught-free accommodation the better. Consequently, the decks had already been scrubbed white, the midshipmen and master's mates were attending their customary classes with Brehaut, and all the other minor rituals common aboard a ship of war continued as if the nearest Frenchman was several hundred miles off, with no chance of *Prometheus* going into battle that day, or any other.

And the same rules should apply to him, Banks decided. He already had a full day's work planned, and there was a punishment to be witnessed in under three hours. So when he sent for Franklin, the newly failed acting lieutenant, he did not wish to spend a great deal of time with him.

"I was sorry to learn of your board," he said, once the man

was seated. "They are a chancy business at the best of times; doubtless you shall fare better on the next occasion."

"Thank you, sir," Franklin's reply came readily enough although, when he added, "I hope so," there was an element of finality that Banks was quick to notice.

"You are settling down in the aft cockpit again, I trust?"

Franklin was about to respond, but Banks did not wish for a long discussion, and spoke over him.

"You must not think your unofficial duties as senior of the mess are unappreciated," he said. "Indeed, guiding young men in their careers, and seeing them become efficient officers is worthwhile work, and should never be underestimated."

Banks was unsure how to phrase the next part. He had discussed it long and hard with Caulfield the night before, but was still not wholly behind the idea. Unfortunately that meant allowing a pause in the conversation; something that Franklin was quick to take advantage of.

"I have visited Brown and Briars, if that is what you are referring to, sir." he said, innocently.

It wasn't, and Banks had to hold back a curt reply. Instead he drew a fresh breath and forced himself to relax. He might think a pursuing force of French warships did not concern him but that was clearly not the case, and he wondered if this really was the right time to handle other matters.

"Brown and Briars will be dealt with in due course," he finally replied. "I would chance their eventual return to Gibraltar will be called for; they are intending to plead guilty, so no prosecution witnesses shall be required."

"Though someone should surely speak in their favour," Franklin persisted, and Banks was mildly surprised by the remark. He had forgotten it was every man's right to have his divisional officer, or any member of the ship's company, stand for him. Presumably the same provision would be made in civil courts, and was an important consideration; it would be terrible if he consigned both youngsters into the hands of the authorities, only to find he was also losing King, or another favoured officer.

The thought lowered Banks' mood still further, and he knew he was in danger of losing his temper. The man opposite might be no more than a midshipman, yet was attempting to impose his opinion on him, a senior captain. And it was doubly annoying that, in this one small matter at least, he appeared to have been successful.

"Little can be said in their favour," he began, controlling his tone manfully. "They are condemned by their own mouths; we must let justice take its course."

Franklin made no response and his face remained entirely neutral, although Banks still drew the impression the warrant officer held a strong opinion. He could not fail to be reminded of similar conversations held with Adam Fraiser, his former sailing master. Franklin might be old for his post, but remained considerably younger than Fraiser, although the similarities were strong.

"But we shall let their future be for now," Banks continued, reclaiming the conversation. "It was a different matter entirely that I wished to speak with you about."

Franklin looked back with interest but said nothing, and Banks found himself becoming more frustrated with every passing second.

"It has come to my notice that, in addition to your normal duties, you have been undertaking a degree of pastoral care."

"Yes, sir," Franklin admitted. "Mr Kennedy and I organise regular meetings for any who wish to learn more of the Christian faith. Mr Caulfield is aware, and has no objection."

"I am sure of it," Banks replied automatically. Whatever his personal thoughts about the value of such assemblies, Britain was a God-fearing nation, one in which all were presumed to have a faith; it would be wise to show nothing other than support. "I trust you are receiving a regular attendance?"

"Yes, sir," Franklin repeated. "And it is growing steadily."

"Well, I was to offer you the chance to place such matters on a more formal basis."

The interest was suddenly evident on Franklin's face, and he actually sat forward on his chair as his captain continued.

"*Prometheus* does not have a chaplain at present, neither are we likely to acquire one in the near future. And, whilst you may not have taken holy orders, you are clearly generally respected. Would you consider taking on the position for the length of this commission?"

Now Franklin showed true surprise, his mouth opened as if to speak, but not a sound was heard, and Banks felt suitably gratified to have finally silenced the man.

"It would be strictly unofficial, of course," he continued. "You should continue to draw your midshipman's allowance, and would not be entitled to the monthly groat from the people." He cleared his throat and passed on quickly. "But I would value your assistance at divine service; you may give the blessing and read prayers and perhaps an occasional sermon? And I would chance the people would take more notice of a cleric who was also a fighting officer, especially one who has distinguished himself so conspicuously in action."

Franklin was deep in thought, and Banks started to wonder if he would ever speak again. Then he finally stirred himself.

Thank you, sir," he said, although his gaze was still set in the distance. "It would be an honour, and a move I was actually considering at the end of this commission." The last words might have been spoken lightly but were clearly meant.

"I know little of such things," Banks replied. "Though if it has been on your mind to change your career, a spell aboard *Prometheus* as her unofficial chaplain could only speak in your favour."

Franklin's eyes turned to meet those of his captain and they were strangely alive. "It would indeed, sir," he said.

"And you might return to the wardroom," Banks added. Despite his mood, seeing Franklin take to the idea so wholeheartedly had actually given the captain a modicum of pleasure. And such a concession would not inconvenience him in any way.

Franklin thanked him once more, although now his face had

unaccountably fallen.

"You would be more comfortable in the wardroom, I am sure," Banks added, noticing the change.

"Oh, undoubtedly, sir," the midshipman agreed. "Though in truth I am happy enough in the aft cockpit, and feel that is where I have been placed."

"Well, that is for you to decide," the captain told him. "But I see no reason why we should not start immediately," he continued in a more businesslike manner. "I have already spoken with the first lieutenant, who is ready to make suitable changes to the watch bill. And you can begin by considering a sermon for this Sunday's worship."

As far as Banks was concerned, the interview was over and he raised himself up from his chair. After a second or so Franklin followed, although his mind remained some distance away.

"But I was forgetting," the captain said as the two men shook hands. "You may start considerably before then. We have a deserter aboard; a man name of Butler. We shall be flogging him in less than two hours. You had better make your way to the punishment deck and do whatever is necessary."

* * *

"We might take advantage of this unusual wind and head north," Brehaut suggested softly. "Take us as near as we can go to the Spanish coast, then shelter behind Cape Creus."

"And allow them to sail past?" Caulfield asked. "It is a thought, I suppose, but would the enemy prove so obliging?"

"Properly hid, they should have little choice," King mused.

"A north westerly, which is far more common in these waters, will doubtless reassert itself in time," the sailing master continued, warming to the idea. "When it does, we might come up from astern and track them all the way to Toulon."

"Though it would be difficult to alert the inshore squadron." Caulfield pointed out. "I doubt the captain would condone such a move."

"He has been uncommonly touchy since that affair in Toulon harbour," King reflected.

It was mid morning and the three officers were the only occupants of the wardroom. They sat about the large table with Caulfield at the head, as was his right. Before them lay a chart of the North Eastern coast of Spain, with *Prometheus'* current position shown by three neat pencil marks. But their discussion had already drifted once from the problem at hand, and seemed liable to do so again.

"He has," the first lieutenant agreed. "Frankly I cannot see Sir Richard meekly following such a force; nor shall he stand by while they attempt to join those at anchor in Toulon." There was a moment's silence, before Caulfield delivered the killing blow. "I think it far more likely he will wish us to engage."

"The frigates, do you mean?" King asked.

"Not necessarily," Caulfield pulled at his chin in thought. "Sir Richard has been consistently victorious during his career, both in this ship and those previous. He may well take on the frigates, and is likely to prove successful. Or, if the opportunity presented, I can equally see him making straight for the liners."

"And take on all three?" King was incredulous, while Brehaut seemed appalled and disgusted in equal measure.

Caulfield shrugged. "Such a thing is not unknown."

"But that would be madness," King protested.

"Maybe so, but I have seen it before in other men."

For a moment no one said a word, then Caulfield began to speak softly, and with extreme care.

"When a man becomes captain he takes on a very special role." The first lieutenant pushed himself back from the table, and started rocking slightly on his chair. "Suddenly he is in total control, and there are many who cannot adapt to such power. Those that do are usually blessed with the lighter commands at first. The crews are small, with fewer officers to carry out their wishes. And, of course, far less chance of major victories."

"But when he progresses?" King prompted after there had been further silence.

"When he progresses it can indeed change," Caulfield continued. "Not perhaps with sloops or frigates: the nature of such vessels being that a bold heart and dashing moves are almost expected, while there is usually a close enough relationship between captain and officers to see that nothing too outlandish is attempted. But when given a liner, or maybe the command of a small force of shipping, a captain can do most whatever he likes."

"You are thinking about our taking on the three French battleships in the summer?" Brehaut asked, but Caulfield shook his head.

"No, that was totally legitimate, in my view. The enemy was more powerful undoubtedly, but we had stronger crews and retained the upper hand, even if it were only in our minds."

"The incident in Toulon harbour then?" it was King this time and his voice was especially low.

"I fear so," Caulfield agreed equally quietly. "In truth I do not know why Sir Richard exposed us as he did; the information we obtained was not vitally important, and may have been acquired by a frigate the following morning."

"You think he enjoyed taking the risk?" King again.

"Not enjoyed, but perhaps has become over confident."

"He would not be alone," Brehaut added, after a moment's consideration. "Why we need only look at Admiral Nelson's history to see a likeness. All remember victories such as Copenhagen and The Nile, but who talks of his defeats: San Juan, the Turks, Santa Cruz, or Boulogne?"

"No one accompanied Sir Richard to the flag when Nelson returned," King pointed out. "And I do not suppose his journal gave much mention to how close we came to being captured."

"And if it had, what of it?" Caulfield snorted. "We were not, so it would be judged a chance worth taking. And as the report would have been to Lord Nelson, a man not unknown for taking risks himself..."

"So you don't believe we will be allowing the enemy past?" King asked in a slightly louder voice.

"No, I do not." the first lieutenant replied sadly. "To my mind it is more probable *Prometheus* shall be called upon to intervene in some way. And frankly I cannot see any good coming of it."

* * *

"Hands to witness punishment." The pipe reached members of Flint's mess just as they were looking forward to the end of the forenoon watch, and normally would almost have been welcomed. Sir Richard Banks was not known as a flogging captain; there had been remarkably few times when the entire crew were so assembled since the start of the commission. And most Jacks could tolerate the usual allocation of twelve, or an occasional twenty-four lashes, neither of which took particularly long to administer. But, seeing that the traditional time for such a ceremony was eleven thirty, barely minutes before they would be served their first tot of rum for the day, those on watch usually considered their work period ended.

That morning would be different, though. If Butler were to receive even half his allocation, it must take considerably longer than quarter of an hour. Additional boatswain's mates would be called to relieve those handling the cat, while Butler was likely to collapse and need time to recover. And it wasn't as if this was an ordinary day. Most had heard the captain's conversation with the brig's master, and were fully aware a powerful enemy was on their tail; one that might close on them at any moment.

So it was that Flint and his mess formed a grim and morose little group, as they assembled on the upper deck, and waited beside the grating that was already upturned and rigged against the gangway.

"Bloody disgrace," Bleeden said, when they met up. "Two hundred lashes, an' after what 'e did to secure that pirate."

"An' Butler ain't fit," Cranston agreed. "No matter what the sawbones might say, a man in his condition should never be treated so: it could do for him."

But Flint said nothing. He had seen enough good men abused by bad officers in the past, and sincerely thought Sir Richard to

have been made of better stuff. Two hundred lashes was indeed a
dreadful punishment; one expected from a bunch of stuffed shirts
sitting at court martial perhaps, but not of a captain with any regard
for the morale of his crew. Cranston was wrong, however; Butler
might be undernourished but remained inherently strong. The
punishment would not end his life although, so angry had the
sentence made him, Flint felt it could shorten his own.

The idlers were assembling now, as well as Mrs Roberts, the
carpenter's wife, and all personal servants. Only the minimum
number needed to actually sail the ship were excused attendance,
and even the majority of those would have a prime view of the
proceedings. The wind had yet to increase; *Prometheus* was still
straining to find every last ounce of its power, and it seemed
foolish in the extreme to divert attention from that, to carry out a
punishment which would only lower the spirit of every man on
board.

Then, with a simultaneous click of metal, a marine guard
formed up on the break of the quarterdeck. They carried loaded
muskets, and there were flashes of light from their highly polished
bayonets. A further file stood forward of the main hatch, and more
lined the gangways. *Prometheus* boasted over one hundred of these
elite sea soldiers. All were volunteers, and suitably proud of their
recently bestowed Royal codification, but Flint doubted if their
authority could hold over the combined strength of five hundred
incensed seamen. There could easily be a bloodbath, yet by that
evening they might all need to fight the French; it was a ludicrous
situation.

And then Butler was brought up. Walking between the oldster
Midshipman Franklin, who seemed to have taken on the part of
chaplain for that morning, and Mr Manning, he looked pale, and
remained incredibly thin, despite several weeks of the surgeon's
special diet. His appearance brought forth a rumble of discontent
from Flint's mess, as well as many of the others assembled. With
communication on the lower deck being as good as it was, news of
Butler's treatment had spread like flames in a fire ship, and every
man present felt the same righteous indignation. A lot would

depend on how the sentence was administered, Flint decided. Were the punishment broken into two, three, or even more sessions, there might be no trouble. But if the captain opted for all two hundred to be delivered that morning, there was a good chance it would end in riot.

Officers were now appearing. Flint noticed that all looked unusually smart; full uniform rarely being worn when the ship was at sea and, he had to admit, were suitably grim faced. He had no idea how Butler's sentence had been taken by the senior men, but was sure a few were bound to have objected. Not that Sir Richard Banks would take any notice, of course; aboard any vessel, be it merchant or Royal, a captain's word was law, and every man's life in lay his power. Admittedly he might not be able to order a hanging, but there were numerous instances when men had been so ill treated by their commander that death became a refuge, and one they all too often claimed.

Then, finally, there was the captain. His arrival was greeted by a similar rumble of disapproval and, to his credit, Sir Richard appeared momentarily astonished. But his expression soon became set and, as the first lieutenant began to read from the Articles of War, the tension mounted further.

"Every person in or belonging to the fleet, who shall desert or entice others so to do, shall suffer death, or such other punishment as the circumstances of the offence shall deserve..."

Lieutenant Caulfield's voice rambled on to no apparent regard from the others. All had heard the rules a hundred times before, yet here was the end result in front of them. One of their own, who was about to receive a punishment that had become nothing more than a matter of rote.

Once Caulfield had finished, the captain himself stepped forward to speak.

"Butler, you have pleaded guilty of the charge of desertion, and agreed to accept my judgement and sentence, rather than that of a court martial." Again, a disgruntled murmur, and again, the captain seemed surprised by it. "In coming to the sentence I have taken into consideration your previously good record, and that you, and your fellow captives did much to aid the capture of the Barbary xebec. And it is with these facts in mind that I have decided upon an exceptional penalty." Now the rumble died, and men began looking to each other in confusion.

"But let me say this," Banks was continuing, apparently oblivious to the reaction his words had brought. "If any man present expects to be treated as leniently in future, he may be disappointed. Desertion is potentially a capital crime; men have been hanged for what our shipmate has done, and will doubtless be so again. So let us get this matter over with, and place our attention where it is truly needed. You all know there is an enemy close behind – our energies are better spent fighting them, and not each other. Mr Clement, twelve lashes, if you please."

Twelve lashes: a muttering went about the assembled seamen and some even looked accusingly at Butler's messmates. But those standing with Flint were every bit as bemused, and whispered urgently to each other, in spite of several calls for silence.

There was no doubting the sentence was to be served, however. Butler was strapped to the grating, and a leather apron tied backwards about his waist. Then, with the faintest of whistles, the first blow was struck, and nine separated strands from a length of log line landed squarely upon his bare back.

It was over within two minutes; by then Butler's torso had become a bloody mess although, as was noted by many, the stripes had not cut as deeply as usual. But punishment had been delivered and, as Butler was turned over to the care of Mr Manning, he would now be regarded as innocent as any present.

"What goes, Charlie?" Flint found himself asking one of his mates as the call to disperse came.

"Blowed if I knows," Bleeden admitted. "Matt heard it as two hundred. Pr'aps the cap'n had a change of heart?"

"Or maybe it never were to begin with," Jameson said in a more considered tone. "It was the bootneck, Wainwright what told me the sentence," he mused. "The one what we tied in an hammock and carried up the barrack tower. You don't think he might have been getting even, do you?"

Chapter Twenty

They spotted the topmasts of the first French ship two hours later. It was the smallest, reportedly a sloop, and probably sent as a scout for the rest of the squadron. Corbett had the watch and immediately alerted his captain, although other officers got wind of what was about and soon the quarterdeck was positively crowded.

"I'd say she were a corvette," Caulfield declared when the sighting was finally visible from the deck. "Likely to be carrying less than a sixth rate within a hull even lighter, though much good that'll do us."

"Aye," King agreed laconically. "She'll have the legs on anything heavier than a frigate, that's for certain."

"And she's making absolutely sure of who we are," the first lieutenant continued, lowering his glass.

Certainly the Frenchman was not afraid to close on them. Since first coming into sight off the battleship's larboard quarter, the smaller vessel had steadily crept up to windward and now stood less than two miles off their starboard beam. But though she might come tantalisingly close, while there was space between her and the reach of *Prometheus*' long guns, she would be safe. Banks could order them about, and even attempt to give chase, but it would be as if a cow were pursuing a greyhound; the lithe craft would turn in an instant, and be heading away at more than twice the liner's speed in not much more.

"Mr Hunt, a signal, if you please!" The captain's shout was unexpected and made several jump, none more so than their new official fifth officer. "Make, '*Prometheus* to flag — enemy in sight to windward'."

Hunt glanced at Bentley, one of his midshipmen, and soon the hoist was breaking out from their mizzen.

"And acknowledge," Banks added after a suitable pause. Signalling to non existent companions was now common to the point of almost becoming a tradition but, if the enemy had been sent to take a look, they may as well instil as much doubt as possible. This particular Frenchman was clearly unconcerned, however. The corvette remained on station a further half hour before turning neatly to starboard, tacking, then heading off in a flurry of spray. Soon she was nothing more than a blur of white to those on deck, and then disappeared entirely.

"Doubtless the others will know about us before long," Caulfield muttered to King. "Yet I cannot see French liners making any more speed than us."

"Though they may send their frigates separately," King replied with more caution. It was considered poor form to speak despondently to a superior officer, although any ill feeling between him and Caulfield was long forgotten. And it soon became obvious the first lieutenant had not contemplated such a possibility.

"You mean they might be sent in to soften us up?" he asked. "We would deal with them harshly if so."

"In daylight, yes," King agreed. "But cleverly handled and under the cover of night, it would be a different story."

"Two French frigates could never account for *Prometheus*," Caulfield replied with certainty.

"They need not," the younger man persisted. "Minor damage should suffice – maybe knock away a spar; slow us sufficiently and..."

"Leave the rest for the liners to finish off?" Caulfield finished grimly.

"It is a possibility."

"Like *picadors*, readying a bull so their *torero* might make short work?" the first lieutenant sighed.

"Probably on those lines," King, who knew little about bullfighting, agreed.

"Well, there are still several hours of daylight remaining," Caulfield continued after a pause. "And personally I would doubt the French will relish a night action, although it might be prudent to alter course in case they do. But much will depend on what the captain has in mind."

King said nothing. The bounds of seniority had already been

stretched; it wasn't for him to make further suggestions, and certainly not to the captain. *Prometheus* was steering to raise Toulon in the least possible time. If Banks were intending to run – to stake everything on reaching the British fleet, a significant alteration in course would not even be considered. Yet his theory remained, and he felt it plausible. There were many imponderables, of course, no one could tell the state of the enemy's shipping, nor how well they were crewed. Or the skill of their officers for that matter. But this was a powerful squadron, and had already been taken past one of Britain's main overseas bases, so whoever led it did not lack spirit or determination. The most logical course was for *Prometheus* to make a bid for safety; head for Toulon at all costs and raise the British fleet. But if Banks was determined to follow it, King sensed they would see action long before morning.

* * *

However, when darkness fell with no further sighting of any French vessel, King was having second thoughts. He had dined with Brehaut and Corbett, both of whom were remarkably cheery and, when the time came for him to take the first watch, he did so with fewer doubts.

Christmas was only a few days off; there would be no moon until early morning and conditions could be best described as patchy, with thick banks of low lying cloud rolling in with the breeze. But at least the threatened rain had not appeared, so King settled down to what was likely to be four hours of monotony. *Prometheus* was sailing well; if the French squadron had been just beyond the horizon when the sun went down, they would have to gain over sixteen miles before reaching her, which must take even the sleekest frigate a fair while. And notwithstanding the poor visibility, an enemy should surely be spotted long before it came within range of their thirty-two pounders.

The wind, which was almost directly opposed to the prevalent north westerly, remained unusually constant. Hardly a sheet or brace had been touched for some hours, so it was reasonable to expect the French to be experiencing similar conditions. And with every strike of her bell, *Prometheus* was steadily drawing nearer to the might of the Mediterranean Fleet, where she would ultimately find safety.

The brig that had warned them would also be nearing Toulon shortly. She may even have been fortunate in meeting up with the offshore squadron already, and a considerable force could be beating south to their rescue at that very moment. In the quiet of the night King told himself that was bound to be the case, and wriggled his right hand inside its glove to encourage circulation. Having but one arm held few advantages, he decided, but there was one less limb to grow cold, while mittens should last twice as long. And he was still enjoying the private joke when Bleeden, bellowing from *Prometheus'* main top, brought him back to stark reality.

"Send for the captain," he snapped, as soon as the brief message ended. A sail had been spotted; there was no knowing what class of ship it belonged to, but she was steering off their starboard quarter, which gave more than enough reason to wake Sir Richard. King took an anxious pace or two along the deck as he waited for Banks to appear. *Prometheus* was making her maximum speed in the present conditions, even to the extent of carrying stunsails at night when there was storm in the air, a rare and risky act in itself. His mind ran back over his predictions of the previous afternoon; despite Corbett and Brehaut's confident words, his original theory returned and now seemed far more likely. He supposed Banks could still alter their heading, still seek safety to eastward, in the wastes of the Mediterranean; that or turn to the west and take shelter behind the north east corner of Spain. But both courses of action would have less impact after so much time had been wasted.

"She's closing with us fast," the masthead added, just as Captain Banks made his appearance. "I reckons her to be a frigate. And it looks as if there may be another on her tail."

* * *

"Who is at the masthead?" Banks demanded.

"Bleeden, sir." The captain was wearing a watch coat over his nightshirt and apparently not in a mood to be trifled with. "Sound enough man – a former smuggler, I believe," King added.

"Then he ought to be able to see straight," Banks grunted. "But better send a middie up, just the same."

A glance at Bentley, who had called Sir Richard, was sufficient and soon the lad was clambering the starboard main shrouds with a night glass strapped over his shoulder.

"And she's hull down?"

"She was, sir," King confirmed. "Though coming up fast, by all accounts."

The captain made an odd guttural sound that King was uncertain if he should reply to, but fortunately Bentley's voice was then heard from the maintop.

"I have her," he said, with reassuring certainty. "She's a frigate sure enough, and not more than two mile off."

So much for hull down, King thought, but held his silence.

"Clear for action," Banks snapped, although Bentley had more to add.

"I'd say she were a fifth rate," he persisted, over the scream of pipes and the bellowing of orders. "And there's definitely a further following, though I cannot make her well enough. Carrying quite a tophamper – she may be larger."

The first ship sounded like the lighter frigate, or the corvette; either would be an inconvenience as another vessel of any size must limit their options. But the second would appear to be something bigger. She was conceivably a third rate, similar to *Prometheus*, although a heavy frigate would be almost as bad. The French had a number of forty gun ships built to carry eighteen pounders. They were fast, as well as considerably more powerful than a normal single decker, and it would be just their luck to have run into one of them.

"Very good, Mr King," Banks said, turning back for his quarters. "I shall dress while there is still something of a cabin remaining. But you may send the men to quarters, and have that man Bleeden replaced at the maintop. If he cannot spot a Frenchman 'till she is two mile from our stern, it's hardly surprising he failed as a smuggler."

* * *

"Ahoy, there, Charlie boy," Jameson greeted as he clambered up the main topmast shrouds. "You're for a warm; I'm relievin' you."

"Trick don't end 'till two bells," Bleeden replied, suspiciously.

"Then you should have kept your eyes open," the midshipman, Bentley, who was sharing his tenuous perch, told him.

"How can anyone be certain in weather like this?" the seaman grumbled as Jameson began to shin up the topgallant mast. The other two glanced about; Bleeden had a point; with no moon, the banks of cloud were only really distinguishable by a slight deepening in texture. And they were being carried in with the wind; their movement constantly distracting the eye, and making a misery out of any lookout's hour long spell of duty. The Frenchmen could easily have been hidden, and indeed were currently nowhere to be seen, having presumably slunk back into one of many patches of cover.

"If you two think you can keep a better watch, then I'm a squarehead," Bleeden continued, as he and Jameson delicately changed places on the yard. "This is much worse than a true fog, an' you're welcome to it."

* * *

Within an hour the situation had altered dramatically. *Prometheus* was transformed from sleeping ship to a potent man-of-war, with guns run out and alert hands standing ready at every station. King had disappeared to manage his cherished heavy cannon, while Caulfield stood relaxed and primed next to an equally composed

Brehaut. Only Banks seemed filled with nervous energy, and paced the deck compulsively while considering the various options. Dressed in seaman's trousers and leather waistcoat buttoned tight over a cotton shirt, he was probably cold and would doubtless have noticed had not thoughts of the enemy gained complete control of his mind.

One Frenchman, the smaller frigate, could occasionally be made out off the starboard beam, where she was keeping pace with them beyond the reach of their cannon. She had the wind marginally forward of the quarter, as did *Prometheus*, but was sailing without the aid of studding sails, which would make her more manoeuvrable. Of the other ship, though, the one that had only been properly sighted twice, they knew far less. She was also judged to be a frigate, but appeared of larger proportions and, when last seen, had apparently been making to leeward. But after twenty minutes of waiting, all on the quarterdeck were starting to have doubts. And it was one thing to face a visible foe, admittedly lighter than them, although still able to pack a sizeable punch, but the concealed forty gunner was felt to be much more of a threat.

Mercifully there was still no rain, but the cloud remained patchy and, sailing as they were, the hidden frigate could close at any time. And if she did, it would be hit and run; *Prometheus'* gunners may not have the chance to get a decent broadside in before they were soundly raked, or received a telling sidelong barrage that left their tophamper in tatters and the ship at the mercy of the heavyweights that lay close behind.

Banks stopped pacing abruptly and turned towards Brehaut. "How far off is the coast, Master?"

"No more than ten miles, sir, and would be in sight, were it day."

Ten miles; that did not give them much in the way of sea room if forced to fight. Should the second ship truly be there, *Prometheus* would be going into battle on the edge of a lee shore. But another, and more clearly defined, frigate was definitely sailing to windward. He could make towards that and chase her away, while freeing himself from any threat of land, and the temptation to do so was growing stronger with every passing minute. But such a move might also have been anticipated and even planned for by the enemy: he was just as likely to be playing directly into their hands.

If what they all suspected was correct, the second may close on him to larboard, trapping his ship between two enemies and raking her bow and stern. Even if both were nothing more than fifth rates, the British would be lucky not to be partially disabled, while their own fire was likely to be ineffective. And then the frigates would simply depart with the ease and speed of their class, leaving his ship as easy meat for the oncoming liners.

"Ten miles is not so very much," Banks mused, while his mind continued to wrestle with the problem.

"Indeed not, sir," Brehaut agreed. "Although the coast falls away shortly afterwards, and that would give us more leeway."

"How far?" Banks asked

"I should recommend a further fifteen miles."

Banks waited expectantly.

"As I said, the coast falls away," the sailing master repeated, conscious that he now had his captain's entire attention. "There is a bay, the Gulf of Roses, were we to turn any earlier we may become trapped there. I can show you on a chart, if it makes matters easier, sir?"

"Please continue," Banks replied.

"Delaying for fifteen miles would allow us to pass by Cape Creus. Once that is rounded, more sea room will be gained. The wind is currently against that prevalent in this area; it must inevitably change and, when it does, we might follow the coast all the way to Toulon."

The captain nodded but said nothing. He knew the waters reasonably well, and understood Brehaut's suggestion. It would, as the sailing master said, give them a measure of safety. Passing by Cape Creus should also deny the invisible heavy frigate any opportunity of closing to leeward. She would effectively be scraped off their larboard beam by the outpost of rock. But there would be far less chance of meeting with any alerted ships from

Nelson's fleet and, if the wind did not change and the enemy followed, there remained the possibility they may yet be trapped on a lee shore. And it would be one made from French soil, rather than Spanish.

* * *

The intricacies of the situation were lost on Lieutenant Corbett, although that was not to be surprised at. From his station on the upper gun deck he could see much, and hear most of what was about, but lacked the more comprehensive understanding of those on the quarterdeck. Still he knew enough to accept that his eighteen pounders would soon be in action, and was confident that their servers, who he had personally drilled and exercised, were prepared. As was he; in truth, Corbett had never felt so ready in his life.

At present their opposition were nothing other than a pair of frigates. They might give *Prometheus* a run for her money, but little else – it would be poor form if a British third rate did not see off two single-deckers, especially as they were bound to be poorly provisioned and manned by untrained crews. The fact that the smaller ships could still cause significant damage had missed him completely; Corbett's mind being firmly set on the trio of liners that, he hoped, they would eventually engage.

At St Vincent, Nelson had captured two such battle-wagons with a ship no larger than *Prometheus*. And one of those was a three decker, seized when the first struck, and was subsequently used as a stepping stone to board the bigger vessel. Corbett did not pretend to be a second Nelson, even if in private he considered himself to have many of the Admiral's attributes. But an example had been set and, should the opportunity come his way, he was determined to follow it.

He took a turn up the darkened deck, acknowledging the gun crews, currently divided and resting between their guns, as he went. The men returned his nods or occasional words of encouragement respectfully, and Corbett told himself he had a good understanding of the common seaman. He sensed all were positively spoiling for a fight, while recognising a fellow spirit in the officer that led them. And that, he was certain, was half the battle.

"No sign of a moon," he muttered to Adams, the midshipman who was stationed forward, and under the open spar deck.

"Not for another hour or so, sir," the younger man agreed. "Though I reckons we are better off without it."

Corbett was not sure of the last point. They had been blessed with only patchy cloud, and the promised rain had yet to appear, but he would have liked more visibility if they were to engage faster craft. The upper batteries currently lay in near darkness; light was needed when the guns went into action, and the ticking of closed lanterns told him it would be available. But once those traps were opened, the men's night vision must be all but lost, and it would be a shame if the enemy were able to get in a lucky strike when they were so disabled.

"Well, we should have a bright enough moon by the time the liners appear," he replied.

Adams looked doubtfully at his superior.

"The Frog frigates will detain us, you can be sure of that," Corbett explained, clasping his hands comfortably behind his back. "But I cannot see even a forty gunner making much of an impression on this old barge." He released his grip and patted a timber affectionately. "And if it means we get the chance to fall in with a proper enemy, they shall have served their purpose admirably."

A murmur of approval was heard from the nearest gun crew: Corbett turned to them and acknowledged it with a cheery smile.

"Yes, sir," the midshipman replied in apparent agreement, although inside he was not quite so sure.

* * *

"Very well, we make for Cape Creus," Banks said, breaking the silence, and stirring up the group of officers who had gravitated towards the faint glow of the binnacle lamp.

"But first perhaps play a little game with the enemy?" the captain continued. "Mr Brehaut, take us to starboard, if you please; I intend to run down on that Frenchman and see him move!"

"We shall have to take in the stuns'ls, sir," the sailing master replied, as he collected the speaking trumpet.

"So be it," Banks agreed. "Strike them, they will not be wanted again this session. Any victory we achieve tonight shall be won by cunning, rather than speed."

* * *

Prometheus' gun crews were divided into two teams, each serving weapons on opposite batteries, with a third, and separate, group attending whichever cannon was in action, and reinforcing the servers on that side. Such a system enabled the unused battery to be available at any time, while on the rare occasions when both sides of the ship were engaging an enemy simultaneously, the floating team could be equally split between them.

"Ready starboard battery," Briars called out after the message had been passed down from the upper gun deck, and the transient servers trooped across to join the starboard guns. A few hours ago, Briars had been under close arrest in a Royal Marine storeroom, and was only released on clearing for action, according to the custom. But his confession and subsequent public disgrace, along with a brief spell in custody, had knocked any remaining confidence from the lad, and it was with surprise that he noticed men were actually responding to his order.

"We're changing course," Lieutenant King informed him, from a few feet away.

"Yes, sir," Briars agreed hesitantly, and the ship crept round and began to take the wind more fully on her beam.

"Looks like we're trying to chase the Frogs away," King continued, taking a few steps towards the boy. "Though I'd be surprised if we had the speed to do so with the starboard guns."

King had reached the midshipman and noticed his face

appeared filled with doubt.

"If the enemy maintains their station, we won't have the pace to close with her to starboard," he explained. "It is far more likely the old tub rounds on her stern; then we may chance a raking broadside, but that will be from the larboard battery."

Briars nodded silently in the near darkness and King had a moment of insight.

"Look, I cannot tell how you are feeling," he said more softly, "Though a guess would probably not fall short of the mark. My advice is to put whatever did or did not happen to one side. You remain a warrant officer, and right now that is what the Navy needs and expects. There will be plenty of time to discuss crimes and punishments later: for now, do your duty and leave problems of the future where they belong."

"Yes, sir," Briars repeated, although his expression was more positive.

"Hey, Joe!" the voice came down from above and belonged to Adams, one of the midshipmen on the upper deck. "First luff's changed his mind; its ready larboard battery now."

"Belay that," Briars called out instantly. "Ready larboard battery."

The men paused in preparing the starboard cannon for use and, only grumbling mildly, began to move across to the opposite battery.

"Mr Caulfield's mistake," Briars assured them, although none seemed particularly bothered.

* * *

"Need the Jakes, Mr Corbett," Bleeden informed the third lieutenant. Despite being in Flint's mess, he did not serve in his gun crew, having been switched to one of the upper deck's eighteen pounders to make up for previous casualties.

"Use the pissdale," Corbett told him curtly. "Or a gun port, the Dear knows it's dark enough, and you can't be seen by the quarterdeck."

The last part was certainly true. Bleeden's gun was directly beneath, in what usually constituted the wardroom.

"It ain't a piss I'm wantin', sir," Bleeden replied with rude honesty and to the amusement of others. The lieutenant sighed. It was a lengthy walk forward to the heads, and Bleeden was not a man to be trusted to go quite that far when the ship was cleared for action.

"Oh, very well, you may use the commissioned officers' quarter gallery," he grunted. The first lieutenant's facility was actually closer, but one of the few concessions to Caulfield's rank was a private head, and it would be wrong of Corbett to offer it to a common seaman. "But mind you don't take forever," he added.

Bleeden knuckled his forehead politely, and made off aft, where he slipped open the sliding door of the starboard quarter gallery. Inside it was dark and stuffy, and there was an odd feeling of insecurity about the place, being a lighter structure, and only tenuously attached to the ship's outer hull. A closed lantern was burning from the deckhead, and Bleeden opened it, before glancing about in its light.

Everything was provided for him to take his ease in both comfort and privacy; rare commodities aboard any warship. But Bleeden's mind was ever alert to the main chance, and began to explore further possibilities.

There was a small cabinet set below the ornate window. Within, he found an almost full bottle of lavender water, together with four sets of razors and three unused bars of soap. Of these the soap and cologne was by far the more saleable, and he placed both on one side, intending to pocket them later. He then went to close the lantern, but changed his mind at the last moment. The quarter gallery did indeed offer exceptional comfort, and it had not been a particularly pleasant night that far; he may as well enjoy the light for a little longer.

But when he was finally summoned back to duty by an irate midshipman banging on the door, Bleeden left in such a hurry that he completely forgot about his booty. And the lantern, that continued to burn brightly next to the quarter gallery window.

Chapter Twenty-One

The weather wasn't improving any; low lying areas of cloud were turning to a proper fog which rolled in with the wind, while the scent of rain was also far stronger. But *Prometheus* made good progress as she clawed towards the last reported sighting of the lighter frigate. The enemy might have moved significantly since of course, and was bound to have forereached on her previous position. But with the third rate's mastheads being higher, Banks still hoped she might be taken by surprise. And if the other ship to leeward chose to follow, they were welcome: he would be expecting it. The mist they were sailing into was definitely stronger and Banks knew his ship to be hidden. With luck he should be able to land a devastating broadside on the first, then turn back and be in a perfect position to tackle the second as well.

And if they did not meet, he would simply order the ship back, heading apparently to take up her old course, although he had a far more subtle twist in mind. And one that was inspired, in part at least, by his sailing master.

By that time they should be able to turn to the north west, and just scrape past the coast of Spain. There might not even be a change of heading to slow them, while any enemy to larboard would be forced to pull back, unless they wished to come into close contact with *Prometheus'* heavy artillery. The British would continue, hopefully staying ahead of the increasing fog, and sight Cape Creus by the light of the moon that would be due to rise about then. That landmass would also be clipped as tightly as he dared, allowing *Prometheus* to carry on into more open water, with all their enemies behind and to starboard.

But much was being taken for granted. *Prometheus* may well be damaged in the forthcoming encounter; she might even receive without giving in return: in only a couple of hours he could be facing the entire enemy squadron in a ship unable to manoeuvre. It would be overwhelming odds, with the addition of a wide and encompassing lee shore that also happened to be French territory. But Banks was not particularly downhearted; he sensed his plan would work. There remained a chance of their becoming trapped, but this strange wind must surely change eventually, and the more usual north westerly return. And even if it remained, the south east coast of France was surely a large enough area to hide a single ship while, if they were found, he might at least stretch any action out long enough to enable the British to come to his rescue.

For that was still very much on his mind. The brig was bound to meet up with Nelson's fleet before long, and help would be despatched immediately, of that he was confident. And it would be a sizeable force; one large enough to deal with the French without risking too much damage in return. When the enemy were not in their expected position, Banks was sure any intelligent officer would make the obvious assumption, and turn some of his force to seek them out to the west.

But that was so much conjecture, and some while in the future. Right now he had to fight the immediate action. And, if he were not very much mistaken, one of the French frigates should be discovered shortly, perhaps behind the very next layer of cloud.

"Lookouts have been relieved, sir," the first lieutenant told him.

"Very good, Michael," Banks' response was automatic, and he did not feel the need to say more.

"The weather's worsening, though," Caulfield added. "I've a mind it will be rain afore long."

He was probably right, Banks decided, though rain should not alter his plans; if anything, it might benefit them. But even that was too far ahead, he was waiting, straining almost, for the first sign that they had run down on the enemy.

And it was possible they would not meet at all, he realised. That would put a very different slant on things. If no French frigate materialised, *Prometheus* would be free to seek sanctuary in the wider waters to the east. The idea was actually appealing, and he cursed himself for not considering it before. Then, just as he was starting to plan further, a call that was almost a parody of the customary lookout's bellow, was heard from the main masthead.

"Enemy in sight. The light frigate; we must 'ave passed 'er – she's less'n half a mile off the larboard quarter; I jus' caught a glimpse."

"How is she steering?" Caulfield enquired in what was best described as a whispered shout.

"Seemed as if it were same as before, sir," the lookout replied.

Banks felt his heart begin to race. His opponent was proving anything but intelligent. *Prometheus* had been allowed to change course and effectively creep up while they continued on the same heading, apparently oblivious to any British movement.

"Take us to larboard," he muttered to Brehaut. "Mr Caulfield, I fear it will be the starboard guns after all. We shall run down on her tail."

Yes, that should certainly be the case, *Prometheus* was already a good few hundred yards to windward, and more would be gained while they were turning. With the breeze in their favour they must close at speed, and should still deliver a sound raking even if they were spotted at the last moment.

Brehaut began ordering the manoeuvre as Banks allowed all on the quarterdeck a brief smile; this was going to be easier than he expected, and there would be no call to endanger his ship on a lee shore. If fortune were still on his side, he should shortly disable one of the frigates. The other Frenchman, however powerful she may be, would then have to pull back, leaving *Prometheus* free to continue to Toulon, and the safely of Nelson's fleet. The ship's head was turning, they would soon be round and could then pick up speed. Caulfield caught his eye, and Banks actually saw him open his mouth to speak. But he never heard what his friend had to say, as it was then that the broadside struck them.

* * *

It came across their stern and starboard quarter, and proved as devastating as it was unexpected. For all their thoughts about being elsewhere, the larger French ship must have been following her companion, on the same course but to windward, and was completely missed by *Prometheus'* lookouts. Consequently she had come out of nowhere, and there was no doubt she carried a heavy armament.

Banks went to pull himself up from the deck where he had fallen. He had a sharp pain to the left side of his skull, and he needed to grit his teeth to make his brain think clearly. When the enemy fell upon them, *Prometheus* had been in the process of recovering from her turn. Even now her canvas flapped wildly; the ship was without control, yet remained trapped between two enemies.

He tried to rise further, but something was stopping him and the effort caused the pain in his head to increase until he was forced to let out a pitiful moan. He brought a hand up to discover his scalp was torn and bleeding. All about the deck was scattered with debris, both human and otherwise. There were several blocks and other pieces of tophamper amongst the detritus, and Banks guessed one of those must have struck him.

Then vague but troubling thoughts that they were about to be targeted again took precedence. "Starboard the helm," he yelled, despite the pain doing so caused. It was important – vital – that the ship was brought back to the wind and then hidden: there was a convenient bank of fog to larboard that should suffice for the time being. He levered himself up to his knees although was unable to progress further, and there was a ringing in his ears that he normally associated with the sound of his own ship's gunfire. "Starboard, I say!"

But no acknowledgement came from the wheel and, even in his disorientated state, Banks could gauge the ship's motion. The rudder must either be unmanned, or was no longer functioning.

A lantern was uncovered from the area under the poop that usually accommodated his quarters and, by its light, Banks was able to make out a little more of his surroundings. Of Brehaut and Caulfield he could see nothing; there was a midshipman, clearly wounded and making an odd primeval crying sound as he nursed his belly. And the crew of the nearest carronade would appear to have been entirely wiped out, partly by French shot, and partly by their own, upturned, weapon. Several marines lay on the deck in attitudes of peculiar abandon, and there were seamen staggering, dazed and confused, at almost every quarter.

The captain blinked and drew breath. "Quartermaster, take her to larboard," he repeated in desperation while trying, yet again, to stand. But still there came no reply, and he was about to begin crawling forward when he saw the reassuring form of Brehaut, the sailing master, approach.

"We are back under rudder, sir," he said, the Jerseyman's voice sounded wonderfully matter-of-fact as he squatted down to his captain's level. "Wheel was hit, but I have stationed men, and we are using the auxiliary tackle in the gun room; they are putting the helm across now." He glanced up, seeming to ignore Banks for a moment. "Braces there – meet her as she comes. Mr Knolls, set your men to attend that mizzen stay!"

"Where's Michael Caulfield?" the captain found himself asking, but there were more important things for Brehaut to do.

"Mr Hunt, we appear to be short of waisters, I should be glad if you would send a party to the main braces."

Banks waited while the sailing master brought the ship back under proper control, then tried to rise yet again as they entered a bank of dense fog.

"You should be taken down to the surgeon, sir," Brehaut told him in his usual, unaffected manner, although Banks would have no such thing. He gave himself another heave, and was finally able to stand, by gripping onto the sailing master's watch coat.

"You must have been knocked cold," Brehaut said, one hand cautiously supporting his captain. "I had thought you dead, and considered it best to attend the steering."

"You did right," Banks murmured, adding, "what of the enemy?"

Brehaut looked out into the cloud filled darkness. "Not seen sight nor sound," he said. "And it must be a good five minutes since they first struck. I'd say it were a true hit and run; her captain probably didn't relish returning to the wasp nest he'd disturbed."

Despite Banks' dazed state, that made sense. The heavy frigate would have no way of knowing the damage they had caused and even a partial broadside from a two decker could do them serious harm.

"We must secure the ship," Brehaut continued, conscious that he was the only one capable of reasoned thought. "Mr Hunt is unhurt and attending our damage. I should like your permission to summon Mr King from the lower deck."

Yes, King would take the situation in hand, Banks supposed. But there was something nagging at the back of his mind. Something that was at once important, yet also indefinable.

"Do that," he said, and noticed an immediate return of strength. "Take me to the binnacle," he added. "I can rest there and support myself."

Brehaut duly dragged his captain the few paces to where the wooden structure stood, mercifully untouched, even though the remains of the ship's double wheel, as well as those who had attended it, were strewn about the deck in an unspeakable mess. Banks gripped the cabinet and took consciously deep breaths; his head still ached but he was definitely growing stronger and felt able to assess himself properly.

Apart from the head, there was a universal ache that encompassed his entire body, almost as if he were suffering from a fever. That and the darned ringing in his ears which seemed to be putting a block on all constructive thought. But about him men were working. He could hear the crack of axes on wood, shouts of orders or complaints and the occasional sob. Someone was attempting to brace up the mizzen mast, but it was impossible to tell if they were being successful.

"I'm going to have to leave you now, sir," Brehaut's apologetic voice came from nowhere, indeed Banks had already thought him gone.

"Very good," he replied automatically. Then what he had been searching for was suddenly found; he looked towards the departing sailing master and asked the question yet again.

"Where's Michael?"

* * *

King had been taken by surprise as much as anyone, although the damage to his gun deck was not significant. The frigate's broadside struck them at an angle, most of her shots were high and none penetrated the heavy timbers of the lower wales. But the unexpected attack had unsettled his men, and he was still calling for order when a white faced midshipman appeared at the aft companionway.

"Captain's callin' you to the quarterdeck, Mr King," he told him. It was Brown, the other lad implicated in the assault on *Prometheus*' passenger. "They've been hit bad," he spluttered. "Our wheel's taken and first luff's split in two by a round shot."

"Shut up," King snapped in a mixture of anger and horror. To speak so in front of two hundred men trapped on a gun deck was foolishness of the highest order, and he was so enraged that the loss of his friend hardly registered. But as he clambered awkwardly up the companionway, King found he was breathing hard, and there was a pain in his chest as if something far too large was being contained within. He did not doubt Caulfield was dead, but already knew he would take a while to totally accept the fact.

Conditions were much the same on the upper gun deck; King decided it must have been the quarterdeck and above that had taken the brunt of the damage. Corbett raised a hand and made to step in his direction, but there was no time for delay and King turned for the next companionway. And when he emerged into the cold night air, it was just as he feared.

Necessity had caused lanterns to be lit, which showed the true devastation. Rain was now falling, and bodies lay at every station, but King was experienced enough to look beyond these. Their wheel being out of action mattered far more; that and the work some of Knoll's men were carrying out to the starboard mizzen chains.

"We've lost five shrouds and the starboard backstays," the boatswain reported without being asked. "I'm rigging preventers, but don't expect the mast to hold if you're thinkin' of any fancy sailing."

King had no plans for anything of the sort; his only intention was to secure the ship, and fully assess her damage.

"Tom!" It was the captain's voice, and he turned to see him standing unsteadily next to the binnacle. His face was oddly distorted, and there was a stream of blood flowing freely through his hair and down the side of his face.

"How is it with you, sir?" he asked, although the words seemed to have been spoken in the midst of some terrible dream.

"The wheel is taken," Banks replied, foolishly pointing in the direction of the nearby wreckage. "And I cannot find Michael."

"How are we set?" King asked, turning to Brehaut who had appeared from out of the gloom.

"All plain to the t'gallants," the sailing master reported promptly. "Steering nor-nor east. The Spanish coast is just off our larboard bow, but we should clear that for sure, and Cape Creus lies twenty five miles beyond."

"Will we round that?" King asked, as Hunt lumbered up to join them, his face badly bruised.

"I believe so," Brehaut chanced. "Though the moon shall be risen by then, so we should know for certain."

"And the enemy?" For all King knew, one or more of the liners might easily be hiding in the mist.

"Two frigates," Hunt informed him. "The heavier is probably still to windward, the other was in our lee, but has not been sighted for some time."

"Very well," King drew breath; this had all happened so quickly his mind was reeling, although there remained something strangely comforting about being on the quarterdeck. And the fact that he apparently had control did not concern him in any way.

"You have made arrangements for the wheel?" he demanded.

"Yes, the auxiliary tiller is manned and in position on the rudder head." Brehaut replied. "There is a midshipman and a master's mate stationed to pass directions. A quartermaster's mate is in the wardroom and will supervise steering."

King glanced round and noticed Adams had been brought up

from the deck below, and now stood under the lee of the poop. Despite his relatively sheltered position, the midshipman's watch coat was billowing softly in the breeze. King looked further and saw three massive holes in the bulwarks, presumably made by shot that had caused such carnage on the quarterdeck.

"The lookouts are manned?" King grunted.

"Both mastheads have reported," Hunt told him, "and the forecastle. All guns are loaded."

"So tell me exactly, when was the last proper sighting of the enemy?"

There were several seconds' delay, as if neither officer wished to speak.

"Not for a fair while," Brehaut finally confessed. "And we saw nothing of the ship that caused the damage," he elaborated.

"Didn't even see her when she did," Hunt confirmed, gloomily. "Just the flash of guns. But she were powerful – for a frigate, I am meaning."

"And where was she steering – what course?" King snapped; really this was frustrating in the extreme.

"She struck as we were turning," Hunt again. "So assume her to have been on the starboard tack."

King took this in; the situation was not quite as bad as he at first thought. *Prometheus* had been hit some while before; if either of the French had a mind to close, they should have done so by now. And no tell-tale fire had been started to give their position away. There were lanterns in use for sure but most hung below the level of the bulwarks and hammock stuffed side netting, while he could trust the reflected light to be lost in the ever increasing fog.

"Ask Mr Roberts to report, if you please," he ordered, but the carpenter was already approaching from the break of the quarterdeck.

"No significant damage to the hull, sir," the man told him. "Though the starboard mizzen channels is weakened. Mr Knoll is attemptin' to rig preventer stays, an' it's a new lower mast, but I should not like to trust it at present."

King nodded impatiently. He supposed they had been lucky,

but he would so much rather *Prometheus* to have been badly holed, than suffer the effective loss of her captain and first lieutenant.

"See to that, as soon as you are able, Mr Roberts," he said, pointing at the savage holes in their starboard side. "Stretch a bolt of canvas across, if nothing more permanent can be achieved." The damage was high above the waterline, but he did not wish for the glint of lanterns to betray their position. It remained vital the ship stayed as invisible as possible. As it was, the enemy had found them, even though they were completely darkened; he could not afford for that to happen a second time.

* * *

On the deck below, Bleeden and the others left at his gun were watching with detached interest. The broadside had shocked them as much as anyone aboard, and those previously nominated had gone to assist. But it was the duty of the rest to remain with their weapons, and they were happy to do so. Let those detailed for such work make the repairs, and clear away bodies. All knew the first lieutenant was dead, however, and there were rumours about the captain being hit into the bargain. But now Lieutenant King had arrived, things seemed to be getting back to normal. Something more personal was worrying Bleeden though, and he was particularly keen to settle the matter as soon as possible.

"'Ere, you're wrigglin' about like a bucket load of eels." Carter, a Londoner, informed him. "You needin' the 'eads again or somethin'?"

"Aye," Bleeden confirmed. Mr Corbett was distracted and this seemed as good a time as any. "Cover for me, will you?"

There were men stationed at the auxiliary tiller gear, but none took notice of him. Bleeden slipped past and, after a careful look about, into the officers' quarter gallery once more. Inside it was just as expected, and he pulled a face in private remorse. There was his planned booty, where he had left it; Bleeden pocketed everything bar one of the cakes of soap, leaving the third out of politeness: it wouldn't do if all the lieutenants had to go about unshaven, now, would it? Then, finally, he reached up to the open lantern and deftly shut the small door, closing down the light and returning the quarter gallery to its rightful darkness.

Chapter Twenty-Two

"Michael Caulfield's dead, I suppose," Banks pondered a while later. "We served together for so long, it will seem strange without him."

King shifted uneasily. The captain's wound had been attended to; a wide canvas bandage having been placed about his head by one of the loblolly boys, as Banks refused to quit the quarterdeck. And now he stood, or rather slumped, against the binnacle, occasionally blocking sight of the compass that Brehaut was so keen to keep under his eye, while making occasional comments that varied wildly in their relevance.

"Moon's due in forty minutes," Brehaut commented softly, and King was reassured that the remark had been addressed to him and not the captain. But could it really be so long since they were hit? No French vessel had been sighted in the meantime and visibility was still poor, although the masthead had reported a glimpse of the coast some time ago, and *Prometheus* remained set on her course to clear it, as well as Cape Creus that lay beyond.

For King was, unknowingly, following his captain's plan, if for subtly different reasons. He held few hopes the British would rescue them, his main intention in seeking the southern French coast, was simply to disappear. To King's mind such an extreme move would put *Prometheus* out of sight of all enemy warships by the time the moon rose, and may even leave them safe to proceed more directly towards Toulon when dawn finally broke.

"He was my premier aboard *Pandora*, don't you know?" Banks told them conversationally. "That would have been in 'ninety-six, or was it seven?"

King was about to respond when a call came from the masthead.

"Sail ho! Ship in sight, fine off our starboard bow," it was the voice of one of the midshipmen, King could not be certain who, and carried the edge of urgency that would have made all listen, even if it had been spoken in another language. "Less'n a mile off," the lad added, "an' steering more to the north."

King automatically looked to the captain, then away again, as the man had clearly not understood.

"I'd chance that to be the larger frigate," Brehaut said, in a reassuringly level voice. "She will probably be searching for us."

"So I was thinking," King replied. "Should we engage?"

"Not for me to say," the sailing master began. "Though I would not persuade you against such an action."

King waited.

"We shall be more vulnerable as soon as the moon rises. But at least this gives the chance to settle one before then; the other will be of little menace on its own, and might yet disappear before daybreak."

That made sense and King felt both glad and relieved that Brehaut was proving such a stout ally.

"Then take her a point to larboard," he said softly. "And let us see if we cannot pay back the earlier compliment."

* * *

Corbett was near enough to understand what was about, yet not be too involved, which actually suited him perfectly. He knew the captain remained on the quarterdeck, although all orders were coming from the second lieutenant, so guessed Sir Richard to be wounded in some way. And he was still every bit as keen to distinguish himself, so long as it could be limited to personal and independent acts of bravado; maybe leading, or repelling, a boarding party, or saving someone from certain death. Surely he felt no inclination to interfere with anything Tom King might have planned. The idea of commanding a damaged warship, especially one lacking both captain and first lieutenant, and currently running from a superior enemy, held no appeal whatsoever.

And on the deck below, Flint was equally happy to be kept out of matters that did not concern him. Mr Franklin, the former acting lieutenant, was now supporting Mr Lewis, who had moved up to full command of *Prometheus*' main guns. Flint didn't know how he felt about the former; he was old to be a midshipman, and had very publicly failed as a lieutenant, yet retained a measure of personal authority that was quite uncommon even in senior men. And Flint, like most seamen, respected such things.

There was a buzz that other principle officers had either been killed, or were out of action, but Mr King had gone to sort matters out. And there would still be a battle, he was sure of that. With at least two Frenchmen in the vicinity and several more besides, their guns would be in use before the end of the night. And this time it would be a proper target – no more long range pot shots at pirates, or pounding away against shore emplacements that had the annoying quality of being unsinkable. He still wanted nothing more than a decent ship to ship action; and preferably one close enough to let him see the damage his efforts were causing. And to kill Frenchmen – that was becoming an all embracing passion.

It was not that he blamed the French for his condition, and actually held no animosity for the people themselves. But the illness was continuing to spread, and no longer confined its efforts to merely sapping strength or taking control of his body. It now left him with an inexpressible feeling of anger and frustration: one that was impossible to exhaust or deny. And if the French, for so long his country's sworn enemy, provided an outlet for both, he supposed they were almost doing him a favour.

* * *

King had little idea what was in the enemy captain's mind, and only a rough notion of his own intentions. But he did know that bringing *Prometheus* close to even a heavy frigate could only be of benefit. Apart from a couple of quarterdeck carronades, the British ship's fire power remained unaffected, while the carpenter and boatswain, though both limited by the caution inherent to their trades, had pronounced the mizzen solid enough for the current state of wind.

The final point was one that bothered him slightly. Their

breeze had been constant for so long he had naturally assumed it would remain so, but in the last fifteen minutes a number of minute variances were signalling a more permanent change likely. In fact, there could be no doubt about it; he had already noticed a slight increase, and the banks of cloud were definitely starting to disperse. If it were to gather strength further, they would disappear completely; in half an hour *Prometheus* could be left in stark moonlight. Then speed would become more important and he must return to worrying about the state of the mizzen.

But at least one minor annoyance had been solved, Captain Banks having finally been persuaded to rest in the chart room, the small cabin set to larboard and under the lee of the poop. He had been gone for several minutes, and King sincerely hoped he was asleep.

"What do you see there?" he bellowed to the maintop, and was reassured by the brief delay that showed those at the masthead were checking before making a reply.

"Nothing of the enemy at present," the young voice which belonged to Bentley, told him. "But there's still a solid bank of fog about their last position, and we thinks them to be hiding within."

"Anything elsewhere?"

"No, sir." The news was hearteningly positive. "We're running a constant sweep and have clear water to windward for upwards of a mile."

King supposed that was also reassuring. Even if the heavy frigate had managed to escape, *Prometheus* was still heading away from what the French would regard as the obvious course. For the British to allow a following wind to take them towards a lee shore was probably the last thing the enemy would suspect.

"Deck there!" it was the main lookout again, but this time the voice held a note of urgency. "The fog's clearing ahead, an' we can see topmasts."

King and Hunt, who stood nearby, exchanged glances; if their masthead could make out the enemy, it was likely to be visible in return.

"It would look to be the frigate, though she appears to have changed heading, and is steering northwards, roughly a mile an' a half off our starboard bow."

Still they waited on the quarterdeck.

"No, she's altering course, and coming round." Then, after a suitable pause. "She's tacking."

* * *

"Very good, gentlemen, I think we may expect action," King said, his voice oddly formal. The enemy were offering battle and, even if the inevitable broadsides banished any thoughts of staying hidden, he would be foolish to pass up such an opportunity. But there were ten minutes at least before the first shots would be fired, and King had something very important to do.

Rumours and tittle-tattle circulated aboard every ship, and one about to go into action was even more vulnerable to the eroding power of gossip. *Prometheus* had a good and loyal crew; men he could trust: men who knew the truth when they heard it, and would appreciate being informed of the situation. He flashed a look at Hunt, who was standing to his right. "Kindly send the upper deck aft; I wish to speak with them. And be sure that my message is relayed to those below."

It took hardly any time before he was looking down from the break of the quarterdeck and into a dark sea of faces that stared expectantly back at him.

"I thought you should all know what is about," he began, only mildly hesitant. "We have taken damage, though not severe, and *Prometheus* is undoubtedly able to fight." There was a rumble of approval, but he did not stop.

"However, many are aware we have lost officers, and I am sorry to tell you Mr Caulfield, our first lieutenant is killed." Now there was silence: he had the attention of every man on the upper deck, and probably most below. "The captain is also wounded, but not badly and will soon recover." He had insufficient grounds for the last statement, but could see no need for making matters worse. "I command at present, and have Mr Brehaut and Mr Hunt as well as the other lieutenants to support me. With luck Sir Richard shall resume his duties before long, but if anyone thinks of behaving differently in the meantime, they must change their minds this instant."

Still the silence, while King was now firmly into his stride.

"And you probably know equally well, there are Frenchmen in the area," this time there was a murmur of comment which King rode expertly. "And quite a superior force – or it would be, if only they were British." He had purposefully allowed an element of humour to creep in, and the men recognised the fact with isolated chuckles. "At present, a heavy frigate is bearing down on us, and will be within range shortly. I need not remind anyone we are a third rate, and can out gun and out man any of her size with ease. All I ask is you do not let me, the captain, or the ship down, and that the enemy is despatched with the minimum fuss."

Now came a muttering of eager anticipation and, as the men were dismissed, King turned back to Brehaut and Hunt who were nodding with approval.

"You hit the right note there, Tom," Hunt told him. "Why even that old smuggler Bleeden seemed happy."

* * *

And Corbett was also encouraged. A French heavy frigate would prove an excellent target for his guns while if, as he hoped, they could lay alongside, he was the perfect officer to lead a boarding party. Reynolds might do much with his marines of course, but Corbett remained confident of taking overall command. And if not that, then at least the glory.

"Ready starboard battery," he ordered, checking his midshipmen and quarter gunners were in position. The enemy had been reported as close hauled off their starboard bow, so there was little likelihood of the other battery being used. His guns were eighteen pounders: as big as any the French might be carrying, while below, on the lower gun deck, twenty-eight thirty-two pound monsters were also waiting to do their business. All any of them wanted was the chance.

* * *

The moon had finally started to rise in the east, and the frigate could now be seen from the deck. She was less than half a mile off, and heading almost straight at them, apparently intending to exchange broadsides as she passed. King could not help but think such an action to be rash for a single decker of any size. Two flashes came from her forecastle as he watched, and shortly afterwards the whine of round shot passed them by.

"Bow chasers," Hunt commented unnecessarily. "Chances are our friend is a touch impatient."

King made no reply, but noted the young officer seemed unusually stiff, and guessed nerves were starting to take control. All about was silent, the men were standing by their guns and waiting patiently, which was undoubtedly the best course of action. He wondered if the lack of Sir Richard's presence had unsettled Hunt, then dismissed the matter from his mind and thought instead of the oncoming battle. There was something in the frigate's headlong attack that worried King, and he knew he would realise what, if only he were allowed to concentrate.

"Okay, lads, it won't be long now," Hunt cautioned the carronade crews, and King was more certain than ever the waiting was affecting him. It must be very much the same in the French ship, he told himself, and *Prometheus* would present a far more imposing foe. He wondered briefly what he would do if some quirk of fate had placed him in command of the frigate, and then, in a rare flash of insight, it came to him.

"Make ready to turn to larboard," he warned, and Adams, the midshipman stationed under the poop, sprang to attention.

"Turn to larboard?" Hunt questioned, and even Brehaut, standing next to the binnacle, looked round in surprise.

"I expect her to tack, and lay across our hawse," King

explained. Watch for the first sign, and move as soon as it is sighted."

He felt his face flush in the cold night air, and was conscious that several hands at the nearby carronades were considering him with interest. He may just have made a first rate fool of himself, but the French appeared too easy a target, and he was convinced a trick was being planned. And then, just as the doubts were beginning, he saw a flutter in the enemy's fore topsail.

"They're turning!" It was Brehaut's voice that rang out but, due to King's warning, all had been ready, and *Prometheus'* helm was put across almost simultaneously with that of her opponent. The frigate must have been no more than a quarter of a mile off by then, and clearly intended to present her entire broadside to the third rate's prow. As it was, both ships eased round until they were abreast of the other, with the British liner having a slight advantage in being a few yards ahead.

"Fire!" King yelled, just as one of the guns on the lower deck reacted early. Still, the remaining broadside blasted out a second later, and the increasing moonlight allowed those on the quarterdeck to see their shots tell.

"Beautiful, Tom, beautiful!" Hunt was bellowing in his ear, and King knew the young man's nerves had been chased away by the gunfire.

"She's taking damage," Brehaut commented more steadily as the enemy's fore and main topmasts tumbled in a muddle of spars and canvas. But even as the French ship was reeling from her injuries, her broadside roared back.

The first shots hit *Prometheus* almost immediately and soon the British ship's hull was comprehensively covered. King had assumed the frigate to be armed with eighteen pounders, although what was landing felt a good deal larger. But whatever its weight, the broadside did significant damage.

Several holes were punched through their starboard bulwarks, carrying seamen, gun crews and marines with them as they continued across the ship. And more material damage was caused to their fittings, with the clang of iron on iron being heard often, while clouds of dust and splinters rose up, and there was the unmistakable scent of burning. The starboard mizzen channels were hit once more, this time taking almost all support from the mast and, when the flag locker was struck, both poop and quarterdeck became littered with gaily coloured bunting. But the command group, such as it was, remained unhurt, and King looked to Brehaut and Hunt in shared relief.

"Upper battery ready!" that was Corbett's voice, and King blessed the fact that he had been able to keep his men at work serving the guns.

"What of the lower?" King asked. There was a pause before confirmation came from his previous station. Then, once more, the battleship shuddered to the mighty rumble of her broadside guns.

"Take us to starboard!" King's mind was leaping ahead, and had already recorded the fact they were steadily gaining. To turn now would allow them to rake the enemy's bows, whilst ensuring *Prometheus* cleared the nearby mainland. They turned slowly, and were late in sending their next broadside. But no shots were received from the French and soon the British ship was once more heading west, and out of the enemy's arc of fire. King watched in bemused silence as the next barrage was taken mutely on the frigate's prow and noted, with unconcern, that deadly flames were now starting to reach up from her inner depths.

"Can we take more sail?" he asked Brehaut, but the sailing master shook his head.

"We're risking much as it is," he told him sadly. "And certainly should not wish to place the mizzen under more pressure."

King glanced back to where his opponent, now stationary and very much ablaze, was effectively acting as a beacon to her fellows. He had won a minor victory, although there had been no merit in it – for a two decker to silence a frigate carried limited kudos. But soon the area would be swarming with Frenchmen; he could expect attention from the liners, all three of which were untouched, while any one would make a worthy adversary on its own.

"But we'll be clearing the Cape nicely," Brehaut continued, and King supposed he should be pleased. There was no chance of slipping silently to the west, however; their course was now advertised to the enemy who must surely follow. *Prometheus* was also wounded; her mizzen may not take repair, so she would be limited for speed and manoeuvrability. The wind was remaining stubbornly against them, and suddenly being trapped in waters bounded by the French coast, did not seem such a good idea after all.

Chapter Twenty-Three

Banks rose unsteadily from the chart room deck where he had been laid, and tried to think. He remembered *Prometheus* being struck by an unexpected broadside, and his own injury, sustained from the lump of falling tophamper, but little more. Certainly not falling asleep, and having to be helped into the chart room, nor specific details of the danger his ship was in. And there was an additional and undeniable feeling of emptiness deep within which warned that something of incredible sadness had occurred, although he knew not what.

He raised a hand to the tight bandage about his head and felt at the wound. It was tender, and hurt when pressed, but the pain was not unbearable, and there was no fresh blood. And he could stand; he needed to grip tightly to the chart room table, but the initial spinning sensation slowly eased, then he was able to take a step unassisted.

The door to the quarterdeck opened easily and outside the moon was high and gave reasonable light. He looked about. There were some remains left of their ruined wheel, but the bodies were gone – knowledge that it had been hit, as well as his sailing master's arrangements to see the ship remained under helm were slowly returning. There was Brehaut now, he was standing next to the binnacle, along with someone he could not identify who was dressed as a lieutenant. And it was then that he remembered about Michael Caulfield.

Something must have alerted the sailing master, for he turned and noticed him.

"Sir Richard," Brehaut called out, as he approached. "Are you all right, sir; should you be up?"

For a moment Banks gave no response, his mind seemingly elsewhere, and all on the quarterdeck were sure the concussion still affected him. Then he seemed to shake himself free of his thoughts, almost as if he were coming back to life, and Brehaut at least sensed he was returning to normality.

"Thank you, Master; I am much improved," he replied, and it turned out to be true; Banks was actually feeling a good deal better. He made for the binnacle to check their course and automatically took in the damage to his ship, while casting a critical eye at those about him.

"What of the mizzen stays?" he demanded, indicating Roberts and his men who were at work nearby. "Are they lost?"

"Not lost, sir," Brehaut told him. King had appeared from the darkness of the main deck, and the young fifth lieutenant – Banks could not recall his name – joined the others in staring as if he were an exhibit in some travelling fair.

"But will they serve?" He was in danger of losing his temper.

"In due course, sir," King said with his usual assurance. "Mr Roberts thinks there a chance all will be sound by mid-morning, and the boatswain has rigged auxiliary preventers to the starboard rabbets until then."

Banks nodded and was relieved when there was no answering pain. "And the rest of the ship," he snapped. "How is she set?"

"We are steering from the wardroom," King told him. "And have taken minor damage as well as some casualties, though only three guns are not in use."

"From that one broadside?"

"No, sir; we were in action since," King's voice now carried a measure of awkwardness.

"We fought the heavier frigate, sir," Hunt chimed in more boisterously. "And Mr King set her to rights. Took down her topmasts, then laid us across her bows and dished out the finest raking I have ever yet seen."

"She is taken?" Banks again, while he privately remembered Hunt's name.

"Not taken, sir" King confessed. "There was no time, and we still had the second frigate in the area."

"And three more liners thereabouts," Brehaut pointed out.

"Of course," the captain agreed, remembering the situation; then adding, "and you did well, Tom, I am confident."

"At present we are off the Spanish coast," Brehaut continued, indicating to larboard, although nothing could be seen beyond the bulwark. "Nearest land lies fifteen miles to the west, though we will soon be rounding Cape Creus. Then we may choose to shelter in its lee, or turn and continue across the Gulf of Lyon, as you wish, sir."

"What of the enemy?" the captain demanded.

"No sight for some two hours," Brehaut answered calmly. "And the moon's been up nearly three. The last we saw of them was the damaged frigate, and she were afire. Not seen the smaller ship at all, and never properly did, if the truth be known. Nor anything of the liners or that corvette."

But they had done well, Banks decided. *Prometheus* had been handled competently in his absence; she may have taken damage, but no man could be blamed for that. The important point was they were relatively safe and, once clear of the Cape, would be able to shelter. Come daylight, *Prometheus* was bound to be in sight of French territory, but it would take an age for any message to reach the searching ships, and by the time one arrived, the British should be with them also.

"Very good," he said after considering a little longer. "How long until dawn?"

"Three hours," Brehaut replied. "By then we should be past Cape Creus, sir."

"Then so be it," Banks grunted. "Gentlemen, you must take some rest. Have the watch below stand down, and make arrangement to turn in yourselves."

"There is the matter of the first lieutenant, sir." King began, but Banks interrupted.

"That he is dead?" he asked. "Yes, I do recall, and indeed am sorry." There was a pause and all three appeared mildly uncomfortable until the captain added, "Mr Caulfield was a fine officer and will doubtless be missed," almost harshly.

* * *

The following morning did indeed see them safe, with the hard and rugged outline of Cape Creus behind, while the blue waters of the Gulf of Lyon stretched out north and east. There was no trace of enemy shipping, and a gentle sun had chosen to bless them. But no one aboard *Prometheus* was fooled and seemed to sense this to be nothing more than the calm before the storm.

A French frigate had been severely damaged, and the powerful squadron it belonged to would doubtless be searching for them. Confined, as they were, to the western section of an inland sea, it could not be long before they were found; the only question lay in who would do so first, the French or the British.

Prometheus' watch system had been re-established, but the ship remained cleared for action so, taking advantage of the unseasonably warm weather, Banks called a meeting of senior officers on the ship's poop. They were seated about a mess table covered with one of the captain's best damask cloths. David had served them coffee and hot rolls – still acceptably fresh – while the carpenter's team were putting the final touches to their starboard mizzen channels, and working especially quietly to enable them to overhear.

"Mr Brehaut informs me we are slightly over one hundred and twenty miles off Toulon," Banks told them, although all present bar Marine Captain Reynolds would have been expected to know as much. "The wind is currently in the east and contrary. It would seem likely to change, but we cannot rely on that. If not, the best we can make is north by nor-east."

This was also well known, but still evoked a rumble of comment.

"Were we to steer so, I feel it likely the French would find us," the captain continued, his tone intentionally flat. "And, though Mr Roberts and his team are doubtless doing all they can, I understand the mizzen channels and their settings will require extensive repair, and cannot be fully relied upon until we make a dockyard."

At the mention of their name, the carpenter's men paused and gave self-conscious smiles, only to hurriedly continue as it was realised they were giving themselves away.

"So, we may stay where we are, in the hope the French shall not find us. Or head north, and further into the Gulf, in search of a more favourable wind."

This time the captain's statement brought no comment. Even Reynolds was sufficiently aware that to do so meant sailing into a dead end. And it would be a dead end with the wind effectively blocking them in.

"So what are your thoughts, gentlemen?" Banks asked.

* * *

But before the meeting finished, fresh news made the decision for them and, once more it was carried by a call from the masthead.

"Deck there, I can see topmasts beyond the Cape!"

King, who had been in the midst of suggesting they stayed put, closed his mouth mid-sentence, and all about the table held their breath.

"There are two ships at least," Jameson, who was on lookout duty, continued. "Though I thinks there a third about to round the headland."

The main landmass of Cape Creus was ten miles to the south, which meant the sighting would be little further away. And, as the wind had been steadily veering, the enemy were gradually gaining the windward gauge.

"Send a middie aloft with a glass," Banks ordered, and King caught the eye of Adams. *Prometheus* was currently hove to under top and stay sails; it would take no time at all to add top gallants and courses and possibly stunsails, at which point they should be able to match the speed of any French liner. But he was forgetting that Roberts, the carpenter, had yet to pronounce their mizzen safe, while he could only truly travel north for considerably less than a hundred miles before the southern coast of France rose up to meet them. And then, if the wind was determined to stay contrary, they would be firmly wedged against a lee shore.

"The first is clearing the land," Adams reported to a silent but intense audience. "I'd say she was a frigate." All at the table let out a sigh; frigates were in short supply in the Mediterranean Fleet; the sight of one must surely mean the squadron was French. "And at least three ships lie beyond."

Really the news could not have been worse, and Banks allowed himself a brief moment of anger, before rising up and addressing his officers.

"Very well, gentlemen, it seems the French are closer than we had thought. Mr Brehaut, we will be making sail as soon as I have spoken with the carpenter. And then I think we should prepare for battle once more."

* * *

Half an hour later *Prometheus* was under topsails, topgallants and staysails, with the bulk of the French ships now identified beyond doubt and in clear sight off their tail. King had the watch, as the captain intended delaying sending the hands to quarters, and was becoming accustomed to the slight delay and lack of sensitivity in the steering. Once more Brehaut stood by him, and the sun was still shining. Indeed it had turned into a very pleasant morning: doubly welcome this close to Christmas. King could not help glancing back at the enemy, their sails seemed unusually white in the fresh, clean air, and under bright, though impotent sunshine, they might have been nothing more than a massive yachting expedition, rather than a battle squadron intent on their own death and destruction.

"We should sight what is marked as Cape Béar at any time," Brehaut stated calmly. "Once that is rounded it will be up to the captain. There are two or three miles to claim to the west, but only that, and the coast begins to curve steadily eastwards from then on."

"I can see no benefit in allowing ourselves to become cornered," King added. "Though the Gulf itself is as much of a trap, if on a larger scale."

"It is fortunate the wind has changed, however," Brehaut mused. "At least we can make some semblance of an easterly, though not enough to raise Toulon."

"Nowhere near," King agreed. "And with three prime liners to windward..." He was too tired to finish his sentence; there could not be many aboard *Prometheus* unaware of the situation, and that it was hopeless.

The ship's bell rang and both men knew they had only an hour of duty left until claiming what comfort there would be in a ship cleared for action. To starboard, Roberts and two of his mates were still annoying the damaged mizzen channels, even though the carpenter had declared that nothing more could be done on more than one occasion. The mast should hold in anything up to a steady breeze – above that little could be guaranteed, so it was doubly irritating that any future change of course must be to starboard while, in normal circumstances, they would have been praying for a decent storm.

"So what are the options?" King asked finally, his voice now low.

"Remarkably few, I fear," Brehaut replied, equally softly. "We can make as much as we can for the east, but that will only bring the enemy about our necks the sooner, while to continue steering north must end on a lee shore, and somewhere near a town named Narbonne, if I'm any judge."

"We might yet be rescued by the Med. Fleet," King reminded him, but the sailing master gave a dismissive shrug.

"It is something to be borne in mind, Tom, and may well cheer the people, if the captain feels the need," he spoke in barely a whisper. "But do you seriously think it an option?"

King said nothing. Brehaut was right, to be rescued so would entail such a series of unlikely coincidences that he really should discount the prospect. No, far better to take a mature view: they faced impossible odds, and were slowly, but steadily running out of sea room. That there would be a battle was as inevitable as the fact they must surely lose.

But much depended on how they did so. Captain Banks could take what many would see as the sensible option: fire a couple of token broadsides, before striking his flag and surrendering the ship in an effort to save life on both sides. That was probably the most civilised ending, although one that King at least did not expect to see, as it would mean handing over a prime line-of-battleship to the enemy. Some would consider such an act a minor defeat, but to those aware of the current situation, it spelt disaster on a far larger scale.

Were the enemy then able to avoid the scaled down blockading squadron off Toulon they could bring their capture home in triumph, where *Prometheus* would be refitted for French service. Then she might sail in company with a revitalised fleet, one large enough to take on all of Nelson's ships and crush them by sheer numbers. With the Mediterranean Squadron so destroyed, the French would be free to head south for the Atlantic where they would cause total havoc with each blockading force in turn, until a fleet capable of holding the English Channel was assembled. Three days was all Bonaparte claimed necessary to see an invading army across that narrow strip of water: with such combined power, the enemy might hold it for three months.

Or *Prometheus* could be scuttled; that would be preferable to seeing her serve under an enemy flag, and there should still be a general saving of lives. But King was equally sceptical about Sir Richard Banks ordering such an action, and doubted whether many of his officers or men would obey him if he did. Ignoring the political implications, and an imaginative French press would make much from the meek self destruction of a British line-of-battleship, it would also burst the illusion of invulnerability the Royal Navy had established over this, and the previous war.

No, the only option seemed to be a full scale action; one where *Prometheus* was effectively sacrificed in exchange for as much damage as could be caused to her tormentors. If they were lucky, the French may be wounded enough to make their own destruction inevitable. And if not, if the battleship was destroyed without leaving a suitable mark on the enemy, she would still have gone down fighting. It might be considered a wasteful gesture, certainly when the loss of life that must surely follow was assessed, and the war would not be brought to an earlier close. But neither would the battle have been given up entirely in France's favour. And, when judging the options Sir Richard Banks faced, King was reasonably certain which would be chosen.

* * *

"I don't care what private arrangement you have with Mr Manning," the surgeon's mate told Flint. "Laudanum ain't a drug we're allowed to dispense on an ongoing basis, an' without anything official written up, I can't give you nothing."

Flint snorted in disgust. It wouldn't have been so bad if he'd known about this before declining his grog ration, but one of the stipulations Mr Manning insisted upon when giving the magic elixir, was that he remained stone cold sober. Flint understood rules were being broken, or at least bent, although was now at the stage when the twice daily dose, one taken at midday, and the other at the end of the second dog, was all that kept him going. It gave rest – sleep even – and, most of all, a temporary reprieve from the pain that otherwise ran rife about his entire body. With those few hours of peace to look forward to, Flint could continue: without them, he may as well end it all now. And then a jumped up loblolly boy from the Smoke says there is nothing written down...

"I want to see the surgeon," he muttered.

"You can, eventually," Blake told him. "But will have to wait in line. We've been up to our armpits in wounded since last night, and there's still a good few what needs further lookin' at." The young man was about to turn away but, seeing the pain in Flint's face, relented slightly. "Look, Mr Manning's asleep right now, and I ain't the one to wake him. But he's expected back by six bells, arf-noon watch. Why not try then, and I'll see if I can't get you in?"

Flint gave a grudging thanks, and stumbled off along the orlop. There were indeed a lot of men lying wounded; all seemed to have been attended to, but some might still be in more pain than he was. And his own ailment had been around for quite some time now, so really he should be getting used to it.

* * *

"Gentlemen, I think we should beat to quarters," Banks addressed his officers with some formality. No one knew what the next few hours would bring, but it was likely to be the last time he gave such an order, certainly to those about him, and on that particular quarterdeck. In twenty-four hours some were likely to be dead, with *Prometheus* herself nothing more than a wreck. A few may make it into captivity, and even find themselves exchanged, although such civilised arrangements had been scarce so far in the current war. But the French squadron was gaining on them and, now that the southern coast of France was not only in sight, but steadily spreading until it stretched across their starboard bow, all knew the time for their final action was close.

But at least the wind was being compliant to some extent. Since mid morning it had veered slightly, and Banks would be able to take the ship further to the east. Not much, and nowhere near enough to place Toulon in their sights. But it might allow them time to force a night engagement.

All that was in the future, though; for now Banks stood motionless while three Royal Marine drummers beat out a stirring rhythm, and the ship's bell sounded. The hands swarmed to their battle stations eagerly enough. They had hot food inside them – he had ordered the oven lit especially, while the noon grog issue would still be having some effect. And most, he was quite convinced, were actually looking forward to the action. They might not regard themselves as potential victors – only a fool would be so misguided when the enemy's strength was there for all to see. But they had a good ship, with sound officers, and the slaughter of one frigate remained fresh in their minds. Whatever the afternoon brought, it was not going to be boring.

"Do you wish for me to remain on the quarterdeck?" King asked. With Caulfield gone, he was officially the first lieutenant, and had every reason to leave the command of the lower deck to Lewis.

"No, Tom. Much as I would appreciate your presence, we

shall need our guns working at maximum efficiency; you are better placed below."

"Very good, sir." King replied, before adding, less formally: "and are you quite well in yourself?"

The captain gave a brief smile. "I am splendid, thank you." In fact his head was hurting once more, but Banks felt he could at least think straight, and was fit to command – which was probably what the young man had meant. "And have yet to thank you personally for what was accomplished yesterday."

"She were only a frigate," King replied, mildly abashed.

"But we were damaged, and both Michael Caulfield and I were not at hand." At the mention of the first lieutenant's name, both men gave a slight start, as if having briefly forgotten.

"I heard from Brehaut that you spoke to the people: that was exactly the right course," the captain continued. He noted that King was actually blushing now, despite his tan, and guessed him keen to get to his post on the lower battery. But although the two had served together a good while, Banks suddenly realised there was much that had never been said.

"Some men must be trained, and others contained," his voice was unusually soft. "You tend towards the latter, Tom, and that can only be for the good. And you were born to be a sea officer; it has been a pleasure having such a man under my command."

It was too much; King was acutely embarrassed, but Banks would not have taken back a word. Then they shook hands in the early afternoon sunshine, and both were fully aware that they did so for the last time.

Chapter Twenty-Four

As soon as Lieutenant King returned to the lower gun deck, Franklin was free to resume his usual duties. In the past, when an acting lieutenant, these had been as signals officer, and he still kept a fatherly eye on that station. But there would be no call for communications in the next few hours, besides Franklin now had new responsibilities, and ones he actually considered more important.

He made his way aft where a companionway led to the orlop and, once down on the deepest, darkest deck, took stock. The place was barely half filled and seemed unusually well ordered, bearing little resemblance to the horror that was his personal vision of hell, and all too common during a lengthy engagement. Two well spaced lines of men lay on canvas sheeting and, in the main, they seemed as content as any in their position could expect to be. At one end, three groups of sea chests waited under the doubtful light of a line of swaying lanthorns, and Franklin knew this to be the surgeons' operating area. It was empty now, but the stained sailcloth coverings showed that had not long been the case, and there were piles of what might as easily have been carpenter's tools on hand for when they were needed once more.

Franklin started forward, stepping carefully past the feet of recumbent patients, to where the surgeons would be found. To most, he was still just another warrant officer – at one time a temporary lieutenant, but since returned to his old duties, and nursemaid to the ship's young gentlemen. Only a few realised his obligations now also covered *Prometheus'* spiritual welfare, but those that did were pleased to see him.

One was Briars; he lay quiet and motionless between the body of a snoring holder with a bandaged head and Wainwright, a Royal Marine, who was singing softly to himself and might possibly have been drunk.

"What cheer, Joseph?" Franklin asked, seeing the lad.

"Well enough thank you, Mr Franklin." Briars replied. "Are you stayin' with us now?"

"I'll be here a spell," he told him, very much in the manner of a returning father. "But how's it with you?"

"Surgeon says I've lost my right leg," Briars announced in a mixture of surprise and doubt. "One moment I were walking the deck, the next, being carried down here."

"Well, I'm sure you're being looked after." Franklin said. "Mr Manning's a fine surgeon – he accounted for Mr King's arm after all, and he is now an active officer and as healthy as can be."

"It were Mr Prior," Briars explained. "Least that's what they told me; I can't remember much beyond the pain. Mr Manning has seen me since though and declared it to be a prime wound of the first rank."

Franklin wondered how such an injury to a young boy could be described so, but let it pass. "I have to check with the surgeons," he said. "But, if not needed, I might come back and sit with you, should you wish it," he suggested.

The lad nodded weakly, and Franklin rose up and headed forward once more. There could be as many as thirty bodies on the deck, some would have died without being brought down, with more returned to duty suitably strapped or bandaged, but still it was a fair haul. However, Franklin was aware of the ship's position and knew the number would grow before the day was out. There was no sign of Manning, but his assistants, *Prometheus'* two surgeon's mates, were seated at the farthest end of the orlop, and Franklin approached them.

"Happy to see you back, Mr Franklin," the older one, Prior, called out although he also raised an eyebrow at the irony in his greeting. "Nothing for you at present, though there are those who might benefit from a word, and you would be welcome to assist the loblolly boys when we see action once more."

"I thought I might read a passage or two," Franklin explained, holding up the brand new volume of the New Testament that Kennedy had kindly provided. "For those who care to listen."

"That would be fine, Mr Franklin," Blake, the other surgeon's mate told him. "There's bound to be a few who'll appreciate a decent story."

* * *

"Take her to starboard – as far as she will go," Banks ordered, and the sailing master looked up; first to the sails and then the weather vane.

"Port two points," he said, translating the captain's orders to the correct helm command, before listening while his words were relayed to those manning the tiller below. They would actually be steering north-east by north, which would hardly take them out of danger, but was as near to an easterly heading as *Prometheus* could make with the current wind. Probably more importantly though, it brought their broadside round; again, not ideally – only one of the Frenchmen would fall within their arc of gunfire, but at least it gave them a mild advantage.

Prometheus' weakened mizzen had allowed the three French liners to catch her. They now stood off to starboard, and were closing steadily, apparently intent on driving the British ship against the dark shore that blocked her way east, as well as to the north. The enemy were well spaced with the closest, to the north east, placed to deny any chance of their turning, while the most westerly was far enough back to risk a long range barrage. Brehaut guessed they would continue to be squeezed until *Prometheus* touched bottom or was forced to tack into the hateful wind. And then the French would present their broadsides as an impenetrable wall that spat devastation on the British ship's prow. But even if they turned, and allowed her to slip between any two, *Prometheus* would never survive the combined fire of a liner to either side. She would be dreadfully wounded, and must shortly die; probably without inflicting any major damage in return: a requirement that, Brehaut guessed, would be very much on his captain's mind.

But while there was sea room to claim, they might as well do so and *Prometheus* was still turning steadily until her bows pointed at a slightly thinner line of black which was the more distant shore to the north. Brehaut's charts gave scant indication of soundings, but what there were indicated a good depth. He estimated they had three hours before coming into any real danger of striking, and in that time the wind may even have changed.

But that was wishful thinking, he told himself. Little short of a miracle could stop those liners from inching ever closer. And it would not be long before they decided themselves near enough to a lee shore. Then each would turn and present their full broadside towards the stricken British ship, and the final chapter in *Prometheus'* distinguished story would have begun.

* * *

On the lower gun deck, King was totally up to date with the situation. It was daylight, after all; a delightful afternoon actually, and the enemy were in plain view from the starboard gun ports. Little could be seen of *Prometheus'* eventual destination, of course, but there was land visible to larboard, and King was sufficiently acquainted with the area to know matters had not eased. And even in his darkened underworld, he was seaman enough to realise the wind was not coming to their aid, and that such a thing was growing less likely. But there still remained the tantalising target of the nearest ship, that lay just within reach of his battery. And it was then that he suspected Flint must have been reading his mind.

"When we going to get a chance to fire on that Frog, then, Mr King?" the man asked, as King was taking his habitual walk behind the line of waiting cannon. The officer stopped and considered him. All were now aware of Flint's illness, but there seemed to be something extra in the pale, weather beaten face that afternoon. His individual muscles were working terribly, and there was an odd, translucent sheen to the skin, although Flint's eyes seemed more alive than usual.

"All in good time," King said, trying to make his words both consolatory and encouraging. Yet the others at Flint's gun seemed every bit as concerned and, as he looked along the dark, low deck, King realised that every man was standing ready at his station, apparently keen for the work to begin.

As was he: it could not be denied. In most actions a delay in sending off the first shots was customary: guns that had been loaded without haste were considered more potent, and it was generally acknowledged that an opening broadside would wreak the most damage. But King still found the temptation to fire almost irresistible. If they did so it would be at long range; few, if any, shots would tell, and those that did were unlikely to disable the enemy. But this was not the pairing of two roughly equal forces; the French were at a decided advantage and, with the time in which they had to fight being limited by an ever closing coast, King could see no reason to wait. He was even considering sending a request to the quarterdeck but, before he could, they received a welcome order instead.

"From the captain," the midshipman told him breathlessly. "We are to open fire on his signal."

"Close up there," King bellowed. "Target the nearest Frenchman, and set your pieces to maximum range."

The last instruction was a personal one. Each gun captain knew his weapon and some were bound to compensate for what they regarded as a tendency for it to shoot high. But King was having none of that; even ignoring the fact most gunners failed to allow for the tapering of the barrel, he intended every shot to go as far as possible, and would brook no argument from any with illusions of marksmanship. The men seemed to understand, and slipped their quoins out without a word. And as each captain began squinting over his cascabel, they allowed only for the speed of the ship and that of the target. There was hardly any roll; even if they fired at the very peak, it was unlikely every shot would reach the distant Frenchman. But should a few go high and damage tophamper, it would be for the better, as far as King was concerned.

Then there came the unmistakeable scream of a whistle, sounding shrill and urgent in the still afternoon air. The guns were cleared, each captain held their firing lines taut and, on the final order, the lower deck erupted to the sight and sound of their entire starboard battery being despatched in a simultaneous barrage.

Most immediately turned to serving their smoking charges, and there was the hiss of steam as sodden lambswool mops were plunged into iron that had suddenly grown too hot to touch. Fresh shot was drawn from the garlands, and relays of lads raced along the crowded deck in an effort to keep the hungry giants fed. But a few were spared the time to consider their handiwork, and several seconds later there came a muffled cheer.

"Straddled 'er nicely, sir!" Flint told him with a rare beam, and King noticed much of the colour had returned to his face. The other servers were just as pleased, and a premature sense of victory seemed to flow round the entire lower deck. They might be fighting a doomed battle, but at least their guns were now in action and, for most, that was more important than anything else.

* * *

"I can't see them allowing us another chance like that," the captain stated flatly as he surveyed the results of his gunners' shooting. They had caused no visible damage to the enemy; all spars appeared intact, and neither was there the tell-tale sign of smoke. But Banks was not downcast; he had been tempered in the furnace of battle and knew well that more subtle harm could have been done by the bombardment.

The French might have been shaken and, if not experienced, panic could easily set in. And some were likely to have been injured or died; the British shots might even have taken out an important member of the enemy's command group although, before that thought could turn into a hope, Banks rejected it. No, he did not wish for that.

But he had meant what he said; the enemy would not continue closing while *Prometheus* remained capable of hitting them; he should expect a change of tactics and, barely a minute later, was not disappointed.

"They're turning," Brehaut reported. "Yawing to starboard; I think they are intending a reply."

314

"Then we shall have to wear!" Banks ordered, and immediately the sailing master's attention returned to his proper duty.

"Stations for wearing ship!" he called, before glancing up at the sails. It would be a procedure not helped by the remote command of the helm, and the fact they were making such stately progress made it harder still. But the main fear was their mizzen mast. The complex combination of spars and yards was only lightly supported, and would inevitably be placed under strain. Once they were about, the wind would be taken to larboard, and *Prometheus* should be safer, but in turning they risked losing the entire structure, leaving them at the mercy of the oncoming enemy.

"Main clewgarnets and buntlines!" Brehaut called. "Spanker brails – weather main lee crossjack braces!" The procedure ran smoothly, with the sailing master never having received such attention from *Prometheus'* hands before, but they were yet to reach the moment of true danger.

"Up mains'l and spanker. Clear away after bowlin's. Brace afterwards." Then the clincher. "Up helm!"

The main topsail was full, while the mizzen had begun to shake, and *Prometheus* started to turn, with her afteryards being guided round as she did. Brehaut held his breath. And then, just as the ship was heading directly away and her vulnerable stern was exposed, there came a general gasp and he knew the enemy had opened fire.

* * *

So immersed was he in watching Brehaut handle the ship that Banks was also caught by surprise. He turned to see the first cascade of water erupt close by, but considerably to starboard of their taffrail. It must have been exactly the right moment to wear; either the French were oblivious to his intention, or had not bothered to delay their fire in order to change aim, but the nett result was the same and most of their shot fell harmlessly into the sea. Only one was taken aboard *Prometheus* and that, probably poorly cast and a stray, thudded hard against their larboard quarter gallery. The frail structure exploded into a cloud of splintered wood and fittings but the hull was not affected, and *Prometheus* could sail on, effectively undamaged.

"Overhaul the weather lifts, man weather headbraces – rise fore tack and sheet!" Brehaut was continuing as if nothing had happened, something that came as no surprise to the captain, while *Prometheus* still steadily changed direction. They were losing sea room, of course, but somehow that did not bother Banks. And he could also listen to the creaking and groaning of the mizzen with no more than mild interest. This action might not end well; the odds were simply too high for such an outcome. Already he was totally discounting the prospect of support from friendly vessels – even if British topsails were spotted, it was probable that *Prometheus* would be forced to strike before rescue arrived. But despite doubts felt in the past, he now sensed that not all his personal luck was exhausted. There remained a modicum of good fortune left, and it seemed likely to hold out, at least for the next few hours.

* * *

The feeling stayed with him long after *Prometheus* had made her turn and was heading, somewhat faster now, on the larboard tack. She was still close hauled, and rather nearer to the oncoming shore than before, but at least two of the French were being left behind as they clumsily turned in her stead. The third was very much in hand, however, and effectively blocking any chance they may have of ultimate escape, while the light frigate and corvette were standing further out to sea, mute spectators to the British ship's final hours.

"Ready larboard battery!" Banks ordered grimly. The nearest enemy was now heading for a spot in front of their bows, and it was strange how the afternoon sun made her appear such a thing of beauty. She was still upwards of a mile off, so there was small chance of significant damage, but it would be good to hear the guns in action once more, and he gave the order quite casually.

The ship rocked gently to the combined recoil and again the target appeared to have been covered. Too much water erupted in front to be totally certain however and, when it cleared, no major damage could be discerned. But two enemy ships had now received long range drubbings, whereas all *Prometheus* had suffered was a reduction in her officers' sanitary arrangements.

That situation could not last long, however. The southernmost enemy ship was closing on them fast and *Prometheus* had been comfortably in her range for some time. So when the Frenchman's starboard side finally began to glow with a fire that rippled down from bow to stern, it was almost a relief.

And this time *Prometheus* was hurt, and hurt badly. Her larboard side suffered a series of frame jarring thumps that made the fittings rattle and, in several places actually penetrated her sides. Two quarterdeck cannon alone were put out of action, their carriages and servers smashed into one horrible mess, and her brand new mizzen took a hit eerily similar to that which had accounted for its predecessor. This time the damage was considerably worse though; enough of the fresh pine having been removed to make the carpenter's attendance almost unnecessary.

"I should not trust it, sir." Roberts told Banks plainly after the most cursory of inspections. "She might go at any moment; it would be better if we struck all canvas."

But the captain would have none of it. To discount their mizzen while it remained standing would be a nonsense; once *Prometheus* was reduced to a fore and main, she may as well surrender, and he had more mischief in mind before that happened. The two further French liners were creeping up from the east; there would be no avoiding them, but still Banks felt he could stretch things out a little longer.

"Larboard battery?" he enquired, and Hunt, who was fully involved in sorting the damage to his carronades, broke away to glance down to the upper deck.

"Not yet, sir," he replied briskly. "A moment longer."

Banks grunted to himself and turned away in apparent disgust, although inwardly felt a little chastised. He might be the captain, and this was almost certainly his last engagement in the present war, but there was no reason why he could not have checked on the state of the eighteen pounders himself.

Then there came the shout from Corbett, and he did take a step or two towards the fife rail to hear what he had to say.

"We are loaded with round, sir," the third lieutenant told him frankly. "Can you name a target?"

Banks looked up at the oncoming ships. "Middle of the three," he shouted, pointing out to larboard before adding, "and see Mr King is informed."

Corbett touched his hat in response, and Banks turned to the sailing master. "Mr Brehaut, I believe she will stand a point or two further to larboard, if you please."

The liner they had fired upon last was now steering to ensure they remained totally trapped to the south, and the northernmost remained well beyond their arc of fire. As was the middle ship, although she should be within range by the time they turned.

"Ready upper..." Corbett began, as the ship's head came round, but Banks interrupted him with the order to fire. The larboard eighteen pounders and carronades were despatched almost simultaneously, with King's battery following a second later. And this time there was visible damage.

The enemy's mizzen topmast was struck and fell, and some degree of confusion must have been caused further forward, as the jib began to fly, apparently freed of all support from the bowsprit. Banks looked on with satisfaction; he could see no significant changes to the hull, but it would be strange if at least a few shots had not told there. And now the game was truly in play he gave no thought as to the number of killed or injured. They were trying to kill the ship; nothing more.

"I should normally suggest turning once again," Brehaut began hesitantly, and Banks immediately switched his attention to other matters. The sailing master was right, they were making better progress on that tack than he realised: the shore would soon be dangerously close.

He might simply call it a day, fire off another couple of broadsides at the southernmost ship, then run *Prometheus* aground as gently as possible, but Banks thought not. No, they would wear once more, he decided in a surge of exuberance. It might cost them their mizzen, but his command would remain a floating fortress; one able to do damage to anything foolish enough to approach. And he still had the overwhelming urge to make this last as long as he could.

* * *

On the lower gun deck, things were moving so quickly and giving him such satisfaction that Flint almost forgot about his ailment. He had fired his own gun at the enemy and pretty much seen the shot strike home. Then after they turned, Cranston, the official captain of the larboard piece, had very gallantly handed over the firing line. So two more shots were let off with that gun as well, one of which he was certain had hit.

And there was no chance of Flint sharing any of Captain Banks' finer feelings. He had lost mates in the past, and was no stranger to the emptiness of bereavement. But in his case the memories only deepened his resolve, and he wanted above anything else to kill Frenchmen.

There was no shame in his desire; he would be dead himself soon, if not that very day. And the French, being the traditional enemy for so much of his seafaring life, were a natural target for his anger. With luck *Prometheus* could even close, as he had long ago decided. The barky might be boarded, or send boarders herself. If so he was determined to be involved. Get to grips with the devils, and show them that, though he may be ill and weak, there was still plenty of fight left in him, and all would be used against them.

* * *

Brehaut took the order to wear once more in good heart. It went against his natural inclinations as a seaman but, since joining *Prometheus*, he had become accustomed to ignoring all but the most basic instincts. Besides, should Sir Richard have pushed matters too far and the mizzen fell, they would have to surrender; that part was obvious.

Prometheus would then be taken; she may still be of use to the enemy, although the French must first find a replacement spar, which would not be easy when every major port was under blockade. And he was professional enough not to wish for such a thing of course, even if it would save lives and bring an end to the action. Brehaut was not against killing or fighting in general but, when in such a hopeless situation, he could see little purpose in continuing. In fact he wished more than anything that it might all end shortly.

And his next command might achieve exactly that. The wind was steadily growing: he would be turning the ship through its eye, and exposing the now doubly weakened mizzen in the process. And then they must take up the starboard tack once more, and so return to having their sternmost mast left barely supported. He was no carpenter, but could see the damage; the spar was a new one, and might be expected to hold out longer than most. But it would not do so indefinitely; perhaps time enough to see them aground off that slight prominence he had already noted, or it might as easily fail in the next few minutes. But whatever happened, it should be over before nightfall; of that he was certain.

Chapter Twenty-Five

Banks had other ideas, however. To him it was important – vital even – they maintain the engagement for as long as possible. There were numerous reasons for this, and all perfectly valid. Further damage would be caused, making the eventual destruction of three powerful enemy warships that much more likely. And by prolonging the action he was also detaining them; the British fleet were bound to come looking: when they did, the French would be as neatly trapped as he currently found himself. Then there was the final, indisputable argument, even if it was perhaps a little more sensitive. For as long as *Prometheus* continued to be fired upon, her value as a prize was also being debased. Even now it would take an English yard several months to set her to rights, and French shipwrights, working with erratic supplies of fittings and materials must surely spend longer.

But Banks' true reason surpassed all of these, and included an element he would hardly admit to himself. Ever since being caught too far inside Toulon harbour, his recurring dread had been to be found in dereliction of his duty. An early surrender would have brought just such an accusation; there were numerous cases of commanding officers being tried for the very same offence, and Admirals had been shot for less. To that point he felt he had done as much as could be expected, although there would still be gossip amongst fellow officers; men who could fight the most gallant of actions with the aid of pepper-pots, sugar casters and knowing nods from their dining companions. Banks had no intention of being so criticised and, while there remained any risk he might be, was determined to string matters out to their inescapable and bloody conclusion.

It was six bells in the afternoon watch. The sun was already well on its way to being hidden behind the nearby land, and failing light could only be to his benefit. He had no plan as such, just an instinct that told him darkness would be his friend, something that might not only draw the enemy closer, but also allow his personal luck one final crack.

And so far he was being blessed; twice *Prometheus* had changed tack without problems, and this was despite the now decidedly fragile mizzen and Brehaut's obvious reluctance. Reefing the mizzen topsail and striking their aft staysails had made the ship less weatherly, but still she made reasonable progress, and might be able to claw enough to the east to clear the oncoming promontory of black rock that grew steadily closer.

Not that so much safety lay beyond; even without reference to the sailing master or his chart, Banks knew the coast well enough. From then on the shore continued in a north easterly direction, something which they might feasibly follow for a while with the current wind. But in less than thirty miles it turned savagely east, ending in an unnamed bay set on the northern shore of the Gulf, that must surely become *Prometheus'* final resting place.

First though, he needed to gain another point to windward. Banks glanced up at the sails; there was certainly room there; an alert helmsman could have squeezed two, possibly three points without risking a luff. But to do so required sympathetic hands on the wheel, and their current method of steering was far too remote for such sensitivity.

"We need to clear that headland, Master," he said, raising his voice slightly to counter the wind.

Brehaut nodded, and looked forward. "A point now might do it," he said. "I shall try for more, but may lose her."

"Better to do so while we have space," Banks agreed.

"And we may try the forecourse, sir," the sailing master added. "Although there is the enemy to consider." Banks glanced to starboard, where the second of the French liners was steadily forereaching on them and might be expected to open fire at any moment. It was long range once more; when wearing, *Prometheus* had lost the sea room gained on the larboard tack, and the French were growing cautious enough not to take up the slack. But forward lay the first ship they had damaged. She was steering slightly to the west, and would be of more danger should Brehaut find that extra speed.

"I think we should," Banks said finally. "There is little to lose."

* * *

Once more the starboard battery was being called for, and Flint returned to his favoured gun with relief. The enemy had released a broadside in their general direction, but it lacked range, most of the shot falling short, with only one skimming off the water before bouncing impotently against their starboard upper wale. He had no idea where the French learned their gunnery but each ship seemed in equal want of practice. They must be unused to holding the windward gauge, and were failing to allow for the rising breeze. But Flint was not particularly bothered: as long as the enemy continued to miss, he would be happy. Besides, it looked as though he would soon be given the chance to teach the Frogs a proper lesson.

"Keep your aim high, lads," Lieutenant King cautioned. "In a race like this, knocking away a spar or two can account for an entire ship."

King was unconsciously working the stump of his left arm under his tunic, and Flint wondered if the strain of being in action was starting to affect the young officer. There was no shame in the reaction; he had noticed all manner of men be touched by the stress of battle in the past, although never had the symptoms been exhibited in such a way. But there was no doubting King knew his stuff. Flint, like all of *Prometheus'* gunners, would have much preferred to aim for the enemy's hull, such a target appealing to him as being somehow more British. But he duly pulled the quoin a little further out, and set his piece firmly on the French liner's foremast.

"Ready on the roll," King warned, and then there was a pause before the entire battery was released in yet another savage broadside.

* * *

"We shall make it with ease," Brehaut confirmed a while later, as he leaned over the larboard top rail and stared out towards the oncoming promontory. "Though I cannot speak for our depth."

Banks said nothing as the sailing master returned to the conn. Their captured charts were being annoyingly vague when it came to soundings. A hand, stationed at the larboard chains, was dolefully calling out no bottom with his line but, when so close to a headland, all knew the likelihood of grounding on a single pinnacle of rock, and it was probably significant that the French were staying comfortably offshore. But at least they were in the Med. – there was little to worry about as far as tides were concerned, and the only other current actually appeared to be working in their favour, as they would surely pass the Cape with almost a cable to spare.

The ship vibrated to the sound of another broadside, and once more the second of the enemy liners was neatly bracketed. Each French ship was releasing two barrages for every three fired from *Prometheus*, so were winning, if only on account of their superior numbers. But most of the enemy's shot continued to fall short. This could only be due to the angle of the enemy's decks as their ships heeled in what was now a sizeable wind. Such a situation could not continue, however; *Prometheus* would soon be clear of the headland and then benefit from a measure of sea room. But that would be eaten up in less than an hour, and then they must once more try to claw an extra point or two back. And this time it might not be possible; this time they could find themselves in the shallows, then aground – a sitting duck for enemy gunboats to finish off at their leisure. And even if they did not: even if fortune shined once more, and they were allowed to continue, the coast itself soon turned sharply for the east. Banks knew that must be the end of their game; the shore would form a solid barrier and only an extraordinary change of wind could save them from an ignominious end.

But darkness would be upon them before then, he reminded

himself, and was more determined than ever not to become downhearted. In the past twenty-four hours he had benefitted from more good fortune than he had a right to expect, yet still remained convinced there was a little extra remaining. If only he knew where, and how it should be used.

* * *

Two hours later much was changed. The wind had continued to rise, forcing them to strike their forecourse, and rain now came in tiny drops that were liable to increase in both size and number. And they were in darkness, or as near as could be found that close to sunset. For the sky was still light enough to show the three enemy ships to windward, with the pair leading having moved eastwards slightly, making further fire from *Prometheus'* starboard battery impossible. And soon they would pull back further: that was as predictable as the oncoming rain, for the British ship was about to be forced into a small bay, and they could already make out a glow of phosphorescence that was the lapping of waves against a cruel and deadly beach.

Banks sensed that time was running out, and knew his duty lay in securing the wounded. The injury to his head was hurting once more, and he pressed at the bandage in an effort to think. There must be a way to secure his people, while destroying the ship, and causing as much annoyance to the enemy in the process. And then it all suddenly ceased to matter.

He turned to Brehaut, who was standing as straight as ever, and noticed for the first time how devilishly tired the man appeared.

"Take her about once more, Master," he said, almost gently. "I intend to run her aground."

Brehaut blinked several times, before following his captain's gaze to larboard. They were close to the shore and there was hardly room enough to wear, but there were less signs of breakers in that direction and, on the few occasions when the lead had struck, the bottom had been revealed as sandy.

"Once round we can make the final provisions for abandoning ship," Banks added, enunciating the words slowly and with care. It was the worst speech any captain could make and, in doing so he actually felt to be betraying his calling. He turned to Hunt."Have the wounded brought up from the cockpit, and clear away all boats."

"Fire!" Corbett's command, shouted up from the main deck, conflicted so dramatically with his thoughts that it took Banks by surprise. For a moment he found himself watching bemused as their shots flew towards the enemy. There was still one Frenchman in range, and she was briefly masked by the water that erupted about her. But the feeling that all fighting must now cease was growing within him, and he muttered a gruff order to belay which almost went unheard amidst the fifth lieutenant's shouted orders and Brehaut's preparations for bringing them about.

He continued to view his enemy dispassionately. The ship that had received their last broadside was already badly battered, with a foreshortened bowsprit that lacked a jib boom, and it seemed that, for no obvious reason, the forward half of her lower deck guns were out of action. Her sisters were in no better condition: one was missing a mizzen with a small fire being fought aboard the third. Watching, Banks decided he must surely have done enough, and was content to let who cared to say otherwise. *Prometheus* had fared worse than any; being the leeward ship, she had taken far more shots to her hull and, even ignoring the carpenter's repeated warnings about the level in the well, Banks knew from her feel that she was starting to settle.

Brehaut was still bringing them round, and Banks stood in silence while his ship finally declined battle. It would be her last turn, and one that inevitably lead to her death on the nearby shore.

He reached into his pocket where his hand found one of Sarah's letters. It must have been written in their home near Portsmouth while she was still deciding when their child might be born. If all had gone well, he would probably be a father for the second time by now and, at that very moment yet so many miles away, his young family would be preparing for Christmas day.

The present war could continue for another five, ten, maybe fifteen years; Britain would be victorious eventually, but he should not expect exchange until then – such civilities being rejected by the new French regime. In that time his children would grow up with little concept of him as a father; he would be nothing more than a target for reluctant letters while, if he were to return, it would be as a muttering old man. One who only wished to talk about his exploits in wars that would doubtless have been forgotten and speak of the men he had known, and knew no longer.

Banks didn't relish the prospect of confinement, even though he knew it would be tolerated in the same way as other hardships had been during his career as a sea officer. But it was a shame that Michael would not be there to share the time with him.

* * *

Flint received the order to secure his cannon with disgust. His piece was gloriously hot, while he breathed in the acrid smoke that clouded the darkened reaches of the lower gun deck as if it were an exotic perfume.

"Ditch all ready-use charges and prepare to abandon." Mr King was still walking down the deck and giving the dreadful orders, but Flint made no move to obey. The gun was being heaved up one final time and, rather than presenting through the port in the usual manner, his men now secured the muzzle above it, before locking the train tackle as if for heavy weather. There would be the wounded to attend to; they being the special responsibility of those on the lower deck, and Flint supposed he should at least make an effort.

Despite missing out on his midday dose of Mr Manning's magic elixir, and with the evening's allowance almost being due, Flint actually felt better than he had for some while. All muscles and limbs seemed to be moving freely, and the intense physical exercise of the last few hours had reduced his chronic and nearly universal pain, to a bearable numbness. There was no change in his attitude, though; the ship might be about to surrender, with all preparing to meet an inglorious end, but Flint had a mind to continue fighting.

He moved away from the gun and started towards the aft companionway that lead to the orlop. There were no convenient weapons he could carry that would also allow him to deal with a wounded man, but his eyes soon picked up on something discarded on the deck that would do just as well. It was a pusser's dirk, the standard hand knife carried by every competent seaman. Flint was accustomed to wearing his on a lanyard, but always removed it when they cleared for action. Someone had not been so thoughtful and must have lost theirs in the heat of battle. He bent down and picked it up. It held a fine edge and, contrary to protocol, the point had not been rounded off. A perfect fighting tool in fact and, as he placed the line about his neck, one that Flint was determined to put to good use.

* * *

Fortune was staying with them; the ship completed her turn within a cable of the land, and was on the larboard tack once more. But it would not be for long. The wind whistled through the rigging, and all on the quarterdeck knew they must surely be swept aground at any time.

Hunt drew a deep breath, then raised his eyes aloft, calling for the tops and mastheads to be cleared in the same tone he would have used for a change of helm or canvas. Then the captain himself bellowed the final order that must see them wrecked.

"Strike the weather shrouds!"

Prometheus would be travelling in excess of five knots. When she did touch, it was important her masts and tophamper carried away. Many of the spars would probably be snapped or sprung, making them of less use to the enemy, yet the wreckage might provide support for those forced to take to the water.

The deck was unusually well lit, there no longer being any need for secrecy, and everything was being done with commendable efficiency. All boats, including Banks' brand new and freshly painted barge, now trailed to larboard, while the upper deck and forecastle already appeared crowded with bodies, both fit and injured, who were only waiting for the order to abandon. And on the nearby beach, dozens of lanterns showed where groups were assembling in expectation of the inevitable disaster.

"I see no reason to prolong," Banks said quietly to the two officers by his side. "Mr Hunt, you will oblige me by striking our colours; Mr Brehaut, call in the hand with the lead. And then you may take us to starboard."

Chapter Twenty-Six

Prometheus grounded less than two minutes later and the shock, though expected, was enough to send even the most sure footed seaman staggering. It may have been an outcrop of rock, or perhaps the sea bed was even shallower than anticipated, but the nett result was as if they had suddenly been sent sternwards, while the abrupt and odd solidity of the decks was almost as disconcerting. The masts groaned and cracked: to no one's surprise, the mizzen went first and in its entirety. Toppling sideways, and straining at the main with its stays and brace pendants, the whole affair crashed onto the dark waters to starboard, and was soon joined by its taller associate. The fore topmast followed, and *Prometheus* actually righted herself slightly, even though there was now a considerable tangle of tophamper that effectively tied her to the land.

From his position on the upper deck, Corbett glanced about; the captain was on the quarterdeck, and there was King coming up from below, amidst a mass of scrambling gunners from the lower deck. The ship's bell was ringing continually, but no one needed further persuading; their battle was over, all they could do was make the best of it – and friends with former enemies.

Corbett pressed his way to starboard through a mob of moving men. He peered through an open port and down at the dark water below. Some had already jumped and were keeping alive by swimming or gripping on to whatever piece of wreckage lay close by, but others were very definitely struggling. A few splashed ineffectively while screams from the rest were regularly cut short as the crowded sea closed over them. He looked up; the shore was still a fair way off but there were lamps ablaze and signs of rescue parties forming up, while three small fishing smacks were in the process of being launched. But *Prometheus* carried several hundred people and, unless something more practical was arranged, a good proportion were about to die.

Corbett supposed he might clamber through the port and join those in the water below. He was able to swim relatively well, and should keep one, or maybe two afloat, providing they did not all sink together. And then it struck him that this was probably the opportunity he had longed for. Order was required, and he was an officer; there must be a better way to organise a rescue, he only needed to discover it.

It would not take much to direct men into groups and set one or two swimmers with each. Make sure they had hammocks, or the like, and enough line to see they did not become separated, then send them off towards the shore. Or perhaps take charge of the ship's boats, all were launched, but would be unable to approach those struggling due to the tangle of lines and spars that littered the water to starboard. He might get himself aboard one, and have it rowed to the edge of the debris, then cut their way through and bring whoever they could to the shore. There was Adams; the midshipman stood by the remains of the sprung mizzen and seemed to be examining it with interest. Corbett was about to call for his assistance when someone else attracted his attention.

"That's your answer, sir," the voice might have come from the heavens, but in fact belonged to Charlie Bleeden, one of the gunners. Corbett turned to him.

"The main'll make an escape route," the former smuggler continued. "Get the lads down that an' they'll end up a darn sight nearer the shore, and in clear water, where the boats can reach 'em."

Bleeden was right; Corbett could see that instantly, and made straight for the forecastle ladder, yelling for others to follow. He was soon on the gangway and heading aft where he encountered the stump of the fallen main. It actually hung down below the level of the top rail but was far longer than the mizzen, and would be so much more suited to the task. The spar was wedged quite solidly; a number of lines being attached to the foremast, while still more draped down its length and would doubtless be of use.

"That's the ticket," Bleeden agreed, joining him. "You can be sure the lads will be more comfortable walking down a spar than swimming; get them to the end, an' the boats can carry 'em the rest of the way."

Corbett nodded, conscious that a crowd of men were already gathering and looking to him, as an officer, to set an example. "Follow me," he ordered, then swung himself over the side and began feeling with his feet for the mast beneath.

He was almost certainly the least able, but there were some things a commissioned man must do. And do successfully, he reminded himself. Were he to slip and plunge straight into the crowded depths below it would be the end of all thoughts of using the mast as a means of escape. At first his boots slipped on the weathered surface, but soon he was balancing upright, and starting to totter down the sloping trunk.

Then there were men behind him; their weight made the mast wobble, but Corbett kept his sights fixed on the nearby fighting top that would at least give him the chance to rest. One boot slipped, but he immediately felt support from the man behind and was able to recover. Then he was only a matter of feet away, and even broke into a slight run as he made for the top.

"That was well done, sir," Bleeden, who had been following, told him. Corbett nodded, even though his breath now came in gasps, and there was an odd giddy feeling that would not go. But the lower mast was already filled with more capable climbers, and he was holding things up.

"Come on," he said, heaving himself past the heavy structure of the top, and finding the main topmast beyond. This was thinner, but they were also closer to the water, so any slip need not be so devastating. And Corbett felt he had already set a sufficient example; he walked down the spar with far more confidence, and actually slid the last few feet as he reached out for the smooth timbers of the crosstrees.

"Grand work, sir," Bleeden told him with rare bonhomie, but Corbett was breathing too hard to reply. He hung on for slightly longer than before and, only after being totally certain of his safety, did he glance back.

The entire main mast was filled with escaping men, their bare feet being far better suited to balancing on the wide, but slippery, spar. And the first group were already past the top and would be with them shortly. Encouraged, Corbett nodded once to Bleeden, then pulled himself around the crosstrees, and onto the topgallant mast.

Now the sea was close and lapping beneath his feet while spray splashed against him as he tottered on, hands stretched wide to aid balance. The mast might end in the sea, but was clearly touching bottom, and there were only fifty or sixty feet of black water beyond before the first of the waves crashed against the shore. The mast bowed; Bleeden was behind and another followed, with more than twenty or so after. Men who would have panicked had they taken straight to the water, but felt comfortable enough walking along a yard at any height.

The sea met him half way up the mast. Corbett lowered himself in but could not touch the bottom which he guessed to be several feet below his boots. He felt about the spar as Bleeden joined him.

"Are you a swimmer?" Corbett demanded, but the seaman shook his head with a grin.

"Very well," he told him, "I have a line – probably a brace pendant." Corbett gasped, holding it up for Bleeden to see. "And will try for the shore. Do not let anyone go until I am safe, and it is secured – do you understand?"

Bleeden, who was clinging onto the spar, nodded in agreement, and Corbett began to reel in the sodden Manila. He could not judge its length, but guessed it to be sufficient. Then he slipped his tunic jacket off and tied the brace securely about his waist, before pushing off and making for the shore in an improvised and ungainly doggy paddle.

After no more than fifteen seconds, Corbett knew it had been a mistake. He was no swimmer and, despite the lee of the ship, the waves were high and made him splutter and cough. And there was a current; the beach was apparently moving sideways as he struggled, while all the time more water ran up his nose and into his throat. Then, just as hope was about to be extinguished, he felt the glorious touch of land beneath his feet. It disappeared almost as soon as it came, but gave encouragement, and Corbett pressed on until his breathless body was finally rolling in a rising surf.

A strong hand lifted him up and clear of the water. There were two men who had come out to meet him and both began to babble in French. Corbett pulled at the line to show them; they seemed to understand and the brace was released from about his waist, then passed back to an unseen group further up the beach.

He coughed and choked some more, but allowed himself to be gently guided up the dark sand. Someone wrapped a rough blanket about him and he nodded in appreciation, before sinking down onto the welcome solidity of dry ground. He was exhausted and had nearly died, but the inner glow of satisfaction was undeniable. Out to sea the shattered husk of his former ship was hardly recognisable with her foreshortened masts and distorted hull. But there was already a constant stream of seamen coming off her down the main mast, and more would be rescued afterwards. And this was down to him; it might have been someone else's idea, but his example that had been being followed. Corbett pulled the blanket closer about him and knew an ambition had finally been realised.

* * *

Meanwhile Flint was lowering himself through a starboard gun port and into the darkness below. He had already helped carry one wounded man on deck before, on returning for a second, discovering the orlop to have been cleared. In fact the barky was almost empty, with a heel to starboard from which she would never recover that made movement about her decks difficult. And so he had chosen that gun port, it being nearest to the companionway, with the water barely inches below.

But once he was fully immersed a change seemed to come over him. The pain that had been blunted by exertion was awakened as cold water enveloped his body and Flint gasped in surprise. But he knew the beach to be close, a matter of a few hundred yards away in fact, and there were boats, their own, and those of the French, nearby. Flint pressed himself from the hull, and made to swim. There were lines tangled all about, and getting through took time and energy, but eventually he was in open water. Then he struck out, although after only two strokes his arms became unaccountably heavy. For several seconds Flint struggled, the water lapping against and into his mouth, before he turned back in desperation for the ship, only to find her well beyond his reach. Still he fought, crying out as the water closed above and feeling the darkness draw in about him. And it was then that an iron grip found his shoulder.

It was a boat hook, and had actually bitten into the flesh of Flint's upper arm, but the seaman could feel nothing but relief. He was steadily being pulled backwards through the water until his body was caught by professional hands, before being half lifted, half dragged over the stern of a small boat.

The craft tipped under his weight and that of its crew as they struggled to bring him aboard. Then he looked up and into the faces of unknown men.

"*Êtes-vous blessé?*" one of them asked, and Flint's eyes opened wider as he instinctively fingered the pusser's dirk that still hung about his neck.

"He is asking if you are wounded," another voice explained, although the accent was strong and hard to understand. "Jacques is the apothecary, and will care for you," the man continued.

"No, not wounded," Flint told them softly, and released his hold on the knife. "Not wounded at all. Though I am so very grateful."

Epilogue

"I have received a message," Kate announced importantly as she entered Poppy's room. "It is from Mr Franklin, he served aboard *Prometheus*, as you may recall."

The girl shook her head; the name meant nothing to her, but then she had long ago taught herself not to remember such things. And faces.

"He was writing from Marseilles but expects to be moved to Briançon shortly," Kate continued, holding up the papers for Poppy to see. "The French have him prisoner, and the letter took only a fortnight to arrive," she added in wonder.

"What news is there?" the girl asked from the comfort of her bed. It was gone ten in the morning but, since Mrs Manning put an end to her private enterprises, Poppy had become accustomed to rising late.

"Well some good and some not so," Kate replied, considering. "None of Mr Manning, I fear, though there are many still unaccounted for; indeed this is the first true information we have received." She moved on quickly. "But the captain is captured also," she said, glancing at the letter again. "Oh dear, poor Sir Richard shall not enjoy that. As is Mr Corbett, he was a lieutenant, and turned out to be something of a hero, it would seem. Mr Dawson the purser, Mr and Mrs Roberts and Mr Kennedy are safe as well. He lists a lot of other officers and seamen, which is kind, and there will doubtless be more to add."

"That is good," Poppy replied without enthusiasm.

"But some are sadly dead," Kate continued, flipping through the sheets of paper in a businesslike manner. "Michael Caulfield, the first lieutenant, Mr Knolls the boatswain, Mr Blake – I think he was the new surgeon's mate, though we never met. Maxwell, the quartermaster, Clement he was a boatswain's mate – far too many, and it is not a complete list."

There was a pause while Kate surveyed the girl more

carefully.

"And there is news of Joe Briars," she said at last. "Along with Jackie Brown; they were midshipmen: you will remember them, I have no doubt."

Poppy was silent, but her dark eyes had become fixed on those of the older woman.

"Mr Franklin says Briars asked after you," Kate continued. "I cannot truly tell from what he has written, but assume much to have been said after we left the ship. Certainly he is aware of a wrong done by the boys and you would seem to be in some way involved."

Still the girl said nothing, although Kate noticed she had settled a little deeper into her bed.

"Poppy, I have no idea what this is about, but it seems the lads expressed regret for whatever they did."

"Regret?" Poppy snorted. "They didn't seem so very sorry at the time."

"Probably not," Kate agreed, "But please have some understanding. I can only suppose the circumstances, though were young myself once – and there is no need to look at me like that, miss." She paused and sighed. "As I say, I know not what went on, but accept that things can get out of hand..."

"No, you were not there," Poppy agreed. "Yet are content to believe the word of a boy and what some man tells you in a letter."

"How can I do otherwise when you will not say?" She sighed. "And however terrible it might have been, was what they did truly enough to send you back to your previous ways?"

"You do not know – you can not tell." Poppy turned away and began to address the wall. "And I am not able to explain."

"If you try, I will listen."

Time seemed to hang in the small room but in fact it was only a few seconds later that Poppy began to speak.

"I know how you feel about me and my trade," her words were slow and delivered so softly they could barely be heard. "And it must be fine to have right on your side; to know absolutely your opinion is correct. But you *are* right, I do not dispute it. No woman would wish to do the things I did for money. But it was that and survival, or something infinitely worse: I could choose whether to or not."

"Poppy, I am sorry, I don't see what you mean..."

Her head swung back and she stared her mistress in the face. "I mean I could choose who I lay with and on what terms. With the boys there was no alternative – they held me down."

"And that is different?" Kate asked.

"Oh yes," the girl replied. "That is very different."

Silence returned for a moment, then the girl placed both hands upon her belly, closed her eyes and appeared to lapse into a sulk. Kate considered her professionally; if the dates she had given were correct, Poppy should really be far larger than that.

"You are quite right," the older woman agreed as she looked at the letter once more. "This is just what one person has written. Although I do have every reason to believe Mr Franklin when he says they were truly repentant."

"It don't change a thing," Poppy declared. "There were four of them..."

"So I gather, and agree it was wrong, terribly wrong. I wish you had said something at the time, action could have been taken."

"And who was I to tell?" Poppy turned back, her eyes opening wide. "The captain? Do you think he'd have wanted to know his midshipmen behaved like animals? The ship were full of men, there was only you, and Mrs Roberts. I should have been a laughing stock in no time."

"You might still have told me – indeed I am a mite disappointed you did not: the Navy takes such things more seriously than you think."

"There were four of them," the girl repeated.

"I would have believed you," Kate maintained. "As would any woman. And I would have made the officers listen – you should have known me well enough for that."

Poppy's glance fell away once more and for a moment she appeared more interested in the edge of her sheet.

"Well, that's as maybe, but there is nothing that can be done,"

Kate continued. "It is a shame, but then you could say the same about the whole sad affair."

"Why?" Poppy returned angrily. "Because I am with child?"

"No," Kate said sadly. "Because they are all dead."

The statement reverberated for several seconds before Poppy focused once more upon her mistress.

"Young Cross died during the attack off Toulon, as you well know," Kate began. "And Mr Franklin reports both Brown and Briars were lost when the ship ran aground. Carley drowned in the action with the pirate ship – surely you must remember?"

"I see," she said, but no more. Then Kate spoke again.

"Poppy, you are correct, I was not there and don't know what happened. And nothing can make up for what they appear to have done. But they were boys, you must see that. Why Brown was barely older than you, and the others far younger – were you aware Briars only turned fifteen a few days before Christmas?"

There was now a total lack of response from the girl; she had settled under the sheet and might not even be listening. But Kate continued, if not entirely for Poppy's benefit.

"I knew all four relatively well and, though they undoubtedly behaved badly, that was as a group. I do not believe any one of them would have contemplated such a dreadful thing had they been alone. It must have been a shared madness; I have seen it amongst women as often as men, and girls as well as boys. They were in the wrong, it cannot be doubted, and you may not find it in yourself to forgive; that is your right. But perhaps consider those who have accepted your faults, and forgiven them. And, as I have said, they were just boys."

"Just boys?" Poppy questioned, from under the covers.

"Just boys," Kate confirmed.

"And they are all dead?"

"I fear so."

Poppy's head reappeared, and she seemed to be considering the matter for a moment. Then her eyes returned to those of her mistress.

"Good," she said.

Kate turned and walked quietly out of the room. She could understand the girl, and indeed had every sympathy; not just for what had happened with the midshipmen, but how she must be feeling in her stage of pregnancy. Kate could remember the misery she herself felt the first time, and was secretly relieved that, on this occasion, everything seemed so much better. In fact she was looking forward to the child with a joy impossible to describe, while an inner certainty told her this time things would be well.

But it was a shame that Franklin's letter had not brought more positive news of Robert. What she had told Poppy was correct; the French authorities were being annoyingly slow in confirming those held, although it was doubtless better to think her husband missing than dead. And not only Robert: Tom King, Lewis, Brehaut: so many of the men she had come to know were unaccounted for. Kate was no stranger to bereavement and understood the tricks a mind could play, but somehow she simply could not accept that they were all drowned. There must be another explanation: this could not be the end of the story.

Selected Glossary

Able Seaman	One who can hand, reef and steer and is well-acquainted with the duties of a seaman.
Back	Wind change; anticlockwise.
Backed sail	One set in the direction for the opposite tack to slow a ship.
Backstays	Similar to shrouds in function, except that they run from the hounds of the topmast, or topgallant, all the way to the deck. (Also a useful/spectacular way to return to deck for a topman.)
Backstays, Running	A less permanent backstay, rigged with a tackle to allow it to be slacked to clear a gaff or boom.
Banyan Day	Monday, Wednesday and Friday were normally considered such, when no meat would be issued.
Barky	*(Slang)* A seaman's affectionate name for their vessel.
Belaying Pins	Wooden pins set into racks at the side of a ship. Lines are secured about these, allowing instant release by their removal.
Bilboes	Iron restraints placed about an offender's ankles, allowing him to be of some use, picking oakum, *etc.*
Binnacle	Cabinet on the quarterdeck that houses compasses, the deck log, traverse board, lead lines, telescope, speaking trumpet, *etc.*

Bitts	Stout horizontal pieces of timber, supported by strong verticals, that extend deep into the ship. These hold the anchor cable when the ship is at anchor.
Blue Lamp/light	Common night signal, often used as a sign of distress and a term borrowed by evangelical officers when referring to themselves.
Block	Article of rigging that allows pressure to be diverted or, when used with others, increased. Consists of a pulley wheel, made of *lignum vitae*, encased in a wooden shell. Blocks can be single, double (fiddle block), triple or quadruple. The main suppliers were Taylors, of Southampton.
Board	Before being promoted to lieutenant, midshipmen would be tested for competence by a board of post captains. Should the applicant prove able they will be known as a passed midshipman, but could not assume the rank of lieutenant until they were appointed to such a position.
Boatswain	*(Pronounced Bosun)* The warrant officer superintending sails, rigging, canvas, colours, anchors, cables and cordage *etc.*, committed to his charge.
Bob	*(Slang)* A trick.
Boom	Lower spar to which the bottom of a gaff sail is attached.
Bootneck	*(Slang)* Term for a marine. Also guffies, jollies and many more...

Braces	Lines used to adjust the angle between the yards, and the fore and aft line of the ship. Mizzen braces, and braces of a brig lead forward.
Brig	Two-masted vessel, square-rigged on both masts.
Bulkhead	A partition within the hull of a ship.
Burgoo	Meal made from oats, usually served cold, and occasionally sweetened with molasses.
Bulwark	The planking or wood-work about a vessel above her deck.
Canister	Type of shot similar to case. Small iron balls packed into a cylindrical case.
Careening	The act of beaching a vessel and laying her over so that repairs and maintenance to the hull can be carried out.
Carronade	Short cannon firing a heavy shot. Invented by Melville, Gascoigne and Miller in late 1770's and adopted from 1779. Often used on the upper deck of larger ships, or as the main armament of smaller.
Cascabel	Part of the breech of a cannon.
Caulk	*(Slang)* To sleep. Also caulking, a process to seal the seams between strakes.
Channel	(When part of a ship) Projecting ledge that holds deadeyes from shrouds and backstays, originally chain-whales.
Chasse Marée	A small, decked commercial sailing vessel.

Chips /Chippy	*(Slang)* Traditional name for the carpenter. Originally from the ship builders who were allowed to carry out small lumps of wood, or chips, at the end of their shift.
Close Hauled	Sailing as near as possible into the wind.
Companionway	A staircase or passageway.
Counter	The lower part of a vessel's stern.
Course	A large square lower sail, hung from a yard, with sheets controlling and securing it.
Cove	*(Slang)* A man, often a rogue.
Cutter	Fast, small, single-masted vessel with a sloop rig. Also a seaworthy ship's boat.
Dale	Drain aboard ship, larger than a scupper.
Deadeyes	A round, flattish wooden block with three holes, through which a lanyard is reeved. Used to tension shrouds and backstays.
Diachylon tape	An early form of sticking plaster, often used by surgeons.
Dismal Jimmie/y	Admiral James Gambier (1756-1833) a noted "Blue Lamp" admiral known to be most insistent on regular worship.
Ditty Bag	*(Slang)* A seaman's bag. Derives its name from the dittis or 'Manchester stuff' of which it was originally made.
Driver	Large sail set on the mizzen. The foot is extended by means of a boom.

Dunnage	Officially the packaging around cargo. Also *(Slang)* baggage or possessions.
Fall	The free end of a lifting tackle on which the men haul.
Fen	*(Slang)* a prostitute.
Fetch	To arrive at, or reach a destination. Also a measure of the wind when blowing across water. The longer the fetch the bigger the waves.
Forereach	To gain upon, or pass by another ship when sailing in a similar direction.
Forestay	Stay supporting the masts running forward, serving the opposite function of the backstay. Runs from each mast at an angle of about 45 degrees to meet another mast, the deck or the bowsprit.
Glass	Telescope. Also, an hourglass and hence, as slang, a period of time. Also a barometer.
Gun Room	In a third rate and above, a mess for junior officers. For lower rates the gun room is the equivalent of the wardroom.
Go About	To alter course, changing from one tack to the other.
Halyards	Lines which raise yards, sails, signals *etc*.
Hammock Man	A seaman or marine employed to tend the hammock of a junior officer.
Hanger	A sword, similar in design to a cutlass but usually carried by an officer.
Hard Tack	Ship's biscuit.

Hawse	Area in the bows where holes are cut to allow the anchor cables to pass through. Also used as general term for bows.
Hawser	Heavy cable used for hauling, towing or mooring.
Headway	The amount a vessel is moved forward (rather than leeway: the amount a vessel is moved sideways) when the wind is not directly behind.
Heave To	Keeping a ship relatively stationary by backing certain sails in a seaway.
Idler	A man who, through duty or position, does not stand a watch, but (usually) works during the day and can sleep throughout the night.
Interest	Backing from a superior officer or one in authority, useful when looking for promotion.
Jib-Boom	Boom run out from the extremity of the bowsprit, braced by means of a Martingale stay, which passes through the dolphin striker.
John Company	*(Slang)* The East India Company.
Jollies	*(Slang)* The Royal Marines. See Bootneck.
Junk	Old line used to make wads, etc.
Jury Mast/Rig	Temporary measure used to restore a vessel's sailing ability.
Kuffar	Term for someone not of the Muslim faith.
Landsman	The rating of one who has no experience at sea.
Lanthorn	Large lantern.

Larboard	Left side of the ship when facing forward. Later replaced by 'port', which had previously been used for helm orders.
Leeward	The downwind side of a vessel.
Leeway	The amount a vessel is moved sideways by the wind (as opposed to headway, the forward movement, when the wind is directly behind).
Liner	*(Slang)* Ship of the line (of battle). A third rate or above.
Lubber/Lubberly	*(Slang)* Unseamanlike behaviour; as a landsman.
Luff	Sail closer to the wind, perhaps to allow work aloft. Also the flapping of sails when brought too close to the wind. The side of a fore and aft sail laced to the mast.
MacLaine	Alexander MacLaine, an 18th century cleric who compiled several books of sermons for general use.
Martingale Stay	Line that braces the jib-boom, passing from the end through the dolphin striker to the ship.
Miller	*(Slang)* Seaman's name for a rat when it is to be eaten, in the same way as deer is known as venison.
Mot	*(Slang)* Term, usually derogatory, for a young girl.
Orlop	The lowest deck in a ship.
Packet / Packet Service	The HEIC employed a number of fast sailing vessels to maintain communications and carry light cargo.
Pipeclay	Compound used to polish and whiten leatherwork.

Point Blank	The range of a cannon when fired flat. (For a 32 pounder this would be roughly 1000 feet.)
Polacre	Small merchant ship common in the Mediterranean.
Portable Soup	A boiled down mixture of beef and offal that could be reconstituted with water.
Pusser	*(Slang)* Purser.
Pusser's Pound	Before the Great Mutinies, meat was issued at 14 ounces to the pound, allowing an eighth for wastage. This was later reduced to a tenth.
Quarterdeck	In larger ships, the deck forward of the poop, but at a lower level. The preserve of officers.
Queue	A pigtail. Often tied by a seaman's best friend (his tie mate).
Quoin	Triangular wooden block placed under the cascabel of a long gun to adjust the elevation.
Ratlines	Lighter lines, untarred and tied horizontally across the shrouds at regular intervals, to act as rungs and allow men to climb aloft.
Reef	A portion of sail that can be taken in to reduce the size of the whole.
Reefing points	Light line on large sails, which can be tied up to reduce the sail area in heavy weather.
Reefing Tackle	Line that leads from the end of the yard to the reefing cringles set in the edges of the sail. It is used to haul up the upper part of the sail when reefing.

Rigging	Tophamper; made up of standing (static) and running (moveable) rigging, blocks etc. Also *(slang)* Clothes.
Running	Sailing before the wind.
Salt Horse	*(Slang)* Salt beef.
Sea Daddy	An older, more experienced, seaman who teaches a youngster the lore of the sea.
Scarph	A joint in wood where the edges are sloped off to maintain a constant thickness.
Schooner	Small craft with two or three masts.
Scragged	*(Slang)* to be hanged.
Scran	*(Slang)* Food.
Scraper	*(Slang)* Bicorne hat.
Scupper	Waterway that allows deck drainage.
Sheet	A line that controls the foot of a sail.
Shrouds	Lines supporting the masts athwart ship (from side to side) which run from the hounds (just below the top) to the channels on the side of the hull.
Smoke	*(Slang)* to discover, or reveal something hidden.
Soft Tack	Bread.
Spirketting	The interior lining or panelling of a ship.
Squarehead	*(Slang)* a Dutchman.
Squealer	*(Slang)* A youngster; a term often applied to midshipmen or volunteers.
Stay Sail	A quadrilateral or triangular sail with parallel lines hung from under a stay. Usually pronounced stays'l.

Stern Sheets	Part of a ship's boat between the stern and the first rowing thwart; often used for passengers.
Stingo	*(Slang)* Beer.
Strake	A plank.
Tack	To turn a ship, moving her bows through the wind. Also a leg of a journey relating to the direction of the wind. If from starboard, a ship is on the starboard tack. Also the part of a fore and aft loose-footed sail where the sheet is attached, or a line leading forward on a square course to hold the lower part of the sail forward.
Taffrail	Rail around the stern of a vessel.
Ticket Men	Hands employed aboard a pressing tender to see the vessel safely to harbour, replacing those crew that had been seized.
Timoneer	One who steers a ship.
Tophamper	Literally any weight either on a ship's decks or about her tops and rigging, but often used broadly to refer to spars and rigging.
Tow	Cotton waste.
Trick	*(Slang)* A period of duty.
Veer	Wind change, clockwise.
Waist	Area of main deck between the quarterdeck and forecastle.
Watch	Period of four (or in case of a dog watch, two) hour duty. Also describes the two or three divisions of a ship's crew.
Watch List / Bill	List of men and stations, usually carried by lieutenants and divisional officers.

Wearing	To change the direction of a square rigged ship across the wind by putting its stern through the eye of the wind. Also jibe – more common in a fore and aft rig.
Wedding Garland	An actual garland that would be raised when a ship was expected to remain at anchor for some while. It signified that the ship was not on active duty and women were allowed aboard. This was considered a preferable alternative to granting shore leave, a concession that was bound to be abused.
Windward	The side of a ship exposed to the wind.
Windward	The side of a ship exposed to the wind.
Yellow (Admiral)	The rank of Admiral was achieved solely through seniority. Following a man being made post (captain) he gradually rose on the captains' list as those above him died, retired, or were promoted. On attaining flag rank he would normally be appointed Rear Admiral of the Blue Squadron, the lowest level of flag officer other than Commodore. But should the officer be considered unsuitable for such a position, he would be appointed to an unspecified squadron; what was popularly known as being yellowed, and a disgrace to him so honoured.

Principle Characters

HMS *Prometheus*

Captain:	Sir Richard Banks
Lieutenants:	Michael Caulfield, Thomas King, Simon Corbett, Lewis, Anthony Hunt, Franklin
Sailing Master:	Brehaut
Midshipmen and Volunteers:	Jack Brown, Joe Briars, Carley, Bentley, Cross, Adams, Steven
Surgeon:	Robert Manning
Surgeon's Mates:	Prior, Kate Manning, Dodgeson, Blake
Loblolly boy:	Wells
Purser:	Dawson
Purser's steward:	Rigget
Quartermaster:	Maxwell
Boatswain:	Knolls
Boatswain's Mate:	Clement
Gunner:	Hurle
Corporal:	Musgrave
Cook:	Olivier
Coxswain:	Ashley
Carpenter:	Roberts
Captain's Steward:	David
Wardroom Steward:	Kennedy
King's Steward:	Keats

| Seamen: | Flint, Charlie Bleeden, Rogers, Carter, Sanders, Peterson, Bolton, Greg, Beeney, Harding, Cranston, William Butler, Matthew Jameson |
| Marines: | Captain Reynolds, Sergeant Jarvis, Wainwright, Mason |

also:

Mrs Roberts:	Wife of carpenter
Poppy:	Kate Manning's maid
Judy:	A former passenger aboard *Prometheus*

Additional:

Captain: HMS *Canopus:*	Captain John Conn
Commander HMHV *Aries*:	Jefferson
Toulon blockade:	Vice Admiral Nelson
	Rear Admiral Bickerton
	Captain Hardy
Naval Commissioner (Gibraltar):	
	Captain William A Otway
Staff:	Commander Stewart
	Lieutenant Hoskins
Naval Storekeeper:	Pownall
Dockyard Supervisor:	Cawsgrove
Superintendent of the Wharf:	Kendall

About the author

Alaric Bond was born in Surrey, and now lives in Herstmonceux, East Sussex. He has been writing professionally for over twenty years.

His interests include the British Navy, 1793-1815, and the RNVR during WWII. He is also a keen collector of old or unusual musical instruments, and 78 rpm records.

Alaric Bond is a member of various historical societies and regularly gives talks to groups and organisations.

www.alaricbond.com

About Old Salt Press

Old Salt Press is an independent press catering to those who love books about ships and the sea. We are an association of writers working together to produce the very best of nautical and maritime fiction and non-fiction. We invite you to join us as we go down to the sea in books.

More Great Reading from Old Salt Press

The Scent of Corruption by Alaric Bond

Summer, 1803: the uneasy peace with France is over, and Britain has once more been plunged into the turmoil of war. After a spell on the beach, Sir Richard Banks is appointed to HMS *Prometheus*, a seventy-four gun line-of-battleship which an eager Admiralty loses no time in ordering to sea. The ship is fresh from a major re-fit, but Banks has spent the last year with his family: will he prove worthy of such a powerful vessel, and can he rely on his officers to support him?

With excitement both aboard ship and ashore, gripping sea battles, a daring rescue and intense personal intrigue, *The Scent of Corruption* is a non-stop nautical thriller in the best traditions of the genre. Number seven in the Fighting Sail series.
ISBN 978-1943404025

Blackwell's Homecoming by V E Ulett

In a multigenerational saga of love, war and betrayal, Captain Blackwell and Mercedes continue their voyage in Volume III of Blackwell's Adventures. The Blackwell family's eventful journey from England to Hawaii, by way of the new and tempestuous nations of Brazil and Chile, provides an intimate portrait of family conflicts and loyalties in the late Georgian Age. Blackwell's Homecoming is an evocation of the dangers and rewards of desire.
ISBN 978-0-9882360-7-3

Britannia's Spartan by Antoine Vanner

It's 1882 and Captain Nicholas Dawlish has taken command of the Royal Navy's newest cruiser, HMS *Leonidas*. Her voyage to the Far East is to be peaceful, a test of innovative engines and boilers. But a new balance of power is emerging there. Imperial China, weak and corrupt, is challenged by a rapidly modernising Japan, while Russia threatens from the north. They all need to control Korea, a kingdom frozen in time and reluctant to emerge from centuries of isolation. Dawlish has no forewarning of the nightmare of riot, treachery, massacre and battle that lies ahead and in this, the fourth of the Dawlish Chronicles, he will find himself stretched to his limits – and perhaps beyond.
ISBN 978-1943404049

The Shantyman by Rick Spilman

In 1870, on the clipper ship *Alahambra* in Sydney, the new crew comes aboard more or less sober, except for the last man, who is hoisted aboard in a cargo sling, paralytic drunk. The drunken sailor, Jack Barlow, will prove to be an able shantyman. On a ship with a dying captain and a murderous mate, Barlow will literally keep the crew pulling together. As he struggles with a tragic past, a troubled present and an uncertain future, Barlow will guide the *Alahambra* through Southern Ocean ice and the horror of an Atlantic hurricane. His one goal is bringing the ship and crew safely back to New York, where he hopes to start anew. Based on a true story, *The Shantyman* is a gripping tale of survival against all odds at sea and ashore, and the challenge of facing a past that can never be wholly left behind.
ISBN978-0-9941152-2-5

Eleanor's Odyssey by Joan Druett

It was 1799, and French privateers lurked in the Atlantic and the Bay of Bengal. Yet Eleanor Reid, newly married and just twenty-one years old, made up her mind to sail with her husband, Captain Hugh Reid, to the penal colony of New South Wales, the Spice Islands and India. Danger threatened not just from the barely charted seas they would be sailing, yet, confident in her love and her husband's seamanship, Eleanor insisted on going along. Joan Druett, writer of many books about the sea, including the bestseller Island of the Lost and the groundbreaking story of women under sail, Hen Frigates, embellishes Eleanor's journal with a commentary that illuminates the strange story of a remarkable young woman.

ISBN 978-0-9941152-1-8

Water Ghosts by Linda Collison

Fifteen-year-old James McCafferty is an unwilling sailor aboard a traditional Chinese junk, operated as adventure-therapy for troubled teens. Once at sea, the ship is gradually taken over by the spirits of courtiers who fled the Imperial court during the Ming Dynasty, more than 600 years ago. One particular ghost wants what James has and is intent on trading places with him. But the teens themselves are their own worst enemies in the struggle for life in the middle of the Pacific Ocean. A psychological story set at sea, with historical and paranormal elements.

ISBN 978-1943404001

Captain Blackwell's Prize by V E Ulett

A small, audacious British frigate does battle against a large but ungainly Spanish ship. British Captain James Blackwell intercepts the Spanish *La Trinidad*, outmaneuvers and outguns the treasure ship and boards her. Fighting alongside the Spanish captain, sword in hand, is a beautiful woman. The battle is quickly over. The Spanish captain is killed in the fray and his ship damaged beyond repair. Its survivors and treasure are taken aboard the British ship, *Inconstant*.

ISBN 978-0-9882360-6-6

Britannia's Shark by Antione Vanner

"Britannia's Shark" is the third of the Dawlish Chronicles novels. It's 1881 and a daring act of piracy draws the ambitious British naval officer, Nicholas Dawlish, into a deadly maelstrom of intrigue and revolution. Drawn in too is his wife Florence, for whom the glimpse of a half-forgotten face evokes memories of earlier tragedy. For both a nightmare lies ahead, amid the wealth and squalor of America's Gilded Age and on a fever-ridden island ruled by savage tyranny. Manipulated ruthlessly from London by the shadowy Admiral Topcliffe, Nicholas and Florence Dawlish must make some very strange alliances if they are to survive – and prevail.

ISBN 978-0992263690

The Guinea Boat by Alaric Bond

Set in Hastings, Sussex during the early part of 1803, *Guinea Boat* tells the story of two young lads, and the diverse paths they take to make a living on the water. Britain is still at an uneasy peace with France, but there is action and intrigue a plenty along the south-east coast. Private fights and family feuds abound; a hot press threatens the livelihoods of many, while the newly re-formed Sea Fencibles begin a careful watch on Bonaparte's ever growing invasion fleet. And to top it all, free trading has grown to the extent that it is now a major industry, and one barely kept in check by the efforts of the preventive men. Alaric Bond's eighth novel.
ISBN 978-0994115294

The Beckoning Ice by Joan Druett

The Beckoning Ice finds the U. S. Exploring Expedition off Cape Horn, a grim outpost made still more threatening by the report of a corpse on a drifting iceberg, closely followed by a gruesome death on board. Was it suicide, or a particularly brutal murder? Wiki investigates, only to find himself fighting desperately for his own life.
ISBN 978-0-9922588-3-2

Lady Castaways by Joan Druett

It was not just the men who lived on the brink of peril when under sail at sea. Lucretia Jansz, who was enslaved as a concubine in 1629, was just one woman who endured a castaway experience. Award-winning historian Joan Druett (*Island of the Lost, The Elephant Voyage*), relates the stories of women who survived remarkable challenges, from heroines like Mary Ann Jewell, the "governess" of Auckland Island in the icy sub-Antarctic, to Millie Jenkins, whose ship was sunk by a whale.
ISBN 978-0994115270

Hell Around the Horn by Rick Spilman

In 1905, a young ship's captain and his family set sail on the windjammer, *Lady Rebecca*, from Cardiff, Wales with a cargo of coal bound for Chile, by way of Cape Horn. Before they reach the Southern Ocean, the cargo catches fire, the mate threatens mutiny and one of the crew may be going mad. The greatest challenge, however, will prove to be surviving the vicious westerly winds and mountainous seas of the worst Cape Horn winter in memory. Told from the perspective of the Captain, his wife, a first year apprentice and an American sailor before the mast, *Hell Around the Horn* is a story of survival and the human spirit in the last days of the great age of sail.
ISBN 978-0-9882360-1-1

Turn a Blind Eye by Alaric Bond

Newly appointed to the local revenue cutter, Commander Griffin is determined to make his mark, and defeat a major gang of smugglers. But the country is still at war with France and it is an unequal struggle; can he depend on support from the local community, or are they yet another enemy for him to fight? With dramatic action on land and at sea, *Turn a Blind Eye* exposes the private war against the treasury with gripping fact and fascinating detail.
ISBN 978-0-9882360-3-5

The Torrid Zone by Alaric Bond

A tired ship with a worn out crew, but *HMS Scylla* has one more trip to make before her much postponed re-fit. Bound for St Helena, she is to deliver the island's next governor; a simple enough mission and, as peace looks likely to be declared, no one is expecting difficulties. Except, perhaps, the commander of a powerful French battle squadron, who has other ideas.

With conflict and intrigue at sea and ashore, *The Torrid Zone* is filled to the gunnels with action, excitement and fascinating historical detail; a truly engaging read.

ISBN 978-0988236097

Blackwell's Paradise by V E Ulett

The repercussions of a court martial and the ill-will of powerful men at the Admiralty pursue Royal Navy Captain James Blackwell into the Pacific, where danger lurks around every coral reef. Even if Captain Blackwell and Mercedes survive the venture into the world of early nineteenth century exploration, can they emerge unchanged with their love intact. The mission to the Great South Sea will test their loyalties and strength, and define the characters of Captain Blackwell and his lady in *Blackwell's Paradise.*

ISBN 978-0-9882360-5-9